THE LEGEND OF GASPARILLA

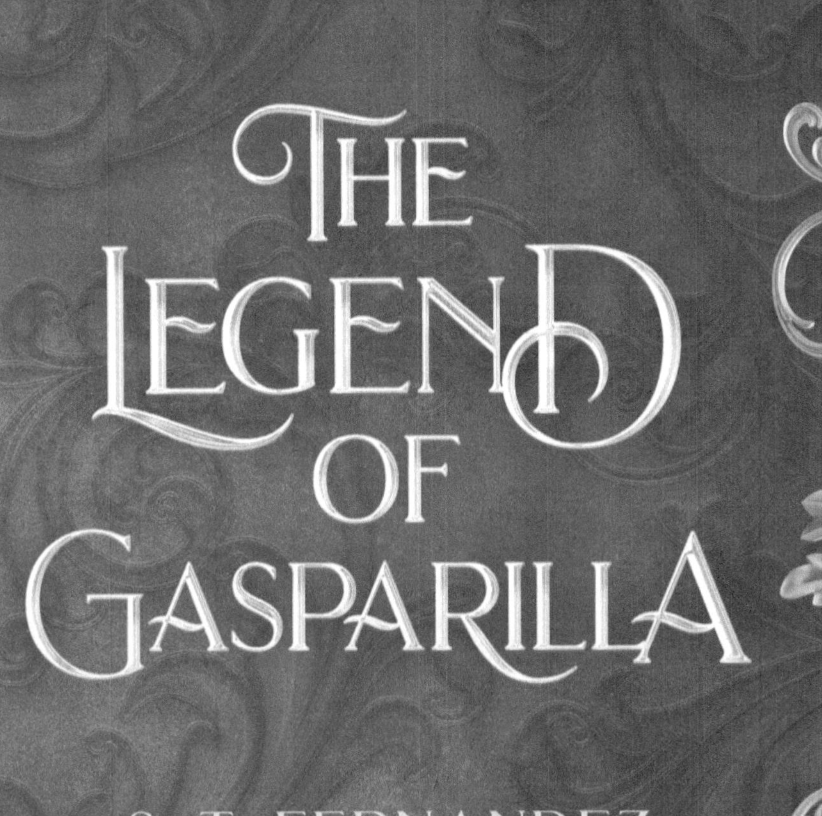

THE LEGEND OF GASPARILLA

S. T. FERNANDEZ

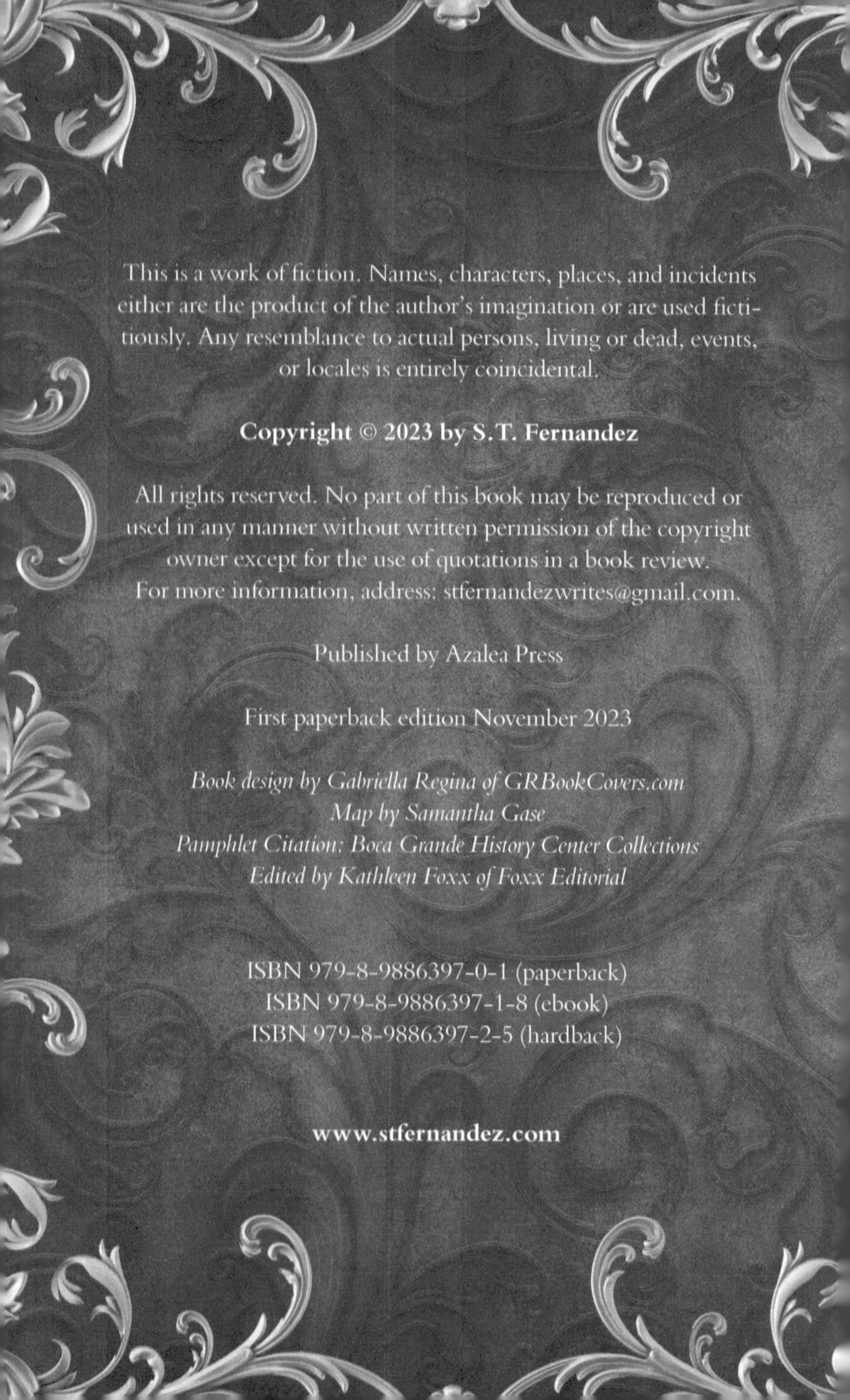

This is a work of fiction. Names, characters, places, and incidents either are the product of the author's imagination or are used fictitiously. Any resemblance to actual persons, living or dead, events, or locales is entirely coincidental.

Copyright © 2023 by S.T. Fernandez

All rights reserved. No part of this book may be reproduced or used in any manner without written permission of the copyright owner except for the use of quotations in a book review. For more information, address: stfernandezwrites@gmail.com.

Published by Azalea Press

First paperback edition November 2023

Book design by Gabriella Regina of GRBookCovers.com
Map by Samantha Gase
Pamphlet Citation: Boca Grande History Center Collections
Edited by Kathleen Foxx of Foxx Editorial

ISBN 979-8-9886397-0-1 (paperback)
ISBN 979-8-9886397-1-8 (ebook)
ISBN 979-8-9886397-2-5 (hardback)

www.stfernandez.com

For the people of Tampa Bay.

Hoist the sails and fire the cannons!

El Cazador
Captain Rodgers Hid
Spanishtown
Creek
Gasparilla's
Pirate Haven
Havana, Cuba
San Juan,
Puerto Rico

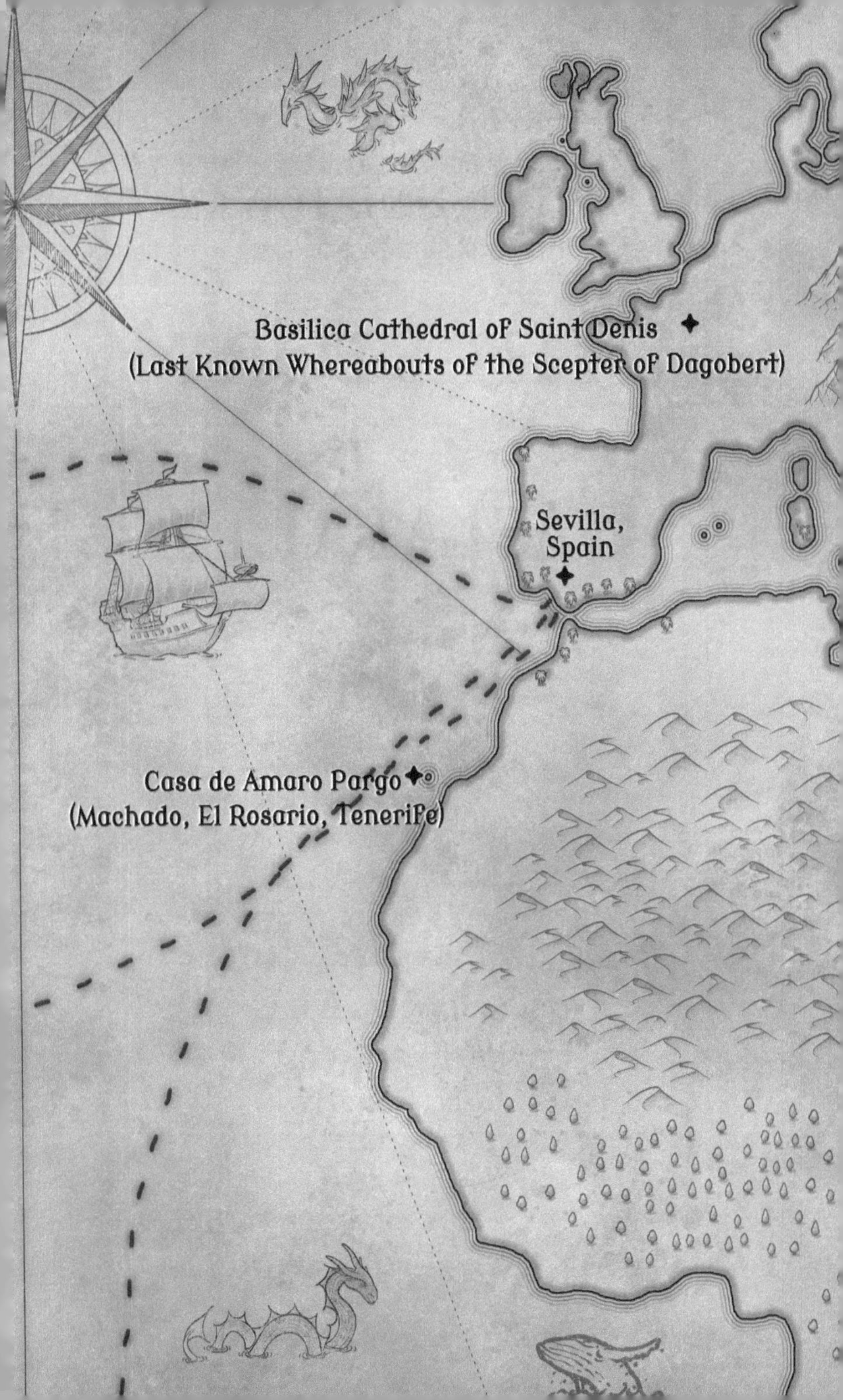

Basilica Cathedral of Saint Denis
(Last Known Whereabouts of the Scepter of Dagobert)
Sevilla, Spain
Casa de Amaro Pargo
(Machado, El Rosario, Tenerife)

C. H. & N. RAILWAY

"BOCA GRANDE ROUTE"

THE STORY
of
GASPARILLA

ISSUED BY

C. B. McCALL

Gen'l Passenger Agt.

C. H. & N. Ry.

BOCA GRADE, FLA.

C. H. & N. RAILWAY

"BOCA GRANDE ROUTE"

Spring 1928

NOTE

The writer compiled this narrative from events relayed by John Gómez, also known as Panther Key John, the last living crew member of the infamous pirate José Gaspar. Gómez passed away at the age of one hundred and twenty years at Panther Key, Florida, in the year of our Lord 1900. Further chronicles were obtained by John Gómez Jr., who lived and cared for his father until his death.

While it is almost unfeasible to collect precise information regarding the infamous outlaw due to numerous conflicting interpretations, the writer has attempted to put into readable form the story concerning José Gaspar, his origins, and his life. Naturally, the writer has used only those accounts where two or more sources are similarly compared. However, it is well to remember that due to the long lapse between the death of Gaspar and the current year, nearly all old landmarks and sources have gone or passed, though the legend lives through the tales retold by the residents of Gasparilla Island.

With the above aforementioned, this is the story of José Gaspar.

Pat Lemoyne
Publicist
Charlotte Harbor and Northern Railway

PART I

THE JEWELS
&
THE WOMAN SCORNED

Chapter 1

Gasparilla Island, Florida
1816

"This is silly," Lawrence muttered to himself. "Absolutely ridiculous." The sand crunched underneath his feet as he walked toward the front porch. The sunset cast shadows across the large wooden door encouraging the dips and crevasses to play tricks on his eyes. He was just about to knock when the hairs on his neck rose. His head snapped around, peering into the fading light of day, but he was met with tall palms and a light summer breeze. He could swear someone was watching him. Shaking his head, he turned back and knocked firmly on the door, toggling from foot to foot as the seconds ticked by.

The weathered hinges of the door slowly creaked open. A young man stood in front of him with eyes reminiscent of those he was responsible for sending to the bottom of Hillsborough Bay so many years ago. His brows furrowed at the sight of a U.S. Naval officer—a reaction not entirely unwarranted. It wasn't Lawrence's first time on the island, and he wasn't about to hold his breath for an invitation. Their secluded *rancho* welcomed only those who were *his* companions—the very same man who shared the face of the young man before him. The sight of the light olive skin, the dark brown hair, and a chiseled jaw just shy of shedding off the fat of his youth gave Lawrence chills.

"May I help you?" he asked.

"I am here to speak with Mrs. Gaspar. I am Lieutenant Kearny of the U.S. Navy. It is an urgent matter." *Urgent.* He mentally scoffed at himself. But there was no turning back now.

The man opened the door enough to allow himself to lean against the door jam, looking upon Lawrence with amusement. "Lieutenant Kearny?"

"Yes, sir, Captain of the USS—"

"Enterprise. Yes, I know who you are," he said with contempt.

Lawrence cleared his throat. "It appears my reputation precedes me."

"Indeed, it does. Of course, I've never had the…privilege… of meeting you, despite your ransacking of our village shortly after my father's death. I fail to see what *urgent* matter would bring such a prominent naval officer to this island at dusk."

His voice dripping with condescension left no doubt in Lawrence's mind. This was José Gaspar's son. "Well, that is the matter I wish to speak to Mrs. Gaspar about," Lawrence said firmly. His fists expanded and contracted at his side. "My apologies. I didn't catch your name."

"That's because I'd never freely give it to the man responsible for my father's death." He glared at Lawrence with the fire of a thousand suns.

Lawrence went from feeling foolish for appearing on their doorstep to fuming with anger in seconds. "I assure you, young man. Your father was responsible for the actions that brought about his demise."

"Iván! Who are you talking to?" a feminine voice called from inside the home. A hand gripped the partially open door, pulling it open. The woman's beauty transcended time, for he was sure she looked the same every time he encountered her. Her skin glowed, the smooth peaks of her cheekbones more prominent than the last time he was here. Her long brown hair cascaded down her back in soft waves, complimenting her beauty. Her hazel eyes—which appeared more brown than green in the porch gaslight—glared at him with curiosity. There was a time he would have wed this woman. Whether it was for re-

venge or his own pleasure, he could not tell. But one thing was
for certain. Lawrence always got what he wanted, and not having Joséfa as his wife had stung at the time. Perhaps it still did.

"Lieutenant. What a surprise. Won't you come in?"

"Thank you, Mrs. Gaspar."

"Iván, please move aside and let the Lieutenant in. Suppose
you wouldn't mind telling *Señora* Lopez to prepare something
to eat for our unexpected visitor. I am sure he is hungry after
such a long journey."

Iván remained leaning against the door jam, glaring at him.

"My son. Do as I say," she demanded.

Iván turned to her, their eyes speaking a silent language
only mother and son could talk before he made his way inside.
Lawrence thought the home itself looked largely out of place.
The house appeared to have been plucked off a well-inhabited
area and plopped into the depths of the tall palms that populated
the small island. He wondered who else occupied Gaspar's pirate haven and whether their homes were as lovely, having only
caught glimpses of it during the USS Enterprise's investigation
of the island. The hardwood floors gleamed and stretched long
to the back of the house—the foyer opening up to a large sitting
room with very wealthy furnishings. Given that Mrs. Gaspar's
brother was a wildly successful merchant, he couldn't blame all
the abundance on the thieving of piracy. Some of it, in any case.
The rest of the house was a mystery, with only the hallways on
the right and left of the room visible. This made proving his
theory and his mission more difficult.

Something caught his eye in the corner cabinet of the room.
It was lovely. Well made. A vase of wild bamboo sat decoratively
on one shelf; a long sword lay on display just above it. He swore
he had seen that sword before. As if attracted to it by some weird
magnetism, he stepped toward the cabinet.

"Please. Take a seat." Mrs. Gaspar sat gracefully in her
wingback chair and gestured toward the couch. He abandoned
his musings and joined her.

"What can I do for you, Lieutenant?" she asked.

Despite his initial courage, he was at a loss for words. He was spared a few moments to collect his thoughts when a stout woman carrying a tray filled with biscuits and tea entered the room, setting it on the table before them. Her mouth was placed in a tight line as she asked, "*Crema?*"

"*Si, por favor. Gracias*," he replied in his best Spanish. It left much to be desired but was necessary as long as the Spanish still occupied the area. The woman handed him his tea and left the room.

"Mrs. Gaspar," he said, figuring this was an excellent place to start. When he noticed her brow arching, he smiled gently. "I imagine my appearance here is a bit of shock."

"To say the least," she agreed, taking a small sip from her cup.

"Yes…well…you see, there seems to be quite a bit of… piratical activity lately. There are some signature marks to the raids, and there seems to be a pattern."

Joséfa placed her cup on the side table, looking at him with interest. "A pattern, Lieutenant?"

"Yes, they are identical to that of your husband's."

"I see. That does sound interesting, but it doesn't explain your appearance here, I'm afraid."

Lawrence placed his teacup on the table and leaned back, observing her facial features for any telltale signs. He listened to the house to see if it would give him any clues—the moment stretched on.

"Lieutenant?"

He snapped his attention back to her. "Yes, Mrs. Gaspar. The thing is, I do not believe these instances to be a coincidence in nature. I have seen glimpses of a man resembling your husband in ports like Galveston and New Orleans. More recently, I was close to a man of his exact features in the settlement of Spanishtown Creek but could not identify him."

"Well, you know us Spanish. We all look alike."

Lawrence noted the sarcasm in her tone but continued. "I wonder if my eyes are deceiving me or if I have been duped."

"Duped?" she asked in amusement.

He exhaled slightly, unease creeping into his bones. He pressed on. "I will spare you and your child from any harm or repercussions. I understand how difficult it must be to be manipulated by one's husband to have him keep you hostage all these years."

"Hostage?" she asked incredulously.

"Now, I empathize with your desire to protect him, but I can assure you amnesty.

She looked at him, bewildered. "Sir, what exactly are you asking?"

"Is José Gaspar still alive?" he exclaimed. "Does he still live?"

The lingering silence grew so thick one could cut it with a knife. Her eyes locked on him. Then quite suddenly, she burst into laughter, startling Lawrence. After catching her breath, she continued. "Lieutenant, did you come all the way here to ask me about *ghost* stories?"

"Ghost stories! I assure you, Mrs. Gaspar. I saw this man in the light of day."

"It sounds like your ghosts mean to haunt you even in the light of day, for my husband no longer walks this Earth. You, of all people, should know that. You saw him go overboard."

"Indeed I did…but could he have survived?"

"I assure you, Lieutenant, my husband is at the bottom of the bay where you put him," she bit out. "Furthermore, I fail to see how you could believe José is alive after searching this island from grain to palm looking for treasure he allegedly had in his possession at the time of his death."

At that moment, Iván came out of the hallway and stood behind his mother, ire dripping from his gaze.

"Now, if you are quite done questioning the widow of the man you tracked down and killed, I will have Iván see you and your ghost stories to the door. I'm sorry you went through the trouble of coming. Rest easily, for José Gaspar no longer lives." Her stern look indicated the conversation was over.

So stupid! You daft, idiotic imbecile! Of course, he's not alive!

Lawrence rose from his seat when something in the neighboring hallway caught his eye. Not something. Someone. A little girl with features that resembled Joséfa's so closely. She stared at him in curiosity. Lawrence squinted, trying to make out any features of the little girl that could possibly be that of José Gaspar.

Joséfa followed his stare to the hallway. "Alejandra, go to your room and wait for me there. Now."

Alejandra scurried down the hall, a door slamming shut moments later. Lawrence's eyes bore into Joséfa's. "I wasn't aware you had any other children."

"It isn't unheard of for young widows to have additional children after the death of their first husband."

Lawrence raised his arms and motioned around the room. "And yet, there wasn't a single male beyond your son here to greet me upon my arrival. How curious. She looks an awful lot like you. And if my eyes hadn't deceived me, she almost resembled Gaspar. Of course, that would be impossible, seeing as how he died decades before the girl was born."

Joséfa's rage could be felt across the room. Her gaze narrowed. "I fail to see how I owe you an explanation. Our family has been through enough tragedy, and now you stand here forcing me to face my grief once again. I am through with this conversation." Joséfa rose from her chair and motioned toward the front of the home. "Please, leave."

Lawrence bowed respectively toward her, his heart racing with the revelation that he might have been right after all. "I'm sure we'll be seeing each other again very soon." And he meant it because, with Alejandra's appearance, it was clear that José Gaspar was not dead and Lawrence's journey to the island had been a fruitful one. He would return with his men and tear apart every inch of this filthy pirate haven.

As Lawrence entered the foyer with Iván and *Señora* Lopez trailing closely behind him, the floorboards above the entry creaked with footsteps. He stopped in his tracks, causing Iván to run into his back. No one else introduced themselves save *Señora* Lopez. He looked up at the ceiling. The steps from above suddenly stopped. He turned to Iván with a devious smirk, the boy's breathing accelerating slightly as his ire remained steady. Iván straightened his spine. "As my mother said, take your ghost stories with you."

He huffed at Iván and proceeded out the door.

"Ghost stories, indeed," he murmured, walking briskly down the trail to the shore. Lawrence's mind raced with the prospect of bringing down his nemesis again. How could he have gotten away? He saw him sink below the water's surface. No one could have survived it. He recalled the intense jubilation at besting Gaspar. He thought he had won.

Lawrence was too busy trying to figure out how Gaspar could have escaped that he failed to notice the rustling in the bushes lining the pathway. He glanced around, the towering palm trees caving in on him. His breathing accelerated, and sweat soaked through his clothing. He shuffled back a few steps, his hand immediately grabbing the gun on his waist. Lawrence pulled it out and aimed it all around him. "Who's there? Show yourself!"

Raucous laughter erupted. "You hear that, boys? He wants us to show ourselves."

Dozens of figures emerged from the shadows, blocking any possible escape. "You cannot harm me! I am a U.S. Naval officer!"

"Oh. They know who you are, Lieutenant."

A single gunshot traveled through the darkness and hit the gun in Lawrence's hand. It flew from his grip, leaving him defenseless. He held his hand to his stomach, wincing from the impact. Then, the sea of figures parted, and a large and imposing shadow strolled toward him—the torch in his hand casting flickers of light against his face. Lawrence's eyes widened when the man came into view, and he forgot how to breathe.

Gaspar was free of the beard he used to wear so proudly, but his long dark hair grazed his shoulder, the strands dancing to and fro in the wind. His jaw tensed, and his eyes darkened with each step.

"You," Lawrence squeaked.

"Yes. Me."

Lawrence's initial shock began to fade, and his lips twisted. "It cannot be! How did you ever survive?"

Gaspar handed the torch to his fellow pirate, the rest of his crew tightening around him. "That is privileged information."

"And I demand it!"

"And you'll not get it," he seethed. Gaspar unsheathed his sword, the very same one he had seen in the living room just moments before. "You dare to come here and harass my family for the last time, Lieutenant. You're a fool to come here alone. You are but a lone sheep in a pasture, and I, the wolf coming to devour." As Gaspar pointed the tip of his blade, Lawrence's heart hammered in his chest. "I told you that fateful day, José Gaspar dies at his own hand. No one else's. And now, you will die at mine."

Lawrence barely registered his threat before the sword cut across his throat. His eyes went wide—the blood pouring rapidly from his mouth. The torchlight flashed in Gaspar's dark eyes, and the depths of hell reflected back at Lawrence. It was the last thing he saw before he faded forever from this world.

Chapter 2

Iván José Gaspar watched with intense curiosity from the second-story window—arms folded tightly against his chest as Lieutenant Kearny's body disappeared from the shores of Gasparilla Island. "What a sorry son of a bitch." He shook his head. "I still don't understand. How could you let a sniveling man like that claim to have driven you to your death?"

"Hmph. He did not drive me to my death, Iván." José said, smirking mischievously from where he sat in the dark corner of the room—freshly bathed and in clothing not drenched with blood. "He only thought he did."

Iván huffed his displeasure. "The man roamed around all of *La Florida* bragging about how he had taken down the great José Gaspar and disparaged your image as this hateful, vengeful, nasty pirate. Everyone on Gasparilla Island knows you are much more than the image he painted."

"Make no mistake, Iván. I am everything he had painted me to be."

Iván regarded his father, biting the inside of his cheek. "Will you still not tell me?"

He sighed. "You know the answer."

Iván threw his hands in the air. "But Papa, I have been asking for years. Am I not old enough to know what happened?

You're my father, and you guard your secrets so close to your heart that I often wonder if I really know who you are. I am your blood. Don't I deserve to know your true story?"

José appraised his son. He still couldn't believe he had grown into the young man before him, knowing he was Iván's age when he first courted Joséfa. He rubbed at his chest, where his heart began to ache in denial. He wasn't ready to let him be…well…a man. There's no contesting he already was, given that he had to grow up quickly to be head of the household when José appeared to be a ghost, only coming out at night or when necessary to the populace of Spanishtown Creek. After all, when his family visited the mainland for Iván's education, José needed to watch over them despite having people at his disposal to do this for him.

The loyalty of the inhabitants of Gasparilla Island provided him the cover he needed to survive beyond the confines of his home, most of the remaining crew of *La Floriblanca* closely guarding his secrets and respecting his desire to keep those secrets from his children. This was the one thing he held on to if only to protect them from the knowledge of his descent and that fateful day on Hillsborough Bay, the events too terrible to recall. They often plagued his nightmares, causing long spates of sleep deprivation, much to Joséfa's dismay. As he sat contemplating whether Iván was truly ready, he feared his son's judgment, but he saw the determination in his son's eyes. The time had come.

"Very well."

Iván's eyes widened. "*De verdad?*"

José nodded. "Yes. It is time." José rose from the chair. "But let us go to the sitting room. A few ounces of your *Tio Armando's* strongest rum are in order for a tale like this." José and Iván made their way downstairs, where they found his daughter, her long brown hair just like her mother's, brushing the ground as she played with a spinning top by Joséfa's feet. His wife sat, a scowl still on her face as she stared at the front door. She was still just as beautiful today as she was when they were young.

He never saw a woman age so gracefully, despite the frown lines currently creasing her forehead.

Joséfa turned to them. "He was a wretched, weak man. I should have been quicker with a response when he saw Alejandra."

José inhaled deeply. "Do not fret, *mi amor*. We no longer have to worry about him. The crew is discarding his body in the depths of the ocean as we speak." José shook his head. "It was his own fault for coming here with only a fisherman for a witness, one that is happily on my payroll. Someone as prideful as Kearny would have never whispered his intentions to travel to Gasparilla Island to chase a ghost. We are safe." He gazed at his wife, the next words falling out uneasily. "I was about to tell our son the story of my previous life and what happened to *La Floriblanca*."

Joséfa's eyes traveled between Iván and José and then her daughter. "Alejandra? Why don't you find Elena? Ask her to tell the villagers the threat is gone. Can you do that for me?"

Alejandra continued playing with the top. "I want to hear Papa's story, too," she said without looking up.

"Absolutely not," Iván protested. He turned to José. "She's barely ten years of age *and* a girl. If I had to wait, surely she has to. Much, *much* longer."

Alejandra rolled her eyes dramatically. José covered his mouth to hide his laugh.

"Your brother is right," Joséfa interrupted before the siblings started a feud. "We will tell you eventually." She shot her son a judgmental look, "At precisely the same age as Iván is now. We play equally in this house regardless of being a boy or a girl." She returned her attention to Alejandra. "Please do as I asked you."

Alejandra rose from the floor with a huff and exited the front door. José took a moment to pour a little rum into his tumbler and a little less into his son's, handing it to him where he sat on the neighboring sofa. "Why don't you start with what you already know?" he asked.

Iván looked down into his glass. "I hear whispers of a deathly pirate around town, one with swordsmanship so exceptional, it is legendary. I hear stories of how you brought down fleets of men to their knees, despite being unable to bring the crew the USS Enterprise to theirs."

"All of that is true."

"But if that is true, how did you manage to escape?" he asked, looking at his father in awe. "The whole town thinks you dead." He paused, shaking his head. "How?"

José smiled. "Because every well-thought-out plan has the potential of going wrong. Always have a backup plan, *hijo*. Remember that," he said, taking a long sip of his drink. "What you know is only what you have heard from the crew of the USS Enterprise. I made the inhabitants of this island promise to keep this secret. They did so out of respect for me, not only because I wished to tell you myself when the time was right but because I couldn't let anyone know that I was still alive, that I had actually bested Lieutenant Kearny. You saw how he was when he thought me dead. He managed to find the island and harass everyone here despite not knowing I was alive. Given the spectacle that transpired this evening, I couldn't let him live." He gazed at his son uneasily. "A man like Lieutenant Kearny would have never stopped. You understand why I just killed him?" Iván's face was grave, but he nodded his understanding. With a sense of relief, José continued, "Secrecy is most important. It is why I must ask you to keep this to yourself for as long as you live, even long after I pass. Do I have your word?"

"Of course, Papa. I wouldn't dream of uttering a word of it," he declared.

Joséfa reached out and squeezed José's free hand. "Perhaps it is best to start from the beginning when you were an Admiral."

Iván's eyes lit up. "An Admiral?"

"Yes, an Admiral…and consultant for the king." He glanced back at Joséfa, his brow furrowed. "In *Sevilla*?"

Joséfa nodded with a slight smile. "*Si. Sevilla.*"

CHAPTER 3

SEVILLA, SPAIN
1783

THE AFTERNOON SUN WARMED JOSÉ'S FACE AS HE STEPPED OUTside *El Palacio*. He closed his eyes and welcomed it, breathing deep into his lungs. Sweat beaded on his brow, but he could hardly blame the sun. A deep sense of uneasiness was his reliable companion when in the king's presence. José exhaled with a sense of relief and made his way home through the streets of *Sevilla*—the bright colors emanating from the flower boxes that lined the Juliet balconies along the road surrounding him on either side.

"Gaspar! Wait!" Felipe galloped at full speed, his sandy blond hair riding the wind, blue eyes alight with mischief.

José glanced behind, chuckling. "*Buenas tardes*, Felipe. Be careful. You're going to fall over and break something."

Felipe halted on the cobblestone, heaving for air—exhaustion heavy on his face. "You're a tough man to catch up to."

José assessed his friend. "You know, if you picked up the art of the sword, you wouldn't be so out of breath."

Felipe looked at him incredulously. "Heavens no. Who has time for all of that? I leave all the heavy lifting to you." He straightened his jacket. "I wouldn't want to risk cutting my clothing. You know I am fond of it. Or my face. I don't want to risk cutting my face. What will all the ladies of Sevilla do then?"

"Oh no. We mustn't have that." José smiled, shaking his head.

They continued down the crowded street, their discussions jumping from the decline of trade routes to the freer trade between Europe and the Colonies to the fall of the fleet system. All of these factors weighed heavily on José.

"You worry too much. You are a consultant for the king for a reason."

"I just wonder how important my consultation with the king will be in the upcoming years," José said.

Felipe moved aside for a group of *damas*, his eyes observing the ladies a little too long. "With all due respect, *Admiral*. Your men are completely loyal to you. The king cannot overlook this. Not to mention you're the son of one of the most successful merchants in Sevilla…may God rest his soul. No one knows these waters better than you—your expertise with the continued fight with the British, the French, and the Portuguese over Atlantic trade cannot be ignored."

José weaved through the scores of people, Felipe trying to remain at his side. "I've been contemplating my options, is all. My father always told me it was wise to have a backup plan. Perhaps I'll bounce some ideas off the other men at the ball this evening."

"Do you plan to escort Mariana to the ball?" Felipe smirked.

"Mariana?" José shook his head, a few strands of his long brown hair sticking to his brow. "Mariana only had my affections for a short time, my friend. That relationship has been over for more than a year. And you know I'm planning on courting someone else."

"So, you're truly willing to risk Armando cutting off your *cojones* when you ask for his sister's hand in marriage?"

José's face fell slightly. "Armando and I have already discussed this. My intentions to marry Joséfa are not new to him. We grew up together. Our families have been close our entire lives."

"But Gaspar," Felipe lowered his voice, "Armando knows of the rumors, too. If they are to be believed, Armando may change his mind. And no one will give a second glance at Mariana. She will never be made to wed.”

José smirked.

“I already have Armando’s blessing. And I have no doubt Mariana started those rumors to force me to ask for her hand in marriage. Why would she do that? I have absolutely no idea. My initial perception of her was off.” José shrugged. “Perhaps I never really knew her at all.”

“For the love of everything, José. She’s a woman—a Spanish woman at that. And *that* woman is in love with you. The torch she carries in your honor blinds the whole town. She will seek redemption, that one. Mark me.”

“Once she realizes I am no longer available, she will welcome plenty of suitors, rumor or no rumor. And the rumors are just that. Rumors.” *Sort of.* José knew the feel of Mariana’s soft lips and the warmth of her breasts against his chest. He remembered tracing the hills and valleys of her body in his youth, over her clothing and unwitnessed. It was a lapse of judgment on José’s part. He shook off the memory.

“I would have absolutely no issue taking a woman—or two—like her to my marriage,” Felipe winked.

José sighed. “Mariana, while beautiful in every way possible, doesn’t hold my attention in the most important ways. There must be *some* common interests—the arts, music, history. We can’t spend every waking moment of our lives naked in our marriage bed ‘til death do us part.”

“I see nothing wrong with that,” Felipe murmured.

José purposefully ignored him. “Getting her to talk about those interests was impossible. All of our conversations were completely one-sided. Instead, all she wanted to do was gossip about *this family* and *that girl* and *did you see what she was wearing* and *did you hear what so and so did* and on and on and on. It was exhausting. She never had a good thing to say about anyone. I cannot imagine being married to someone like her for the rest of my life.”

"And I'm guessing you never told her about your change of heart?" Felipe asked skeptically.

"Well, no. But, as I said, I'm an afterthought to her anyway. You'll see, my friend. When we arrive at the ball tonight, she will likely be courted by some other handsome gentleman."

Felipe looked at José, puzzled. "For your sake, I hope you're right. There's no telling what a woman in a rage will do. Not exactly the chance I would take, but I'm not a dashing, handsome Admiral built like a warship whose swordsmanship is known across the country."

"And I'm not the heir of a Count with a lifetime agenda of taking multiple women to his bed."

Felipe shrugged. "True, but only the widows and the ones married to men older than my *Abuelo*."

José laughed. "You're impossible."

Felipe's words churned in his mind in the hours leading up to the ball. *Would Mariana seek revenge after so much time has passed?*

Chapter 4

A cool breeze drifted into the room. The muslin fabric brushed her ankles. Mariana pulled her shawl around her shoulders and glanced out the window admiring the sunset over the Guadalquivir. Deep, rich colors of orange and red painted the sky. Her thoughts wandered to the upcoming ball. Butterflies erupted in her stomach, trying to break free from her body. She would finally see José, and her plan had better work. If not, she didn't know what to do. Her hand drifted to her abdomen, her hand laying gently upon it. If her parents found out, it would be an absolute nightmare. Papa would disown her immediately. She needed to do this. Mariana Rodriguez Diaz deserved the best. Only the best.

"Mariana, did you hear a single word I said to you?" Lorena asked—a brow lifted to the heavens.

Mariana was startled and turned toward her. *Shoulders back, chin up, clasp hands.* "No, so sorry dear cousin. My mind was drifting."

"Well, perhaps you should try to stay here in the present instead of letting your mind drift to a man who doesn't deserve the space you're providing for him in your head."

Mariana glared at her cousin. "Whatever do you mean by that?"

"Nothing." Lorena avoided her eyes, placing her shoes on her feet.

Mariana rolled her eyes. "Lorena, what is with the dramatics? Out with it."

Lorena clasped her hands at her waist. "There are rumors, *prima*. I'm wary of even telling you because it will take you seeing it for yourself before you believe what I'm telling you." Lorena rose from her seat, turning her back on Mariana. "José Gaspar is courting Joséfa de Mayorga."

Mariana froze, refusing to believe what she had just heard. *It couldn't be. She's so….*

"There's no way that is true, Lorena. That's just nonsense."

"See!" Lorena turned, throwing her hands in the air. "This is why I didn't want to say anything to you in the first place. There's no point."

"José Gaspar is the biggest rake ever to grace the shores of *España*. He has probably had more women in his bed than pillows throughout his short lifetime. *La Familia Mayorga* will never approve of their marriage."

"Oh, hush. He's not *that* bad. And he comes from a wonderful family."

"Why would he want to marry her over someone like me anyway?" Mariana continued. "There's nothing special about her. She's completely dull." Even though Joséfa did have a fantastic figure that curved in the best places, Mariana's much thinner body didn't…and Joséfa had those green hazel eyes that men couldn't seem to resist looking into compared to her deep brown eyes. And perhaps Joséfa did have the long, flowing hair, but undoubtedly Mariana's was better. Joséfa de Mayorga was just too…. "She's too *boring* for a man like José. He'll forget her when I'm on his arm, dancing with him and when she sees us, she'll have to accept what we have together. Besides, he barely knows her."

"They have known each other since childhood. Don't be delusional," Lorena said, plopping herself on the vanity chair.

"He's been friends with Armando since childhood, and I highly doubt Armando would let a man like Gaspar anywhere near his sweet, innocent little sister. She couldn't handle a man like Gaspar. Please, Lorena. It's complete nonsense. What José and I have is *real love*. It's passionate. The kind you cannot live without."

"Oh, *sí*? If he couldn't live without your love, he'd be dead by now. You haven't been seen together for over a year. Really, Mariana. Why do you want him so much?"

Mariana's heart raced—the seed of doubt creeping into her mind. Would her plan work? What other options did she have? This had to work. She stood completely still. A deep sense of anxiety rested in the pit of her stomach. She breathed deeply, "No. No," she said, shaking her head. "He could not." Mariana glanced up at Lorena, tears glistening in her eyes. "Cousin, he and I…we…well…."

Lorena's eyes widened. "You didn't."

"Of course we did." They didn't, but the less Lorena knew about her plan, the better. "And I intend to go to him tonight as well. He told me how beautiful I was and made me feel things. He worshipped my body as I worshipped his!"

"Keep your voice down, Mariana. Do you want your parents to find out?"

"Oh, let them. I couldn't care less."

"You are blinded by lust!"

"So what if I am?"

"And what happens when lust withers away? What do you both plan on talking about? Hmm?"

Mariana shrugged. "There are plenty of families in this town with scandals."

Lorena rubbed her temples, breathing deeply. "Mariana, your naiveté is something profoundly upsetting. What you have done is completely reckless, and you'd better pray no one finds out about this."

"No. It wasn't reckless. I *love* him. And he loves me. You will see it tonight. At the ball. All of this nonsense about Joséfa will be put to rest."

"Did he tell you he loves you?"

Mariana shifted back and forth on her feet. "Well…no. But I know he does."

They stared at each other for a long time. "Perhaps it's best if we stay home tonight," Lorena suggested.

"Enough! We are going to the ball, *prima*. You will see. Everyone will see. José Gaspar belongs to me."

They spent the rest of the afternoon preparing for the ball in silence, but the seed of doubt had already sprouted in Mariana's mind.

CHAPTER 5

José's carriage rolled through the streets of Sevilla. He leaned his head against the wall, sighing. Despite looking forward to the ball, he couldn't help but think of his earlier conversation with Felipe. His brows furrowed, thinking of Mariana. The last thing he wanted to do was hurt her. José couldn't understand her ongoing obsession. He hoped she could tell the difference between infatuation and a real relationship. She would find someone else if her heart allowed. He hoped his appearance with someone else would make his position clear to her.

The carriage pulled up to the Palacio Alcazar. His sour mood shifted with a distraction that made his heart soar. Joséfa de Mayorga, daughter of Viscount Mayorga, stepped gracefully out of her carriage. Her brother, Armando Mayorga, held her hand in aid. Her long legs peeked from underneath her peach muslin ball gown. José grinned at the sight.

He rushed out of his carriage and quietly glided to her side. Armando glanced up at

José. "*Buenas noches*, Admiral Gaspar," he said, bowing to José.

"*Buenas noches*, *Señor* de Mayorga." José bowed in return, then reached for Joséfa's free hand, placing his lips softly upon it. She smiled warmly. José held her gaze for a few short moments, relishing her beauty.

"*Buenas noches*, Admiral," she replied with a smile. A gentle blush crept across her cheeks. He could have died right there. She had always been Armando's younger sister, but now, she was a woman—a charming woman. Her gorgeous deep brown hair was pinned up in curls at the back of her head. José didn't know the name of such styles. All he knew was that he couldn't take his eyes off her.

"You look exquisite tonight and always, Joséfa." He dropped her hand ever so slowly.

Armando swatted José's shoulder. "Quit your gawking, José. You act like you haven't seen her in ages."

"I cannot help it. When I was away, rumors of your sister's beauty reached even there. They described her in a way that would make Infanta Maria Joséfa jealous. How can I *not* gawk?"

"*Dios Mio*. You never stop with all the romanticism. You've known her since she was a child," Armando goaded.

Joséfa kicked Armando gently in the ankle without taking her eyes off José.

"Well, *Señor* Mayorga," he smiled, glancing his way. "She has grown into the most intriguing and intelligent woman. I've been deprived of her being away at university and then my travels with the Royal Navy. I will need to catch up on all her world history knowledge. She would undoubtedly be one of our time's greatest scholars if she were a man. But of course, you know that."

Armando nodded begrudgingly. "Yes, I do."

"All right, the both of you. I'm right here. Quit talking over me."

"Shall we go inside?" José held out his elbow. Without looking away for a moment, she wrapped her arm in his. They walked into the palace, her brother in tow. José considered himself the luckiest man in the world just then. Joséfa de Mayorga was about to receive the proposal he had always wanted to give her. Would she say yes? He hoped she would say yes. What if she said no? *Dios Mio!* She very well could, given his less-than-reputable history with women. Joséfa was a good woman, decent.

From a most respected family. Would she mind that he had his fun while he was away?

"You're quiet, José." She breathed into his shoulder, sending shivers down his spine. He almost knelt right there at the entrance of the Palacio and asked her to marry him.

José looked down at her with a warmhearted smile. "It is nothing. I am just nervous, I suppose."

"Nervous? Whatever for? How many of these balls have we been to over our lifetime? Same Sevilla, different ball. And with you away, you had to have been at worse events than this."

José laughed heartily. "You are completely right, of course."

"Then why so nervous?" she asked with a sparkle in her green hazel eyes.

A mischievous grin broke. "You'll find out soon enough, my dear."

CHAPTER 6

MARIANA GLANCED AROUND THE ROOM EVERY FEW MINUTES hoping to catch a glimpse of him. Lorena spoke true—she hadn't been with José in close to a year, but the memory of their brisk encounter stuck fiercely with her. Images of his body molded to hers flashed in her mind and sent shivers down her spine. The way he wrapped his arms around her, the way he kissed her neck, and the possessive way he kissed her lips gave her sensations her body had never felt before. It didn't matter that the encounter itself was juvenile. It didn't matter that Mariana had entertained other men. Nothing compared. She didn't mind planning to go beyond their initial rendezvous after the ball. It served both the purposes of her pleasure and his entrapment. Everything needed to go perfectly. She closed her eyes momentarily, letting out a long sigh.

"I'm so sorry, Mariana. Am I boring you with my conversation?"

She opened her eyes to find Coronel Bautista staring at her with serious offense on his face. She plastered a shy smile on her face feigning all the innocence she could muster. "My apologies, Coronel. As you might imagine, I have been on my feet far too long today. I find your conversation stimulating. You were saying that—" Mariana paused abruptly. Her eyes could not take in what she was seeing. Her heart beat violently against her chest. She forgot how to breathe and felt the walls caving in on her. *It was true. It was all true.*

José entered the front of the room in uniform, looking exceptionally handsome but with a tiny, annoying flaw. Joséfa. She was by his side on his arm, on display to the whole of Sevilla as a couple. The shock began to dissipate, followed by a rage bubbling up inside her. Her vision went red. Mariana wanted to run from the room but remained frozen in place. It would have been stimulating if she could walk over to José and throw her drink in his face. Perhaps claw his eyes out. Claw *her* eyes out. The plan she carefully thought out went up in smoke in the blink of an eye.

"Yes, he *is* a bastard, isn't he?" Coronel Bautista said, snapping Mariana out of her ire.

"More than you know."

Bautista huffed. "It is far past time something is done about the pompous ass. He has spent way too long under the protection of the king. Look at him as he struts around, all arrogance," Bautista seethed.

Mariana dared to glance in his direction. Her fury began to peak again at the sight of the two of them—of the way he looked at Joséfa as if almost ready to devour her right there in front of everyone. Her breathing spiked. Right then, all she wanted was revenge. It didn't matter that she had other priorities that needed to be addressed soon. All she could taste was sweet, sweet revenge. "I want nothing more than to see him fall," she hissed. She clenched her fists tight, nails cutting into her palm. Just moments ago, she reminisced over him intimately. What they shared was risky, yet something that would make any man wed a woman in an instant. And yet, here he was, courting another woman right before her. "I thought there was something real between us, but apparently, my feelings were not returned."

"You should know, Mariana. Word was already spreading about the two of you."

At that precise moment, with fury pouring out of her, José glanced in her direction. They locked eyes, the smile falling from his face. She must have looked exactly how she felt. She narrowed her eyes at him.

A hand wrapped around her clenched fist, bringing her back to the present. The Coronel brought her hand to his lips and kissed her gently. "He's not worth the time you have already spent on him and certainly not worth any more of your glances. Your beauty, mind, and soul are far too much for someone like him."

Mariana's eyes went wide in bewilderment, her anger dissipating. She studied him as if for the first time, taking in his dark brown eyes and straight black hair tied neatly back. *He is quite handsome. Why had I not noticed before?* Mariana wondered. He would do just fine for her plans.

"Mariana, if it is revenge you seek, then why not help me?" A sinister gleam shined in his eyes, matching the feeling she had in her broken heart. She glanced one last time in the direction of the Admiral—her gut twisting in betrayal and sadness. And as he held Joséfa proudly at his side, a deep yearning to make him hurt the same way took hold.

"Coronel Bautista."

"Please, my dear. Call me Rafael."

She turned fully toward him, a sly smile on her face. "Well, Rafael. If you mean to cause Admiral Gaspar any harm, I am at your disposal." Her eyes trailed down his jaw, across his lips. She needed revenge. She needed a husband, and it seemed Rafael needed her as well. "There are a few things besides revenge that I need, Rafael."

He leaned to her ear, his breath warm across her neck. "Whatever it is that you are seeking, you may have it. Revenge? A lover? A husband?" He leaned back and briefly glanced down at her abdomen. *Did he know? He couldn't possibly know.* "I am here for you if you will work with me."

With that, Mariana's new plan began to unfold. *Shoulders back, chin up, clasp hands.* "My dearest fiancé, what would you like my assistance with?"

Chapter 7

José navigated the onslaught of greetings when he entered the Palacio's *Salon de Embajarores*. Joséfa and Armando stayed by his side as they made their way around the room, greeting some of the most influential people, including King Charles and Queen Maria Joséfa. His mouth moved with words, but his mind rested on the warmth of her arm around his, the glances, their eyes meeting with unspoken feelings between them. They finally tucked themselves in the corner of the salon with Felipe and some other Spanish Naval officers. Armando and Felipe's ongoing chatter regarding merchant routes and the instability of the Spanish American trade carried on in the background. The rhythmic sounds of feet hitting the ground in unison echoed around them as couples danced. José would randomly put his hand on Joséfa's arm and softly squeeze, his actions having to speak for the words he couldn't presently profess.

Their mutual feeling of longing was cut short when he was tapped on the shoulder. José didn't need to turn around to know who it was by the scowl on some of the officers' faces but did so as a courtesy. "Hello, Coronel Bautista. I didn't think you would be here," José lied. He had hoped not to run into Rafael at all.

"But of course, I would be here. I wouldn't miss any of this for the world." Rafael grinned maliciously.

"Really? I hadn't noticed that you enjoyed balls so much, Rafael. Have you practiced your dancing talents with your mother in your spare time? I'm sure your little sister, Gabriela, would amuse you with a dance or two." José teased. Felipe and the men and women around him broke out in laughter.

Rafael turned beet red. "Laugh all you will now, Gaspar. I doubt there will be any room for humor in your coming days." Rafael glared at José and then turned, disappearing into the crowd. José's smile fell from his face. An uneasy feeling grew.

"What exactly did he mean by that?" Felipe whispered.

José touched the bridge of his nose and sighed. "I don't know, but I've got a bad feeling."

"Who is that man?" Joséfa asked.

"Rafael is a despicable human being who only seeks to bully and demean others while stomping his way through the ranks like the brat he is," Felipe answered. "He's arrogant for no good reason and only fortunate to be born into an aristocratic family. Otherwise, I doubt he would amount to anything at all."

"As of late, I have felt his desire to derail me," José confessed, "which is laughable on the surface. He cannot stand that I have the confidence of the king. There's little he can do, which angers him. Although, I can't help but feel he is up to something."

"I agree," said Felipe. "I will keep an eye and an ear out for you."

"Thank you."

Felipe wove through the revelry of dancers, following in the direction in which Rafael had disappeared. Whatever he was up to, something told José that he would find out soon enough. An uncomfortable feeling grew in his gut and passed through his body. A squeeze of his arm broke through his dread.

Joséfa leaned toward him, their faces only inches apart. "Do not worry yourself. We shouldn't let him ruin the evening," she said softly—her voice like honey.

He smiled. "Yes, you are right."

"I'm quite enjoying myself," she said, smiling.

José took in her deep brown eyes with flecks of green around the irises and forgot how to breathe. "You are so beautiful." He felt victorious when a deep blush swam across her face. He was dying for a moment alone with her. "Perhaps we should get some air on the patio," he suggested.

"That would be lovely." Joséfa shifted toward her brother, never letting go of José's arm. "Armando, we're going for some air."

Armando eyed his sister with one brow raised to the sky and then glanced at José. "Don't go too far. And don't even think about doing anything untoward, *Admiral*."

José laughed. It raked Armando to have to call him by his title even though they'd known each other for so long. Lord knows he had called him names far worse. "Your sister would kick me in my manhood before I could even try."

"That's correct. I taught her well." He pointed at José. "Don't forget that."

"You have my word." He winked and walked with Joséfa toward the doorway leading to the gardens.

The Patio de Los Doncellas held some of the most beautiful gardens in the world. They walked casually, taking the time to stop and admire every flower they passed. The light from the surrounding torches painted a magical orange hue on the moon-shaped arches that lined the courtyard. José and Joséfa noticed a couple hiding in the shadows sharing a quiet embrace. A soft moan echoed from the corner. Joséfa looked up at José. He knew she was blushing even with the limited light. She looked away suddenly, causing him to chuckle. To his amusement, he could swear he heard her murmur a curse.

Joséfa took a seat on the ledge of the reflecting pool. The torchlight danced across the water. José's heart beat fiercely in his chest as he sat next to her, taking in every beautiful feature this woman possessed. He wanted to make this moment special for her in every way. It was a moment they would both remember for the rest of their lives—a moment they would tell their children. The thought made his heart soar.

Joséfa's high cheekbones flushed as a cool breeze moved around the courtyard. The top of her breasts peeked from under her shawl. Her curves were perfectly proportioned and inviting. The wind shifted a strand of hair in front of her face. José reached out and tucked the soft strand behind her ear, causing her to gasp. She glanced down at her lap, her hands fidgeting.

"You know," she started, "it is said that the palace is haunted. One is never truly alone here."

"Is that so?" he asked, amused.

"Oh yes. It is said that many souls who lost their lives to Pedro the Cruel never really left Alcazar. Eleanor de Guzman, his father's mistress, was one of the first people Pedro the Cruel killed shortly after his father died. Did you know Eleanor had ten children? But I digress. Pedro and his mother accused Eleanor of trying to stir up a rebellion. They kept her in the dungeons," she rambled rapidly, barely taking a breath. "Nobody knows how she died. They may have slit her throat. Some say they tied her to a post with a rope, leaving her there for days until she perished. Countless women who refused Pedro the Cruel's advances were also executed here. Can you imagine? Executing a woman because they do not share your affection? I don't think I've ever met someone who would sink so low."

He laughed. "Men in power have been known to be outrageous sometimes."

"That is true. History does provide the evidence."

"And these ghosts, Joséfa. Have you seen them with your own eyes?"

"*Dios Mio*! No, and I pray that I never do." She shivered.

José noticed the hairs on her bare arms rising. A devious plan began to form in his head. He stared beyond Joséfa, his eyes growing wide—his jaw slack. He started breathing rapidly—his body going stock still.

"What is it, José?" Joséfa asked in alarm.

"*Fantasma! Fantasma!*"

She jumped up, looking behind her expecting to see an apparition. She squealed as José's arms wrapped around her from behind. He bellowed with laughter—the sound echoing throughout the garden. Joséfa playfully slapped his arm.

"*Hombre malo*! You scared me half to death."

"My apologies," he said between fits of laughter. "It was just too easy." She turned in his arms. José's laughter died as he saw the sudden heat in her eyes. "You take my breath away."

She smiled. "I bet you say that to all the *damas*."

He pulled her tightly against him. "I may have politely commented on their beauty. But what I will never say to any other woman is how intelligent, intriguing, or intoxicating they are." He bent, bringing his lips to her right cheek. "You, *mi querida* Joséfa, are intelligent." He glided across her face, his lips lightly grazing her lips before reaching her other cheek, "you are intriguing." His lips traveled back to hers, leaving barely any space at all. Joséfa stood still, barely able to breathe. "And you are most intoxicating."

His lips crashed into hers—his tongue exploring hers. José gripped her tighter as her knees buckled beneath her, his evident arousal pressing into her stomach. José groaned when she twined her fingers in his hair. His absolute need for her had him succumbing to his want, dispelling all civility. The intensity and passion filled his body and soul with a desire for her.

She pulled away, breaking his trance. He rested his forehead against hers, their chests moving up and down as they gasped for air.

"You promised my brother you wouldn't do anything untoward."

"So I did." He breathed across her lips. They held each other's gaze as he cupped her face, his thumbs caressing her cheeks.

"What do you want with me?" she whispered.

"I want a life with you, *mi amor*. I want it so bad that it hurts."

"I will not be taken advantage of. I am not that kind of woman," she declared fiercely.

"And I would never dream of debasing you. I want more than just your body."

A slight tinge of insecurity swam in her eyes. "Do you want more than that with *just* me?"

José's brow furrowed, his heart sinking into his stomach. "Yes. You don't believe me?"

She looked down at the ground. "What about Mariana?"

"Mariana?"

"Yes, Mariana."

José placed his finger under her chin, lifting it to meet his gaze. "Mariana and I are not a couple. I admit to having an interest in her. We had a brief affair when I was in town for a short time a year ago. While what we did was inappropriate, I never took her to my bed. I realized we weren't a match. I began to keep my distance. Mariana could not accept that my feelings were not the same. She wrote to me constantly, and I wouldn't respond to her letters. When I returned, she immediately sent a letter to my home expressing her feelings for me. I never replied. My involvement with her was daft on my part, a momentary lapse in judgment. Does my explanation suffice?"

They stood silent for what José felt was an eternity. Then, Joséfa nodded. José let out a breath. He held her face in his palms once again. "Joséfa, you have to know how much I adore you."

She smiled. "I do."

He went down on one knee. "Marry me, Joséfa."

Her mouth dropped, and her eyes went wide.

"Make me the happiest man on Earth, and be my wife. I want to spend my days bearing witness to your joy when we visit new places, when you learn new histories, and explore new cultures. I want the pleasure of witnessing you bearing our children as you become the world's greatest mother. I want the privilege of growing old with you. I swear to honor you, to love you immensely all the days of our lives together. You have captured my soul, and I never want you to release it. Say you'll be my wife."

The tears streaked down her cheeks. José's heart leaped when she nodded. "*Sí.* I will marry you."

He sprang up, kissing her passionately, her tears coating his face. He pulled away, placing soft kisses down her neck.

Joséfa sighed. "You need to ask for my hand in marriage."

José laughed, pulling back to look at her. "I have already asked your brother, and I have his blessing. I plan to ask your father formally when he returns to Sevilla. The man is like a father to me. I doubt he will say no. When does the Viceroy Mayorga return from *Nueva España*?"

"Former Viceroy," she corrected. "He returns soon. His last letter was sent just before he left. We expect his ship should be arriving any day now."

"Excellent. I will be waiting at the port when he arrives so that I may ask for his daughter's hand in marriage."

Joséfa's smile grew. It was so lovely, he etched it in his memory. "This will be an evening I will never forget."

"Nor will I," José agreed. "But we'd better get inside before your brother murders me, and then I will never get to ask your father for your hand." She giggled as they strolled arm in arm, heading for the sounds of music, dancing, and laughter. They would give them another reason to celebrate.

Chapter 8

Felipe's efforts to find out more about what Rafael was up to were a failure. He roamed around the ball for nearly half an hour and then departed. "Nothing unusual," Felipe remarked, but José couldn't let it go. It put a damper on an evening that should have been one of the best of his life.

He paced the length of his study and back again, stopping in front of the books lining the wall. They were his father's. José kept all of them. The books on a shelf told the observer everything one needed to know about a man. It was a gateway to one's soul, and in some small way, it kept him close to his father.

With great luck, José became an Admiral—the son of a prosperous merchant. It was the reason for his successful career with the Royal Navy. His father taught him everything about shipping routes, popular ports, and places to avoid. That, of course, was most important when carrying his Majesty's goods and other items that could never be revealed to the public. They were sensitive, and the king would have his head if any pirate were to rob one of those ships. José shuddered. *Blasted pirates.* They were always a nuisance. José didn't understand why any man would choose a life so low.

Suddenly, there was a knock on the door of the study. José's brows furrowed. "Come in."

Anna Luísa—his caretaker—peeked her head in the room, her eyes wide and alarmed. "Admiral," she said, a little short of breath, "you have a message from the king. It appears it is urgent." She walked briskly across the room, handing him the letter with the king's seal. He took it from her and opened it, wondering what the king could want at this hour. José quickly scanned over the letter and then reread it. He was to report to the Palacio immediately. He couldn't understand what would prompt such an urgent request. Perhaps something went wrong with one of the shipping routes he suggested.

Cristo, I hope nothing was stolen.

He put the letter in his pocket, pausing at the door. He completely forgot Anna Luísa, whose face was tight with worry. "*Gracias*, Anna Luísa. I'm sure it will be fine." A growing sense of unease had him doubting his words.

Two of his Majesty's guards greeted his carriage when he arrived. Climbing out, he greeted them, but they responded only with, "This way, Admiral Gaspar." They walked down the quiet corridors, their footsteps echoing against the walls. They opened the doors to a room, motioning for him to enter. The scene he was met with stunned him. The king sat in an opulent chair, Mariana sitting to his right, Rafael standing by her side, sneering. His ominous warning from earlier in the evening came back to him: *Laugh all you will now, Gaspar. I doubt there will be any room for humor in your coming days.*

"Admiral Gaspar, thank you for joining us," the king said, his eyes unusually cold and distant. He beckoned José, and he cautiously stepped forward.

José glanced at Rafael, who wore a smug expression José wanted to punch off his face. Mariana, however, didn't look at him at all. She stared at the ground before her feet.

"A matter of grave concern has been brought to my attention." The king reached into his pocket and pulled out the most beautiful necklace with rubies that glimmered in the torchlight. "Admiral Gaspar, do you recognize these?"

José's brows furrowed. "No, your Highness. I've never seen them before, but they are quite lovely." He glanced at Mariana, who was still staring at the floor. "My apologies, your Highness. What is this about?"

"He's lying, your Highness." Rafael protested. "To make matters worse, he put *Señorita* Rodriguez, a woman of noble birth, in danger by asking her to keep them at her house. This poor woman has been subjected to his thievery."

José couldn't believe what he was hearing. "Your highness, this is madness. I did not do what he accuses me of."

Rafael's eyebrow shot to the sky. "Oh? I have it on good authority that you visited Mariana several times during your stay nearly a year ago. What *exactly* were you checking in on, if not the missing jewels? Your majesty, some witnesses can attest to José's appearance at Mariana's residence."

"And who's authority is that, Coronel Bautista? *Yours*?" José replied, his composure slipping. "Because if it is, it is more than likely fabricated."

"Admiral Gaspar, are you accusing Coronel Bautista and *Señorita* Rodriguez of lying to their king?" The king glared at him with disdain.

José's entire body froze. His majesty had never looked at him like this—with such contempt. "Yes. I am Your Highness."

"Then, how do you explain the comings and goings at *Señorita* Rodriguez's house, Admiral Gaspar?" the king asked, one eyebrow raised to the sky.

José's mouth opened and closed. He glanced at Mariana, who had not moved. He could now see the tears welling up in her eyes. She knew he was innocent, but everyone in the room knew he wasn't there to hide jewels. That grave error that fateful night was coming back to haunt him. "I went to her home to court her."

"Court her?" the king replied aghast. "Do you think me a fool?" The king stood slowly, coming face to face with José. His gaze, which generally held such warmth toward him, held an intensity he had never seen from him before. José broke out in a sweat, his body turning cold. He glanced down at Mariana. He studied her as she breathed heavily. José's eyes narrowed when he glanced at Rafael, who stood out of the king's view, grinning evilly.

He looked back at the king. "Your Majesty, I am one of your most trusted advisers. You have trusted my guidance before. I am asking you to trust me now. I am innocent."

The king glared at him and nodded. José breathed a sigh of relief. He returned to his chair, spine straight. "Admiral José Gaspar, you stand accused of stealing jewels from your king. Guards, please take Admiral Gaspar to the dungeons, where he will await his sentence." José's entire body went numb as his whole world fell away.

"Your Majesty! I am innocent!"

The king flicked his hand in the air. "Guards, get him out of my sight." The guards grabbed his arms, yanking him. He didn't miss the smirk on Mariana's face before he exited the room.

CHAPTER 9

THE SMELL OF THE FILTH OVERTOOK HIS SMALL SURROUNDINGS penetrating his nostrils, courtesy of the rancid fumes emanating from the chamber pot. As his stomach flipped, his anger rose. He remembered Mariana's face, how she wouldn't even look him in the eye. As he sat in the dark corner of his cell going over the events that led him there, he begrudged himself for not seeing it sooner—Mariana wanted revenge. He should have listened to Felipe. He never realized the depth of Rafael's hatred of him. It was a bold move on their part. Rafael and Mariana devised the perfect plan pinning José in a corner with no way out. Checkmate.

He sighed, slamming his head back against the stone wall several times—the final time a little too hard. "*Carajo*," he exclaimed, rubbing the back to ensure he wasn't bleeding.

"I doubt that will solve much of anything except to give you a bruise and a headache," a man's voice called to him from the adjacent cell.

"Yes, but it does remind me that this is not a nightmare," José responded.

"No, this is not a nightmare. This is reality," the man replied sadly.

José sat for a few moments welcoming the distraction from his over-analyzing. "What is your name?"

The man emerged from the shadows of his cell, approaching the bars that separated them. The moonlight hit his face, and José could tell he had been there for some time. His beard was an inch long, his hair matted, and his face was streaked with dirt. He couldn't be more than a decade older than José. His eyes looked upon him with a welcomed gentleness. "Rodrigo Lopez at your service, sir," he said, bowing his head. "And you are?"

"José Gaspar at your service."

Rodrigo's eyes widened a bit.

"José Gaspar? *Admiral* José Gaspar?"

"The very same," José sighed, looking down at the ground. "Although, I do not believe I am an 'Admiral' for much longer."

"For someone like yourself to be sitting in a filthy cell?" Rodrigo sat on the cold ground, resting his arms on his knees, and gazed intently at José. "Seems like quite the story."

"Yes, it is quite a story."

"Care to share? It may feel better to tell it," Rodrigo offered sympathetically, the corner of his mouth lifting in a smile.

José contemplated just how much he should divulge to this stranger but decided that letting him into the inner workings of his mind might be beneficial after all. Perhaps Rodrigo could see what he wasn't able to.

And so, José started from the beginning with his lust for Mariana, his courting of Joséfa, the warnings from Felipe, and the accusation of stealing, ending at the cell he sat in.

Rodrigo took in every detail with interest, a *v* forming on his forehead as he frowned. He opened his mouth and closed it, then winced a little. "Admiral Gaspar," he finally said, "forgive me for being so forward, but a man as handsome as yourself probably had many women interested throughout your years. Didn't you expect this type of reaction from the lady? Surely, you didn't think that *not* saying anything to her could've ended in anything but disaster?" he asked, somewhat amusinged.

José sighed. "Clearly, I hadn't thought everything through. I truly wish I had." He rose from the ground and started pacing the length of his cell. "And that sniveling, despicable little man encouraged her. I just know he did."

"Does it matter if he encouraged her or not? And can you blame her? The whole town believed her to be promiscuous. You didn't leave her with many other options," Rodrigo concluded. "Coronel Bautista is quite the resourceful bastard. You should have seen this coming, given the lengths he has gone to rise in the ranks."

"I should have. I'm mad at myself for not recognizing his will," José replied, perturbed. He couldn't determine if he was more annoyed at himself or Rodrigo. His brows furrowed as he continued to pace in deep concentration. Then, something Rodrigo said in his previous statement distracted his thoughts.

"Rodrigo? How is it that you know so much about Coronel Bautista?" he asked, surveying him curiously.

Not even the mass of shaggy, matted hair could hide the welling of tears in his eyes. He stood from the ground and began pacing. "That's a long, sad story."

"Care to share? It may feel better to tell it," José replied, using Rodrigo's words.

Rodrigo smiled, but the sadness in his eyes remained. "I know of you and Coronel Bautista because I, too, was in the Royal Navy once," he confessed. "On the day I was to set sail for the *Nueva España*, I failed to report for duty, risking a certain arrest for abandoning my post." Rodrigo's eyes brimmed with tears. "I couldn't leave her," he spoke softly. "My wife. She…she was so very ill. Had I left, I knew it would have been the final time I would see her. I wanted to hold her as she took her last breath. I would've never been able to do so had I left."

Rodrigo moved toward the barred window of his cell. The faint moonlight highlighted his features—his face heavy with pain and anguish. "I would do it all over again," he professed. José couldn't help but feel sympathy for his cellmate. If his Joséfa were dying, there would be no question. He would have done the same.

"On a night I was sure to be my wife's last, Coronel Bautista came to collect. Despite my pleading to permit me a moment to say goodbye to my wife, he took me there and then." Rodrigo's anger seeped from him in waves. "He refused. I begged him, yet he still refused," he seethed.

"I received word of her passing the next day. The pain over not being there when she passed will live with me forever," he said softly. The silence stretched on, José not daring to move a muscle. The man poured his soul out for what may be the first time since losing his wife, and somehow José could relate. In a way, he'd just lost Joséfa. The reality of their situation filled José with a sense of dread. He was in a cell awaiting a sentence that was likely death. Joséfa would move on. They would never be, not after all of this. A hollow feeling grew in the pit of his stomach.

Rodrigo sat once again, leaning back against the wall of his cell. "Even though I abandoned my post, even as I was refused the privilege of holding her as she departed from this world, I would change nothing."

They didn't talk again that evening—each man left to their thoughts. The cool summer night air crept into the cell. Up until the summons, he'd had the best day of his life when Joséfa agreed to marry him. All he waited on was her father's return to make it official. All of it was gone now—making her his wife and creating a family with her. He wished desperately for a way to fix it, but José couldn't understand how the accusation of thievery was believed in the first place.

How had the king believed the scheme Mariana and Rafael cooked up? And so easily! The question plagued him long into the next day as the darkness claimed his cell once again. No one came to march him to his death. José's entire body went slack against the cold stone wall. He thanked God that his mother was not alive to see this. May she rest in peace. And his father would be even further disappointed. What must they think of this as they watch from the heavens? *You're a complete disgrace. That's what they're thinking.*

The soft shuffle of steps sounded down the hallway, drawing him from his thoughts—a dark figure emerging to stand in front of his cell.

"Admiral Gaspar?" the man whispered.

"Yes?"

A set of keys rattled against the cell door. It sprung open to reveal a short, round man—his bald head shining in the moonlight. "You need to come with me. Quickly."

José sprung from the ground and approached the cell door. "Who are you? Who sent you?" he asked in a hushed tone.

"My name is Manuel. And your men sent for me," he said with a warm smile.

José glanced at the cell next to him. Rodrigo sat in the corner, a smile tugging the corner of his mouth. A sense of guilt grew at the thought of leaving him behind.

"What about him?" he asked, pointing to Rodrigo.

Manuel's brows furrowed. "I am not able to free him."

"Why ever not? His crime is minimal."

"Piracy is not minimal, Admiral."

José's head snapped in Rodrigo's direction. "Piracy?" he bit with disgust.

Rodrigo shrugged. "They believe I am responsible for a raid that took down one of the Royal Navy's ships." Rodrigo slowly rose from the ground and walked to the bars dividing their cells. "Every word I told you was true. But my wife died some time ago. I was pulled from a merchant ship the minute we arrived. Admiral Gaspar, given what you told me, it will be difficult to prove your innocence. You will need to escape Sevilla if the king is not swayed. Before my capture, I was due to set sail on a British merchant ship. It is still in port. I can get you out," he said confidently.

"And what? Be in a lot with someone accused of thievery?" he hissed in a whisper.

Rodrigo looked him dead in the eyes. "Are you not accused of thievery as well?"

José studied him; his words sank into the depths of his mind. He shook his head. "I can't believe I'm considering this."

Manuel tugged José's sleeve. "Admiral, we must go. We are pressed for time."

"Release him," José demanded. "Now."

"But Admiral!"

"Do it."

Manual eyed him speculatively and then moved to Rodrigo's cell door, opening it. Rodrigo quickly stepped out, resting his hand on José's shoulder.

"I am your most humble servant."

"I know," José replied.

"Come this way!" Manuel instructed.

They followed him down the hallway to a side door. It swung open, and the fresh air assaulted his lungs. José took a moment to appreciate the rancid-free air. The three silently moved through Sevilla's dark allies—distancing themselves from the Palacio Alcazar—when Manual stopped abruptly. He turned, facing José.

"We are to go to Casa Mayorga. Your friends are waiting for you there." Manuel glanced at Rodrigo uneasily, and it dawned on José—Rodrigo would not be welcome.

"Admiral," Rodrigo interjected. "I will go to the docks and arrange our passage to *Nueva España*."

José nodded, and Rodrigo whirled around, disappearing down the dark street toward the docks.

"Come," Manuel instructed. José followed Manuel to spend what would prove to be his final time with Joséfa.

CHAPTER 10

THEY TREKKED DOWN MULTIPLE SIDE STREETS, REACHING CASA Mayorga within half an hour. Manuel carefully opened the wooden door. It creaked slightly as they made their way into the room. José took a deep breath, not knowing whether he was fully prepared to see Joséfa—not knowing how she had taken the news of his arrest. He shook his head. *How had it come to this?*

Manuel led him down the hallway—light spilling from a room at the end. As he entered the room, he found Armando looking out the window. Joséfa sat on a chair by the fire biting her fingernail—eyes rimmed red. Felipe, pacing with his gaze toward the floor, looked up. "Thank God!" Felipe exclaimed.

Joséfa's head snapped in his direction, tears building in her eyes. She ran to him, throwing her arms around his waist—sobbing uncontrollably into his chest. José gently squeezed her, stroking her hair. "It's all right, *mi querida*. It's all right. I'm here now."

Armando turned to them—his face ridden with worry. "How did this happen, José?"

"To be honest, I haven't the faintest clue how the king managed to believe the farce," he said, still consoling Joséfa, whose sobs were ebbing.

"I'll be taking my leave," Manuel said, turning to leave the room.

"Manuel," José called after him. Manuel paused in the doorway.

"I know this is a great risk," he acknowledged. "Thank you."

"Do not waste any time, Admiral," Manual warned. "It is only a matter of time before the guards recognize you are no longer in that cell. You will need to come up with a plan. If I can be of any assistance, your friends know how to find me." He left down the hallway—the door clicking shut a moment later.

"Come, Joséfa. Sit down." José guided Joséfa back to her chair, where she plopped down into it. Felipe handed him a dram of whiskey, which José accepted gratefully—the amber liquor burning as it slid down his throat.

"Well," Felipe began as he sat opposite Joséfa, "it would appear that while the king easily believed Mariana, your fellow officers did not." He smiled weakly. "The king took her word as a bond. But of course, we know Rafael had everything to do with this."

"That *bruja* is just as much to blame for this!" Joséfa snarled.

"Yes, well. There is little we can do about it now," Armando said. "The only way to prove José's innocence is for Mariana to confess that Rafael manipulated her into framing José. The woman was scorned." Armando glanced pointedly at José. "I doubt she'd do anything that proves José's innocence. It would mean she lied to the king. It could mean her death—not to mention an admission of theft because Rafael *did* steal the jewels. Mariana never had access to them."

Joséfa glared at Armando, a tear streaming down her cheek, her face growing red. "Do not look at José like that. He is not to blame."

"I'm looking at him like that because he knows better," Armando protested.

José patted Joséfa's shoulder. "Armando speaks true, *mi querida*. I made a mistake. I shouldn't have been in Mariana's home in the first place." She sighed, slumping deeper into her chair.

"So, what options do we have?" asked Felipe.

Armando clasped his hands behind his back, turning to the window. Joséfa stared into the fire biting her fingernail again. José leaned against her chair, brows furrowed in contemplation—the silence stretching into precious minutes.

"We should sneak José back into his cell, go to Mariana, and convince her to confess," Joséfa suggested. "She could say it was all Rafael's idea. She wouldn't be implicated. The blame would be placed on Rafael. She can pretend she was coerced into the plan."

"It's the middle of the night," said Armando. "Much too late to accept guests."

"It would appear Mariana is accustomed to accepting late-night guests," Felipe chided as he rose from his seat. "It's as good a plan as any, but it doesn't leave us much time. We need to go now." He looked toward José. "I assume you know how to get a hold of her at this hour?"

José blushed as Joséfa eyed him uneasily. "You will *not* be going. I will," she demanded.

"That's not going to happen," Armando turned, glaring at her with conviction. "I won't have my sister involved in this."

"It's not your decision, Armando. It's mine."

"The hell it is! Until our father returns, you are in my care!"

"I'm a grown woman!"

"Barely!"

"I'm twenty! I'm not a damned child!"

Armando stared at her, willing her to back down before he turned his pleading eyes to José. "Surely you don't agree with this plan?"

He sighed. "It's a solid plan. And while I'm not too fond of Joséfa being involved any more than you, it cannot be me. And I don't think she would respond well to you or Felipe. If Joséfa goes, she may be willing to listen to her. I think she can convince Mariana. Joséfa's good at communicating."

"Good at communicating," Armando mimicked.

Joséfa rolled her eyes.

"Will you go with Joséfa?" José asked Felipe, relieved when he nodded. "Then it's settled. Joséfa and Felipe will go to Mariana's. Armando and I will wait here. We may need to have a different plan should this not work. We'll think on it."

José reached down, gently brushing Joséfa's cheek, smiling in a way he hoped would ease her nerves. "Everything will turn out fine, *mi amor.*"

She reached up and squeezed his hand. "I truly hope so."

CHAPTER 11

THE CARRIAGE ROCKED STEADILY BACK AND FORTH. FELIPE LOOKED pensively out the window as they arrived at Mariana's. Joséfa breathed deeply a few times—her heart thumping rapidly against her chest as they pulled up to Mariana's residence.

"Come on," he said.

She nodded, and they silently stepped onto the street. Felipe reached into his coat pocket, pulling out a few *pesetas*. He glanced at the second-story window closest to them. The breeze moved the drapes, gently grazing the flower bed on the balcony railing. Felipe launched the first *peseta*. It clanged on the bedroom floor. When she didn't come to the window, Felipe found the second *peseta*. Another clang. Suddenly, the drapes moved aside. Mariana's scowl was visible despite the lack of light on her face. Felipe pointed to the home's side door, Mariana disappearing moments later.

"This way," he whispered.

They walked to the side of the home. Joséfa's heart was hammering a staccato beat. Felipe stood behind her, giving her a tender nod of encouragement when the door opened. Mariana stepped out into the night—her eyes narrowed. She glared at Joséfa as if her eyes could dissect her body. Mariana crossed her arms over her chest. "What can I do for you all?"

"Admiral Gaspar has been accused of stealing the king's jewels. I understand you had something to do with this?" she asked.

Mariana smirked. "The *former* Admiral. And yes, I did."

Joséfa's nails dug into her palms. Her knuckles went white. "How could you?"

Mariana's eyes turned venomous. "How could *I*? After the man took my heart and shattered it? How dare *you* come here in the middle of the night and try to shame me when José is the one who led me on."

"Yes, he did," Felipe interjected. "And believe me when I say that he has been thoroughly scolded for doing so. He should have never done that to you, but you know very well that the two of you were never intimately involved beyond that late-night visit. He never shared in your affections, and while your intimacies went beyond kissing, you never consummated the relationship."

Mariana's eyes went wide. "He told you that?"

"Of course he did," he replied.

"He had no right," Mariana hissed.

"And it is not your right to accuse a man who broke your heart of a crime he never committed," said Joséfa, her patience dissipating.

Mariana stepped closer to her. "I couldn't care less about your judgments. I loathe him. I take no shortage of satisfaction in delivering what he deserves. He believed himself untouchable—always taking whatever opportunity he wanted, *whomever* he wanted. He's paying for it now, isn't he?"

"Have you no place in your heart for forgiveness?" Joséfa pleaded, her vision blurring with unshed tears. "You know he is innocent. You are sending him to a most certain death with these accusations. I beg you to please see it in your heart to forgive him and end this charade. Please."

Mariana gave her a once-over—a smug grin on her face. "And what if I do? He'll crawl back to you without giving me a second thought." Mariana leaned toward Joséfa, disdain hanging on every word. "He should have been mine. You couldn't

possibly know what to do with a man like Gaspar. You've probably never been kissed by a man—sweet, little Joséfa. I have no
idea why he would waste his time on you. And here you are,
standing at my doorstep in all your self-righteousness, asking
me for a favor? You have lost your mind."

"That is quite enough, Mariana." Felipe scolded. "Joséfa
has done nothing wrong."

"She took him from me."

"You never had him in the first place!" he exclaimed, his
voice echoing across the walls of the neighboring homes.

Joséfa expected to be verbally assaulted, but hearing the
nastiness in Mariana's tone exercised every ounce of patience
she could muster. "Why not turn in Rafael?" she asked, determined for Mariana to see reason. "We all know he orchestrated
this. We know it; Admiral Gaspar's men know it. You are the
only reason the king so easily believed the lie. But you can
change that. Tell the king this was Rafael's idea."

Mariana studied her fingernails. "I'm afraid I cannot do that."

"You cannot, or you will not?" Felipe asked.

Mariana shrugged. "Both, perhaps. First, the damage is
done. I refuse for the people of this town to view me as a liar."

"But you *are* a liar," he countered.

"And secondly, but most importantly," Mariana continued,
"I will not implicate my betrothed in a crime."

The ground fell out from underneath Joséfa. Felipe reached
out to steady her. "You're *marrying* Rafael?" she asked.

"Yes, the date is set. So, no. I will not implicate my future
husband," she smiled coldly. "My sincerest apologies, but it appears your efforts here are worthless. I do hope you both have
a most pleasant evening." She turned on a heel, slamming the
door without a backward glance.

All the hope drained from Joséfa, an overwhelming feeling
of disbelief filling its void. A tear escaped down her cheek. Her
future with José slipped away, and there was nothing else she
could do.

CHAPTER 12

THE FIRE CRACKLED, SENDING BITS OF ASH DANCING ACROSS THE ceramic tile floor. The whiskey burned José's throat—a reminder that this was all real, and he was a fugitive if Joséfa and Felipe returned with bad news. If they could not convince Mariana, he would have to flee with a man he hardly knew he could trust. Dread crept down into his stomach, churning with whiskey. He breathed deeply, attempting to calm his flailing nerves.

"What is the backup plan?" Armando asked. He tapped mindlessly against his glass, staring into the fire.

José braced himself for Armando's reaction. "A man is waiting for me at the docks. He was in the dungeons with me. I set him free, expecting him to stay true to his word. He is to secure passage on a merchant ship if we can't prove my innocence."

Armando's head snapped in his direction. "You freed a criminal? Have you lost your mind?"

"What other options do I have?" Armando stared at him, his face heavy with worry. José continued. "He knows a Captain that will take me to *Nueva España*. Perhaps I can be of some use on their ship."

"That could be disastrous! How do you know this man is trustworthy? He could be a murderer, for all you know. Or worse—a pirate."

"Well, he was *accused* of piracy, although he claims to be a sailor on a British merchant ship."

"*Carajo*, José," he exclaimed before slamming his tumbler on the table. "Are you mad? If he is lying, your reputation will be ruined forever. There will be nothing Joséfa or I can do to save your honor. The both of you will never have a future."

"At this moment, there is no future. She cannot marry a thief."

"But if the king finds out…." Armando sank into his chair in defeat.

"What other choice do I have? Do you have any grand ideas that you want to share? Because if you do, I would love to hear them."

The grandfather clock ticked in the corner of the room without abandon, the fire casting deep shadows across Armando's face, deep in concentration. José poured more whiskey into their glasses and sat back in his chair.

"You understand then?" he asked.

Armando sighed. "Yes, I understand."

"If there were any other way, I would have considered it already."

"And what of my sister?"

"What am I supposed to do? There is no future with her."

"It doesn't have to be that way."

José's heart leaped slightly with hope. "What do you mean by that?"

Armando rose from his chair and moved toward the fire, placing his free hand on the mantle. "Felipe and I are going to *Nueva España* once my father arrives. Joséfa can do some more investigating into who the players are in this ruse. They didn't work alone. Someone has to know something. Joséfa is smart. She will figure out how we can prove your innocence. In the meantime, we'll meet in *Puerto Rico*. From there, you'll be part of my crew under a different name. When we return, hopefully, Joséfa will have this resolved.

"You think she can do this on her own?"

"Oh, I know she is fully capable. But she won't be alone. She'll have the help of your men."

José shook his head, his heart aching in his chest. "They're not my men anymore."

"Yes, they are, Admiral. Those men have more respect for you than their King. They know you didn't do this. Everyone does."

"Then why does the king believe Rafael? This part still remains a mystery to me. It's driving me mad."

"He doesn't believe Rafael. He believes *Mariana*."

José buried his head in his hands. "I cannot understand how I got here."

Armando placed a hand on his shoulder. "It will all work out. You are a good man, José. Taking care of my sister is a big responsibility. I've been doing it all my life. There are very few men that I would trust with her. You are one of them."

José's brow rose. "You trust me with her after what I did to Mariana?"

"Psst…really, José. Don't you think I know who Mariana is? Mariana is a scandalous woman. You weren't the first man she developed an obsession for. I was the object of her infatuations before she turned her attention to you. I'd be lying if I said a part of me is grateful, no offense."

"None taken. I'd be lying if I said a part of me wished Mariana's affections were on you instead. Why did I have to go and get involved with her? How I wish she kept obsessing over you."

Armando shrugged. "I never paid her any attention. But I digress; one thing is for certain—you value who Joséfa is as a person, not just for her beauty," Armando said as he smiled warmly. "One of many reasons I never protested your match with Joséfa is because I knew you would honor her all the days of your lives together. I'm aware your marriage to her is dependent on us proving your innocence, but I should like to call you brother one day. Let us hold on to hope."

The front door banging open against the wall with a thud made them jump to their feet. Footsteps shuffled rapidly down the hallway. Joséfa burst into the room, tears streaming down her face. "She refused. That evil, wicked woman refused!"

Felipe strode into the room behind her. "She is engaged to Rafael. She will not turn on him."

José's chest tightened. He had no other options. Finding Rodrigo became imminent. He was leaving for *Nueva España*.

CHAPTER 13

THE INCOMING SHIPS LEFT GENTLE RIPPLES IN THE GUADALQUI-vir, reflecting the oncoming dawn in their wake—pale pinks and purples rolled over the water. A cool breeze lapped around José's face causing the hood of his cloak to tickle his forehead. He held Joséfa in his arms for what might be the last time. His heart ached as her gentle sobs vibrated against his shoulder.

"I truly hate that woman," she said between sniffles.

José backed away from her, cradling her face in his hands. "Do not give her the privilege of space in your mind, *mi amor.* I want you to paint a picture of our future together with you as my wife, our children—all ten of them, like Eleanor de Guzman if you wish. You continue your history studies and all the things that bring you joy. Hold *these* thoughts in your head. When all of this is resolved, we will be married. We will have that. I promise you."

"Do not make promises you cannot be sure to keep," she said. Her tears ran over José's hands.

"*No llores, mi amor.* You're breaking my heart."

"I cannot help it. I don't want to lose you."

"You will not lose me. You have me forever." His lips crashed onto hers. Passion, helplessness, love, and fear of what may come all poured into the delicate dance of their lips. The taste of salt melted on his tongue. The prospect of this being their final kiss made him dizzy with desire. José pulled her tightly to him, his hard length digging into her belly through the cloak. Joséfa gasped, lost to José's command of her body. He broke their kiss— both willing the air into their lungs. Both left wanting.

He placed his forehead softly against hers. "I love you, Joséfa. I have no right to ask you to wait for me. But you are right. I cannot be certain we will find each other again. It would be selfish of me not to encourage you to move on. Your happiness is more important. If you ever grow tired of waiting for me and you can have the life you dreamed of with someone else, I will not be upset. I will understand completely."

"I will do no such thing."

"But you must if something happens to me and I cannot return home."

She shook her head. "I cannot even bear the thought of anyone else."

José chuckled. "As much as I love hearing the words leave your mouth, I am serious."

"As am I."

He pulled back, his gaze fierce. "You cannot wait for me forever. A part of me wants to live in the beautiful world you create for us in your mind; another part feels guilty for even suggesting it."

Joséfa cupped his face, and he saw all the love she possessed reflected in her eyes. "I am yours, José. I will wait for you. And if you do not return, I will never wed another. I am not capable of it. I love you too much."

He placed a gentle kiss on her lips. "Your words have embedded themselves in the depths of my heart where they will remain until my death."

The birds chirped as the sun breached the morning sky. From a distance, the ships began to unload and load various goods. Men moved with synchronized precision—some rolling barrels—others carrying crates of food heading to the ships' kitchens. Joséfa pulled away suddenly, her brows furrowed. "Is that my father's ship?"

José strained to make out Martin de Mayorga's ship settled in the port. "Yes, I believe it is. Come, I will bring you to him. Your brother and Felipe must already be waiting for us." She grabbed his hand reluctantly. He smiled in encouragement. "Everything will be all right, *mi amor*. You will see."

Armando and Felipe came into view as they made their way to the docks. Armando's face was buried in his palm, Felipe placing a supportive hand on his shoulder. A young sailor looked on warily.

"What is it? What's happened?" Joséfa asked when they reached their side.

The tears welled up in Armando's eyes. "He's dead. Our father…is dead."

Joséfa shook her head. "No. No. No! It's not supposed to happen this way. He resigned. His last letter said he was coming home."

"He's not coming home, *hermana*. He's dead."

Joséfa sank to the ground. José knelt and held her to him, rocking her like a child. Her wailing echoed against the walls of the ship. There were no words José could provide her—nothing would make it better. Having lost both his parents, he knew the feeling all too well. He caressed the top of her head. His shirt grew damp with her tears. Time passed them, but he could hardly care. Sailors continued loading and unloading items around them, but all he could do was sit on the dock until the sobbing ebbed.

A hand came down gently on José's shoulder. "Admiral?" a familiar voice asked. José glanced up to find Rodrigo cautiously taking in the scene around him. "The guards. They are on their way down to the docks. You can see them in the distance." Rodrigo pointed toward the town, where guards raced down the streets. "If they see you with your friends, they will know who helped you escape. I'm afraid we need to go," he said apologetically.

"Go, José," Joséfa protested, her voice rasping.

José cupped her face. "I am so sorry. I hate to leave you like this." He glanced at Armando. "I will meet you in *Puerto Rico?*"

Armando nodded—his eyes red-rimmed and brimming with tears. "Look for the *Gloriana*. We'll arrive a little later than anticipated, but I will be there. You have my word."

"And mine as well," said Felipe reaching down to clasp José's hand. "I will look after Joséfa. We'll make this right somehow."

José's heart swelled with gratitude. "Thank you, both. I am eternally grateful for your friendship."

"You need to go, *mi vida*," Joséfa warned. "Please. I will not lose you, too."

His lips met hers briefly, trying to convey all he felt for her. "*Te amo.* And I will forever."

"I love you, too. Now *go!*"

José jumped up and followed Rodrigo down the docks—Joséfa's kiss still fresh on his lips. He barely noticed the crew or the conditions of the vessel. He didn't have time to ask who the captain was. None of that mattered. He was at their mercy now. He scrambled his way to the deck and watched Joséfa held tightly by her brother with Felipe at their side—until they were nothing more than a speck in the distance, until the only home he'd known his entire life disappeared, possibly forever.

Part II

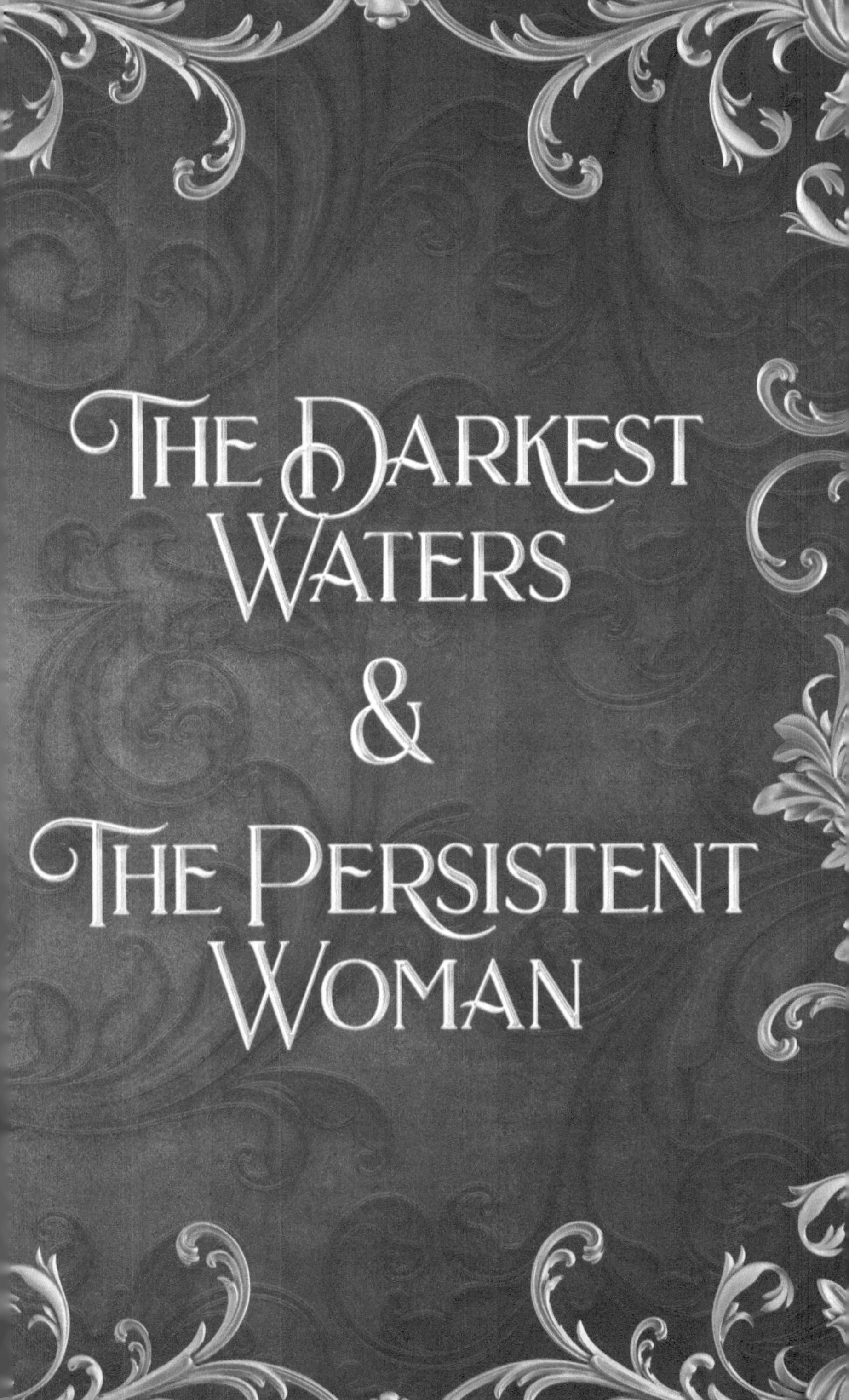
The Darkest Waters
&
The Persistent Woman

Chapter 14

Over the next few days, José kept to himself. The ship was filled with sailors who would scare the bravest of men if caught with them in a dark alley. Aches and pains shot down his arms from the lifting, pushing, and heaving—the daily life of a sailor he thought he had left behind. The ache in his heart had not subsided. He thought of his Joséfa often. Brave and determined, she was sure to find a way to vindicate him.

One particular evening, José lay in his hammock as it rocked slowly from side to side. Heavy snoring echoed from the back corner of the crew's quarters, making it difficult to sleep as tired as he was. A silhouette descended the steps below deck, which he had no trouble identifying as Rodrigo.

"José? Are you awake?" he whispered.

"Clearly," he said, gesturing to the symphony of snoring in the far corner.

"Come. The Captain would like to speak with you."

José slowly rose from the hammock—pain shooting through his lower back. They ascended the stairs to the deck in silence. The Captain had barely said two words to José the entire two days he'd been on the ship. It seemed as if he wanted to avoid him, turning away from him when he got close or leaving the room altogether when he entered. The fact that he was an

Admiral for the Spanish Royal Navy had everything to do with it. Trust, it seemed, would be an uphill battle.

Uneasiness coursed through every step as they entered the doorway of the Captain's quarters. The Captain sat at a desk riddled with mountains of maps and food. A brown dog sat by his feet eating scraps—his ribs reflected in the lamplight. By the back window, objects sparkled in the moonlight—objects that looked distinctively like mounds of gold pieces, jewelry, and chalices worth more than the Vatican.

José slammed Rodrigo against the wall. "You brought me on a God-forsaken pirate ship?!"

"I was trying to save your life," Rodrigo protested.

A gun cocked behind his head.

"Put him down, Gaspar."

José eased his grip on Rodrigo, releasing him to the ground. The Captain flicked the gun to the chair in front of his desk. José moved to the chair, his anger restrained in his chest.

"Now, Gaspar. I wanted to bring you here to formally welcome you to the crew."

"Welcome me to the crew? You are mistaken, Captain. I never requested to join, nor was I asked."

"I wasn't exactly asking."

José glared at him. "Why in the world would you want me to join your crew? The men on your ship know who I am. They know I'm part of his majesty's Navy that—"

"*Were* part."

The heat emanated from his head. "I *was* part of his majesty's Navy that put pirates like you in jail—*pirates* like Rodrigo here." Rodrigo stared at the ground avoiding eye contact. "So, please tell me how this is supposed to work because this crew— if you can call it that—is not going to welcome me with open arms like we're one big happy *familia*."

"I was just getting to that," the Captain said, waving his finger in the air.

"Well, thank you, Captain…?"

A smug smile pulled at the corner of his mouth. "Captain Jonathan Rogers," he bowed mockingly, "at your service."

José's hands tightly gripped the wooden armrests of his chair. "Rodgers? *The* Captain Rodgers who led multiple pirate attacks against Spanish merchant ships? Like my father's?"

"Yes, the very one. Although, I take issue with the word *pirate.* My crew and I prefer the word *privateer,* if you will."

"You're a filthy pirate to the Spanish."

"And now, so are you!"

Waves gently lapped the side of the ship as they sat motionless in a stare-off—the tension in the room growing thick. The Captain's words struck his heart and cut deep, the realization of his current circumstances sinking in. To the Spanish Royal Navy, he was now the enemy sailing the waters, not as a British privateer but as a pirate. "What happens now?"

Captain Rodgers stood from his desk and began pacing casually. "Your reputation precedes you, Gaspar. When Rodrigo came to me and asked if I would take you in as part of my crew, I recognized it as an ideal opportunity. To have the son of one of the most successful merchants, *Spanish* merchants, on my ship was a treasure in and of itself. I simply couldn't refuse. Your knowledge of the trade routes is invaluable. You are my most prized possession. How unfortunate it must have been to lose the king's favor, but I can't say I'm upset about it." Captain Rodgers stood at José's side. "The crew will take kindly to you because they know, just as I do, that you are now the most important crew member on this ship. That is why you are now my first mate."

"First mate?"

"Rodrigo? You don't have a problem being my second mate, yes?"

"Of course not, Captain," Rodrigo quickly replied.

"Then, it's settled."

"*Mierda. No puedo creer esto.*" José buried his head in his hands. Cold medal prodded his skull. He peeked through his fingers to find Captain Rodgers' gun aimed straight at his head.

"My Spanish is a little weak, but I'm sure that wasn't gratitude you just gave me, Gaspar."

José rose from his chair, unintimidated by the gun held at his head. "I will do my duty. Forgive me if I'm not thrilled about the circumstances. I will, of course, assist you until we reach Puerto Rico."

Captain Rodgers' laugh echoed against the wall. "This ship is not bound for Puerto Rico. No, no. We're on our way to Havana. Eventually, that is. There is the matter of securing our goods along the way...."

"You mean *stealing* them," José snapped.

Captain Rodgers tucked his gun back in his belt. "Once we have secured our goods, we will be on our way to Havana."

Fury pulsed in his temples. It took everything he had not to murder Captain Rodgers on the spot. José bowed. "Have the most pleasant evening, *Capitan*." He charged out of the room.

CHAPTER 15

In Sevilla, news spread far and wide of José Gaspar's fall from grace, and there was nothing Joséfa, Felipe, or Armando could do to combat it. The king had declared him a thief, and so it was that he was a thief. But the three of them knew better.

While Armando and Felipe were busy with their upcoming plans to sail for *Nueva España*, Joséfa pondered daily about what she could do to clear José's name. It helped to suppress the grief over losing her father. She imagined it did the same for Armando. Weeks had passed, but her feelings of loss and grief remained. Every time Joséfa went to the market, she was met with stares and whispers, but wouldn't every fiancée of a thief be met that way?

One evening, the sun cast its final rays into the sitting room of Casa Mayorga. Frantic with anxiety, Joséfa moved about reorganizing the room for the millionth time when she heard a knock at the door. With Armando still not home, she made her way to the front of the house to answer. She was surprised at who she found on her doorstep.

"What are you doing here?" Joséfa looked upon a set of the richest brown eyes that matched those of her cousin, Mariana.

Lorena Sariego Diaz curtsied before her. "*Señorita* de Mayorga, I was hoping to have a word with you."

"I do not think it wise for the both of us to speak, considering your cousin is responsible for the fall of my fiancée based on entirely false accusations."

Lorena wrung her hands at her waist, shifting uncomfortably from foot to foot. "I understand why you are angry and why you might feel it necessary to hold me accountable for my cousin's actions. But I am here with information that you deserve to know." She sighed before looking at Joséfa with pleading eyes. "Please, Joséfa. May I come in? I do not wish to discuss this out in the open."

Joséfa paused momentarily before moving aside and motioning her through the entry. She led them back to the sitting room, gesturing for Lorena to sit at the neighboring chair by the fire. Lorena looked around, her hands still fidgeting in her lap. She closed her eyes and breathed deeply. When the silence was too much, Joséfa spoke. "Whatever it is, please tell me. I have spent these past few weeks in agony, determined to find a solution because of what happened. I doubt your information will help our situation, but I am willing to hear you. So please, speak."

Lorena shook her head. "It is just not right."

"Nothing about this situation has been right, so you must be more specific."

"There is so much more to this story."

"Tell me," Joséfa demanded.

Lorena exhaled. "I understand you continue to seek an audience with the king, and I am here to tell you that your efforts to clear José will never succeed. The king will never dismiss the accusations."

"I will not give up."

"And I do not blame you for continuing to try, but you will not succeed because there is far more going on than you understand. Far more that involves the king himself."

Joséfa felt pale. "What is it that I don't know?"

The seriousness in Lorena's eyes had Joséfa's anxiety peaking. "As you know, Mariana is set to marry Rafael in a few weeks' time. She is pregnant but not with Rafael's child. She is pregnant with her lover's."

Joséfa's heart raced. "It is not José's. He assured me they weren't intimate."

"That wasn't what I was implying. The child is the king's."

Joséfa stared wide-eyed in shock. She couldn't believe what she was hearing. Mariana's pursuits knew no bounds. "*Dios mio. This is far more terrible than I thought. The king himself.*"

"Yes, the king takes what the king wants," Lorena huffed. "So you see, there's little that can be done. The king knows she holds his child. Rafael knows it is *not* his child but has agreed to marry Mariana; it worked out well for the three of them."

"But if she had a supposed father for her child, why accuse José? She could have left it at that."

"Do you remember the night of the ball?"

Joséfa nodded.

"Mariana was obsessed with José for many years. I warned her of José's intentions to wed you, of how he had moved on, and so should she. It fell on deaf ears, and I couldn't figure out why she had been so insistent. Other men had taken an interest in her, but it appeared she was so deeply in love—or in lust, in my opinion—with José that she refused to see he no longer took an interest in her.

"That night, she planned to seduce José to claim that the child was his and finally have the man she always wanted. When you entered the ball with José, you essentially ruined her plans. To her, you were a problem she didn't see coming. She was beside herself with anger. So, when Rafael approached with a plan to assist her in her pursuit of revenge and rid himself of the one man standing in his way, Mariana agreed. And now Rafael has what he wants."

"Lord, how I hate them both," Joséfa exclaimed. She sat stewing in all the information that had just been revealed. Something kept nagging her. "I still don't understand why the king would believe José had stolen the jewels." Her vision blurred as she stared at the fire.

"I'm afraid I will be of no help there. For an Admiral who has served his majesty's Navy and served him well, it makes no sense to me either." Lorena stood and approached Joséfa, crouching before her and placing her hands on hers. "What I can tell you is that I will help you in any way possible."

Tears streaked down Joséfa's face. "Why?"

"Because you are a good woman caught up in a situation you knew nothing about. Because you come from a good family. You and Armando do not deserve this. I suspect the past few weeks have been challenging for you both, with losing your father and José. Please know that despite my being related to the cause of your pain, I am here for you." She squeezed Joséfa's hands.

Just then, Joséfa heard the hinges of the front door. Armando and Felipe appeared in the doorway moments later and paused at the scene before them. Lorena stood up and faced them. "*Señor* de Mayorga, *Señor* Santos Torres." She curtsied.

Armando looked at her with confusion but bowed in greeting nonetheless. "*Señorita* Sariego. What brings you to our home this evening?" He glanced over at Joséfa. "And why is my sister so distraught?"

Lorena sighed. "Perhaps you both should take a little whiskey and a seat. This is quite a story, and the liquor will help."

Chapter 16

The moon cast light upon the ocean surface, providing a certain calm José desperately needed. José rested his arms upon the railing of the ship's deck and breathed deeply, soaking in the warm sea air. *I will not yield to this life. I will not be a pirate. I will prevail.* This became the mantra he repeated at the end of each day. It became his new routine. Every evening, the bow of the ship was his new sanctuary, a place where he could quietly collect his thoughts and reign in his rage.

It had been weeks since the incident with the Captain and just as long since he uttered a word to Rodrigo. As he went about his duties on the ship, he tried desperately to hold on to his rage, but he found it dissipating with each passing day. He could not deny that there were good men on this ship, despite his knowledge of the bad ones. He avoided them and their sneering. It was clear they were loyal to Captain Rodgers. He had no intention of breathing the same air as them if he could avoid it, but the others were not awful. In fact, he found that many of them were cordial, asking him about his time in the Royal Navy, wondering about his life, and sharing details about theirs. He could feel himself empathizing with some of the crew, which was both surprising and irritating. They were pirates and thieves. José could not let them get close. *I will not yield to this life. I will not be a pirate. I will prevail.* He willed his mantra to set into his veins.

The floorboards creaked behind him, breaking his attempt at a peaceful moment to himself. Rodrigo moved beside him. Rage pumped through the vessels of his heart, and anxiety grew in the pit of his stomach. He breathed deeply into his lungs, followed by a slow exhale.

"I am sorry, Admiral."

"I'm no longer an Admiral."

"But you are still a great man."

"I'm a disgraced man." He turned, glaring at Rodrigo. "How could you not tell me what type of vessel this is, Rodrigo? You knew what this would mean for me. You must have known of the captain's intentions."

Rodrigo breathed out a long exhale. "I am truly sorry, José. I did not see any other options given your situation. I was trying to be helpful. I never meant to deceive you. And I thought he would likely see some value in your presence on his ship. I did *not* anticipate that he would make you his first mate."

"And this does not bother you?" José asked.

Rodrigo waved a hand in the air. "No, no. Not at all. I have no intention of ever becoming a captain. It is the freedom that drives this life. So, being first mate or second is not of consequence to me."

"You speak of freedom like we won't eventually have it stripped from us once we are caught."

"Nonsense. Of course, this is freedom. Do you not notice the kind of life you were living? Always having to impress people, work for something, and get close to people that would otherwise not have time for you—giving your life up for a fight that isn't yours—always honoring a king who is honorable only because he was produced from some other nobleman who was honorable only because he was produced from some other nobleman, and so forth. And why? Because they're God's chosen ones simply by the blood that courses in their veins? Did God not give you the same nose and mouth to breathe? The same eyes and ears to see and hear?"

"Yes, they are God's chosen. He is the king. And you should not speak ill of him."

Rodrigo huffed his displeasure. "Noble birth is such a disease. Why should you defend him? Because he honors you at this time? Is he sending someone across the seas to rescue you? Please, Gaspar. He would execute you if he ever got his hands on you again."

José dipped his head in his hands. "You'll have to forgive me if I don't seem inclined to join your merry band of thieves so quickly."

"Like it or not, you've already joined."

"Involuntarily, that is." He sighed. "Understand, I just left the only life I knew, and I was *good* at that life. Very good."

"And you'll be good at this, too."

"I'm comfortable at sea. I feel as if I'm in a different world out here—my world. The ocean is my second home. But I still lose *her.*"

Rodrigo nodded. "Ah, your lady friend."

"My fiancé."

"Oh, I see." Rodrigo fidgeted silently, looking out to sea.

The pungent smell of the sea entered José's nose and ticked his hair across his forehead. He wasn't yet ready to resign to this life. He held on to the slightest bit of hope. *I will not yield to this life. I will not be a pirate. I will prevail.* "Joséfa will fix this," José remarked determinedly.

Rodrigo chuckled. "I have no doubt that she will. More often than not, men underestimate a woman's abilities. And any woman who has obtained your adoration has to be quite a woman."

"She is that."

Rodrigo held a pensive look. "I can't help but think that if the world were ruled by women entirely, there would be no war. I believe we got it deeply wrong somewhere in our past, letting men rule the world."

José smiled. "What do you mean by that?"

"Well, think about it. If women are smarter than men—I believe this to be true—what purpose does a man serve in this world? We have been blessed with the strength of our muscles and the build of our bodies. So, what does that make us?"

José arched a brow. "Fighters, warriors, and the like, of course."

Rodrigo laughed. "Ah, *mi amigo*. That is where you are wrong. It is not what we are born to be but what we are born to *protect*. We were built with strong hands, large muscles, and great bodies to protect our women."

"Well, yes, but clearly to fight," José protested.

"And that's where the world went wrong. Men were never meant to rule. There would be nothing to fight, save wild animals if women were our rulers and we, men, their protectors."

José laughed, shaking his head. "You are quite the forward thinker."

"I have been told that a time or two.' Rodrigo turned to him, resting one elbow on the railing—his face growing serious. "I will leave you with this warning. As much as I admire women for their minds, as much as you admire your woman for hers, do not go on thinking that the Captain shares the same sentiment. This is not the time for chivalrous acts that will get you killed. He does not see women as we do."

A shiver crawled down José's spine. "What do you mean by that?"

"The captain is likened to a king here. He takes what he wants, including women. He doles out punishments if you do not obey or get in his way. He has no loyalty to anyone but himself. He will not show you mercy. He is a ruthless son of a whore."

José let the information sink in. "And yet you say we are free out here? It sounds like we've traded one King for another."

Rodrigo shrugged. "Perhaps. To me, it is far better to be a prisoner at sea than in a cell."

Rodrigo's ominous warning about the captain stayed with him long into the evening as he lay in his hammock, attempting

to sleep. His entire life, his father raised him to respect women first and foremost. It was the code that he lived by. His father lived by that code until the day he sailed away and was murdered at sea. José could never imagine not interfering if something happened in his presence. He wondered if he could bury his instincts to protect those the captain might harm. *How could the crew let him do it?* He wondered. They must have been raised with some calling to respect and protect those who cannot fight for themselves. It begged the question whether the crew had been desensitized to the captain's monstrosities. The fear of turning into one of them loomed heavily in his mind. *I will not yield to this life. I will not be a pirate. I will prevail.*

CHAPTER 17

"It's hopeless." Armando sat staring at the floor, unable to move after Lorena gave all the disastrous details of the king, Mariana, and Rafael. "It's completely hopeless."

Lorena winced. "I'm afraid there's more. It appears the ship he's on belongs to a pirate named Captain Rodgers."

"My apologies. Did you say Captain Rodgers?"

Lorena nodded.

Felipe pinched the bridge of his nose. "This is worse. This is so much worse.

"There must be something we can do," Lorena said.

Armando's head shifted in her direction, an incredulous expression on his face. "You mean to help us?"

Lorena straightened her back, glaring at him. "Yes, I absolutely will. It is not fair to Joséfa or you. Or to your family. What she has done is horrific. I cannot stand by her side."

"But she is your cousin."

"Cousin or no. I value my integrity. Would you stand by *your* cousin if they attempted something like this?"

They continued to stare at each other. Joséfa glanced at Felipe, lifting a brow in question. He shrugged slightly. Armando finally acquiesced. "No, I don't suppose I would. You have risked a lot by coming here. I...we are eternally grateful. You are a good woman, Lorena." Joséfa watched the both of them studiously, his look altering as if seeing her for the first time, and he held it there longer than necessary. A blush crept up on Lorena's face before turning her head toward the fire.

"That dirty scoundrel. I could wring Rafael's neck for doing this to José," Felipe seethed.

Armando patted Felipe's back from where they sat on the sofa. "Do not give up hope just yet, *mi amigo*. There must be some other angle we can use."

"What other angle? The king himself is working against us. The old bastard. He's more than twice Mariana's age. I'm even surprised his nether regions are still working!" Felipe exclaimed.

Lorena's hand came to her mouth to presumably hide her laughter. It seemed their strange, new ally had a sense of humor. Joséfa liked that, and she was grateful for the small moment of laughter before the heaviness of the situation settled back in. "Does anyone have any other ideas?"

The room fell silent. Felipe opened his mouth to speak but then shook his head, thinking better of giving his idea voice.

"Perhaps we are going about this all wrong," said Armando. "We know we do not have the support of the king. That is not an option. Somehow, we have to get José back from Captain Rodgers. Perhaps that is what we should explore first. Once we have him, we will need to determine our next steps. The only option could be *Puerto Rico*."

"*Puerto Rico*? To live, you mean?" Lorena asked, her tone laced with the barest hint of shock.

"Yes, our family owns a *rancho* on the island," Armando answered. "It's our best option to get him back."

Lorena tried to hide her disappointment as her gaze traveled to her lap, but Joséfa noticed. *How curious.*

"If we choose this course, we have to better know our enemy and what motivates him," Felipe said.

"He's a God damn pirate. Gold and expensive things motivate him," Joséfa said helplessly.

"Of course, but what kind of expensive things? We should visit the tavern by the docks, see if we can discover anything useful," Felipe suggested.

"*We* means you and me, correct? I do not want my sister anywhere near a seedy tavern," Armando demanded.

"Hello? I'm right here. And yes, I'm going. This concerns my fiancée."

"Like hell you are," he protested.

"Perhaps it would be best if I went as well," Lorena interrupted.

Armando's face was heavy with shock. "Lorena, you have done so much already and put yourself at great risk by coming here. If the king discovers that we know about his affair with Mariana, he will execute you. I will not have you risking your life."

"I understand, but if the four of us go together and are well concealed under cloaks, I do not see how this will be a problem."

"Are the both of you sure? There are a lot of… nasty things that can happen in seedy taverns," Felipe warned.

A smile grew on Joséfa's face. "Sounds like an adventure to me."

"*Mierda*!" Armando exclaimed. "This is what I was afraid of."

"It will be fine, Armando," Lorena reassured him. "You will be there to protect us."

"Ahem."

"Eh…you *and* Felipe, of course," Lorena said, acknowledging Felipe.

Armando sighed. "Very well then. But both of you are to stay by our side at all times. We will meet here at dusk tomorrow."

Joséfa and Lorena exchanged a smile before Lorena glanced at the clock upon the mantle. "Oh, dear. It's getting late. I need to be going."

Armando stood from the couch, making his way to Lorena. "I will escort you home." He held his hand out to her, helping Lorena to her feet, both unable to keep their eyes off each other. Joséfa glanced at Felipe, who was smirking. It looked like some good was brewing amid their drama.

CHAPTER 18

TABERNA DE LOS SUENOS SORDIDOS SAT AT THE END OF THE DOCK, hidden where no light could reach it in the evenings while the occupants came and went. This was mainly because said occupants didn't want to be seen. The loud moans of a woman carried from the second-floor window just above the front door. Apparently, they didn't mind being heard, however.

"Whatever you do, keep your head down and do not leave my side," Felipe warned, grabbing for the front door. He held tightly to Joséfa's arm as he had from the moment they had stepped out of the carriage a few blocks away. Armando held Lorena's arm just as tightly as they entered. Joséfa didn't know what to expect, but this was much more than she imagined. She had never seen so many men gathered in one spot—drinking, screaming, and punching. Many of them were already drunk on ale, slurring lyrics to the songs the guitarist played in the corner. The women were in various states of undress. One sat on the lap of a man playing cards; his left hand held five cards in front of him while the right one disappeared under her skirt bunched at her thigh. She closed her eyes, tipping her head back against his chest— her mouth dropping slightly while her chest moved rapidly. The man placed the cards on the table while whispering in her ear. Joséfa felt the heat crawl up her cheeks. She was suddenly steered in the opposite direction.

"I knew we shouldn't have brought them here," Armando murmured to Felipe as they reached a table in the far corner, mostly away from the crowd. Armando sat firmly at Lorena's side, tucking her close to him. Felipe scooted Joséfa's chair closer and threw his arm over the back.

"Really, Armando. It is not like we do not know what happens in taverns like these," Joséfa said.

"Be that as it may, I do not need you witnessing it and getting any ideas."

"Better to have some idea, no?" Lorena teased. Armando's jaw went slack, and a deep red blush crept on his cheeks. Lorena chuckled behind her lifted hand.

A lady in a dress of the deepest purple approached the table. "What will it be for you all?" she asked, barely acknowledging them.

"Five ales, *por favor.*"

She turned without another word. "Ales?" Joséfa asked. "Since when do you prefer beer over your whiskey?"

Armando rolled his eyes. "This is not the type of establishment that would carry the whiskey I prefer. Best to keep it simple." He glanced over at Lorena and adjusted her hood slightly over her face. She smiled at him appreciatively. He reached out to Joséfa, attempting to do the same. She swatted his hand.

"Calm down, Armando. You will attract more attention to us with all of your fidgetings." She pulled her hood a little more over her face to satisfy him.

"When does your man get here?" Armando asked Felipe. "And how exactly did you find this heathen?"

Felipe glanced at the door. "He works for a merchant I frequently play cards with. The situation with Gaspar seems to be the only thing this town can talk about, so I dared ask if he employed anyone on his ship who had previously worked for

Captain Rodgers. He said one, which was rare since most don't make it off Rodgers' ship." Joséfa's stomach sank at his comment. "He'll be here soon. I told him to look for someone who sticks out like a sore thumb."

"The women under hoods?"

"No," Felipe smirked. "I told him to look for an uptight male who looks like he has a colony of insects in his pants."

Armando shook his head, turning his attention to the room around us. The barmaid returned with the drinks, and the group sat silently. Lorena didn't dare to look up, not wanting to make Armando more nervous than he already was. But Joséfa's curiosity took over. She turned her head, taking in the surroundings. Felipe gently grabbed her chin with a smile, guiding it back to the table to the waiting glare of her brother. She sighed and quietly drank her ale.

"There he is." Felipe raised his hand, summoning the tall, scraggy sailor to the table. He glanced around at them, his face heavy with dread. The thick stench of the sea wafted off of his clothing, smelling for all the world like he had just bathed in a barrel of fish. Felipe pushed the extra ale across the table. "We took the liberty of getting an ale for you."

"Thank you. But I much prefer coin to ale for my services." He smiled, revealing a set of teeth that were white in very few spots. Felipe reached into his pocket and dropped a bag of coins on the table. The man glanced into the bag, seeming satisfied, and inserted it into his pocket. "What is it that I can help you with?"

"I understand you were a…sailor on Captain Rodgers' ship?"

The man's face fell, and his hand went for the knife at his waist, but Armando was quicker. His blade dug into the side of the man's throat. "Good man, we have paid for your services, so you will answer our questions. Trust that your secret is safe with us. We don't exactly roll around in the hay with pirates."

The man's eyes traveled down Lorena's body. "Are you certain about that?"

Armando dug the tip of the blade into his throat. "Are you certain you want to insinuate anything negative about the women at this table with my knife at your throat? Don't look at her." He nodded toward Joséfa. "Or her. Just answer his questions, and we'll be on our way." He lowered the knife. The man glared at Armando before turning his attention back to Felipe.

"Yes, I was a *sailor* on his ship." He smiled, amused at the reference.

"What can you tell us about the manner of items he likes to steal?" Felipe asked, cutting right to the chase.

"Collect?"

"Steal." Armando bit out.

The man rolled his eyes. "He liked to collect rare treasures, items of historical value as well as coin and goods to keep his crew going."

"Treasures to trade to collectors?" Felipe asked.

The man began laughing. "Not unless the occasion called for it. He hated parting with his treasures. Had a weird obsession with them. That's why he would rob merchant ships of their goods every now and then to pay for his obsession."

"And *collect* their items as well?" Armando said, a smirk on his face. "What kind of merchants did he go after?"

"He wasn't too picky. But he did have a thing for the merchants with the good liquor."

"Like barrels?"

"Wine. Whiskey. Rum. The man didn't discriminate when it came to liquor or women."

Armando's gaze snapped to Felipe, an idea blossoming. Felipe nodded. "I think that will do it for us. Although, I did have one more question. Purely for curiosity's sake. How did you get off his ship alive?"

The man looked around and leaned into the table. "There are only two ways to get off Captain Rodgers' ship. The first is death, of course. And the second is pretending to be dead. Either way, you're dead."

Joséfa gaped at him in shock. "And how exactly did you pretend to be dead?"

He didn't glance at her when she asked the question but directed his attention back to Felipe. It appears he was smart enough to heed Armando's warning. "One day, Ol' Man Jeffy, a sailor on his ship who had worked with Captain Rodgers for many moons, passed away of old age. God rest his soul." He made the sign of the cross in a backward motion. "On the night they planned to throw Ol' Man Jeffy to the fishes, it just so happened we were close to land. I seized my opportunity. Praying for Jeffy's forgiveness, I took his body out of the wrappings tossing it overboard in the dead of night. I made sure my knife was sharp to the touch and wrapped the tarp around myself, waiting until they threw my body overboard early the following morning.

"The ball and chain around my ankles was the hardest obstacle next to my breathing. I placed extra tunics around them to ensure I could cut and wiggle them free when the time was right. It was very close, and I was almost out of breath. Cutting through the fabric was easy. I then had to cut through the tunics around my ankles while sinking deeper into the sea. Not exactly the most calming situation, mind you. Just when I thought it wouldn't cut through, my strength leaving me, I broke free, swimming as fast as my limbs would take me. My head breached the water, and those first few breaths were like being reborn; in a way, I was. Because I would never be who I was. I couldn't. No one ever escapes Captain Rodgers' ship."

He glanced around the table, now daring to look at the women. "I know who you all are. I know of Gaspar's escape and why you want to know about Captain Rodgers. He is an evil man." He reached for the hem of his shirt, lifting it to expose his stomach. Deep lacerations long since healed were riddled across his chest. Lorena gasped. "This is what he does to men who are loyal to him. This is how he shows his appreciation. You need to think long and hard if you plan to go after him." He nodded toward Lorena. "Keep your woman well out of his sights. There's no telling what will happen if he gets a hold of her. He is the devil himself and only knows how to take. And take he will." With that, the man dropped his shirt, stood up, and left the tavern. Despite the commotion of the bar, the four of them remained silent, drowning their sorrows in ale before getting up, their limbs numb as they departed *Los Suenos Sordidos*.

CHAPTER 19

"Gaspar!" José turned to the Captain, who was calling for him across the deck. "Come to my quarters!"

José sighed and walked across the crowded deck, the crew tending to the ship as they approached what they hoped would be a successful raid of a French merchant ship. He walked into the captain's quarters, closing the door behind him. "You wanted to see me?"

The captain sat, head down, dissecting the map in front of him. "I want to go over this one more time." They had gone over the route several times in the past few days. Despite the captain's usually confident demeanor, José could sense the nerves radiating off him. It puzzled him how a captain of his reputation could be showing any nerves at all. "Now, you say the new route the French are using is bound for Venezuela, correct?"

"That is correct. We should intercept within a week."

"And you know this how?"

José thought the answer to this would be obvious but held back in remarking his sentiments. "Because it was my job to know, Captain."

Captain Rodgers nodded. He tapped his finger repeatedly on top of the desk; a worn mark lay just beneath his finger, indicating this was his practice. "Yes, yes. You've said as much. But how do we know this information is accurate?"

"Because it was my job to know these routes like the back of my hand. I was Consult to the king," he snapped.

"Watch your tone with me," Captain Rodgers warned, his head jerking up. "Let's not forget whose ship you're sailing on now, Gaspar. You're on my ship and follow my orders. You are now a privateer for the British. You serve a different King now."

I will not yield to this life. I will not be a pirate. I will prevail. José ground his teeth. "I understand, sir."

Captain Rodgers observed him, his face unreadable. He stood abruptly out of his chair, walking hurriedly toward the door and yanking it open. "Fredríco, Jasper, Willy. Get over here now." Three sets of hurried footsteps pounded on the deck until they were standing in the room with José. All three men sported long beards; Fredríco's black, Jasper's a fiery red, and Willy's a pale blond. They were all bald, whether by choice or by God's design, José did not know.

Captain Rodgers slammed the doors shut. "Jasper. Willy." He flicked his head toward José, and within a second, José was forced against the wall, his head and arms pinned against the wood, splinters digging into his cheek. José struggled against them as they ripped his shirt apart, exposing his back. The sheer terror of the situation began to make his pulse race as he realized their intentions.

Slow steps made their way to José's side. Moments later, the captain's reeking breath blanketed his ear. "I want you to remember this moment every time you have the slightest inclination to speak back to me in a tone undeserving of the captain of this ship. I want you to remember this moment when you think you have bested me, when you think yourself a better captain. I want you to re-member this moment for all the days of your pathetic life. You are nothing, José Gaspar." He motioned to Fredríco and stood in front of José's view, an evil smirk upon his face. "Ten lashes."

The first lash landed on his back with a deafening crack, the pain causing his eyes to well with tears, but he didn't dare cry out. The second came down, and José held Captain Rodgers' gaze, forcing his face to remain stone-still. The same went with the third, fourth, and fifth—and still, José did not scream. He never called out in pain. He took every lash, boring his eyes into the captain with intense anger.

When the tenth lash landed, the captain smiled. "You're awfully quiet, Gaspar. Does this mean you have learned your lesson?"

José sighed dramatically, his breath hitting the wall in front of him where his head was still pinned. "I just wonder why you would choose to be a coward and not do the lashings yourself?"

The captain's smile dropped, his face turning scarlet red—his breath pumping in and out of his lungs. "Is that the way of it then?" He leaned closer to José. "TEN MORE LASHES," he bellowed, spraying José's face with spit. "And make no mistake. I'll be the one with the whip this time. Give me the God damn whip!"

The captain moved out of his preview, and moments later, the lashes began anew, but this time José smiled through the pain despite feeling like his back was being torn apart. *I will not yield to this life. I will not be a pirate. I will prevail.*

CHAPTER 20

José lay on the cold, wooden floor of the crew's quarters as Rodrigo applied a salve to his back. While he was gentle about it, José couldn't help but wince from time to time.

"*Lo siento*," Rodrigo said for the hundredth time.

"*No te preocupes*. I appreciate the help," he said, with no short amount of gratitude. The salve gave him instant relief.

Rodrigo sighed. "You really shouldn't have provoked him like that. Luckily, they only broke the skin in a few places. It shouldn't scar too badly."

"In truth, I think Fredríco did more damage than the captain. I could sense the captain wasn't too pleased about it." Rodrigo chuckled softly above him, causing José to smile through the pain. "The man seems offended by anything I do. Men like him are threatened by men like me. He knows it. I know it. The crew knows it."

Rodrigo rose from the ground and grabbed the clean tunic lying on José's hammock. "All done. I doubt you will be able to sleep on your back this evening." He helped José stand from the ground and handed him the tunic.

José gently pulled the shirt over his head, making sure not to disturb his back's open wounds. "I'll sleep on my side. I'll be fine." José met his gaze to find a worried expression on his face. "What is it?"

"I want you to understand. It is not that I disagree with your observations. I, too, believe the captain feels threatened by you, and yes, I understand why. If you cannot learn to navigate him, you must plan to eliminate him."

José's brows rose. "You mean kill him?"

"Yes. If you continue down this path, you two cannot exist in the same space. He knows you can run this crew better than he can. It is either you or him, and he will not hesitate to ensure you are the one who falls. He doesn't play by the same rules you are used to. He is not a gentleman. He plays a vindictive game. I am here by your side as promised. I say this because I have deemed myself your humble servant. You are a target now. The men have heard how you challenged him. You will need to watch yourself."

José's back throbbed in pain as the words poured out of him. "I have no intentions of running this crew. The fault is his with the first mate nonsense. But if the moment comes, I will not hesitate to take his life. Anything that is a threat to the future I have with Joséfa will not get in my way."

Rodrigo shook his head. "Gaspar, you must realize that a reunion with your beloved may not be possible."

"It must be possible."

"It may not," Rodrigo said firmly. "Think on it. We are set to raid a ship. Your reputation will be tested, and if successful, there's little doubt everyone will know who José Gaspar is if they do not already. Your skill with the sword alone will cause them to challenge you. If the whole of Spain believed you to be a fierce Admiral, it would be nothing compared to who you become as a pirate. You will cross a line with this raid you cannot come back from regardless of what your friends may or may not be able to achieve back home."

José's body tensed. "Why are you saying this?"

"Because innocent blood will be spilled by your blade. That changes a man. I know because it changed me. The person I was no longer exists. There's a darkness that comes with this territory.

It seeps into your veins and crawls through you until it reaches your mind and warps it. I had a loving wife and a wonderful family—a career I was proud of. I was well known in my beloved town of Salamanca, and now I can never return. That life is gone along with my wife." Rodrigo placed his hand on José's arm, squeezing softly. "You will realize that you may not feel worthy of her when this is through. I tell you this not to hurt you but to prepare you." He moved to gather his salve and rag, placing them on the corner table that sat against the wall. He turned and motioned to the hammock. "Rest now. We have a week's time to heal your back. Sleep. Think later."

But José could do nothing but think that evening. He lay on his side in his hammock as it swayed slowly throughout the evening, like a cradle. Perhaps he should have felt comforted by it, but nothing could soothe his tumultuous thoughts or his soul.

CHAPTER 21

Joséfa, Armando, and Felipe sat in the sitting room at *Casa Mayorga,* still digesting all of the information that Captain Rodgers' escaped crew member had provided. Joséfa still reeled at his ominous warning. No one leaves Captain Rodgers' ship alive. The warning, although grave, did not deter her or her group.

"So, we attract his attention with wine exports. Shouldn't be too hard," Felipe said, sitting in the adjacent chair, swirling the liquor around in his glass pensively. "That's your line of business."

Armando's hand rested on his hip, staring into the fire. "Yes, but with my father no longer with us, it presents a little bit of a problem." He glanced warily at Joséfa.

Her eyebrows rose. "Me?"

"Yes, of course. I cannot leave you here."

"So take me with you."

"Like hell. You heard the man. We are not to bring any women within Captain Rodgers' vicinity."

"Then what do you suggest I do?"

He sighed. "I have a suggestion. But you're not going to like it." He turned to look between Felipe and Joséfa.

"Oh no," Felipe said, shaking his head. "No, no, no."

"What?" Joséfa asked, confused by Felipe's reaction. "What is it?"

"Come on, Felipe," Armando pleaded.

"Absolutely not."

"And why not? What's wrong with my sister? She's beautiful, intelligent. I'll admit, she can be a little bullheaded at times, but she's still a catch!"

His words sank in, and she gasped. "Please tell me you are not suggesting what I think you are?"

Armando huffed. "What is wrong with you two? You're acting like the suggestion is the most awful thing in the world!"

"IT IS!" they exclaimed simultaneously.

He turned his attention back to the hearthside. "What other options do we have for her protection? I cannot leave her here alone. You marrying my sister is a good option."

"I know you have the best intentions. I truly do. But doing so signals that I've given up on my best friend. I refuse to give up hope. Not yet. We should try out the plan first."

"And when hope runs out? Will you marry her then?" Armando asked.

"I think I should get some say in the matter," Joséfa asserted. "This is my life we're talking about, and I'll not be treated like a piece of property to be bartered away."

Armando sighed. "You know how it is."

"Do I?"

He turned to her, his face more serious than she'd ever seen in her life. "If you don't, you need to learn. I am responsible for you now. I have to protect you. I have to look out for your well-being. What do you not understand?"

Joséfa swore she saw his eyes glisten. She turned to Felipe. "Would you mind if I had a word with my brother, please?"

Felipe nodded, getting up from his chair. "It's probably time I head home anyway. I must let the family know I am alive and breathing every now and then." He stood in front of Joséfa, , eyes penetrating. "It would not bring me any joy to give up this pursuit to give you and José the chance you both deserve. But please know that if this doesn't go as planned, I am at your disposal. I would honor you as my wife as he would honor you."

Joséfa reached out and grabbed his hand, squeezing it. "You are a good man, Felipe. I thank you for being there for me."

He sighed, rolling his eyes. "Of course, I don't know what the ladies in this town would do without my charms at their constant disposal. It'll be dreadful for them. I had big intentions of being Felipe, the Forever Bachelor of Sevilla."

Joséfa swatted his arm. "Get out of here, you devil."

Felipe chuckled on his way down the hall, leaving Armando and Joséfa in the room, the dreaded conversation looming before them. "You know I'm not going to marry anyone else, correct? I'm José's fiancée."

Armando plopped down in Felipe's vacant chair, burying his face in his hands. "Please, Joséfa. Be reasonable."

"Reasonable?"

"Yes," he said, throwing his arms in the air. "Reasonable. José Gaspar is no longer an Admiral in the Spanish Navy. He is a fugitive, and they'll call him a pirate before long. What life do you expect to have with him? Do you really think he could ever return here?"

Her vision blurred, and her throat tightened. "We'll go to *Puerto Rico*."

"*Puerto Rico* is Spanish territory. It is only meant to be a stopping point until we figure out what his future will look like."

"Then we'll go to the Americas. I don't know, but we'll figure out something. I will not give up."

"And then what? You become Mrs. Gaspar, wife of a former Admiral, fugitive accused of thievery turned pirate?"

"He is not a pirate."

"But he is now, Joséfa. There's no turning back from this. Do you have any idea what he can do with a sword? Do you know what he will do to survive? He'll do it. For you, he'll kill any man that stands in his way. Good or bad. I have seen the way you both look at each other. The way he looks at you. He is akin to a man silently possessed by love."

"Then you understand."

"Understand what?"

"That there is nowhere he can go, no circumstances that will ever stop us from finding each other, in this life or the next. I am his."

Armando sighed, his head falling back on the chair. The minutes rolled by without a word exchanged between the two. It seemed to go on forever.

"Perhaps there is another way to keep you safe."

Joséfa cocked an eyebrow. "Well, do tell."

There was a slight lift at the corner of his lips, his hands fidgeting around a bit. "I could marry Lorena, have her be the head of this household, and have Felipe look after you both in my absence."

"Oh, such a sacrifice for you, I'm sure," she said with a knowing smile.

He smiled, then looked down at the ground. "She is intriguing to me."

"You don't say. I couldn't tell. But the question is, how do you know she's intriguing, dear brother?" She placed her chin in her palm, resting her elbow on the armrest with a knowing grin.

"It's not what you think."

"And what am I thinking?"

"Something scandalous, I'm sure." He shook his head. "I've been courting her, *properly* and with her parents' permission, for weeks. She is a lovely creature. Nothing like her cousin at all. She is kind and gentle. She has a quick wit like no other. She calms me."

"That's quite the task."

His smile grew brighter. "She is someone I see myself sharing a million sunsets with."

"I am very happy for you, brother." Tears of happiness escaped her eyes, dropping across her cheek. "You deserve to be happy."

The smile dropped from his face. "As do you. You must see that is why I am suggesting marrying Felipe. I know how this pains you, but you are my *hermanita*, and I love and admire you fiercely. *Papá* would never want you to be alone for the rest of your life. You have so much more to offer."

She rose from her seat and crouched before him, placing her hands upon his. "Know that I love you too. And know that I recognize your efforts come from a place of love. But what you feel for Lorena doesn't begin to describe the enormity of my feelings for José. Imagine that you are young and developing feelings for a handsome, strong, and wonderful person at that tender age. Imagine waiting to grow older, a little wiser, and patiently waiting for him to return so you can show him how much you've grown—just how much you've learned about the world. Imagine he's captured your family's attention, respect, and admiration, especially an overbearing brother with good intentions. Would you be able to walk away then?"

Armando huffed gently under his breath. "Well, I don't know about *admiration*," he replied.

Joséfa clucked her tongue in disapproval.

"However," he continued, "he did have my approval. And I know he would have been…will be a good husband to you." He reached out, cupping her cheek. "As hard as it is to believe, I understand you. I was just trying to do what was best. I will help you find him, and we'll cross the bridge of what to do next as a family."

His words went straight to her heart. She reached up and hugged him tightly, letting hope enter her heart again.

CHAPTER 22

La Félicité was visible from the deck. Anticipation grew among the crew like starving wolves looking to sink their teeth into their prey. Their energy infected José, the nerves extending throughout his chest and into his bones—his mantra silent in the back of his mind. He could not bring himself to say the words, for he knew his next actions might change him forever.

La Floriblanca approached her on the starboard side with the slight advantage of thirty-two guns. The men held their daggers at the ready. José's sword extended from his arm as if it were a natural part of his body, prepared to defend whatever awaited him on *La Félicité*.

Memories swirled in his mind as they approached. His father cautioned in the depths of his soul, *"Remember to always observe the angle of a man's shoulders when he swings a blade in your direction. They tell you everything you need to know."* Countless hours were spent in his youth swinging his blade repeatedly until the blisters on his hand burst open with pus and blood staining the handle. José had accepted the idea of taking a man's life for his King and country long ago. But this was no country, and the captain was no king. His stomach dropped with the pending attack. *How am I to do this?* He shook his head, dispelling the thoughts of a man who no longer existed. Whomever he was at this moment, it wasn't that man.

The morning sun cast rays on the deck of *La Félicité*. A loud boom of a cannon shot at their ship, making contact on the side of *La Floriblanca*. Men scrambled below the deck to assess the damage.

"Hold steady, mates—we're gaining on her," the captain bellowed.

Rodrigo and José gathered the wooden planks to board the ship—groups of men ready to rush themselves from *La Floriblanca*. In the blink of an eye, they were next to *La Félicité*, which had slowed, likely acknowledging that this would be a fight fought with more than just cannons.

The men yelled as they threw the planks across and ran onto *La Félicité*. José watched as one of his own was unceremoniously pushed off into the depths of the water, but any of their attempts would be futile. *La Félicité* was outnumbered, but despite the lack of crew, they fought. José dearly wished they would stand down.

A tingling sensation drove through his arms as the first man he encountered ran at him, sword pulled back and ready to strike. "You'll not have anything on this ship without a fight, you filthy pirate!"

Time stood still, the phrase catching him off guard, but he then submitted to his fury. José observed the man—his posture, his next move. And the dance began. He ducked the man's blade, cutting him across the torso in his wake. The next man came and went with the same ease. And the next. And the next. Blood splattered on the deck and sprayed across his clothes, but he killed with the grace of a flamenco dancer circling his partner with ease. He could hear the sound of the *castañuelas* clicking their rhythm in his head as he moved to the dance of death.

His blade cut across the neck of another determined victim. The light of his eyes focused on some distant place José would never reach. The blood seeped through the man's collar as he dropped to the deck with a thump. José turned to fight the next man who dared to challenge him, but he found the ship blanketed in silence—the crew of both vessels staring at him in amazement.

Captain Rodgers stepped forward, grinning villainously. "Well, then. It appears I have more than just a savvy merchant-man on my ship. You are quite the treasure, Gaspar. Quite the swordsman. I'm not likely to part with you. Ever."

José stood still, his mind numb. The innocent blood soaked his tunic, dripping onto the deck from the hem in a steady beat. His grip on his sword loosened, and it fell to the floor with a clank. The bodies littered the deck, some still twitching with the last bits of life leaving their body. "What have I done?" he whispered. At that moment, José realized the future he held on to with Joséfa—the possibility that Armando would rescue him with Felipe by his side—was now gone. He was no longer a man but a beast. *I yield to this life. I am a pirate. I have succumbed.*

CHAPTER 23

SEVERAL MONTHS LATER...

"I will find you," she whispered. The waves of Joséfa's light brown hair framed her face as she looked down at José. Subtle rays of sunshine filtered through the room, grazing her face. "I promise. I will find you." Hovering over him, her fingertips lightly traced his jawline and traveled through his hair. She leaned in, placing her soft lips on his. When she pulled back, her eyes welled with tears. "I will find you."

José was startled awake. "Joséfa!" A roar of laughter erupted around him. He took in his surroundings and was disappointed to find he was not in bed with Joséfa but in the crew quarters.

"Ooooooooh, Joséfa!" John Gómez taunted from the corner of the room. "It sounds like you had a nice time in dreamland, Gaspar." John rolled with laughter—his round belly, larger than the rest of him, jiggled up and down, sending the hammock swinging until it accidentally rolled over. He hit the floor with a thud. The crew laughed hysterically.

"So graceful, John," José teased.

Footsteps thundered down the stairwell. "What in God's name is going on down here?!" Captain Rodgers stood at the foot of the stairs glaring at the crew. "Pull yourselves together, you scoundrels! We'll be arriving in Havana at mid-day. Get the ship ready!"

The crew shot out of their hammocks. The ship suddenly came alive with the creaking of floorboards and shouting. The eagerness of the crew to step foot on land for the first time in months was evident in each step they took—each rope they pulled. The morning sun broke through on the horizon, revealing a landscape in the distance so breathtaking that José forgot how to move his feet. His heart had become cold, and his soul dark. He had forgotten how to let beauty in.

"You think you're special, Gaspar? Keep it moving!" Captain Rodgers called from the helm. José internally seethed at the captain but kept his emotions in check as he resumed his work until there was nothing left to do but dock in Havana. He and the rest of the men stood on the deck admiring the view.

"This Joséfa. Is she waiting for you?" John asked, breaking into his thoughts.

José looked down at him, his curly black-haired head barely reaching his shoulder, and sighed. "I wish, but it is highly unlikely." He smiled sadly. She would be a fool to wait for him, and Armando would never allow it. "I suppose I need to keep reminding myself that there's no turning back from this life, and there's no place for her in it." His cold heart hardened. *I am a pirate. I am no longer worthy of her.*

John clapped José on the back. "Bah! Women. You have a sea of women to choose from. I've seen them flocking around you like the gulls at every port we've been to." He closed his eyes, tipped his head back, and breathed deeply. "And what a life it is indeed! Nothing like the freedom of the seas to energize the soul!"

"Hmph, forgive me if I do not share your enthusiasm."

La Félicité sat in the port when *La Floriblanca* arrived. It had been months since he'd seen Rodrigo, who led the crew of *La Félicité* to Havana, selling various items and goods along the way. When José's legs finally descended onto the dock, he wobbled a bit and had to steady himself.

"Careful there." Rodrigo stepped out from the crowd of the dock's merchants.

José laughed. "It's always a bit unsettling, isn't it?"

"They say you get used to it eventually, but I have yet to," Rodrigo replied, leading José toward the town. They dodged through the crowded streets. An army of men loaded and unloaded goods from the various ships. Families stood just a few paces away, stretching their necks to view the passengers walking off the ships. "Not to worry. I'm sure a little rum can cure the wobbling. What do you say we grab our rooms at the inn and settle for a good meal and a drink?"

José's stomach grumbled. "I think that would be an excellent idea."

They passed a group of women standing just outside a doorway. Their breasts spilled from their dresses. Eying José and Rodrigo, one of the women in a deep red dress smiled, licking her lips and gently caressing her breast. Rodrigo locked eyes with her, turning until he faced her, walking backward with ease. "I hear the women in Havana are just as delicious as well."

José pulled Rodrigo out of the way of an oncoming cart, turning him back around. "That is not in my plans, but by all means, do whatever suits your needs."

Rodrigo's eyes softened. "You know there's no better way to rid your mind of a woman than to take another?"

"I'll take your word for it."

Rodrigo patted José on the back. "Come. We already procured our rooms."

José followed Rodrigo down the cobblestone streets. The savory smells of food trickled through the windows of the houses. Clothing was strung between every balcony and arched window. It was a short walk until they arrived at *La Posada*.

Multiple worn tables and chairs decorated the main floor. Men drank heavily and bellowed with laughter. One man—a crew member who traveled with Rodrigo on *La Félicité* to Havana—went stock still at the sight of José. He nudged his companion in the arm and pointed his way. The nudging continued until silence fell throughout the room. José turned to Rodrigo, raising an eyebrow.

"It appears word about your skills has traveled," Rodrigo whispered.

"My skills?"

"As a swordsman. Naturally, the crew—both ours and *La Félicité* who surrendered—bore witness to it. And it *was* something to witness. As Captain Rodgers said, you are quite the swordsman."

José sighed. "Excellent."

Rodrigo clapped José on the back. "Relax, Gaspar. Look at it as a badge of honor. It is tough to earn their respect. Besides, the more pirates and sailors know about your skill, the less likely they'll be to fight."

The barmaid, a short, round woman with a scowl, made her way to José and Rodrigo from around the counter, seemingly less impressed than the rest of her patrons.

"Don Gaspar. Don Lopez. *Bienvenidos.* Your rooms are just up the stairs. Last two doors on the right. Once you are settled, you can come down for some warm *sopa* and some rum." She handed José two sets of keys and turned without another word. With immense relief, José walked briskly out of the rooms avoiding the stares sent in his direction.

The men gathered in the dining room of *La Posada.* It was the first time they had gathered together since the raid, and it seemed all they could do was talk about José like a fantastical character in an adventure book, much to José's displeasure.

John leaped on top of his chair, brandishing his invisible sword. "He killed five men in just one swing!" John yelled over the crowd in the corner. "They couldn't lift a finger to Gaspar!"

"Sit down, Gómez!" José grabbed John's shirt, yanking him down to his stool. "I would like to have my drink in peace."

"I doubt you'll be getting much of that while in Havana. It appears the captain is also hard at work telling the tale." Rodrigo nodded to the opposite corner of the dining room. The men surrounding Captain Rodgers snapped their heads in his direction, mouths open slightly. The room grew dark with the pending nightfall, but he could still make out their faces.

José buried his head in his hands. "We haven't even been on land for a day."

"As I said, Gaspar. Try to relax." Rodrigo grabbed their empty glasses. "I'll go get us some more. In the meantime, eat up, or *Doña* Alfonso will be highly displeased."

José glanced up to see *Doña* Alfonso cleaning her counter, glaring at him with disapproval. He grabbed his spoon and gulped his *sopa* with delight, ensuring she could see him eating. He gave her a little wave, and she huffed, going about her business.

Captain Rodgers hobbled his way to their table—a slimy grin fixated on his face. "It looks like we have the proper effect on our fellow pirates."

"And what effect is that, Captain? To have everyone running away from me like mad? As if I'm Blackbeard?"

Captain Rodgers made the sign of the cross in reverse motion. "May he rest in peace."

"I no more want their attention than a bitch in heat wants the attention of all the dogs *en el barrio.*"

"I beg to differ on that," John said.

"What? The part about the attention?" José asked, grabbing the drink Rodrigo placed in from of him.

"Imagine being a bitch in heat, having all those little doggies coming to you." John sighed wistfully.

"Instead of having to pay for them, you mean?" José teased.

John straightened up. "There's nothing wrong with that."

"Well, John. Be sure to keep those prayers up; perhaps God will see fit to save you some coin and grant you your bitch wish," Rodrigo said as the entire table roared with laughter. John scowled, rolling his eyes.

"Enough, you imbeciles!" Captain Rodgers yelled. The table fell silent immediately. Captain Rodgers glanced behind him and leaned into the table. "I have it on good authority that *El Cazador* will be setting sail from Veracruz in just a few days' time." *Doña Alfonso* made her way to the table, her brows furrowed. Captain Rodgers fell silent, the entire table straightening in her presence. She glared at the group conspiratorially, grabbing José's empty bowl with a huff and turning abruptly away. Captain Rodgers leaned into the group again. "It is said that this ship carries Spanish *Reales* meant for the worthless paper currency in Louisiana. In other words, the funds to provide for the entire populace of Louisiana is on that ship." *Doña Alfonso* made her way back to the table. Captain Rodgers fell silent, and the crew straightened in their chairs again. She placed the bowl in front of José.

"*Para ti. Come te lo!*"

José grew red, trying to find a polite way to refuse. "*Pero, Doña Alfonso.* I am no longer hungry."

"*Si? Bueno*, it is best to get your fill now. Who knows how many swords you'll be swinging around tomorrow? Eat."

José knew better than to argue with a matriarch. He grabbed the spoon and started downing his already filled belly with more *sopa*. It wasn't an awful task seeing how rich and flavorful it was. The woman could cook. She huffed her approval and walked away—a satisfied smile breaching her face.

Captain Rodgers scooted his stool closer to the table. "This is colossal. With this much coin, we can disappear for a while and enjoy the fruits of our labor. We take her, and no one will be the wiser."

"How do you suppose that?" Rodrigo asked.

"I suppose it is because no one *knows* of the *El Cazador* and its mission."

"But then, how do *you* know of it, Captain?" John asked.

"Because I'm the captain, that's how," he bellowed. The entire room went quiet and stared at him. "What are you looking at, you fools? Mind your own." The buzz in the dining hall resumed, and the captain turned his attention back to his table. "Now, I am not one to reveal my sources, but *El Cazador* is making its passage, and *we* are going to rob it. And given the fine work of Gaspar with *La Félicité* and the spread of the tale, they will be daft to even to try and fight back."

"So you assume," José interjected, shoulders weighted with the impending mission.

"Hah! Chin up, Gaspar. This will be the moment of a lifetime as a pirate."

"And here I thought we were privateers."

A sinister smile grew on Captain Rodgers' face. "Two sides of the same coin, are they not?"

José glared at him. *Oh, how I loathe this man.*

"It's settled then. Gaspar, Rodrigo. We will finalize the details beginning tomorrow morning. The rest of you, make sure you lot are finding buyers for *La Félicité*'s cargo. We have a lot of work to do in the coming days." Captain Rodgers stood from the table. "Now, if you'll excuse me, I have an appointment with the loveliest harlot in Havana. Best be on my way." The captain hobbled out the door of *La Posada*.

CHAPTER 24

HEART HEAVY AND EXHAUSTED, JOSÉ MADE HIS WAY TO HIS room, leaving a drunken crew in the dining hall below. A light rustling came from behind his door. He stepped cautiously, gripping his dagger at his waist. Slowly turning the doorknob, he entered to find a young woman lying across his bed without a single piece of clothing on her body. Her long, curly brown hair hugged her entire body down to the curves of her hips. Her olive skin glistened in the firelight—the sweat dripping off of every delicate inch of her body. His mind implored him to believe this woman to be his Joséfa, but he noticed the slight differences. Stepping outside in the hallway, he double-checked that his door was the second to last on the right. "I'm so sorry, *Señora*. I believe you have the wrong room."

She smiled seductively. "You are the man they call Gaspar."

José closed the door behind him and leaned against it keeping his hand on his dagger. "I am. Who sent you?"

She eyed his hand on the dagger at his waist. "I am not sent here by your enemies but by your companion, Rodrigo."

José huffed his disapproval. "I appreciate the gesture of goodwill from my companion, but I'm afraid I am promised to another, and I do not believe she would approve. I am very sorry he troubled you."

Her hand traveled over her breast circling slowly around her nipple. "She doesn't have to know. This can stay here. You have been at sea for a long time. A man must have his…needs met."

His breath hitched. It had been a very long—too long—since José had been with a woman. The liquor worked on his inhibitions as he watched this alluring woman before him, filling him with pulsing need, urging him to disobey the demands of his heart. "I am not asking for a marriage vow, Gaspar. I can be anyone you want me to be," she said, voice dripping with lust, her eyes hooded.

José swallowed, his eyes glued to her hand, which had taken up residence on her other breast. He shook himself, taking his eyes off her. "Truly. As beautiful as you are, I do not wish to take advantage of you."

The young woman stood up from the bed, gliding effortlessly toward him—her long brown hair swaying behind her. José took a few short breaths as she stopped just inches from him, her head barely coming to his shoulder. Cold hands traveled up his arms and lightly touched his neck until she gently placed a piece of his hair behind his ear. "It is not taking advantage if I am offering it."

He reached up and grabbed her hand, sighing deeply. "I cannot."

The woman paused but then nodded, looking slightly dejected. She turned to grab her dress, if you could call it that, from the back of the chair, dressing with haste. She moved to leave, but he reached out and grabbed her hand. He looked down at her. "Will your…employer make you give back the coin if they find out nothing happened here?"

She nodded. "I cannot get paid for a service I didn't provide."

"Fair enough." He twined his fingers with hers guiding her toward the chair by the fire, motioning her to sit. "Then you will serve me the only way I can permit." Confusion crawled across her delicate features. "By conversing with me," he said with a friendly smile, one she returned.

José moved for the bed, grabbed the quilt, and walked over, placing it around her shoulders to keep the temptation of her body hidden. "Can I offer you some wine?" She nodded. José moved to the bar cart in the corner of the room, poured wine for two, and placed one glass in her waiting hands.

"Thank you," she whispered.

"For someone agreeing to have a conversation, we'll have to muster a few more words out of you beyond nodding and a 'thank you,'" he said as he sat in the neighboring chair.

Her hair fell over her shoulder as she looked down at the glass in her lap. "Forgive me. As you can imagine, I am not used to such politeness."

"What is your name?

She smiled coyly at him. "Whatever you want it to be." José gave her an anticipatory look. She sighed. "Jesenia. My name is Jesenia."

"Pleasure to meet you, Jesenia. My name is—"

"Gaspar," she interrupted. "I know who you are. We've heard of you here."

"All great things, I hope."

She laughed, taking a sip of her wine. His eyes roamed over her curiously, assessing her. "You look very young for this type of profession."

Her spine lengthened. "I'm old enough to know how to bring a man to pleasure in a quarter hour." She smirked. "Twice."

José hid his smile behind his cup. "Very well, old enough. Tell me, what are your dreams?"

My dreams?"

"Yes, you must have some dreams."

Jesenia looked thoughtfully at the fire. "I don't know that anyone has ever asked me that."

"Why not?"

She cast him an incredulous stare. "Because I'm a *whore*."

"And because you're a woman of the night, you are not permitted dreams?"

"I am a woman of the day sometimes, too. Have you not met many prostitutes, *Don* Gaspar?"

"A few." He smiled coyly. "Back in my youth, of course."

"Did you make it a habit of asking all your prostitutes what their dreams are?" she teased.

"Only the pretty ones."

She burst into laughter, which was incredibly therapeutic to José's soul. "So, tell me. What are your dreams?"

Her smile fell, her shoulders curving slightly inward. "To be free. There's a whole world out there beyond Havana. I want nothing more than to leave here and start a new life." She chuckled under her breath. "Sounds silly, but…."

"But?" he urged.

She squinted thoughtfully. "But I always believe there's a way. There's always a solution. You just have to find it."

José gazed at her, astonished that such a young being had life all figured out. "Jesenia, I would like it very much if you would stay here. To sleep, nothing more. You can have the bed. I'll lay here by the fire."

She shook her head. "Oh no. I couldn't."

"I insist." José motioned her toward the bed and took the floor on the rug by the fire.

She sighed, appraising him for a few moments. "Very well. But you will need to let me return your courtesy."

"No, no. I have already told you—"

She shook her head. "No, Gaspar. Nothing like that, but you could use my help with your new persona."

José looked down at himself. "My persona?"

Her brow rose. "Yes. You are one of the most fearsome pirates, and you look too refined. You are in desperate need of a new look."

José felt his face heat. "In what way?"

"Well, I would assume the length of your hair is new to you, given how you casually reach for the long curls at the base of your neck, and you're scratching your beard like it's a foreign object to you. Let both of those grow out. You will need to get used to it. If you are going to be Gaspar the pirate, your beard is your armor. Wear it proudly. As for the clothes," Jesenia continued, smiling mischievously, "I believe I can make you just as fearsome as your reputation." She leaped from her chair. "Wait here. I will return shortly."

And that was how José found himself standing in front of the reflecting glass late into the early morning hours, being transformed. A black wool tricorne sat on top of his head, and a slightly loose white muslin shirt, adorned with ruffles at his wrists, was tucked into black velvet breeches. Jesenia wrapped a ruby-red sash around a black waistcoat. José took in his new image with interest. "Wherever did you get these clothes?"

Jesenia motioned to the large knapsack she had brought back with her. "They were a former lover's." José couldn't help but notice the smile drop from her face. She scoffed. "I know that sounds silly coming from a whore."

He looked at her seriously. "Not silly at all. No one can dismiss your feelings, regardless of your circumstances. I take it he is no longer with us?"

She moved to grab the jacket resting on the back of the chair. "*Sí.* He was a pirate, like you." José opened his mouth to correct her terminology but stopped, realizing he could no longer deny it. She gazed at him in the reflecting glass. "His mother gave me all his clothing and a few other items I would like you to have."

José looked at her incredulously. "I couldn't possibly."

"You can, and you will. It is what he would have wanted; someone as legendary as you wearing his armor. At least, that is what I like to call it. He was a good captain." Her eyes glistened as she held up the coat for José to put on. He slid his arms into the sleeves as she pulled it up until it rested on his shoulders. The black velvet coat complimented the waistcoat and breeches, and the gold stitching traveled up the hem of the coat in a unique design that stood out in the firelight. José hardly recognized himself.

Jesenia took his hands and placed various gold rings upon them. José frowned at her. "These have to be worth something."

"They likely are," she confirmed. "But these were not

meant to be bartered. They are to be revered." She turned and pulled one more item from her knapsack, a long gold chain with a medallion. Once she had the item around his neck, she turned him toward the reflecting glass again. "There you are." Jesenia smiled widely. "Gaspar."

As the evening rolled into the hours before dawn, he stared at the ceiling, eyes wide open. The moonlight cast shadows in the room as the embers from the fire died down with the impending rise of the sun. Jesenia stirred in the bed where she lay.

"What troubles you now, Gaspar?" she whispered.

He jolted from his trance and looked up at her. Her silhouette almost looked like his Joséfa…almost. "Nothing at all. Simply wondering how deep into hell I am to fall—a question I'll be asking myself a lot in the upcoming years. Perhaps for the rest of my life."

She chuckled. "*Bueno*, if you are going to hell, then I will certainly be there with you."

"Nonsense. You've done nothing wrong."

"I'll tell the good Lord you said so." José watched her trace circles absentmindedly on the thin fabric over her torso. "You will not go to hell."

"I will not?"

"No. You are doing what you have to do to survive. We all are."

He sighed. "I'm not sure about that."

"No? Are you not doing whatever you can to be with your beloved? I would think your actions tonight prove that you're holding on to hope."

They stayed silent for a long while. "I suppose I see your point. My thoughts are always on losing the life I had intended."

"With Joséfa, you mean?"

"Yes."

She sat up, resting her head on her palm. "Try not to worry so much, Gaspar. These things have a way of working themselves out."

José's brows furrowed. "I pray you don't take this wrong, but how do you stay so positive in such a profession?"

"You mean a woman of the night and sometimes of the day?" She smiled softly. "Yesterday, I sat in my humble home that the Lord provided, wondering how I would feed my family. Then, Rodrigo came into the brothel asking for a woman of a certain description. It so happens that I met his description. Now, I have the means to feed my family. We will not go hungry tonight."

José's heart fell heavy in his chest, the realization of her circumstances unfolding on him. She rose from the bed and cleansed her face in the basin before drying herself with the neighboring cloth. She looked down where he lay by the banking fire. "Keep your spirits up, Gaspar. You hold a torch for your lady. God will find a way to bring you both together one day."

José sprang from the floor before she reached the door. "Wait." He rummaged through his belongings, retrieving a few gold coins from his latest raid. He placed them in her hand, folding her fingers over them. "Thank you."

"But Rodrigo already paid me."

"Yes, but this is for you. For dealing with my troubled mind."

She giggled. "Very well then. I'll take it." She let go of his hand, reaching for the doorknob.

"Good luck to you, Jesenia. I truly hope you and your family make it out of Havana one day."

She glanced at him over her shoulder. "If not, we'll be sure to make the best of this life," she replied, closing the door behind her.

CHAPTER 25

THE LATE AFTERNOON SUNLIGHT INVADED THE SMALL ROOM. José's eyes took in the surroundings as he slowly woke from his dream. It was her again. Joséfa appeared to him, telling him to be patient and have faith. Perhaps the events of the night before influenced the hope he awoke with. Her presence still clung to his mind.

After using the cool water in the basin to freshen up, José adorned himself with all the clothing Jesenia provided him. Giving himself one more glance in the reflecting glass, he descended into the mostly empty dining hall. Rodrigo sat with a cup of tea, observing a map with merchant routes. Seeming to have had quite the night, John sat slumped in his chair, glassy-eyed. Rodrigo looked up at him, his mouth dropping slightly and his eyes sweeping over José's clothing. "*Mierda.*"

John's glassy eyes swung to him, going wide. "Oooh, the captain's not going to like that."

A smile grew across Rodrigo's face. "Worth…every…*peso.*"

Pulling out the chair next to John, José sat, reaching for a piece of bread on the table. Rodrigo and John continued to stare at him. "What news?" José questioned.

Rodrigo's brow rose. "Oh really? We're just going to try and brush off your complete transformation?"

"Yes, we are," José said, glaring.

Rodrigo grinned. "Remind me to send her a large thank you in gold. You look positively savage, Gaspar. Perhaps I should ask her to come back this evening?"

"I thank you, but that won't be necessary." He hoped Rodrigo wouldn't push any further. He didn't want word spreading throughout the small town that he had let Jesenia take the money without providing her services. Or that he gave her any extra.

"You lucky bastard. If I were you, I would take him up on the offer," John grumbled.

"It appears you weren't lacking in any entertainment yourself, John," José teased, welcoming the distraction from his ordeal.

"It was entertainment, all right. I got so drunk that I woke up in the street leaning against *La Posada* with a few bruises on my cheek. My first time on land with the comfort of a proper bed, and I couldn't even make it to the room." A rose-colored swell decorated his left cheek.

"Oh, yes. That certainly looks like it hurts."

"It is best that I don't remember it."

Rodrigo continued his study of the map on his desk.

"What do you have there?" José asked.

Glancing around to make sure no one was listening, Rodrigo leaned into the table. "Trying to find the best route for us to approach *El Cazador*."

"Any luck?"

Rodrigo shrugged. "I have a few theories. I'd love your expertise, however. We should probably make it to the ship before Captain Rodgers comes to find us."

"Hmph. If he takes an issue with our delay, he can blame you for sending the young woman my way."

Rodrigo grinned. "But it was worth it, no?"

"Mind your own."

Rodrigo chuckled and gathered the map. "Let's make our way then."

The streets of Havana were bustling with people. Several minutes passed until they finally had the ship within view. Captain Rodgers stood on the deck—a spyglass in hand, a scowl on his face. They scurried up the ramp to the deck. With his hands on his hips and foot repeatedly tapping on the floor, Captain Rodgers glared at them. "You're late!"

"We thought we would give you some time to enjoy the sights of Havana," José pleaded.

"This isn't my first sailing to Havana, Gaspar. And I don't care what you were up to last night or who. I said morning! It's nearly two hours past noon!"

"My apologies, Captain. It won't happen again."

The captain appraised him then with a scowl on his face. "What. Are. You. Wearing?"

José shrugged. "A gift."

"Hmph. You're still not a captain." Rodgers turned toward the town, looking through his spyglass again. José looked at Rodrigo and John, but they shrugged.

Approaching the captain's side, José tried to observe what held the captain's immediate attention. "Eh, is there trouble?"

Captain Rodgers jerked his head to him. "Trouble? No trouble. I am in the middle of lass hunting."

"*Lass* hunting?"

"Yes, lass hunting."

"Didn't you have enough *lass* hunting last night?"

"Hah! One can never have enough lasses. And I intend to have another one this evening." He turned his attention back to his spying.

"Careful, Captain. You'll go broke if you keep spending money on women."

"Who says I'll be spending any money?" A wicked grin spread across his face. "Now, come then. We have much to discuss."

A feeling of unease grew in the pit of his stomach at the captain's words. He followed him to his quarters with Rodrigo and John trailing behind.

When they entered the room, Rodrigo unrolled the map he had been studying earlier, weighing down the ends with bits and pieces of gold chalices and trinkets that littered the desk.

"I believe the main passage for *El Cazador* will be the route between La Florida and Havana," Rodrigo advised.

"I would agree. It seems to be the best passage," José chimed in.

"Yes, and my source tells me they are planning to set sail from Veracruz at the beginning of January, approximately the tenth or the eleventh," Captain Rodgers relayed. "We'll have a more accurate date as we draw closer."

"How accurate is your source?" José asked.

Captain Rodgers huffed. "None of your concern. Now, I believe the more pressing question is, what *time* of day will this take place?"

"The daytime, no?" John asked.

"No."

"No?" Rodrigo asked.

"No," he exclaimed and then glared at José. "And don't you go asking me either, Gaspar."

José glanced up from the map, shrugging. "It doesn't necessarily have to be during the day, but the night raid does pose more risks. How do we board the ship? What approach do we make? By *La Floriblanca* or by other means? It is quite a risk with so many men on board."

"Yes, but the risk is far worth it in this case. The element of surprise will be on our side." The captain rapped his fingers on the desk, debating his next words. "My informant is the lookout."

"*Cristo!* The lookout?" José asked, aghast. "You have a Spanish Royal Officer in your pocket?"

"Don't look so shocked, Gaspar. I have you, don't I?"

José's blood boiled in his veins. He refrained from commenting. The lookout posed another risk—exposing José's identity to the Spanish Royal Navy. The nerves set in his bones. He shook and ignored them.

"He knows he will be well taken care of," the captain continued.

"And what of the crew?" José asked. "Surely, this will be a bit of a complication. The second we hit land, they will know who was responsible for raiding their ship. It would be considered an act of war."

"Perhaps you haven't noticed, but we're already *in* a war. Not that any of it matters. There will be no crew to report back."

"What do you mean there will be no crew to report back?" Gaspar asked, aghast. While Rodrigo and John looked at him somberly, the captain glared at him, disgusted.

"What do you think? Maybe you're not as smart as I thought you were, Gaspar."

"You can't mean to kill everyone on board, can you? That's ridiculous. Just how do you propose to do that? With a ship that size, there's no way we could even manage it."

"Not unless we *burn* the ship and let it sink."

"But why?"

"Because we're bloody pirates! And dead men tell no tales. If you have a problem with it, I'd be happy to send you to the bottom of the sea, too. So, what will it be? Are you done trying to save your own skin? Or are you with us?"

José glanced between the three of them, his mouth slack. "I can't possibly."

Captain Rodgers moved with lightning speed, slamming José against the far wall. He unsheathed his dagger, holding it against José's throat. "The time for your little games is over. Rodrigo saved your life and brought you on board my ship. Seems like a pretty ill way to repay him by refusing to do your duty to my crew," he hissed. "Now, either you're with us or against us. Which is it?"

José considered death at that moment. It would be an easier fate than killing the men on El Cazador—men he fought alongside under the Spanish Royal Navy. But he was no longer one of them and never would be again. He sighed. "Yes."

Captain Rodgers increased the pressure of the blade against his throat. "Yes, what?"

"Yes, I will do what I must," he seethed as his soul slipped further into darkness.

Sitting at the bar of *La Piña de Plata*, José, Rodrigo, and John sipped their sugary rum drink courtesy of the finest barmaid in Havana. It was a welcome distraction from the most recent dispute with the captain.

"Does he always have to be such a bastard?" José asked.

"Yes. Yes, he has *always* been a bastard," John advised, shaking his head.

Rodrigo patted José on the back. "Don't let him get to you, Gaspar."

"That imbecile goes against everything I am or have been taught to be."

"You need to let go of everything you were taught and be who you need to be. Besides, he will make you a wealthy man."

"Very wealthy," John chimed in enthusiastically.

"But at what cost? My soul can only take so much. These were my countrymen. I likely know some of the men on *El Cazador*."

Rodrigo glared at him intently. "You must put all thoughts of loyalty to any of those men on the ship aside. Bury it deep within you where you can no longer access it. They see you as Gaspar, the pirate now. Admiral Gaspar is no more. And they will take your life at the tip of their blade without hesitation." He reached out and squeezed José's shoulder. "You are Gaspar, the pirate." José gazed at him wordlessly, feeling the power of the declaration. *I am Gaspar, the pirate.*

Rodrigo continued. "If we can pull this off—and I believe we will—we can disappear for a few years, and that will be a welcome break from the good captain."

"Good captain, my backside," José bit out, taking a cool sip.

"I'd be lying if I said the whole raid doesn't have me nervous," John confessed. "Do you really think this one will be successful, Rodrigo?"

Rodrigo's brow furrowed. "Well, I understand why you would be worried. A night raid is very different from any other raid we've done. A lot can go wrong, but I believe it can be done." Rodrigo stood from his chair, taking a long stretch. "I think I've had enough of these delicious drinks. I'm going to retire. I haven't had much sleep these past few days." He glanced around the floor, pulling the chair out and looking under the counter. "Did I forget the map?"

José glanced toward the floor, finding nothing. "I believe so."

"Damn."

"Don't worry yourself." José stood stretching his long legs. "I'll go back to the ship and get it. I could use the walk to clear my head."

"Are you sure? I don't want to receive word in the morning that the captain is missing a hand or, worse, a head."

"As tempting as that sounds, you have nothing to worry about. I'll place the map in your room when I return."

Rodrigo gave a wide yawn. "Very well. John? Are you coming?"

John sat staring at the lovely barmaid, doe-eyed with a permanent grin. "No, I think I'll stay for one more."

"You know she hasn't paid you any attention," José teased.

"One can admire the beauty," John said without taking his eyes off the barmaid. "Magdalena! I'll take one more!"

"*Vale*, John," she replied with a smile. Apparently, Magdalena knew how to work her charm. José smiled and walked out onto the street.

The cool night air whipped José's hair back. Taking his time, he admired how the moonlight cast shadows over the buildings. In the distance, deep, dark blue waves danced with silver light as they gently lapped against the ships lining the harbor. He never grew tired of seeing the beauty of the ocean

and doubted he could live anywhere where water wasn't within reach. The romantic aura of the night did not escape his notice, and his thoughts traveled to his beloved.

"Oh, how I long for you, Joséfa," he whispered, "and for your guidance." The idea of killing an entire crew of his own countrymen weighed heavy on his heart. He understood he was a fugitive, and the king would likely find out about such a betrayal if any of the crew were to escape. There was no choice left for him. He had to complete this mission. Only then would he be free of the captain and able to make his next move. Perhaps there was a way he could return to Joséfa.

José shook his head. To let her go was the only option, but he hoped her journey to *Nueva España* had not begun. He hoped she was safely in Sevilla, away from the person he was becoming. What would she say if she knew he answered to such an ill-mannered captain? José huffed. *She'd be disgusted.*

Just then, a shriek echoed through the streets coming from the direction of the ships. José sprinted as another muffled scream reached his ears. He found the source of the sounds coming from *La Floriblanca*. He raced up the ramp—his chest pumping. Another cry came from the captain's quarters. It wasn't a cry of passion or lust but one of fear. His steps shook the floorboards as he barreled into the room. His gut turned over at what he found.

A young woman, no more than a girl, lay over the side of the captain's desk—his hand clamped over her mouth from behind. Tears glistened in the lamplight, her eyes pleading for help. Captain Rodgers looked over in shock at José's intrusion. It took José no more than a second to act. Captain Rodgers threw the girl into the wall behind him and reached for his pistol on the desk, but José was quicker. He swept the pistol off the desk with force, and it fell to the floor with a thud. José grabbed Captain Rodgers by the neck and slammed him against the wall, his feet dangling slightly off the ground. He peered over his shoulder at the girl who lay crumpled against the wall in terror.

"Go! Now!" he bellowed.

She scrambled off the ground and ran out the door, her pounding footsteps across the deck and down the ramp the only sound as the two men stared at each other furiously.

José gripped Captain Rodgers' neck tightly, gritting his teeth. "Tell me one good reason I shouldn't end your life right here."

"I should whip you for even thinking of it," the captain rasped.

José slammed his head into the wall. "She was just a *girl*."

"I'll have you know I paid her family good money for her maidenhead," Captain Rodgers spat in his face. "And now you owe me." José once again slammed his head against the wall. The captain groaned in pain.

José's eyes narrowed. "One of these days, your luck will run out."

"Is that a threat?" Captain Rodgers wheezed in amusement.

José leaned in his face. "I sure hope so." He dropped him unceremoniously to the ground, where the captain gulped air into his lungs.

"Let us set the record straight, you pompous Spanish arsehole," the captain seethed. "I run this ship. Not you. May that be the last time you threaten my life. I will have you at the bottom of the ocean with all the others who decided to challenge me. And if you dare come on my ship again and attempt to intervene in my affairs, I *will* kill you."

José glared at him venomously, the corner of his mouth lifting in a smirk. "You can try." He grabbed the map from his desk, rolled it up quickly, and turned to leave the room. As he stomped down the ramp into the dark, empty street, he vowed to remove the good captain from the world one day. That was a promise.

CHAPTER 26

THE COOL NIGHT AIR SENT A CHILL DOWN HIS SPINE. *La Flori-blanca* picked up her speed while cautiously tailing *El Cazador*. The wind was dying down, just as Rodrigo had predicted. There was no doubt there would be hundreds of men on board that ship guarding the king's reales intended for Louisiana. He closed his eyes and breathed deeply. *I am Gaspar, the pirate.*

The sun had retired below the horizon some time ago, and it was time. José made his way across the deck, counting the crew, giving them a pat on the back if they seemed in restless spirits. Chino, a young pirate barely seventeen, patted his dagger at his side, his leg, and then back to his side, exhaling deeply. José chuckled. "Relax, Chino. You must have a clear mind. Do not let your nerves get the best of you."

Chino nodded his head vigorously. "Yes, Gaspar."

"Fear is a great motivator, but only if you own your fear. Do not let it own you."

"Yes, Gaspar."

"You remember where to aim, yes?"

"Yes, aim like the butcher."

"Yes. You'll be quite fine."

"Thank you, Gaspar."

José moved further down the deck.

"Gaspar?"

He turned back to Chino.

"Thank you," Chino said. "I had heard of you before—when you were an Admiral. I heard of your skill and your kindness. Although this is a nefarious mission, I am honored to have your guidance to get me through. You truly are a unique pirate." Chino looked over his shoulder and leaned toward José. "I think that's the root of the captain's jealousy toward you."

"Jealousy?" José asked, amused.

"Oh, to be sure," Chino said enthusiastically. "Captain Rodgers could never have an ounce of your strength, skill, or leadership. Be careful, Gaspar. He may need you now, but that could change. And you ought to be prepared when it does. The man has no loyalty to any of us."

The shock of Chino's warning sank deep into his gut. "I appreciate the notice, young man. I truly do."

"Be careful, Gaspar. And know this," he said, leaning in conspiratorially, "if you ever were to come to blows with the good captain, many men wouldn't mind his fall and for you to succeed. That's all I'll say."

"Well, you've said quite a bit. Now, focus on the task at hand and not piratical politics."

A short laugh left Chino as José turned and moved further down the deck. *La Floriblanca* carried several small boats intended to approach El Cazador in the dead of night. Rodrigo and John walked around roping each boat and assigning men to each—some for lowering the boats to the water, others to board the boats when they reached the water. When José reached Rodrigo on the bow, Rodrigo straightened, wiping his brow.

"I don't think I've ever taken part in something so complex. If I'm being honest, it is much easier during the day. Fire the cannons and be done with it."

José nodded. "Yes, but not with an entire ship filled with Spanish coins. A little bit different."

"True."

"Quit your chatting and get moving," the captain called down to them. "We have a treasure to get."

With that, the two of them dispersed. It was some time before *La Floriblanca* was ready to send its boats. The men climbed down the side of the ship, their boats equipped with small anchors to hoist them up on the deck of *El Cazador*. They rowed in complete silence. Each paddle stroke brought them closer. True to Captain Rodgers' word, the lookout peered down to where the boats lined the starboard side of the ship. His silhouette that revealed nothing but his inaction was justification enough. The men hoisted the anchors over the side of the ship.

The lookout pulled the men to the deck. Avoiding any eye contact, José peered down at the floor. If this man recognized him, it could be a risk, regardless of the beard he now wore.

"What of your men?" Rodrigo whispered to the lookout.

"All down below," the lookout confirmed, his voice barely audible. "I lowered the sails as *La Floriblanca* approached at dawn. *El Cazador* will be at a standstill as it approaches. The exit of the crew's cabin is closed and boarded. They lie asleep and cannot get out. The only person you will have to worry about is Capitan de Campos y Pineda."

José swallowed hard. Gabriel de Campos y Pineda, the officer he initially trained with in his youth, was on board *El Cazador*. The captain of *El Cazador*. Worse, he was to die at his hand. He was surely going to hell. "*Señor, perdoname*," he said under his breath.

"The *reales* are on the deck just below us." The lookout reached into his pocket and pulled out a key, handing it over to Rodrigo. "Use this key on the lock. I strongly encourage you to make haste. De Campos is a light sleeper. He is sure to wake from the noise."

"Gaspar, you guard the door to the captain's quarters."

"Gaspar?" the lookout whispered in surprise.

José moved so fast Rodrigo hadn't even seen the blade as it reached the lookout's neck. "What of it?" José hissed.

The lookout shook his head. "*Nada. Nada.*"

Rodrigo stepped forward, placing his hand on José's arm that held the dagger. "Is this going to be a problem?" he asked the lookout.

"No. No," the lookout shook his head again. José didn't need to see his eyes to know they were wide. He dropped the dagger from the man's throat.

"Go guard the door to the captain's quarters," Rodrigo ordered José. Pointing to two of *La Floriblanca's* crew, "You two go with him. The rest of you, start bringing the *reales* to the deck. We must prepare everything before the sun wakes from his slumber."

José narrowed his eyes at the lookout upon passing but continued without a word. Taking his post in front of the captain's quarters, he watched as the men brought up bag after bag of the *reales*. Each bag landed with a thump on the deck, with dozens of the crew moving in succession. A loud bang sounded from below. José grabbed the hilt of his sword to make ready. The crew of *El Cazador* stirred with the heavy footsteps sounding above them. The men picked up the pace with apparent alarm—the yelling below deck reaching their ears.

José turned to the two men guarding the captain's quarters. "Stay here." Stomping his way to the lookout, he grabbed his arm. "How secure is the latch holding the crew below?"

"S-so-somewhat secure, sir," he stammered.

"What is your name?"

"Cristobal, sir."

"Cristobal, go down below and ensure the latch is secure. You have a crew of outraged men downstairs, and we wouldn't want them to see just how far down the rabbit hole one of their own has fallen, would we?"

"Yes, sir."

Cristobal raced downstairs. Returning to his post, he found the two men standing in front of the captain's quarters, looking concerned.

"I believe he has awoken," one of the men said, hand on his dagger.

"And I believe you will need more than a dagger to take that man down," he advised. The door to the captain's quarters swung open, hitting the wall behind it with a bang. José pulled his pistol from his waist, holding it straight at the head of Captain de Campos y Pineda. The two guards thrust their swords on either side of the captain, forcing him to drop his weapon to the floor.

"*Buenas dias, Capitán.*"

"Just what do you all think you're doing?"

José glanced at the multiple bags of *reales* behind him. "What does it look like we're doing, Gabriel? I'm astonished you need to ask such a question. How very unlike you."

Gabriel squinted, moving toward José. The edge of the guard's sword dug into his side, keeping him where he stood. "Who are you?"

José stepped toward him until he was mere inches from his face. "Surely not that much time has passed between us. Having trouble telling the man behind the beard?" he gritted out.

Gabriel's eyes went wide. "Admiral Gaspar?"

"Just Gaspar to you now."

Gabriel's face twisted in disgust. He lunged at José, but the two men at his side held him back. "How dare you!"

"How dare *I*? How dare the king! It is he who sent me to this life. I will not be shamed by you or any other on this ship for it."

"My, how you have fallen."

"Depends on your perspective. In truth, how many innocent lives have been taken at the hands of the Spanish? Does a uniform change the nature of a man, or are you not a pirate yourself, taking whatever you please?"

Just beyond the ship's deck, the sky grew the lightest shade of purple as it kissed the dark blues of the dying night. "Hold him here," José ordered the two guards. He made his way to the railing. The sails of *La Floriblanca* were up as the ship made its way next to *El Cazador*. Rodrigo appeared beside him.

"The men are pouring the gunpowder on the deck. They placed a few barrels on top of the latch as well. They are ready to move when *La Floriblanca* reaches the ship."

"Excellent. It looks like it should be here at any moment."

"Do you think you're going to get away with this, Admiral Gaspar?! Oh! I'm sorry. Gaspar, isn't it? Do you think you'll get away with this, *Gaspar*?!" Gabriel called from behind them.

José strolled over to him, a smirk on his face. "Actually, I do."

"There is no way the king will let you live."

"That is probably true," he agreed, shrugging. A loud bang came from below deck. "Rodrigo. Go below with a few men and make sure the crew doesn't break through."

Rodrigo nodded and rushed below deck with a few of the men.

"Why?" Gabriel asked in disbelief.

"*Why*? Because there was no other choice. That's why."

"Is that what you think?" Gabriel huffed. "You truly are foolish. And I have to say. I am certainly sorry for Joséfa. She will be sad to learn all of her efforts are wasted."

José rushed to Gabriel, grabbing his shirt and lifting him slightly. "What the hell do you mean by that?"

Gabriel shrugged. "She has been petitioning to clear your name. I guess her efforts are wasted. There's no way the king would clear your name now—not when he finds out about all of this."

José leaned into him. A sinister smile grew at the corner of his mouth. "And who says the king is going to find out?"

The realization grew on Gabriel's face. "You wouldn't."

"I would," José hissed.

At that moment, *La Floriblanca* pulled next to *El Cazador*—Captain Rodgers and the men hoisting the planks across the two ships. The men on *El Cazador* moved the bags of *reales* in a frenzy. Rodrigo and the men below deck ran up the stairs.

"They'll hold," Rodrigo advised. "But only just. We need to make haste."

"You cannot do this," Gabriel pleaded. "Those are *your* men below deck, José. *You* led these men. You dined with their families. You taught them the way of the sword and how to be outstanding soldiers—how to be good men. You taught them to be honorable men. There is no honor in this, José!"

"My honor left the day I escaped Sevilla."

"That is not true. Joséfa can still clear your name, and you know it."

"Be that as it may, I must ensure my reputation doesn't get back to the good King. And leaving you here on this Earth to tell the tale of Admiral Gaspar's fall from grace isn't going to help my beloved clear my name." José aimed the pistol at Gabriel's head. "Goodbye, Gabriel."

"José, don't—"

José pulled the trigger. Gabriel's body landed on the floor with a thump. He turned to find Cristobal and the crew standing behind him, speechless. Without a second thought, he unsheathed his sword, swinging it across the neck of a stunned Cristobal. A gargling sound came from his throat as the blood seeped down his neck. His body dropped to the ground.

José glanced over at *La Floriblanca*. Captain Rodgers eyed him with a smile on his face. Stepping over Cristobal's body, José grabbed Rodrigo by the arm. "Let's go." He turned to his crew. "What are you staring at?! Let's go!"

Grabbing the last few bags, the men returned to their ship. They pulled the planks away and began to set sail, slowly circling *El Cazador*."

"Fire the cannons!" Captain Rodgers called from the wheel. *El Cazador* was destroyed with the blast of cannonballs breaching the ship's side. Just then, Chino emerged with a bow and arrow lit with fire. As *La Floriblanca* pulled away, he sent the flaming arrow of fire into the air. It landed on the deck of *El Cazador*. A few moments later, the entire ship burst into flames. Not a single ounce of the vessel remained untouched by fire.

The crew of *La Floriblanca* watched from the railing in silence as she sailed away from the wreckage.

"That was the most unforgiving act I've ever seen of a man." Captain Rodgers stood beside José.

José sighed. "Which part?"

"The part where you finally embraced the pirate within," he said, smirking. He turned, making his way to the helm.

José stared at the remnants of *El Cazador* until it sank in the distance. His heart grew heavy knowing he had a hand in the deaths of so many of his former men, but the guilt was muted with the knowledge that his innocence still lay in the hands of his beloved. His life with her still held a flame. It may be barely lit, but it was still there. He wondered if she would ever take him back after all he'd done.

Chapter 27

Seagulls of every size danced in the oncoming winds. The waves rolled powerfully onto the beach of their pirate island haven, drifting ever so slowly back into the sea. The warm, humid air of the approaching dusk whipped José's dark brown hair tickling his ears and causing him to shudder. Rodrigo sat silently by his side, admiring the beauty of the Gulf. It was the first proper break they'd had between hiding the coin from the *El Cazador* raid and the discovery of the island they now lived on.

A few days earlier, as they traveled along the coast of *La Florida*, Rodrigo captained *La Félicité* with a few of the crew clamoring to escape Captain Rodgers. They were to travel to the neighboring Spanishtown Creek to sell *La Félicité* to avoid notice. Rodrigo knew of a small, secluded island he had observed in passing. It seemed uninhabited, which was precisely what they were looking for.

With the rest of the crew on their way to handle business, Rodrigo and José scouted the island for a proper space to build their secret haven. Deep in the cluster of palms that overtook the island, they came across a cabin that, from all evident signs, had been uninhabited for some time. They made their way to the side of the structure listening for any signs of life within. As they glanced through the dusty window, they saw a table strewn with maps and a heap in the corner of the room under a tarp. It piqued their curiosity immediately. José thrust his shoulder into the door with enough force to break it down. They would not soon forget what greeted them on the other side.

"*Por Dios in el Cielo*," José whispered. He glanced at Rodrigo, whose eyes were just as wide as his.

"Tell no one of this," Rodrigo cautioned. "Not a living soul must know beyond you and me. Swear it, Gaspar."

José nodded vigorously. "I swear it."

Their discovery would change *everything*.

José was still in awe and could hardly believe their luck. It was the one bright light in a shadow of conflicting emotions coursing through him. José inhaled the salty air. The waves crept around his toes, cooling his feet as they sat comfortably, arms resting on their knees, on the beach.

"It's funny," he said.

Rodrigo glanced at him. "What's on your mind?"

"I'm conflicted. A part of me expects to feel incredibly guilty for what we did a few weeks ago."

"Ah," Rodrigo said, turning his attention back to the sea. "I see."

"However, there's only emptiness. It's almost as if I truly do not have a care in the world. A part of me feels anger and justification. Those were the king's men, not mine. The king turned his back on me when I had given him my life at will for our country. And he betrayed me. I would be a fool to think that the king and I would be *amigos* for eternity like Felipe. Be that as it may, I struggle to understand how he could have done it so easily after the years of consulting I provided him. Taking on *El Cazador* felt like the sweetest revenge. A part of the old me sank with the ship that day. To be honest? I'm not entirely sure I regret it."

"And what of your lady?" Rodrigo asked. "Have your intentions to be with her one day changed?"

José sighed, looking down at the churning bubbles crawling across the sand. "I do not know anymore, and I hardly think she'll choose me after this. I am who I am now. There's not much I can do to change my fate now except for leaving no survivors to report back. That is my only hope." José grabbed sand with his hand, slowly letting it out of his palm. "I do pray one day we shall find each other again. Although she may not like the man I am becoming, I will never give up hope."

Rodrigo chuckled lightly. "I would never expect you to. And knowing as little of the lady as I do, I am still positive she will never stop looking for you."

José smiled. "No, I don't believe she will." Another thought had been sitting heavy in his gut. "Rodrigo, I do have a question for you."

"What is it?"

"How in the world did you come to be in the company of such an evil, ridiculous man as Captain Rodgers? I know you and I have spent less time together than the two of you, traveling the oceans, but you do not seem like the horse's ass that he is."

"Hah! Well, sometimes you cannot choose your ship. You have to take the opportunities where they present themselves. I wasn't in a position to be selective when I came across his ship in Sevilla."

José glanced behind at the unmarked graves set in an open patch of land just beyond the trees. "So, this is home for a while, then?"

Rodrigo nodded. "It is. And the rest of the crew will be back in a few short days with the lumber to build—minus your Captain Rodgers."

"Thank the heavens for that. If I had to spend months upon months with the despicable captain, I might hang myself from the trees."

"Why do I get the impression you're going to be the death of him?" he asked with a sly smile.

José huffed. "You never know. I just might."

The rest of the evening rolled on as the two sat on the shore, welcoming the new reality of their life as pirates in hiding.

CHAPTER 28

ONE YEAR SINCE JOSÉ GASPAR'S DISAPPEARANCE

JOSÉFA'S HEART RACED, AND HER BREATHING BECAME ERRATIC. She tried breathing deeply as she forced her feet one in front of the other. She gripped her sister-in-law's arm a little tighter for support. Lorena's presence calmed her slightly. With Armando and Felipe away on business, she would take all the comfort she could from her new sister. They walked through *El Palacio*, the repeating arches lining the walkway passing them by like soldiers standing to attention. Joséfa had been summoned to the new King of Spain, the son of the deceased king responsible for the charges brought against José. Joséfa didn't know what to make of it. She had held onto hope for so long she could hardly stand to encourage it—José having fled Sevilla so long ago. She didn't have any more strength left in her heart left.

Since José's departure, she had fallen into a depression she couldn't work herself out of. Her days were filled with monotonous routines that made her appear to the world as an ordinary woman in society. Inside, she was dying a little more each day. She wanted to claw at any suitors who dared to court her but remained grateful when they did. The rage she felt took away from the constant pain of José's absence and the injustice of it all.

"Deep breaths, *hermana*," Lorena encouraged.

Joséfa failed to bring words to her trembling lips but nodded her head. It wasn't long before they stood before King Carlos IV, his distinct Bourbon dynasty features coming into view for the first time. They curtsied before him and stood waiting for him to speak.

"*Señorita* Joséfa de Mayorga. *Señora* de Mayorga. Thank you for coming."

"It is our pleasure, your highness," she replied quietly.

His light-gray eyes scanned her, taking in her tiny frame; much slimmer these past two years since food didn't have the same appeal as it once did. Joséfa suddenly felt embarrassed with her appearance, the dress she wore hanging loosely on her frail body. "*Señorita* de Mayorga, I received your petition, and I understand you still seek a pardon for the former Admiral José Gaspar.

Joséfa forgot how to breathe. "Yes, your Highness. I do."

He nodded. "You may be surprised to know your petition was of no shock to me. My father's…relations with some of the women in town were known to everyone, especially my mother. As you can imagine, it was difficult as her son to witness her heartache. No other mistress was as particularly cruel as Mariana. She took great satisfaction in chiding my mother, *her Queen*, at every opportunity. My father permitted it and almost encouraged it as he flaunted Mariana in front of her."

Joséfa could feel Lorena tense beside her at the mention of her cousin, who had been mysteriously missing since King Carlos took the throne, along with Rafael Bautista. King Carlos motioned for his attendant, who handed him a piece of parchment. "I never believed for a moment that Admiral José Gaspar was guilty of stealing our jewels. I have been an admirer of his since I was a boy. I used to watch him as he and the other men trained. He was incredibly talented and even more intelligent. José Gaspar stood by my father's side, guiding him, protecting him. And yet, my father believed the lies Mariana poured into his ear. She brought his jealousy to boil, and he would not listen to reason."

He held out the parchment to Joséfa, and she willed her legs to move, taking it in her hands—her eyes scanning it multiple times. She looked up at the king, her vision blurred with welling tears. The king smiled down at her in the most gentle of ways. "Your pardon as requested, *Señorita* de Mayorga. I do not know what manner of man you will find if you are able to rescue him from the fate that has been thrust upon him, but his name is clear if you all are ever to return home."

The tears spilled over, and she smiled happily for the first time in what felt like an eternity. "*Gracias*, Rey Carlos. I will never forget your kindness." Her heart felt like bursting, the hope she barely held onto resurfacing.

"*Rey* Carlos," Lorena said softly from beside her, "I do not wish to anger you. I only ask this because of the child my husband and I now care for. What of Mariana?"

The smile fell from King Carlos' face. "I advise you to forget she ever existed, *Señora* de Mayorga. Take the child. I understand that *Señor* de Mayorga has procured land in *Puerto Rico*. Start a new life there, far away from all of this. The child may want to know about her father in the future, but it may be safer for her to be away from this life for now."

Lorena nodded her understanding of it all. Joséfa grabbed her arm as they curtsied to their King and left the throne room. They silently traveled through the cobblestone streets until Lorena asked, "And now?"

With renewed and vigorous energy reaching through the depths of the darkness in her soul that had plagued her for years, she proclaimed, "And now we rescue my beloved."

Chapter 29

José & Rodrigo's Pirate Island Haven
4 Years after the El Cazador heist

José scratched his long, scraggly beard while peering at the oncoming boat sent from *La Floriblanca*. Sighing loudly, he looked over to Rodrigo, who he found frowning—likely due to his annoyance with the end of their blissful retreat.

"Well, I suppose we weren't completely unaware this would happen. They did send word with the last men who ventured a visit," he said.

"Does not make it any easier." José glanced behind him. The small abodes were visible just through the trees. It was a miracle they could accomplish all they did with limited resources and manpower. If it weren't for Rodrigo's connections, they would never have achieved the goal—at least not with the type of discretion they enjoyed. The two larger dwellings belonging to Rodrigo and José lay just beyond the dwellings of the other men—some of whom had not yet joined them on the shore. "I suppose I should warn the others that their long hiatus is coming to an end."

"You go ahead. I'll wait here for them to row ashore."

José trekked through the powder-fine sand to the tiny abode belonging to John. As he approached, he heard several voices—some that were definitely not John. A moan of pleasure sounded through the trees. José slowed his pace damning

Rodrigo for sending him to round up the crew, knowing some of them were sure to be partaking in their last carnal pleasures for a time. He waited just a few minutes until the sounds of pleasure died before knocking on the door.

"John? We are being summoned to *La Floriblanca*. They have arrived," he called.

"*Mierda*!" The stomping of feet sounded from the floorboards. A crash of glass—likely the rum they had procured from a shipment a few weeks ago—echoed above the chaos. He hoped it was empty, for that would be a dreadful waste. "*Un momento*, Gaspar!"

José chuckled lightly. "Take your time. The boat won't be here for another quarter hour. I'll go get Chino."

"No need!" Chino called…from behind John's door.

José's eyebrows shot up. "Oh!"

At that moment, the door swung open with John leading the way. Chino followed him out with nothing more than his britches on and shirt in hand. José peered inside to find a woman of promiscuous means named Darla—known for her willingness to please in all kinds of sexual situations and a frequent visitor to their island. She lay blissfully across the bed with nothing more than the skin God gave her for cover. José cleared his throat, his cheeks heating. "I trust someone will be coming to escort you soon. We wouldn't want to leave you alone on this island."

She sat up on her elbow. "No worries, Gaspar. They will be here shortly, per usual."

He nodded, trying desperately to keep his eyes on her face, not what she proudly sported below. "Very well then. Be sure to take care of yourself." He moved to walk away and turned back to her. "And Darla, remember what I taught you. Thrust your foot back on the knee, squeeze the wrist to release any weapon, and jab in his nether regions if you ever come to harm."

"Yes, Gaspar," she replied, grinning. "I remember well. Thank you."

He followed John and Chino to the shore, where they found Rodrigo and *Señora* Elena Perez, who had been on the island with them these years as a matron of sorts. She giggled like a child as Rodrigo wrapped his arms around her ample waist. He whispered something in her ear, and she swatted him on the arm. "*Demonio!*" Rodrigo kissed her thoroughly, her knees buckling slightly.

José noticed the boat gliding onto the sand and cleared his throat. Rodrigo pulled away from *Señora* Perez, a mischievous grin on his face. "Think of me when I'm gone?"

She huffed. "I won't think too deeply. There is much to be done while you're away."

"Speaking of," José interrupted, leaning toward the happy couple. "The coin I left you. You remember where I left it?" he asked her.

She nodded her head. "Of course. And I will take care of everything, Gaspar. Please do not worry." She glanced back at the ship in the distance. "You will have enough on your hands."

He sighed, his gaze going to his future or his doom—he couldn't tell. "You're not wrong."

Elena reached out and squeezed his hand. "May the Lord protect you."

José kissed the back of her hand, smiling warmly at her. "The Lord will be very busy then." He shuffled down to the waiting boat Chino and John had already boarded. With Rodrigo detached from his lady, he pushed off the shore and jumped on the boat.

The uneven bobbing of the boat was a precursor to the life they were set to lead over the next few years. They watched their home shrink in size until they reached *La Floriblanca*.

José looked up to the deck to find Captain Rodgers sneering at them. He nudged Rodrigo with his elbow. "Apparently, his sentiments haven't changed with time."

"And you were expecting that they would?" Rodrigo asked, amused.

"Not in the slightest, but one can hope."

As he climbed the rope ladder to the deck, the dread of dealing with Captain Rodgers again sank into his gut—uncertain of his capacity to deal with any of his ire. The captain, a deep scowl on his face, waited to greet them when they reached the deck, cementing those feelings.

"Had yourselves a nice break, did you? You're looking more like the pirate you should Gaspar. That is quite the beard."

José regarded him carefully, unsure of what to say. '*Thank you*' came to mind, but he wasn't sure if he was being insulted or complimented. He preferred not to respond to his statement at all. "And what of your break, Captain? I trust you found some peace during your time away?"

"Peace? Hah! There's no peace for me. You should know I'm always planning. Always making my next move. Speaking of, I need you and Rodrigo in my quarters immediately. We have a lot to go over." He glanced around at the rest of the crew, who barely stepped a foot on the deck before he bellowed, "What are you all standing around for? This isn't a ball. Get to work, you scoundrels!"

They sprung into action and began their usual tasks while Rodrigo and José followed the captain to his quarters. Crates upon crates of rum lay against the wall—apparently well stocked for the days ahead. A map of the Caribbean lay across his desk. Everything else remained the same as if untouched. José and Rodrigo walked around his desk to glance at his plans.

"It appears there's a merchant ship heading to San Juan," Captain Rodgers said while tracing the merchant route with a grubby finger. José's eyes followed the line across the Atlantic Ocean all the way back to where the line started, in Sevilla. His heart skipped a beat. He glanced at Rodrigo, who seemed to deduce his thoughts.

"Do we know what kind of cargo they carry?"

"Aye, it would appear they are carrying Spanish goods, primarily wine, heading for *Puerto Rico*. The details given by my informant were very vague, and I have to wonder if there's something more on this ship than just goods and wine."

"Could be."

Captain Rodgers glared at José. "Nothing more to say than *'could be'*, Gaspar? I think your tongue would be wagging with insight at its present course and where it travels from. Are you not the king of Sevilla?"

"To suggest such a thing is ridiculous. If I were King, I wouldn't be here on *your* fine vessel." José rested his hands on the desk, not giving into his seething stare. "The king could have sent aid. It's entirely possible. Nonetheless, I believe Rodrigo and I may be able to profit from whatever the ship holds. We are recently acquainted with a few smugglers. It's a sound plan."

"Smugglers, eh?" Captain Rodgers asked. "If I've never dealt with them, I'm not likely to trust them. And just who do you think you are giving orders to? I am the captain of this ship, Gaspar. Not you. I am just as fit to handle the profit through my own smuggling connections." He swiftly reached for his pistol and held it at José's head—a sneer resting upon his face. "Do I need to pull this trigger? Hmm? Perhaps I can set my aim a little lower and remind you of who I am and where you stand on this ship."

José rolled his eyes. "Put your gun down, Captain. I was only trying to be helpful. Of course, you have your own contacts. I was merely making a suggestion." José ignored the captain and the gun pointing at his head, continuing to digest the map before him. Captain Rodgers lowered his gun, his eyes boring into José. "What direction are you looking to take this time, Captain?" he asked, hoping not to lend any more to his anger.

"We take the straights. We plan to circle them and approach them from behind. I've made a few repairs and enhancements to *La Floriblanca*. She's sure to catch them in no time at all."

"Excellent," Rodrigo chimed in. "Then Gaspar and I will take our leave to help the men prepare the ship. Gaspar?" Rodrigo motioned to the door.

Rodrigo turned to him when they were safely out of earshot of the captain's quarters. "You rolled your eyes at him!"

"Yes. What of it?"

"Gaspar, you walk a very fine line when you show any contempt directed at the captain. All of the talk about him, regarding his pompousness, is completely acceptable among mates. But here? On his ship? To his *face*? You are lucky to have your manly sacks still attached to your member. You will do well to remember that. It is not lost on me that he did not shoot you right there and then. He will not hesitate next time."

"Let him. I couldn't care less."

"What has gotten into you?"

José stood there looking Rodrigo straight in the eye. "I haven't the faintest idea, my friend. But what I am feeling inside is pure intuition. And I plan to ride that feeling regardless of the dangers he tries to impose upon me."

"Be careful, Gaspar. I understand why you are excited. But be careful. That is all that I ask."

José sighed, patting him on the shoulder. "Do not worry. I hear you. Come. Let us go assist the crew."

The ocean rocked the ship slowly back and forth. A few snores periodically broke through the pattern of José's thoughts. Looking up at the intricate wood patterns above his head, he repeatedly counted the crevices and cracks to lull himself to sleep—his hammock swinging in unison with the ship.

"You're thinking of her," Rodrigo commented. José turned to Rodrigo, who lay in a hammock beside him.

"It would be very hard not to think of the possibility of this ship being the very one that carries my beloved. And what that would mean," he whispered.

"It would mean she will meet a different person than when she left."

"Very true, but I believe she is smart enough to know it. She's one of the smartest women I have ever encountered. If she is coming all this way, she has a plan. She wouldn't trek across the sea like this without one."

"Yes, I'll give her that." Rodrigo turned slightly to face him. "You know that you have options, Gaspar."

"And what options are those? If there is a way to get off this ship without receiving the ire of our dear captain, then I am open to it. I've been lying here for the past few hours running over every possible scenario in my mind. I'm not sure there is anything I can do to buy my freedom off this ship. You have to wonder if the captain even knows there's a possibility this merchant ship might have anyone I may know on it."

Rodrigo's brows furrowed. "Yes, it is quite curious. He's almost too confident that no one would come looking for you."

"Captain Rodgers will never let me go. I could have run to the ends of the Earth by now, and he would find me. He knows who I am and where I came from. He knows how to bring me down. It would be as easy as handing me over to the Spanish," he replied helplessly. "He is an evil spawn of Satan. But it would be hard to ignore the facts of the circumstances—I am still alive, and he has provided wealth to the rest of the crew and me. Regardless of his strange disdain for my existence."

"That is also true," Rodrigo agreed. "But I have to wonder, what happens when you are no longer valuable to him?"

José swayed silently, contemplating the question. "What are you suggesting, Rodrigo?"

Rodrigo nodded to the far side of the crew's quarters. "Do you see the bastard, Fredríco, over in the corner?" he asked just above a whisper.

José casually glanced over and saw the whites of Fredríco's eyes staring in their direction. José casually glanced back up at the ceiling to avoid attracting attention. '*Si*. But what of it?"

"He's the dirtiest of rats if I ever saw one. Something isn't right about this. The crew has always taken a liking to you, much to the captain's displeasure. I wonder if he hasn't planted a mole to sway the crew's loyalty to him or to keep an eye out for you entirely. And we intend to rob a Spanish merchant ship. There are so many other targets that would have been better worth our time and far more prosperous. I have this feeling in the pit of my stomach. Something is very different."

"*Si, mi amigo.* I would have to agree," he gently rolled to his side in his hammock to face Rodrigo. "Do you think he means to kill me? Or worse, turn me in?"

"Yes, I am starting to think it is likely. With a new King, who knows what his intentions might be? The circumstances of a privateer turning pirate are always changing. Why he would choose to do so now remains a mystery to me, but these things have a way of revealing themselves." Rodrigo rubbed his hands over his beard. "Do not worry, Gaspar. It is like I said, the crew admires you dearly. I have been on many ships and have yet to see that kind of loyalty in pirates. If Captain Rodgers seeks to kill you in cold blood, he will need more than that short, stubby son of a whore over in the corner. Still, do not set Captain Rodgers off. Limit your conversations with the crew. Keep your ears open, and I will do the same. We will figure out what he plans to do."

José nodded, his spirits lifting slightly. "Thank you, Rodrigo."

He softly chuckled. "Words of encouragement do not cost a thing."

"It is more than encouragement. You have been my most trusted companion since breaking out of the cells below the palace in Sevilla. I will not forget it."

"Think nothing of it, Gaspar. You're a good man and a damn good pirate."

They swayed in silence until the waves dancing along the ship finally provided the perfect soothing sound to bring them to sleep.

CHAPTER 30

a dash to prepare. The merchant ship was visible on the horizon, and the moment was upon them. José would soon find out just who was on this ship.

Fredríco stood in the corner, speaking in hushed whispers with a few crew members loyal to Captain Rodgers, to José's knowledge. They occasionally glanced his way while they worked with a look that could cut through the thickest of meat. It was all the confirmation José needed. Captain Rodgers intended to turn him in regardless of who was present on the merchant ship.

José casually made his way over to Rodrigo, bending down where he busied himself with gathering rope. "Have you noticed the men gathering in the corner with Fredríco?"

"*Si*. I'm afraid it is as I have predicted," he whispered without glancing up at José. "You will need to prepare, Gaspar. This is going to get very bloody, very quick. Today is the day the men on this ship will choose between you and him. It will test their loyalties." Rodrigo looked up at him then. "I have alerted a few men to the captain's intentions. You will not be alone."

After the crew had prepared the ship for the imminent attack, José and the rest of the crew stood on the deck watching the merchant ship coming closer and closer into view. The crew of the other ship became visible with each passing minute. He squinted. If he could just make out one of them, he would know—

A pair of hands grasped his forearms from each side and yanked him back. José pitched forward, attempting to shake them off, but they only doubled their effort. "Let go of me!"

"No, Gaspar. I don't think they will." Captain Rodgers broke through the crowd of men gathered around him. Most of the men appeared angered—others confused. José couldn't decipher their loyalties just yet, which troubled him.

"What is the meaning of this?"

"Oh, you know very well what this means." Captain Rodgers stepped closer to José—his face just inches away. His hot breath invaded José's senses, making him cringe at the rotting smell of decay. "Our time together has come to an end, Gaspar," he said with unmistakable disdain. "There is no longer a use for you on this ship. On *my* ship. I have all the information from you that I will ever need. Now, I shall profit from the smug, arrogant being that you are. You will be meeting your maker when you return to Spain. Do enjoy your travels back home." He grinned evilly.

"Filthy pirate!" José yelled, attempting to fight off the crew that held his arms. They yanked on him harder, bringing him to his knees. Captain Rodgers retrieved the gun from his holster, hitting José across the face over and over. Blood dripped from his forehead into his eyes, clouding his vision. Captain Rodgers knelt before him with a satisfied grin on his face.

"A filthy pirate I am. But make no mistake about it. *I* am the captain of this ship, and I always will be. This crew that you see here? They are mine. Not yours. Their loyalty lies with me." Captain Rodgers glared deep into José's eyes, daring him to challenge. "Your days of walking around feeling entitled to everyone's praise and respect are over. "

"I am not entitled. I *earned* their respect. You will never be able to say the same. And that crawls so far under your skin, you evil bastard. Their loyalty to you is simply out of fear. Nothing more."

Captain Rodgers roared with laughter. "I hope they torture you to no end upon your return." He looked up behind him. "Fredríco, Jasper, Willy. You hold him here." Captain Rodgers turned to the crew. "The rest of you! Make ready!"

The next few minutes were a blur. José knelt on the ground staring at the deck. *La Floriblanca* fired a shot in warning forcing the merchant ship to slow and meet its pursuer until finally, a quarter hour later, they boarded the ship with ease. As José glanced up from where he knelt on the ground, most of the crew nodded, confirming what Rodrigo advised earlier; he wasn't alone.

"Come, Fredríco. Bring Gaspar," the captain ordered.

José's feet found their footing as he was lifted by the underarms and hoisted from the floor. He stumbled forward, barely holding himself up as he was pushed from behind. The plank wobbled underneath him. The deep blue waves gently rocked the ships toward each other. The captain was already in discussion with a man still hidden from view. Fredríco pulled him forward to the captain's side. José gasped.

Felipe looked up at him, eyes wide. "So. This is the man you speak of, Captain Rodgers?"

"Aye. As you can see, this is the infamous José Gaspar, fugitive from your crown. There is a substantial reward for his capture. He is to be brought to Spain immediately for sentencing."

"Is he now?" Felipe asked, amusement gently gracing his tone. "And how am I to know whether this is really José Gaspar? Back in Sevilla, it is believed that José Gaspar is dead."

"Well then, if he is thought dead, why would there be a price on his head?"

"You do make a good point there," Felipe agreed. He stepped forward, inspecting José's face. "Still, there's no way to confirm this is José Gaspar. I'd be taking a great risk by taking him on and providing you with the proper payment on behalf of the crown for such a capture."

José resisted the urge to roll his eyes. Captain Rodgers turned to him. "Tell them who you are, Gaspar! Don't make me slit your throat and send the body over as proof, as tempting as that option is."

A pair of voices sounded from the stairwell below deck—one unmistakably female. José's heart sank in his gut. His body stilled. The voices grew louder as the silence grew among them.

"Go back downstairs!"

"I will not go back down. You cannot make me!"

"Oh, I most certainly can!"

"The hell you can! Step aside, Armando!"

"It's bad enough we have a pair of ladies on board, but now you want to boss everyone around. I gave you an order. For the love of God, obey it!"

"A pair of ladies on board? Hah! Let's not forget that *we* have been feeding *that* belly for weeks upon end. Now, step aside!"

"No!"

"Yes!"

A thud sounded against the wall of the stairwell. The top of a woman's head with hair the color of coffee and cream pinned back at the nap of her neck. She stilled at the top of the stairs. Eyes green with hints of brown stared at him, disbelief ridden on her face. "José!"

"Joséfa," José whispered.

Armando appeared behind her—eyes wide.

Captain Rodgers whipped his pistol from his waist, pointing it in Joséfa's direction and facing Felipe. "Not sure if this is José Gaspar, hmm? It seems to me that you all are rather acquainted."

Felipe turned to José. "Oh! *Oh yes*! I see it now. Hard to tell with all of that beard covering his face," Felipe said, scrunching his nose.

Joséfa stalked forward unafraid, anger growing on her delicate features. "Captain Rodgers, I presume?"

The corner of his lips turned up. "Why yes, lassie. Does my reputation precede me?"

She folded her arms over her chest. "Oh, it does, all right."

Captain Rodgers stepped toward them, raking his eyes over her body. José pulled against the men holding his arms. "Don't touch her!"

Captain Rodgers stalked back to José, hitting him swiftly across the cheek, making his head jerk to the side. "You do not speak!" He moved back to Joséfa. "What is it you want to say?"

"Well, for starters, we can discuss how you set José up."

"What?" José exclaimed. He glanced at Rodrigo, who gently shook his head from the end of the walkway between the two ships. He and a few of the crew members came to stand behind José.

"It is true," Captain Rodgers confirmed. "I did. What of it?"

"What of it? *What of it*?! We have spent the past few years tracking you all down! That is years of our life together stolen from us that we can never get back. How dare you take a life that is not yours. José is innocent in this. And you worked with Rafael to have him framed for stealing the crown jewels! You sick excuse for a human being!" Joséfa yelled.

"I'm a pirate! What did you expect?" Captain Rodgers jested, swinging the pistol around in her direction.

"Why?" José asked.

Captain Rodgers turned to him. "Because I needed someone who knew the current workings of the seas, and you just happened to fit my needs. Rafael needed a way to get rid of you, make his way up in the ranks, and take the girl. Who was I to refuse? He wanted to help the woman who was scorned by your actions." He glanced over at Joséfa. "And now I can see why you didn't give the other woman a second thought. She is a beauty."

"You keep your eyes and hands to yourself," José threatened.

"Or what, Gaspar? In case you haven't noticed, you don't exactly have the upper hand. You're not in the position to make demands. As it is, this pathetic merchant ship lacks the crew for you all to overtake *La Floriblanca*." Captain Rodgers sighed dramatically. "I can see this is a wasted attempt at a trade, as everyone on this ship seems loyal to José Gaspar. I've changed my mind."

In less than a second, grunts of pain came from behind him. The hold on his arms gave way. He grabbed the sword from Felipe's side and slit the captain's throat in one swing. A shot rang across the deck. Joséfa fell back into Armando's arms as they hit the deck, blood soaking the upper sleeve of her shoulder. He dashed to her side. "Joséfa, are you all right?"

She nodded. "It's just a scratch," she said as she pulled her hand away, revealing the wound. José immediately eased and helped her from the ground. Joséfa examined his face with a frown. "You have a beard."

He smiled, cupping her cheek. "That I do."

"Hhhmmm, I don't know what to make of it."

He chuckled lightly. "Leave it to you to pass judgment on the state of my facial hair when you've just been shot."

"It only grazed my shoulder. I think it will be all right."

He glanced up at Armando. "Good to see you, old friend."

A warm smile grew on Armando's face. "*Igualmente*. It has been some time."

"And it appears I have much to learn about your adventures to find me. But for now," José leaned in, kissing Joséfa briefly on soft lips he'd dreamed of for years. The taste of her lingered as he pulled away. He rose from the ground, and whatever happiness he felt slipped away. The body of the dead Captain Rodgers lay on the deck—the blood from his neck slowly pouring out. Filled with a certain satisfaction, he stalked across the deck to where Rodrigo, Chino, and John, with a few crew members, held the three men who assisted Captain Rodgers, Fredríco included.

Chino stepped forward, handing José his sword. "Thought you might be needing this, Captain."

His words sank in. Looking around the crew, they each nodded, murmuring *Captain*—all but the three. Fredríco looked upon him with disdain. "I will never call you Captain." He spat at José's feet.

"Nor I!" called Jasper, sitting next to him.

"Nor I!" called Willy.

José unsheathed his sword with lightning speed cutting through the necks of the three crew members in a few quick flicks. Their bodies slumped to the ground, the life leaving their eyes. A feeling of emptiness grew at the sight of the three men—a nothingness at taking life so quickly. But he knew it needed to be done. He glanced up at Rodrigo and stalked forward, holding the tip of his sword at his neck. Rodrigo threw his hands up in surrender.

"Did you know?" José growled.

Rodrigo looked him dead in the eyes. "I had no idea."

"Seems a little too convenient. How did you *not* know he set me up?"

"He only sent someone to tell me to bring you to him, Gaspar. I had no idea he had any involvement in getting you in that cell with me. Remember, we were both there trying to figure it out." He leaned into the tip of his sword. "I am loyal to you. You know that. I swear, I had no idea he set you up."

José glared at him a few moments before lowering his sword and nodding. He turned back to his beloved. Armando, Felipe, and Joséfa looked at him with shock. At that moment, he realized this was their first encounter with the pirate, Gaspar.

"You just killed them," Joséfa said.

"Yes. Yes, I did. And I would do it again if it meant protecting you. And protecting them," he said, pointing between Armando and Felipe. Movement caught his eye from the top of the stairs. A familiar woman in a blue muslin dress stood gaping at the scene on the deck. Realization hit him in the gut as he looked upon the cousin of the woman who sent him to his current fate.

"Lorena?"

She noticed him then. Her jaw fell open. "José!"

He sighed, looking over at Armando. He smiled. "May I present my wife?"

Joséfa wobbled on her feet. José shot forward, wrapping his arm around her waist. "May I suggest we take this below deck? I assume she has a cabin where she can rest?"

Armando pulled Joséfa's arm over his shoulders. "We are headed to San Juan. Will you be staying on our ship, or are we to meet you at the port?"

"I'll stay with you," José declared immediately.

Armando nodded. "We'll be downstairs."

José turned to Rodrigo. "Take *La Floriblanca* to San Juan. We shall all meet there." He turned to his crew. "The rest of you. Give Captain Rodgers and his men a proper burial. We meet in San Juan."

PART III

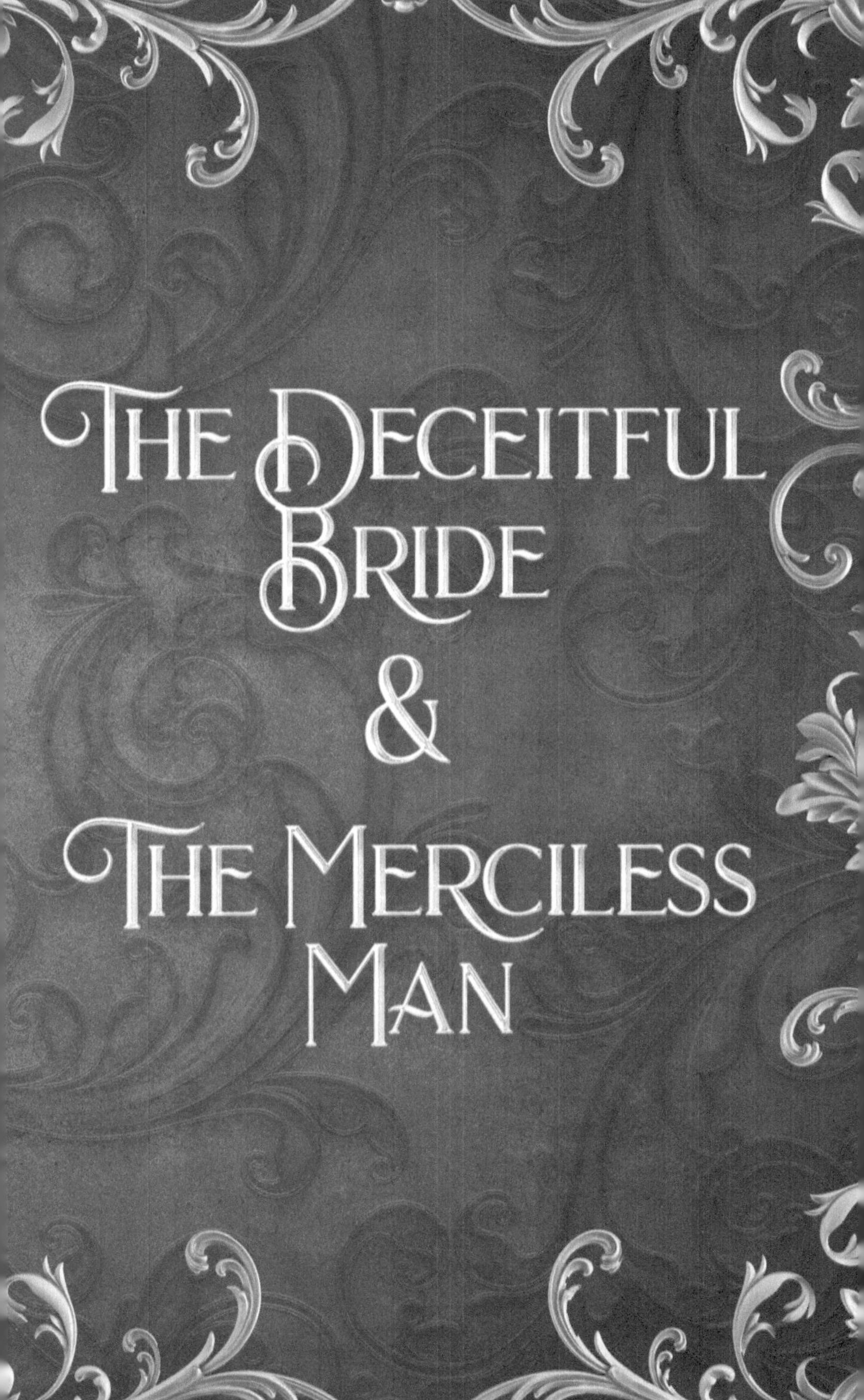

The Deceitful Bride

&

The Merciless Man

CHAPTER 31

HAVING CLEANED HIMSELF UP IN THE CABIN BELOW, JOSÉ discarded his shirt in exchange for one Felipe had left in the room. Coincidentally, a blade was also left on top of the clothing—a sign that the beard may have been a bit much for more than just Joséfa. Not wanting to waste more time than necessary, he kept his beard and made his way to Armando's cabin, where the group awaited him.

When he entered the room, Joséfa was sitting in a chair while Lorena tended her wound. Armando was sitting behind a desk riddled with maps, leather ledgers, and other travel trinkets. He sat back in his chair, elbows upon the armrests and hands clasped at his chest. Felipe took to pacing the length of the room. All eyes were on José once he closed the cabin door behind him, but it was Joséfa's glare that mattered the most. Neither happy nor upset to see him, José had difficulty determining her mood and whether she was ready to face the man that stood before her.

"*Hola*," he said to her.

"A little past the greetings, wouldn't you say?" Armando interjected. He stood up from his chair, leaning over his desk. "Where exactly have you been?"

"Oh, I don't know, Armando. Hiding from the Spanish crown, for starters."

"Well, that's obvious," Felipe said.

"It's been five years!" Armando exclaimed. "We have been traveling these waters looking for you for that long. Where have you been?"

José sighed. "The captain headed for a different port. Once I participated in his plans, there was little I could do. I have been lying low on a hidden island for the past few years. I am now considered a pirate—one with quite a fortune."

"You certainly look like one."

"Yes, Felipe. I do. I can't exactly be clean-shaven, frolicking on the seas, and blend in. I needed to keep up appearances. And if you haven't noticed, I was on a ship with a captain who wasn't about to let me go. What was I supposed to say to Captain Rodgers? *'Oh yes, Captain Rodgers! Lovely day on the seas. By the way, I need to leave your crew because my beloved and her brother—and her brother's wife, who happens to be the cousin of the woman who betrayed me—and possibly my lifelong best friend are traveling the seas to find me so I'll just be leaving now. It has been a delightful time!'"*

"My wife is part of the reason why we have in hand a pardon for you from the king, so I would watch how you regard her."

José stopped breathing. He swayed, feeling his knees go weak. "Pardon? How is that possible? I thought…"

"Yes, that is quite the story. And you look like you've seen a ghost." Felipe pulled a chair from the corner. "Sit. We shall start from the beginning."

José sat with a thump gazing at the floor in a daze—shallow breaths keeping his body going but barely. "Tell me everything."

Lorena placed Joséfa's hand over the cloth covering her wound. Standing straight with her arms crossed over her chest, she began her tale. "It may come as some surprise, but you were not Mariana's only lover."

"I deduced she and Rafael were together, yes."

"No, not Rafael. He was simply a pawn. At least, before they were married."

José frowned. "Who do you speak of then?"

"The king himself."

José's heart sank into his stomach. "*Mierda!*" José could not believe what he was hearing. The pieces of the puzzle he had long been thinking of clicked into place.

"Mariana was pregnant with the king's bastard when Rafael approached her about setting you up for stealing the crown jewels. He told her about Captain Rodgers' intentions to make you part of his crew for a time. Captain Rodgers is…*was*…a man with many resources in Sevilla that were unknown to all of us—some within the highest reaches of the crown. He had the means and the access to complete the task and frame you.

"I knew Mariana was pregnant, but she did not tell me about the king until I walked in on them one morning. The king lay in her bed in all his glory—*old* glory, given his age. I did not think a man his age would still have the…eh…stamina to be with a young lady. I suppose I was wrong.

"He threatened me, saying that if I were to breathe a word of their affair, he would have my head. Naturally, given that Mariana was my cousin, her secret was safe with me. Mariana was betrothed to Rafael and soon-to-be-married. My concern was mainly for the child brought into this world. I wanted him…or her…to have a happy life. Nothing else mattered…

"Until the rumors started circulating about stolen jewels and the accusations made against you. Something about the situation did not sit well with me. I knew you. Or at least I knew *of* you. I knew your family. I learned how you were raised. I never believed you were capable of such a thing. You might be capable of breaking my cousin's heart, but honestly, she brought the heartbreak on herself despite the many warnings I gave her.

"It was at that time I decided I needed to reach out to someone close to you. I went directly to Joséfa, who had already planned to approach the king on your behalf. I had a choice; I could either let her know about the king and Mariana or let her go on thinking there was something that could be done by approaching the king. I decided on the former.

"I cannot tell you how many meetings took place between the four of us. We tried to devise a plan to clear your name. You were gone a little over a year. It was beginning to look hopeless….until the king passed away. And when he did, Mariana, newborn babe in arms, came to me in secret one evening. She feared for her life; the new King knew of their affair and had not taken well to it. He knew the child was his father's, and he was determined to get rid of Mariana *and* the child. She confessed. She confessed every last detail—the jewels, Rafael, Captain Rodgers, just how deep the affair between her and the king went. He couldn't care less about framing you as long as you were gone. He didn't care for the way you drew Mariana's attention. He knew the two of you had been lovers in the past. Rafael wasn't the only one hoping to be rid of you just so that he could have her affection.

"She asked me to look after her child, for the new King had summoned both her and Rafael to the *Palacio*. I'm not sure what happened to them after that, but they never came home. I was left to care for the child. Thankfully, Armando and I were to be married, and he immediately agreed to care for the child, a girl. Isabella." She looked at Armando with a gentle smile. "I will always be grateful to you, José. It is because of you that we fell in love. I suppose I have you to thank."

"Eh…you are welcome?" José did not know how to react to such a statement. The direction his life had taken hadn't exactly been his choice, but he did feel a little better knowing something good had transpired from it.

"After years of petitioning," she continued, "Joséfa received a summons from the new King to go to him immediately. I feared for Isabella's life. I decided to go with her and plead with the king to let the child live."

"When we arrived," Joséfa cut in, "he already knew all about Mariana. He was every bit the son who had to watch his mother suffer as the former King flaunted his mistress in front of her. King Carlos was also an admirer of yours. He expressed that although you couldn't return to your post as Admiral, he hoped to at least give you a chance at a life well lived or what remained of it. He was quite gracious about it all."

José's jaw went slack. "I don't know what to say."

Felipe came up behind him, placing a hand on his shoulder. "You do not have to say anything at all."

"And Isabella? Is she here on the ship somewhere? Does she live?" José asked.

Lorena smiled. "He told us that we were to take Isabella and leave Sevilla for *Puerto Rico*—San Juan, to be exact."

"She lives with us on the island," Armando replied with a hint of pride. "We have been settled there for some time now on our estate. We ship sugarcane from the island and many other products and wine from *España*. Despite searching for you, we have been living a very happy life there."

He looked around the room to the others, all of whom had regretful smiles on their faces—all but Joséfa. His gaze bore into hers. "I don't know how to thank you all for the lengths you all have gone to for my freedom, and I am truly grateful. But my bride does not seem as pleased as most of you in the room. I am wondering why?"

Felipe cleared his throat. "Perhaps we should give these two some time to chat."

"Yes, it is time for my wife to eat," Armando said, coming to Lorena's side and placing a tender kiss on her cheek.

The three of them exited the room leaving Joséfa and José awkwardly staring at each other—the waves cresting against the ship, the only sound in the room for a few long moments.

José stood from his chair and walked across the room, kneeling before Joséfa. He cupped her face. "You are still just as beautiful as the day I left." He moved his thumb gently over her cheekbone. "Perhaps more beautiful."

A gentle smile tugged at her lips. Another long moment passed as they were lost in each other's gaze, but Joséfa still held trepidation in her eyes.

"Please talk to me, Joséfa. I have waited to speak with you for years—to hear your voice. And yet, you remain silent."

She leaned her head into his palm, closing her eyes and sighing with contentment. "It's just…I'm not sure…those men…on the deck," Joséfa whispered. She opened her eyes, brimming with unshed tears. "You took their life without a second thought. You just killed them."

The tears slowly cascaded down her cheek. José gently wiped them away with his thumb. "Yes, I did. And I would do it again."

"But you showed them no mercy."

"And they did not ask for it. They are *pirates*, *mi vida*. They would eventually take what was mine as an act of revenge. They would have done the same to me. They *believed* they were doing the same to me had it not been your ship we happened to approach this day. Word would have gotten out that there was no reward on my head any longer, and they would have killed me either way. They are not good men. I did it for you, your brother, his family, and Felipe. I did it for my men. You must know this."

Joséfa nodded. "When you put it like that, I suppose you are right. It was simply tough to witness."

"Yes, and I am sorry you had to see it. Truly." José looked away from her, fear growing in his gut. "Is that all, Joséfa?"

"What do you mean?"

"Is that the only reason you are detached from me? Is there another?"

"Another?" She pulled his chin with her free hand to meet her gaze, amusement dancing on her delicate features. "Do you mean another man? Are you asking if I have taken another?"

"Well, yes. Of course. I couldn't be upset if you did, given the time I've been gone. I wouldn't blame you all. Perhaps you and Felipe…."

"Felipe?"

"What's wrong with Felipe? I think he's a good-looking man." He attempted to be indifferent, but the very thought made his stomach churn. "And he would look after you nicely if…"

Joséfa leaned forward, placing her lips against his, silencing him with the keen gentleness of her kiss. José could barely move—her lips against his was the only feeling throughout his body. Her warmth seeped into his soul, lighting something he thought long diminished. She pulled away. "No, you foolish man. If you think for one moment that I would go through heaven and earth in addition to the ocean to find you while being promised to another, you are not as wise as I thought you were."

He pulled her to him again, devouring her, the intensity growing with each passing moment until Joséfa winced in pain. "I am so very sorry. I didn't mean to hurt you." He examined the cut at the top of her shoulder; nothing more than a flesh wound. "Has anyone put any alcohol on that?"

"Alcohol? Do you mean rum? As if I could pry that from my brother's hands. Whatever would I do that for anyway?" she asked, baffled.

José shrugged. "An old trick I learned at sea from a healer headed to the Carolinas. Seems to help with the healing process."

"Well, I'm willing to try anything. However, Lorena is quite good with her herbal concoctions. She has brought plenty for the trip."

José sat back on his heels, the gravity of Lorena's story sinking into his bones. "I cannot believe the length Rafael and Mariana went. And the king. It's almost…."

"Too incredible to be true? I agree. That was how I felt upon hearing the news the first time. Well, that and outright fury."

"I can imagine." José intertwined their hands. "I need you to know, Joséfa. I woke up every morning thinking of you. I lived dreaming of the day I would see you again, filling myself with hope I had no business possessing. I have done things— many things—I am not particularly proud of while I was a… pirate and on Captain Rodgers' ship. The gore you witnessed on the deck of this ship is but a fraction of what I am capable of.

That is who I am now. Regardless of the new King's pardon, I will always be this. And while I am grateful for the freedom you have obtained for me, I will need time to figure out where my life goes from here because I had given up hope. The idea that I would one day find you, marry you, and live my life with you in peace. That became something very distant and unreachable. I always knew there was a possibility you would find and marry another. But to see you before me, unwed at that, leads me to believe that you didn't give up on me." He caressed her head, working his fingers over her smooth, thick hair. "Does this mean you will still marry me, Joséfa? Can you take me as I am?"

She placed her hand over his, a broad smile on her face. "To be with you will be the greatest adventure of my life. Of course, I will marry you, José Gaspar."

His heart near bursting, he lifted her from the chair and held her to him, kissing her with abandon. "I love you," he whispered breathlessly.

Tears welled up in her eyes. "As I love you."

Just then, the door burst open. Armando strolled in with a bottle of rum. "I believe congratulations are in order…again!"

"Armando!" Lorena chided from the doorway, with Felipe grinning from ear to ear behind her. "You truly know how to ruin a romantic moment."

"Well, there'll be plenty of romance between the two of them back on the island…*when you're married by a priest*. But there will be none of that here on my ship," he said, handing the bottle of rum to José.

Realization hit José. After so many years around women of looser means, he had nearly forgotten. His lovely bride was still untouched by another. "Oh. Oh! Of course. Yes," he said, pulling his attention back to Joséfa, whose cheeks were aflame. He brushed the back of his hand across her face. "We will wed in San Juan."

CHAPTER 32

José stared at his reflection in the looking glass. This was how he had started his day for the past three sunrises—just standing there, staring back at the man he had become, wrestling with the idea of shaving off his armor. He understood it was just a beard, but to him, it was his armor, his protection. He had long removed all the jewelry and embellishments he wore, a part of him feeling naked at the loss of them. José weathered the glances he received from his fiancée and his friends as they ate their meals together in the evenings. He didn't expect them to understand any more than he expected them to develop compassion for his crew on *La Floriblanca*, at least not overnight.

A knock sounded at the door, disrupting him from his morning routine. When he opened it, Joséfa stood there with a set of clothing in her hands. She appraised him warily, pasting a small smile on her face. "I figured you could use some clothing. These are some extra things Armando, and Felipe conjured up for you." She held them out to him, their hands brushing as he took them from her. A light blush crept across her face. She pointed at his beard. "Would you like my help?"

José looked down to hide the smile on his face. Of course, she wants to help rid him of the beard. She must have sensed his difficulty in parting with it. He nodded, motioning her into the small cabin space. "Please. That would be appreciated." He sat on the small bed that rested along the back wall while Joséfa grabbed the blade and soap. She placed the stool from the corner of the room in front of him; José observed her—a deep swelling of gratitude filling him for her mere presence. He reached down to pinch the skin of his forearm. *Not a dream. That is good.*

Carefully, meticulously, Joséfa guided the blade gently across his skin, removing his armor. She lathered the soap across the contours of his face making sure to take her time, catching every last bit in the cloth in her hand. Those beautiful hazel eyes caught his periodically, and it sent a thrill through him to find the blush making an appearance again. When she was nearly done, he couldn't help himself. He reached up to stop her movement, bringing her hand to rest on his lap. "Lord, how I have missed you. I missed you every day and thought endlessly of your face."

The tears welled up in her eyes. "There are no words for how much I longed for you. There were days I wouldn't leave my room." She shook her head, looking down at their joined hands, the blade and soap resting there. "The dreams were endless. You would be there all the time. There were days I was desperate to fall back asleep so that I could see you again."

José reached out and lifted her chin to meet his gaze. "I'm here now." He closed the distance between them, the last patch to be shaved be damned, and kissed her thoroughly. His hand crawled through the thick strands of her hair that rested in a tie at the nape of her neck. Her tongue was soft against his as he pulled each of her breaths into his being—her full lips driving him to madness.

José moved his hands from her hair and grabbed the outside of her thighs, pulling her toward him—the stool scraping against the floor as she moved.

A loud, repetitive bang sounded against the door. "José! My sister better not be in there with you…alone!"

Joséfa moved away from him with lightning speed, placing herself in the far corner of the room while José opened the door to a fuming Armando taking in the scene before him. His judging eyes traveled between the two of them. José felt like a twelve-year-old being caught by his *Papá*. "We were just…she was… helping me with my beard."

Armando's brow rose to the ceiling. "Your beard? Have you forgotten how to shave it? Well, *clearly*, you've forgotten how to shave it."

"Really, Armando," Joséfa spoke up from her quiet corner, "there was nothing untoward happening."

"Oh, no?" He pointed to her chin. "You have soap suds on your face, *hermana*."

Joséfa paled, her hand swiping off the suds. José thought he might die then when Armando stepped further into the room, but he dragged the stool to the open door and sat watching them both. He motioned to José. "Go ahead. Pay me no attention. Continue what you were doing before I interrupted."

Joséfa huffed her displeasure as she moved toward José, lathering up the last patch of beard and making careful yet quick work of ridding him of the last of his armor—all while her brother watched on.

When she was through, she smiled down at him. "There you are."

He stood from the bed, careful not to come too close to her with her brother's watchful eyes on them as he looked upon himself in the reflecting glass again. It was difficult taking in the image, a face he had known intimately for the many years before Captain Rodgers' ship. Both Joséfa and Armando's reflections appeared behind him.

Armando clapped him on the back. "There's the José we all know and love."

But José didn't feel they truly knew him anymore and wondered if they could love the man he had become.

Chapter 33

Fields of sugarcane surrounded by lush, green mountains spread out in all their glory before him. The warm, tropical air danced around them as their carriage pulled up to Armando's estate. It was another world entirely, and the magic of it seeped deep into José's bones.

It had been a long journey to get here. The weeks passed at an agonizing pace, leaving José longing to place his feet on the ground. Being in the same space with Joséfa day in and day out without being able to truly show her in body just how much she meant to him became more than he could bear. Not even the kisses he managed to steal in the dark corners of the ship's deck would suffice, and they were one kiss too many for Armando, who was constantly monitoring his every move with his sister. Even now, as they pulled up to his home, Armando eyed their clasped hands as if it were the most offensive act in the world. It appears that neither Joséfa nor José were in any mood for his judgment. They were quite over it. José gave her hand a gentle squeeze. She turned to him, smiling slyly. Soon, they would be husband and wife, and he could have her in every way—body and soul.

The carriage pulled up to a beautiful two-story home that sat on top of the hill—the view was one of such beauty that José doubted even the best artists in the world could capture it. He imagined himself peacefully looking at the blues of the ocean long into the evening on the porch surrounding the house. He stepped out of the carriage turning to grab Joséfa's hand but had just a moment to hold it before Lorena tugged her other arm with a grin.

"Come, sister! We have much to do before the wedding! You'll wear my dress. A little altering here and there should do. We need to see what shoes you have. And we must talk decorations..."

Joséfa looked to José for a way out. He smiled at her gently. "Go. Enjoy the moment. We have a lifetime together."

She leaned up to kiss his cheek and left with Lorena to do… well…whatever it is women do. The sound of hooves thudding against the ground grew behind him. He turned to find Rodrigo, Chino, and John coming up the road, stopping short of the carriages. As they dismounted, Chino and John's eyes strayed across the sugar cane fields, their smiles growing wide as they admired the few women at work.

"Behave," José warned.

"Of course, Gaspar!" John said with mock offense. "I will be on my best behavior…but one can admire the beauty, no?"

José leaned in closer. "Behave," he bit out. He looked around at the rest of the men. "You all are guests here. I know you all are not used to acting with any respect for etiquette," Chino spit out phlegm at that exact moment. José shook his head. "But do try to act your best. You all are here because you are my most trusted confidants."

"Confidants. I like it!" John exclaimed.

"You're still a pirate, *hombre*," Rodrigo reminded him.

"Be that as it may, you all are my friends this week as I marry the love of my life. All I ask is don't get us thrown out of here or, worse, be the reason the wedding is called off."

Chino straightened up. "You have our word, Gaspar." He kicked the side of John's leg.

"Ouch! Yes, yes! Of course. You have our word."

"Good. Rodrigo, tell me of the crew," he asked, strolling up to the house.

"Everything appears to be in order. The men will stay in port for a few days until we can give them the next orders." He glanced at José apprehensively. "You *do* know the next orders, don't you, Gaspar?"

"Not a clue."

"Oh..well…that changes things."

"It does. I never imagined or allowed myself more than the smallest hope that I would have any other choice but a pirate's life. This changes everything. The lady will likely want a life with children. Although, the woman I knew *did* always want to travel. Perhaps…"

Rodrigo huffed. "Before you even suggest anything further, bringing a woman on board is bad luck."

"I beg to differ, dear friend. It was a ship carrying not one but two women that rescued me. That has to account for some good luck." He patted Rodrigo on the back. "Come. Let us find you all something suitable to wear for a wedding. And then we can drink some of our host's finest rum and take in the beauty of the island while we discuss our next steps."

Suddenly, a high-pitched scream accompanied by the stomping of feet traveled from just inside the front door. The men hurried toward the house, stopping when a young girl no older than five leaped onto the porch, jumping from the front steps and bound for the fields. An older woman—whose head wrap sat at an angle with dark strands of curly hair hanging in disarray underneath—trailed behind the young girl, her short feet and wide girth hindering her goal of reaching the girl before she disappeared. "Isabella! *Vengance!*" she bellowed in between breaths, but it was of no use.

José sprang into action, sprinting after the young girl just as she reached the tall stalks of sugarcane. She attempted to dodge him, but he grabbed her under the arms and hoisted her in the air making her eye level with him. There was no mistaking

whose child this was. Mariana's dark brown eyes stared at him with such fury that he was sure she had shrunk in size and decided to plague him for eternity.

"And, where do you think you are going, young lady?"

She pouted fiercely. "Away."

"Yes, I see that, but why?"

"I will not take a bath. Tia Lorena says I have to. But I don't want to."

The side of his mouth lifted slightly. "You don't? Why ever not?"

"Because I took one yesterday, of course!" she huffed, glaring at him like the reason was most obvious.

"Ah, I see," José said, pondering the predicament of bath negotiations with the child in front of him. He shrugged. "Just as well, I suppose. It makes it easier for the smaller creatures to find a home. That is *very* thoughtful of you. A few men I sailed with were just as kind as you, having the little creatures stay on them."

Isabella's eyes went wide. "Little creatures?!" The older woman—huffing and puffing with her hands taking reprieve on her ample hips—stopped a few paces behind Isabella. José looked over Isabella's shoulder and winked at her conspiratorially.

"*Si*. Little creatures. Nasty little things. They begin to eat at your flesh because once they have a home on you, they need to eat, of course. So, you are planning on housing them and feeding them? That is *very* kind of you, Isabella," he looked away from her—a quizzical look on his face. "Although, I must tell you. I'm not sure what happens after they begin eating you. You see, the men never actually lived to tell the tale."

Isabella stared at him, her body limp, skin pale. Then, quite suddenly, she began kicking the air, narrowly missing José in the abdomen. "Ramooonaaaaa!"

"*Si, mija*. I'm right here."

José placed her on the ground. "I need a bath, Ramona," she yelled at the top of her lungs while dashing at full speed toward the house.

José and Ramona stared after the child chuckling in her wake. "*Señor*, I do not know how to thank you. It has always been a challenge to have that child bathe."

"I doubt you will have any problems in the future."

She smiled at José warmly. "You are sure to make a fine *papa* someday, *Señor*." She turned on her heels and headed toward the house, leaving a stunned José behind her.

"*Papá*," he whispered—a word that didn't easily mix with a pirate and the life he had long contemplated since reuniting with his beloved. His head became light—his internal tug-of-war between his two worlds becoming too much.

The evening rolled on without much fanfare. José's silence at the dinner table went unnoticed by most except Joséfa, who took every opportunity to squeeze his hand under the table and give him a comforting smile. He squeezed her hand back, giving her a small smile hoping to put her mind at ease.

"What are you two conspiring about over there?" Felipe asked from across the table.

"I assume they are conspiring which positions they will attempt on their....."

"Chino!" José bit out.

"What?! Is the little one running around somewhere?"

Lorena and Armando glared at Chino with disgust. Felipe, Joséfa, and Rodrigo hid their laughter behind their napkins. José pinched the bridge of his nose. "Chino, you do not speak of such things in front of women or at a dinner table."

Chino's confused gaze locked on José. "You don't?"

"No," Lorena spat. "You do not. Surely you couldn't have thought it appropriate."

"Forgive him, *Señora*," Rodrigo interjected. "We spend most of our time at sea and certainly in the company of other sailors and women of…looser means. He meant no offense by it."

"Hmmph…" Armando huffed, his eyes reprimanding his sister for even daring to find Chino remotely humorous.

For the next quarter hour, the silverware clanking against platters and wine glasses placed on the table were the only sounds occupying the dining space. Joséfa began to fidget in her chair, glancing around the table at the other guests. "So, Rodrigo. Tell us of your adventures on the seas. Surely it wasn't all piracy, no?"

Rodrigo dabbed his mouth with his napkin, giving Joséfa and the rest of his guests his full attention. "There was quite a bit of piracy, yes. That in itself is the adventure, in my opinion. There's a certain sense of freedom that comes with sailing the seas. You are the king of your own kingdom, floating on a vast seascape that crawls on forever. The wind is your constant companion. But if you ignore her or take her for granted, she will take her attention elsewhere, leaving your little kingdom to fend for itself."

"The wind is a *she*?" Felipe asked in amusement.

"Oh, certainly! Just as the female is a creature to appreciate in human form, she is reflected in the wind that carries the sails. She is the captain of the adventure—never revealing what lies ahead but always reminding you of the life unfolding before you. The adventure can be peaceful. It can be deadly. But one thing is certain—it is always an adventure at sea, where the shackles of society are lifted."

"Tell me, Mr. Lopez. How does piracy fit into your idea of freedom?" Armando asked, his lips in a thin line.

A small smile grew on Rodrigo's face. "How does overcharging for goods and services not equate to piracy? Or the raising of taxes for no good reason?"

"Well said!" John agreed.

"Nonsense. Taxes are used to enrich the country," Armando retorted defensively.

"More like enriching the kings and queens of the world while leaving mere scraps for the rest of their respective countries," Chino refuted.

"The kings and queens are chosen by God," Lorena said haughtily. John snorted at the end of the table. "Surely, they deserve some compensation for being God's chosen to lead his people."

Rodrigo's brow lifted. "God's chosen? And just what proof do you have of this?"

Armando patted Lorena's hand and directed his attention to Rodrigo. "Understand, we are loyal to the king of *España*. That will never change. Perhaps we should digress to your ideas of freedom, Mr. Lopez. Please enlighten me. How does robbing goods around the globe running from bounties on your lives equate to freedom?" Armando smirked.

"Freedom is completely subjective, *Don* Mayorga. When I speak of freedom, I do not speak of piracy. Piracy is a means to an end. I speak of the ability to create my destiny—something I wouldn't have been afforded had I stayed in *España*. I believe I am more than a class and a rank."

"My goodness. That is quite the opinion," Lorena said, judgment dripping in her tone.

"I think it is refreshing!" Felipe exclaimed.

"I agree wholeheartedly," Joséfa encouraged, smiling wide. "I do enjoy hearing different perspectives. How can one learn if not by conversing with people from all walks of life?"

Felipe grabbed his wine glass, hoisting it in the air. "To Rodrigo, the pirate philosopher!"

The rest of the table, minus a less-than-amused Lorena and a scowling Armando, raised their glasses. "To Rodrigo!"

"I think I like the idea of you being a *pirate philosopher*," Chino mused.

Rodrigo burst into laughter. "I will take it. It's no Blackbeard, but I will take it."

"And what of all the Spanish gold and treasures you have obtained in recent years?" Lorena questioned, souring the mood in the room. "With the pardon given to José, the gold and whatever items your *freedom* has allowed you to take should be returned to the crown."

Rodrigo's face fell. "I'm afraid you are mistaken."

"Oh? How so?"

"It is not I who received the pardon, *Señora*. I am, and will forever be, a pirate. I may be sitting here with you fine people enjoying the pleasures of food and company—sharing stories of the seas and adventures with Gaspar. But there's not much changing my situation. Therefore, I don't owe the crown a damned thing."

Lorena gasped, giving José a stern look. "Surely, you disagree. Given the lengths we went through to rescue you, you could not agree to this robbery."

José's face turned red. "May I remind you, Lorena, that piracy was not of my choosing but was forced upon me by your dear cousin? These men at this table have been loyal to me in a way equivalent to those who reported to me as Admiral. I understand the manner in which we…obtained our wealth may not meet your idea of a respectable way to earn a living, but they do not answer to the crown. And while I am grateful for the pardon, it doesn't close the wound left by the previous king. That wound is still festering." He rose from his seat, dropping his napkin forcibly on the table. "The man you left is not the man who stands before you today. You will do well to remember that. If you all will excuse me, I need a bit of fresh air."

José pushed backed his chair, leaning down to kiss Joséfa's cheek and exited the room, finding his solitude on the wraparound porch just beyond the door. It was the exact reprieve José needed from the exploding storm inside. He leaned against the white, wooden railing. With the slightest hint of the sea, the cool air inflated his lungs as he took deep breaths to calm his frayed nerves. He valued the moment of silence, for he was sure it wouldn't last long.

Sure enough, the door behind him opened quietly, followed by the slow sound of boots hitting the wooden floorboards. Rodrigo came up beside him, mimicking his stance against the railing. Chino and John sat on the front steps resting their arms on their knees and looking out on the grounds joining in José's quiet moment of solitude.

"You understand things can never be as they once were," Rodrigo said, breaking the silence.

"I am not naïve enough to think they would stay the same. I myself have changed so much." He raked his fingers through his hair. "But how on Earth am I supposed to move forward?"

Rodrigo grinned at José sympathetically. "That I do not know, my friend. I do not envy the position you are in. I have always known and accepted that this is who I am for as long as I can breathe. I cannot change it. Even if your family had lovingly accepted us this evening, that wouldn't change my fate. As you can see, the hate for our kind is so deeply rooted it is nearly impossible to break."

"Nearly impossible."

Rodrigo shook his head. "You live in a fantasy world, Gaspar. If you are thinking about having your wife, children, and a family that can go about respectfully in society, you are living in a world of illusion. There is no future that has Gaspar the pirate living among polite society. They expect *Admiral* Gaspar."

"Admiral Gaspar does not exist anymore."

"Yes. You know that. *I* know that." He pointed behind him. "But does everyone in there know that? Do they know you cannot magically turn back time and become someone who doesn't have the scars of the sea embedded so heavily in his soul? Do *they* know you cannot forget who you have become?"

José sighed heavily. "I don't know. They have in their mind one person. A part of me fears them discovering just how much I have changed."

Rodrigo straightened up, turning to him. He patted his back. "Only time will tell, my friend. Take some time to think about it. Remember that you are to marry this woman. She is your soulmate. Of this, I am sure. She crossed the ocean to find you. She thinks the man before her today is the same man she loved before. It is important to let her know who you have become and let her determine if she can still love you as you are."

The door behind them opened again. Joséfa's pale blue skirts danced in the wind, her smile like a caress to his soul. "Is this a private meeting, or may I come out and join you all?"

"Regretfully, we were just leaving," Rodrigo said.

"You will all be staying with us, yes? It is too late to be traveling into town," she said, her eyes somehow relaying apologies unspoken.

"No, *Señorita*. It would be best if we stayed in town with the other men. We will, of course, be back for the wedding in a week's time. We are looking forward to it."

"Thank you, Rodrigo." She looked down at Chino and John, still sitting silently on the steps. "Chino, John. I thank you all for coming to dinner. I cannot speak for the rest of them, but I enjoyed your company. I sincerely apologize for their behavior."

"No apologies are necessary, ma'am," Chino said. "You have done nothing wrong."

"Agreed." John stood from the steps, smiling at Joséfa. "You are very kind. I can see why José spoke of you like his greatest treasure."

Joséfa's cheeks flushed. "Thank you."

José wanted to push them away from her. If they know of her kindness, surely they notice her beauty when she blushes. "All right. Off with the lot of you." He shooed them off the porch.

Rodrigo chuckled knowingly. "Have a good evening, *Señorita*. Gaspar, give some thought to what we discussed." The group disappeared in the direction of the stable. Joséfa took Rodrigo's spot as the sound of horse hooves hitting the ground disappeared into the night.

Strands of hair danced around Joséfa with the gentle breeze. She glanced at José, a small smile growing. "Well, that was quite the dinner party."

"That it was. I'm sure it is one we will not soon forget. Perhaps one day, we will be able to laugh about it."

"Yes, but today is not that day." She sighed. "I do feel awful for how they were treated."

"My sweet Joséfa. There is nothing you could have done. Those are your brother's and Lorena's opinions. I know your heart is different." José came up behind her wrapping his arms around her waist. If Joséfa's heart was big enough to accept his crew, then his crew would accept her or face him. But he did wonder whether her mind could accept the *new* him. What future did she see for them?

José became distracted by the scent of jasmine coming from her hair. Being this close to Joséfa without interruption was an intoxicating treat. His lips grazed her neck, making her sigh in response.

"Armando would be upset if he were to walk out here right now," she said breathlessly.

He proceeded with his slow assault on her neck, his lips nibbling her earlobe. "With all due respect to your brother, I am done concerning myself with what he thinks." She leaned back, purposefully brushing her backside into him, forcing José to groan. He turned her around, caging her between his arms against the railing, his face an inch away from hers. "That was not very kind of you, Joséfa."

Her eyes were hooded with desire. She smirked seductively. "It wasn't intended to be kind."

His lips crashed into hers. All the weeks of constant vigilance by her overprotective brother and years of never knowing if they would find their way back to each other became fused into his kiss. He wrapped his arms around her, pulling her tightly to him. Momentarily lost in each other, they barely made it up for air. He wanted to be inside her so badly, feeling her as they became one—just like he had envisioned so many times before—but his conscience held the reins on his desire. José pulled back, placing his forehead against hers. "Not yet, *mi amor.*"

To José's surprise, she pulled him to her kissing him with just as much want and need. "Why not?" Her hands traveled up his back, driving him mad.

Pulling back again with even more difficulty, he took her face between his palms. "Because you deserve more than a romp on the porch of your brother's house." His hands moved slowly down her collarbone, lightly caressing her breasts and making her nipples pebble ever so slightly as they pushed against the fabric of her dress. She gave a slight flinch at his touch, closing her eyes and lolling her head back. "And as much as I want to explore every inch of your exquisite body and have dreamed of it for so long, I will not dishonor you. I plan to worship you the way you deserve."

"Perhaps we can get married tomorrow," she said, panting lightly.

Although she meant it in jest, the uneasy feeling in José's gut grew anew. He placed a soft kiss on her warm, full lips. "There are a few things we need to discuss first."

She sighed, leaning back against the railing—her hazel eyes looking at him. "The dinner."

"Yes, the dinner. It brought up some things we should discuss. Sit with me for a moment." He intertwined their hands, pulling her toward the two wicker chairs sitting just beside the door. After settling in their seats, he took her hand in his. "Joséfa, there are different circumstances we should consider that weren't part of our life when I fled, leaving you and my life in Sevilla. It doesn't change the life I want with you, but I need to know about *your* wants."

"My wants?"

"Yes, *mi amor*. Perhaps it would be easier if I asked more specifically. Where do you want to settle?"

She sighed, looking away from him. "I thought since you received your pardon that we could make our life here in San Juan. Given your knowledge of the seas, perhaps you could assist Armando with his business. We could have our children here and live a happy life."

José grappled with his subsequent words. "Happy life according to whom?"

Her head snapped in his direction. "What do you mean by asking that?"

"I mean no offense, but you just laid out my life for me without asking what I want."

She blinked a few times. "I suppose I did. I just thought…."

"You just thought that you, too, have given me the gift of a pardon, so I should do what is expected?"

"Isn't that what you want as well? A life with me?"

He brought her hand to his lips. "Of course, it is. But I have more to consider now. I am the captain of *La Floriblanca*."

"*La Floriblanca* is a pirate ship. Everyone knows that. You are signing yourself up for that life."

"That life saved me from a most certain death."

Her brow furrowed. "You confuse me, José. Are you saying that you have chosen a life of piracy over me? After everything we just did to find you. Please tell me that is not what you are suggesting."

"No, I am not suggesting that exactly. But I have to consider that I am now a…pirate."

"You are not a pirate. You have a way out." Even in the dark of night, with only the gas lamps of the porch to illuminate her face, José could see the red creeping up her neck and cheeks. "You cannot have it both ways. You cannot have me and be a pirate."

"But what if I could?"

"Be reasonable, José."

"I am. You cannot expect me to just slot back into society now that I have a magical pardon. It doesn't work that way."

"That could not be further from the truth. You were a respected Admiral."

"*Was* a respected Admiral. Word has spread, Joséfa. Are you prepared to bear the brunt of all the looks we will surely receive when we step into a room?"

"You don't think I have thought of that?" she bit out.

He sighed, placing his face in his palms. "This is not how I saw this conversation going."

"Well, then. The feeling is mutual." She stood, crossing her arms. "I am fully prepared to deal with society looking down on you—looking down on us. I am strong enough to handle it. I always thought we could get through anything if we had each other. Now I'm starting to wonder if I'm enough to get you through it."

"You are enough. Never doubt that."

"Am I? Because it certainly sounds like piracy needs to be part of the equation, too." She turned to face the grounds. "What is it that you want, José? What is your vision for our life?"

He sighed. "I am being pulled at each limb between two very different worlds. You saw how Lorena treated my crew, my friends. You heard the disdain in Armando's voice. They do not speak to me that way because they see me as one of them."

"You are one of them."

"Am I?" he shook his head. "I don't understand, Joséfa. When I proposed to you again, you said life with me would be an adventure. What type of adventure were you expecting?"

She gazed at him silently—a long moment passed before she could form words. "I dreamed of an adventure where we would see the world, have two or three children, teach them the ways of life and all of its wonderful treasures, shower them and each other with unending love." She motioned around the grounds with her hand. "We would settle our roots here and start anew. That's the adventure I was speaking of. With you. Always with you. I just wasn't anticipating *your* wants to be any different."

He stood from his chair, closing the distance between them and wrapping his arms around her. She sighed, laying her head on his chest as he drew circles on the small of her back with his thumb. "Our wants are not that different. I, too, want an adventure with you and our little ones if, God willing, we are blessed to have them. It's just that..." José struggled with his words, unable to will them from his tongue.

"Just what? Please tell me. You can tell me," she gently pleaded.

"It's just that when I was out on the ocean with my men, there was a certain sense of freedom—Captain Rodgers aside. There were times when he was completely insufferable, but most of the time, the crew was no different from the men I served with in the Spanish Navy. Perhaps they were a little looser with their tongue and manner of speaking…."

"Yes, I noticed," she chuckled lightly.

"But truly," he continued, "they were my family. Well… some of them. There were a few I kept my eyes on even in my sleep. Rodrigo, Chino, and John, I must exclude from that party. They have been loyal to me. I used to believe pirates were a bunch of backstabbing lowlifes who would eventually see their end at the tip of a blade or edge of a plank. I found that I didn't fully understand them. And while most of society sees them negatively, I cannot help but see them for who they have been to me." José pulled away from her, clasping their hands together between them. "Make no mistake, I have thought about the circumstances of my life as a pirate and where you fit in it. It has often kept me up at night trying to see a path forward. But I want a path forward. I do."

She nodded. "Very well. Then, I will ask you the same question. What type of adventure were you expecting?"

His hands traveled slowly up and down her arms, the friction heating his palms. "I imagined an adventure where you would be my unofficial first mate."

"First mate?" She burst into laughter. "I think Rodrigo would have an issue with that."

"First mate of my soul, *mi amor.* That is something Rodrigo cannot be. Tell me, Joséfa. You are a lover of artifacts and history, are you not?"

"Of course! I love it all. If an item tells a story, it intrigues me."

"What if I were to tell you that back in my home—*our* home—on our island just off the coast of *La Florida*, I have a treasure trove of items that can tell you all kinds of stories?"

Her eyes widened. "What kind of treasures, José?"

"The very kind that sing to your soul. Would this be the kind of adventure you could see yourself living?"

"Without a doubt in my mind."

"Then, come with me."

"To your island?"

"Yes."

The excitement left her eyes. "But I will be all alone on the island."

"You will have my crew and me. We did leave Elena, Rodrigo's woman, in charge in our absence. I am almost certain she is busy building up the island. You would enjoy her company. You could catalog the treasures we discover. Perhaps see if they are of any value."

"But wouldn't I be rather lonely?"

"Aside from Elena, it would be lacking in some female companionship, but that will change with time. Of course, there are the women Chino and John bring to the island, but I doubt they will be the type of companionship you are hoping for."

"Hmmph," she said, scowling.

"We could live on your island part of the time and part of the time here."

"We could?"

"Of course. I wouldn't want to leave you on the island alone."

"Why would I be on the island alone?" She looked up to find his guilt-ridden gaze—understanding finally dawning. "You intend to continue living as a pirate." She pulled away from him. "You cannot possibly think this will end well, José. A pirate's life is a short life."

"Not if one is careful."

"Careful? Everyone already has eyes on you. You have a pardon and a target on your back."

"I see the pardon as an opportunity."

"How so?"

"Because I can now travel the seas under the guise of a merchant ship."

"Not one of my brother's, surely! You will not drag him into this ruse."

"Of course not. I'm not asking him to be involved in any way."

"But why? Why return to piracy when you can make a decent living as a merchant?"

He sighed heavily. "I cannot let them down, Joséfa. They have sacrificed for me as well."

"Are they all that matter to you? Was my sacrifice not big enough for you?" she snapped. She shook her head, staring at the floor—her ire making the air thick. "I need time to think."

He nodded.

"Tomorrow is the gala of San Cristobal. I hope you can sacrifice the time to accompany me," she said, sarcasm dripping in her tone.

José knew he earned every ounce of her anger. "I will go with you."

Joséfa turned on her heel, leaving a broken man on the front porch, wondering if it was too much to want both his love and his desires.

Chapter 34

tomed to—the polite tip of the head upon arriving, the curt-sy, and the silent whispers exchanged just loud enough to bring light to someone's disastrous attire. Some tale about the mistress gracing their halls to sweep her married lover away while their naïve wife is none the wiser.

This evening, none of the whispers were about dresses and mistresses. That was apparent the moment José and Joséfa stepped into the room. The black tie tugged at José's neck, suddenly two sizes too small despite his and Armando's exact same shape and build. The suit lent to him by his soon-to-be brother-in-law certainly fit his body but didn't quite fit his persona—not anymore.

Everyone snapped to attention, and the whispers died down. Joséfa's chin rose an inch; her arm pulled tighter around his as she smiled and moved them deeper into the ballroom. Felipe coughed behind him, and José turned to find him grinning. "Is something humorous, my friend?" he asked, seething.

"Oh no. Not at all. Just enjoying the show."

"Excellent. I am glad my suffering amuses you."

Felipe patted him lightly on the shoulder. "Come on, José. Try to find the humor in this."

José casually slowed his pace, letting Felipe walk up beside him. "And what exactly is so humorous about this situation?"

Felipe leaned in. "Just look at how many women in the room did one of two things. Either A, they saw you and automatically reached for their pearls as if you would run to them and snatch them off their bosom. Or B, they pushed their bosom into full view, hoping you would snatch the pearls *and* them. I'm not the only one to notice. I've never seen Joséfa so possessive of you in my life." José glanced at Joséfa, who was gripping his arms. She scanned the room, daring any of these women to approach. Felipe chuckled lightly. "Life with you post-piracy will be most entertaining."

José instantly felt like running from the room. He didn't want to be subjected to anyone's attention, much less for the rest of his life. Joséfa tugged on his coat sleeve, smiling at him empathetically.

"Come. Let us get a refreshment. You look like you could use it." She gripped the side of her beautiful pale peach ball gown and led them through the ballroom. Grabbing two glasses off a tray from a passing server, she guided them to a corner. José's shoulders relaxed, and he sighed at the welcomed seclusion. "Better?"

"Much. Thank you."

"Relax, my love. This is the first time you have been reintroduced. It will take some time."

He nodded in what he hoped she would interpret as understanding, but his anxiety grew throughout his body. Fancy balls and the like never used to bother him. He found he enjoyed them. They were a chance to catch up with the other *familias* in Sevilla. While this was not his home, the people were the same—the men with their own shipping companies sizing up the competition, all vying for the attention of the owners of goods from the island whose partnerships they were desperate to win over.

The mothers of high society prowled as usual while their daughters stood by their sides in one of three capacities. The first, willingly at their mother's side, prowling with them. At that exact moment, one of the young ladies caught José's eye and smiled seductively at him, fanning herself vigorously as her breasts almost popped out of her dress that was two sizes too small. Joséfa's arms tightened around his. He patted the back of her hand on his arm and leaned down to kiss her head, letting his affections for his beloved known.

The second daughter sits back, anticipating the moments of laughter. Contempt will inevitably sprout on their face when their mother approaches an eligible bachelor, practically throwing their daughter into their arms. Their eyes nearly hit the ceiling when the said male is old enough to be their father. José shivered. He understood this was society's way, but some of these men had horse excrement for brains, and their looks left much to be desired. *These poor women,* he thought.

Which brought him to the last type—the woman whose sorrow with having to marry is written all over their face. Their stories were always more complex. Perhaps they have a lover they cannot be with. Perhaps they lost the love of their life to war or the sea. These stories remain their own, and he thought they would likely be taken to the grave. He wondered whether Joséfa had looked as sad as the third daughter when she was back in Sevilla.

"You're mighty quiet," Joséfa said, breaking into his thoughts.

He smiled down at her. "I'm just observing."

She nodded in understanding. He was observing what he had been missing during his time at sea. A few weeks ago, he had been on his ship watching his back for Captain Rodgers and his little band of sycophants. A few weeks ago, he feared his life would be over, and now he stood at a ball dressed as a gentleman. *How quickly life can change.*

The time in seclusion in the dark corner of the room was short-lived. Felipe approached them with an older man with strings of gray hair combed over the top of his head and a chubby figure—his bushy eyebrows taking up half of his forehead. He looked at José like he was meeting the king.

"José Gaspar, this is Mr. Janssen," Felipe introduced.

José politely bowed to the man. "Pleasure to meet you, Mr.

Janssen. May I introduce my fiancé, Joséfa de Mayorga?

The man's eyes widened. "Ah! *Señorita* de Mayorga. A pleasure to be meeting you again."

Again? José thought.

"And my sincerest congratulations on your upcoming nuptials," Janssen continued. "I am sure you both are very excited to be married."

"Yes, we have been through a lot to get back to each other," she acknowledged knowing that word had spread throughout the little island about José. "It will be nice to move on to the next chapter of our lives."

José opened his mouth to ask how they knew each other, but Mr. Janssen spoke before he got the chance.

"Absolutely! It is precisely why I wanted to speak with your husband-to-be. I believe I have a proposition for him. One that he would be interested in."

José's brow lifted. "Oh?" Not even five minutes into the room and someone was propositioning him. He dreaded what this might entail.

"I believe I'll take the air for a moment." Joséfa curtsied to them and left José's side, heading to the outdoor area just a few feet away. *Odd…*

"Admiral Ga—," Mr. Janssen began.

"Please. Call me Don Gaspar. I am no longer an Admiral."

"Of course. Don Gaspar, I am a merchant of rare items."

José cocked a brow. "Rare items?"

Mr. Janssen nodded his head vigorously. "Yes, most rare. I take great pride in my investments. I understand you have an appreciation for rare items as well, given your most recent adventures."

"Adventures?"

"Why yes. Your piratical adventures. Now, no need to be embarrassed by such a thing, Don Gaspar. Everyone in this room is familiar with your most recent travels—this being a small island and all."

The heat crept up José's neck. He understood that facing society would undoubtedly be challenging, but he hadn't been prepared for someone to be so untoward. "Mr. Janssen, may I remind you that my most recent *travels* were not my choosing."

"Of course. Of course. I fully understand. It is most unfortunate how it came to be. Getting swept away from the only home you know to be launched into piracy."

"Privateering."

Mr. Janssen waved a hand. "All the same."

José was growing tired of this little man's ability to dismiss his misfortune. He had lived with it for the past five years, after all. "Your proposition?"

"Oh, yes. Dear me. Of course. Of course. Well, the tales of your swordsmanship have traveled as well. It is well known you were a very respected Admiral in the Spanish Royal Navy—"

"…in another life."

"Yes, of course. Another life. But to hear how you demolished an entire crew at the tip of a sword? Now, that is beyond impressive. And that is why I have approached you this evening."

"You approached me because of my swordsmanship?"

The smile on Mr. Janssen's face grew. "Oh, yes. You see, I have the rarest items, and they need the utmost guard against vandals and pirates. It would be most advantageous to have you on board my ship to defend my treasures." Mr. Janssen looked at José as if he were a prized mare, a possession to be hoarded, treasured, and boasted about. José realized it was not the look of someone approaching a king when Mr. Janssen first approached him but the look of someone about to snag a prize.

"While I appreciate the offer, Mr. Janssen, I must respectfully decline."

"I would pay you handsomely."

"I would not need to be paid handsomely."

"But of course, you would. I am a collector of the rarest treasures. I can afford to pay you handsomely for your services."

"I have no doubt you could, but," José leaned in closer to Mr. Janssen, who may have just realized he crossed a line—his chubby face turning redder than a tomato, "like yourself, I too enjoy rare treasures. I enjoy them so much, I took them at the tip of the very sword you're attempting to hire, the very type of being you want to guard against." José straightened back. "Therefore, I do not need to be your swordsman, Mr. Janssen. While I'm unsure of what my next business venture may be, I can guarantee you it will not be a guard dog."

Mr. Janssen's mouth dropped slightly open in shock. "Don Gaspar, you realize your options may be few, yes?"

"I do not see how that is any of your concern."

Mr. Janssen's brows furrowed. "Forgive me. I do not mean to speak out of turn. However, I doubt there will be many who would offer you as good a deal as I have."

"Nonsense. My brother-in-law-to-be has a shipping company, and I have a ship of my own. I am certain Armando wouldn't leave me to the winds. He likely has a plan for my helping the family business."

Felipe and Mr. Janssen exchanged a look—Felipe turning his attention to him. "Uh, José? It was Armando who sent Mr. Janssen to you with this proposition."

José's entire body froze in shock. "I beg your pardon?" he bellowed. A few heads turned his way.

Felipe glanced around nervously. "He sent Mr. Janssen your way with this proposition."

"I heard you the first time, Felipe. But why?"

"I think I will take my leave now," Mr. Janssen said, eying both of them awkwardly. "My offer still stands should you care to consider it, Don Gaspar." He turned and walked away.

With a look that bled with guilt, Joséfa made her way back to us, having supposedly gotten enough fresh air.

José looked back and forth between Felipe and Joséfa. "Someone had better start talking."

Felipe winced. "It's Armando. You know how he is."

"Do I? Because I'm starting to doubt it."

"He has some concerns."

"Concerns?"

"Well, yes. Concerns about how it might look."

Joséfa sighed beside him, muttering something he swore was *Dios Mio* under her breath.

"And how might this look?"

"Lower your voice," Felipe hissed.

José glanced around; sure enough, a few patrons had stopped to gawk at them from a distance. He tried his best to ignore them. "How might this look?" he said in a lower tone.

"You were a pirate. In fact, you just insinuated to Mr. Janssen that you may very well still be a pirate. Your friends are pirates." Felipe paused, inhaling a deep breath. "Armando doesn't want to have you associated with his shipping business," Felipe said, rushing the sentence out of his mouth.

Embarrassment and shame coursed through his veins. "He doesn't want me to be part of his shipping business, but he has no issue with my marrying his sister?"

"I'm afraid he didn't have much of a choice in the matter, *mi amor*," Joséfa said.

"And how is that?"

"Because it was either he let me marry you after we found you, or he would lose his manhood." She shrugged.

José blinked at her. "What?"

"Oh, this I have to hear," Felipe said, his interest piqued.

"There's nothing to tell."

"I beg to disagree," José countered.

Joséfa sighed. "Very well. On one particular day, Armando and I had been arguing for quite some time about what to do once we rescued you. Lorena remained silent while we went back and forth in a spirited debate. He decided he would draw a bath while Lorena went to the *mercado*. It was rare for the two of them to be apart, as she never leaves Armando's side." Joséfa scrunched her brows. "It is slightly annoying, really. How can she want to be in his company *all the time?* I love my brother, but I don't know how she stands it. It's incredibly—"

"Joséfa?" Felipe interrupted.

"Yes?"

"Can you get back to the part where you almost cut off his *cojones*?"

José smacked him on the arm. "Language, Felipe."

"She's like a little sister to me. She's heard me say worse," he protested. José glared at him, causing Felipe to clear his throat. "My apologies. Continue."

"Where was I?"

"He was drawing a bath," José helped.

"Ah, yes. So, he draws a bath. Lorena went to the *mercado*. And I decided to take matters into my own hands."

"Quite literally, from the sounds of it."

Ignoring Felipe, she continued. "We happen to have the most exquisite swords of all sizes. I suppose they were a gift to my father—from one of the many merchants he used to work with. I grabbed the smallest of the bunch and one suitable for holding at his throat. The maids had just finished drawing his bath, and he lay in the washroom for a while. It was a relatively quiet afternoon post-argument. Having grabbed an extra set of the maid's clothing from the laundry room, I slipped on the outfit, placing the dagger on my back and the longer blade in my hand. Grabbing a discarded bucket by the door, I disguised my longer sword behind it, but it turned out it was unnecessary. He was blissfully unaware of my presence when I tiptoed in, his eyes firmly shut.

"One step, two steps. I finally reached him, held the blade just half an inch from his neck, and gently prodded him with the dagger's handle. He flinched. I, of course, had anticipated this occurring. His eyes went wide. *"What do you think you're doing, Joséfa?"* she said in a low voice, imitating her brother. Joséfa smiled mischievously. "Truthfully, I've never seen him so frightful in all my life. It was pretty thrilling.

"I didn't feel his question merited an answer. So, I pointed at his manhood with the smaller dagger. His breathing accelerated, and I had him right where I wanted him. I demanded he give in, let me marry who I truly loved, and stop trying to manage my life. He conceded…but only after telling me that if this is what I truly wanted, he won't help us after finding you. He told me we would have to find our own way if I wanted to be so independent."

"Ah. So, this is why he refuses to let José work for him? Pure pettiness?" Felipe mused.

"I'm certain that's part of it."

"Armando has always been a proud man. He likely didn't appreciate being bested by his sister," José said.

"Or nearly having my manhood nearly cut off," Armando said from just behind him.

José turned and glared at him. Having just learned the reason for his future brother-in-law's opposition to not only employing him but his opposition to their marriage had him seething from the inside out. "Armando. Lorena. How nice of you to join us," he said, sarcasm dripping in his tone. "We just had the most interesting conversation."

"About my *cojones*?"

"No, but that too. We had the most interesting conversation with a *Mr. Janssen*. Care to hear about it?"

Joséfa bristled. "Lorena, why don't we take a turn about the room? I have been dying to see the dresses." Joséfa grabbed Lorena's arm, and the two disappeared into the crowd.

"I think I should like to see the dresses as well," Felipe said, quickly following them.

Momentarily lost in a standoff of ire, they assessed each other—José radiating in cold fury.

"Why?" José asked.

"You know why."

"I truly don't."

"Come on, José. I have to do what's right for the business. My father's business. Employing one of the most famous pirates to sail the seas is a little off-putting for some of our business dealings."

"Oh, we wouldn't want that," he said sarcastically.

"No, we wouldn't."

"And we wouldn't want me marrying your sister either, hmm?"

Armando leaned in, lowering his voice to just above a whisper. "I admit that after everything that had happened back in Sevilla, I may have been a little stubborn about you marrying Joséfa. I was wrong."

"Yes, you were. But tell me, did you come to this conclusion before or after the incident in the tub?"

Armando rose to full height. "After. Oh, don't give me that look, José. This is nothing against you. You have always been like a brother to me."

"Well, you have a weird way of showing it."

"That's unfair."

"Unfair?"

Armando held his hands up. "I have to keep up pretenses. The shipping company is finally doing well with the current trade routes despite the unrest occurring in this part of the world. I have a family to think about, José."

"Funny. I *would have* had a family of my own to think about if it weren't for your wife's cousin ruining my life," he bit.

"Lorena had nothing to do with that."

"You're right. She didn't, and she cannot be held to account for your ignorance."

"Ignorance?"

"Yes," he bellowed, immediately bringing unwanted attention into his fold. From across the room, Joséfa smiled at the other patrons in the hall and began moving through the crowd. José ignored her oncoming approach. Taking every effort to calm his breathing, he continued. "You dare to speak to me of unfairness. Look at what has happened to me. Do you have no empathy?"

"Of course, I have empathy."

"The hell you do. The Armando I grew up with would never attempt to make me feel so beneath him. He would *know* that I am not. What happened to you?"

"Nothing happened to me. My needs are different. And forgive me if I was trying to find some employment for you."

"*Aye, sí!* Find employment *for* me but not *with* me?" He shook his head. "I am trying here. I am trying for the sake of your sister but also for the sake of all of you. To have been away so long from the woman I love and the life I had no interest in leaving. Do you know how torturous that was? And now you want me to be gone from Joséfa for months to be some guard dog for a treasure hunter who is nothing but a thief in fine clothing?"

Armando blinked at him a few times.

"You think I haven't heard of people like Mr. Janssen? Looking to turn a profit at the expense of the actual people who found the treasure?" He scoffed. Suddenly, José stood stock still. Something popped into his head, and he reeled. "Wait...how is it you know Mr. Janssen?"

Armando shrugged. "Everyone in *Puerto Rico* knows Mr. Janssen. He approached me about employing your services. I advised him to approach you directly with my blessing."

José's brow rose to the ceiling—his gut warning him that something was off. "What are you not telling me, *hermano*?" They glared in silence until José felt a tug at his elbow.

"Come, José. Come dance with me," Joséfa said silently, a shadow of a plea in her voice.

"Not now, Joséfa," he said, keeping his eyes on Armando.

"Yes, now."

José looked at her then. He didn't have it in him to continue this fight. Turning his attention back to Armando, he said, "This is far from over." He took Joséfa's hand and led her to the dance floor.

Chapter 35

José & Joséfa whirled with intense precision around the room, maneuvering around other couples lost in a trance to the music of the quartet. They were always so good at dancing together—as if they could reach each other's thoughts through their bodies. All feelings of Mr. Janssen's proposition and Armando's treatment of him slipped away with each step. He let his gaze drop to Joséfa, whose lips turned up in a smile. The small space between them felt like a canyon of significant proportion. This woman he had dreamed about being with—who he thought would never be in his arms again—was his, or would be officially in a few short days. His *esposa*. His wife. The thought had him inching closer with each whirl. The rest of the ballroom disappeared, his entire focus on her.

"Better?" she asked.

"Much."

She nodded. "It will get easier."

"You think?"

"I know," she said, smiling with him with all her confidence.

"Well, then. I am delighted to have you by my side to remind me. I confess I do not share in your confidence."

"Do not worry about Armando. Sometimes he thinks he knows what's best. Being the *jefe* of a merchant company will make anyone think their *pantalones* are far larger than they are."

José laughed. "You have never been soft on him."

A playful smirk crossed her lips. "And I do not intend to start now."

When the song ended, Joséfa and José returned to their quiet corner, where he continued observing the crowd before him. He entirely forgot about the other presence at the ball— the soldiers. It had been some time since he had seen so many men in uniform not trying to take his life. One man was dressed in a uniform different from the Spanish military. If José had to venture a guess, the uniform looked to be American. The man's dark blonde hair was combed tight to his head; his blue eyes scanned the room while he causally conversed with those around him. He certainly had the build of a military guard. *How curious. What was a member of the U.S. military doing here?*

As if summoned by his thoughts, the man in uniform caught his eye and doubled back. He had never met anyone in the U.S. military. The man in question excused himself from his group and made his way across the ballroom to where they stood in their quiet corner. A thrill at conversing with another military officer ran through him until…

"José Gaspar, the infamous pirate. Your reputation precedes you."

"I believe it would be impossible not to have heard of his recent pardon from the king, Señor," Joséfa corrected.

As he laid his eyes upon Joséfa, José noted the sudden change in his demeanor. "Lieutenant, milady. It's Lieutenant Kearny. But you are most welcome to call me Lawrence." Keeping his eyes firmly on her, he grabbed her free hand, placing a kiss upon it. Joséfa pulled her hand away, causing Kearny to smirk. He returned his attention to José, whose anger spiked at the man before him. "I'm sure you'll find that my reputation precedes me."

"Actually, I haven't the faintest idea who the hell you are," José replied, knowing full well who stood before him. Captain Kearny of the United States Navy—a hunter of pirates and a damn good one, too.

He gave José an all-knowing smile. "Well, then. I suppose I should bring you both up to speed. I have been tasked with the honor of hunting down pirates in our waters."

"There is no honor in taking lives," José bit out.

"I would hardly call them lives. They are worthless pieces of excrement that litter our seas."

"How dare y—"

"—speak ill of pirates? Mr. Gaspar, you are pardoned, are you not? Or are you still, in fact, a pirate?"

"I think you already know the answer to that, Lieutenant Kearny," Joséfa interjected.

"Do I?"

"And what exactly brings you to San Juan? It is far off the shores of Virginia," José asked.

Captain Kearny stepped back, his face full of amusement. "Huh, shores of Virginia? Then, you *have* heard of me." José smirked but remained silent. "I am here on behalf of the U.S. Navy. As you can imagine, when news of a pirate… I beg your pardon, *former* pirate…reached our shores, our own proper investigation was warranted. And when I saw the beautiful *Floriblanca* in the harbor, I knew it was true."

"*La Floriblanca* was Captain Rodgers' ship."

"*La Floriblanca* is a pirate ship."

"*Was* a pirate ship."

"Ah, yes. Good ol' Captain Rodgers is no longer," he said with a tsk-tsk. "Such a shame that I didn't get to kill him myself. I had been looking forward to it. Thank you for taking it upon yourself to rid the world of him."

"I did it for my fiancée and for me. No one else."

"Forgive me. I forgot to provide my congratulations. Although," he said, turning to Joséfa, "it would be unwise of me not to ask while I have your audience, milady. A lovely woman such as yourself can have her pick of any eligible bachelor out there. I, myself, am eligible. I have a wonderful sprawling estate with horses and livestock. A gorgeous woman like yourself could spend years of happiness out in the country with someone like myself by your side."

"So humble," she murmured.

"And yet," he continued, "you risk crossing a vast and dangerous sea for *this* man. How is it that you can look past all the…" he waved his hand around in the air in front of José, "piracy?"

"Former pirate," Joséfa corrected, her face set with disdain. "And I would advise you to hold that tongue of yours, for it has done enough insulting. You are standing in front of one of the most successful Admirals—"

"—*former* Admirals."

"—in the Spanish Royal Navy, which he achieved on his own merit—his own talent."

"One of his many, I hear."

José lunged toward him. Joséfa's hand flew up to his chest. She continued, "We have been through many trials and are ready to move beyond what has happened over the last few years. I would ask you to do the same. Now, I must ask you to take your leave if you have nothing productive to say." José and the captain remained still in an exchange of glares full of contempt.

"I have my eye on you, Gaspar."

"By all means, don't leave out the other eye."

He turned and walked away into the crowd. José ran a hand through his hair, sighing. "This was a mistake," he muttered.

Joséfa gently rubbed his arm. "Do not say that, *mi amor.*"

He couldn't bring his eyes to hers. "You are too good of a woman to pledge yourself to me."

"Do not say such things."

"*Es la verdad,*" he said. José searched around the room, finding Felipe in the corner, laughing with a group of men and women. His best friend's ability to make friends where ever he went made him envious. He would give anything for just an ounce of that acceptance right now. He grabbed Joséfa's hand, kissing it softly. "Go to Felipe. He's just there in the corner."

"Where are you going?"

"To meet with my crew.." He turned and left the room without glancing back.

CHAPTER 36

"*QUE PENDEJO*! DID HE SAY THAT TO YOU? AFTER GOING THROUGH all the trouble of finding you? That doesn't seem fair." Rodrigo said.

"Or in character. Armando and I have been friends—brothers since before I could dress with my own hands." He swirled the rum around in his glass, staring at the amber liquid as if it might give him the answers he was searching for. They sat at a corner table of *El Taberna*, the flames flickering from sconces around the room shed just enough light to reveal their faces but not much more. This seemed to benefit some who utilized the various alcoves spread throughout, including Chino and John, who currently occupied them. "Do they never stop—"

"Whoring?" Rodrigo chuckled. "No. They do not."

José shook his head, the dread settling in once more. "I'm wondering if it is a mistake to marry her."

"Oh. I do not know that it is a mistake to marry Joséfa so much as it is a mistake to think that things will be the same. Or that the life you two had planned would be achievable. You have changed, Gaspar."

"Yes, everyone keeps telling me that and yet…" And yet he didn't want to accept in his heart what his mind already knew. He tipped back his drink, feeling the liquid burn down his throat. "I cannot marry her. I have nothing to give her. Nothing beyond the offer to be some swordsman, guard dog for a treasure stealer. I cannot do that."

Rodrigo grinned. "No. I daresay not. I am surprised you didn't take Mr. Janssen's head off right then."

"If I had a sword strapped to my hip, I might have. Instead, I was in a silly suit acting the part of an aristocrat while the entire party scowled at me, dissecting me with their stares and whispers. Some didn't even whisper, speaking loud enough for the whole hall to hear."

"Lieutenant Kearny in San Juan." Rodrigo shook his head. "How curious. He must have been here before we arrived."

"*Claro que si*. But it was almost as if he had been sitting, waiting. How he knew we would be here is beyond me."

"Sent by the U.S. Navy *mi culo*. He is here on his own accord. From what I hear, he's an arrogant bastard," Rodrigo scoffed.

"That he is. The nerve of him advancing on Joséfa as I was standing there." He ran a hand through his hair. "How am I ever going to give her the life she deserves? I thought I would be welcomed into the de Mayorga family business. I would have the means to provide her the life she deserves and, at best, use my skills as a seaman and a merchant to help Armando's business. What am I to do?"

"You can start your own business with our treasure."

"We cannot even begin to get rid of it without being discovered. If half of our treasure were to return to us, they would know we were responsible for a good amount of piracy."

Rodrigo nodded. "Whatever you plan to do, given what you've learned tonight, I suggest you think on it hard. The wedding is in two days, *mi amigo*."

"I know," he said, the panic only held at bay by the amount of rum coursing through his veins.

Rodrigo leaned forward and patted him on the shoulder. "Take my horse and head back to Armando's estate. The ride will give you time to think."

José nodded. "Thank you, Rodrigo."

"*Es nada*. You may not have all the answers, but they will present themselves to you. One can always tell when a change is in the air. It's charged with it. And the air around you is alive with *something*. Your future is not yet determined."

José's brow lifted. "You're not going to reach out and read my palm, are you?"

Rodrigo chuckled. "Heavens no. I'm not that much of a gypsy. Now, go. Get out of here."

Long after the ball had ended, José made his way up to the house from the stables. The thick air gently whipped across his face while the *guahana* danced in the winds. The moon cast shadows across the fields and lit the walkway to *Casa de Mayorga*. As he approached, he heard Joséfa arguing. *This late in the evening?* Armando's voice carried in the mix. He gently opened the door, making sure not to wake the child, although he wondered if Joséfa and Armando were well ahead of him on that front. José made his way to the sitting room, the light spilling into the hallway.

"You cannot expect anything less than ten thousand pounds for it," she demanded.

José stopped in his tracks. *Why was Jos*éfa meddling with Armando's business?

"Seven is plenty."

"Most definitely not. Do you have any idea what it is you are selling?"

"Indeed I do, *hermanita*. Which is why I will accept seven thousand for it."

"*Aye, Dios mio*! Armando. The history. The culture. You are a fool if you accept anything less than ten thousand. Mr. Janssen is not a fool. He knows it as well. You must listen to me. I know more about this than you do."

Armando's sigh carried through the hallway. "Fine. We'll do it your way this time. Your knowledge of the piece better be accurate."

"It always is."

José stepped into the room. "Trouble in the family business?"

Joséfa and Armando's heads snapped up at him. "No," they both exclaimed simultaneously.

José looked between them, his brow raised to the ceiling. "What exactly are you two up to?"

"Nothing at all, *mi amor*," she said, a smile plastered on her face.

His gaze traveled to her hand. "You're fidgeting."

She looked down. "So?"

"You do that when you're hiding something."

"I'm not hiding anything."

"No? Hmmph. Very interesting. Armando?"

"Hmmm?" he answered in a high-pitched squeal.

"Since when do you take your sister's advice in your shipping business?"

His mouth dropped open and closed a few times until he finally answered. "Well, since…you know how progressive these times can be."

"*You*? Progressive?"

"Of course. It is important to take the advice of our outstanding females in the *familia*."

"You wouldn't take the advice of la Reyna if she blessed your front door step with her presence and told you selling slippers would make you a fortune."

"That's entirely unfair," Armando said aghast. "I hear slippers are in high demand these days. Wouldn't you agree, *hermana*?"

"*O, si*." She nodded in agreement.

"Fantastic. So, you'll welcome the advice of a female—your sister, whose suggestions you've never entertained before—but not from a former Admiral who knows more about the merchant business and the sea than his soon-to-be wife?" José rubbed a hand over his face. "You know what? Don't answer that. I don't think I can take any more excitement today. I'm heading to bed."

As he walked out of the room, he thought he heard a collective sigh. Turning back to them, he said, "Don't think for one second that this conversation is over." He turned, leaving a very stunned Joséfa and Armando in his wake. *Just what are they up to?*

Chapter 37

The following morning, the incident with Armando and Joséfa remained fresh in José's mind. Even though the wedding was to take place in a day, his gut gave him nothing but sneaking suspicion to ponder. He stood on the docks observing his crew feverishly preparing the ship to set sail—cleaning the deck, checking the sails. Crates of goods were hauled up onto the ramp one after the other. José's gaze became distant.

"Everything is as it should be, *Capitan*. We can sacrifice another day or two for your nuptials, but the men are itching to be at sea," Rodrigo advised.

"*Si, yo se.*"

"There's a possible raid down the straight that could set us ahead. Maybe take us out of commission for the rest of our lives."

"*Si.*"

Rodrigo placed his hands on his hips, observing José with interest. "They say whoever takes the ship will be the next King of Spain."

"That's good to hear."

"Are you not listening to a word I'm saying?"

José turned to him. "Hhmm?"

"What's with you?"

José sighed. "Nothing of great importance, I hope."

Rodrigo eyed him questionably. "Seems important enough for you to be unfocused. What troubles you?"

José shook his head. "It is nothing to worry about at the moment. Tell me of this quest."

"There's a ship heading to *Inglatierra*. We believe it is in possession of the Dead Bishop's Treasure."

"Do not mess with me this early in the morning, Rodrigo."

"I tell you no lies, *mi amigo*."

José's eyes went wide. "Where did you come about this information?"

Rodrigo smirked. "I have sources in high places too…and so do a lot of other crews."

"Hmph. So, Yanes succeeded. A pirate's every *sueño*." José smiled softly. A treasure of that proportion could bring him and his crew a vast fortune. "You know the treasure hasn't been seen since the fourteenth century. The gold, silver, and jewelry are likely squandered off."

"Not unless it went to the same person. It would be a grave mistake not to go after such a treasure. Honestly, Gaspar. We need to be thinking more like your friend, Mr. Janssen."

"Mr. Janssen is not my friend."

"No," he chuckled. "He is not. But he certainly has a sound business. Now that you've found yourself on the other side of the aisle with the glory of your pardon, perhaps it may be wise to explore this option."

José's brow rose. "And which option is that?"

"Becoming the broker of great treasures."

"Oh, come off it. How would I get away with that?"

"Seriously. Society may view you as a heathen, but that doesn't make you useless. You'd be a fool not to explore the possibility."

"It's a possibility I cannot entertain, not with a brother who has a successful merchant business and his sister at my side for eternity. I will not risk getting caught peddling fortunes at the risk of damning her and her family's reputation. It's already bad enough that he wishes to keep me from working with his company. Besides, men like Lieutenant Kearny are already watching my every move. How would I extract such a treasure without notice?"

"You'd send us to retrieve it for you." Rodrigo leaned against the railing, shaking his head. "You think other countries are not sending out fleets to find the treasure themselves? Do you think they won't keep it? They would. Every ship is a pirate ship on the waters. The naval crew is just better dressed." He reached up, patting José's shoulder. "This information will not stay hidden for long. If we're going to do this, we need to act quickly. You'll need to make a decision."

José rubbed a hand over his face. "I know. I need to speak with Joséfa." He turned, scanning the docks when a familiar face caught his eye a few berths down from where *La Floriblanca* sat. There was no mistaking the tall, muscular build, brown hair, and eyes of Armando de Mayorga. He tipped his hat low to hide his features, which may have worked if it were not for José's familiarity with the man. What he hadn't expected was the company he was in. Standing before him was a man who could not be mistaken for anything but a pirate. His coat looked worse for wear, his shirt crumpled, and he had a beard that looked rather unkempt. His sailor's hat held a feather on the brim. "Who is that pirate with Armando?"

"Armando?" Rodrigo squinted. "Huh. That would be Pierre le Grand."

"The notorious French pirate?"

"*Si*, the very same."

"What interest would Armando have with le Grand?" Armando walked up the ramp and onto this ship, disappearing from view. Fury raged through José's veins. He bolted for the docks, but Rodrigo's steady hand reached out and held him back.

"Patience, Gaspar. Patience. Running onto le Grand's ship will only jeopardize our crew."

José shook free of his hold. "Then I'll be there waiting for him when he debarks."

Rodrigo ran after him. "Think, Gaspar! Do not let your emotions override your logic. What could a successful merchant possibly want with a pirate? Think!"

José stopped. The hairs on his neck stood up, a chill creeping down his spine. Mr. Janssen. Armando's merchant fleet. Joséfa's knowledge of historical facts. His vast fortune had to come from more than just sugar cane. He turned to Rodrigo flexing his fists. "How long have you known?"

Rodrigo shook his head. "I just figured it out, not five ticks before you did." Rodrigo looked in the direction of le Grand's ship. "You need to speak with him. I wouldn't go to him now and cause a stir. Think of your crew's interests and go to him tonight."

José felt his face heat; his gaze zeroed in on the spot Armando had disappeared into. "Indeed, I will." José marched down the ramp.

Rodrigo threw his hands up in exasperation. "Where are you going?"

José turned to him, a mischievous gleam in his eyes. "To do what I do best. Raid."

José sat on the floral wingback chair in the corner of the sitting room, the light from the fire flickering throughout the room. With Lorena putting Isabella to bed and Joséfa in her room making final plans for the wedding, José sat blissfully alone, enjoying the calm before the storm.

He gazed into the fireplace, casually twirling the scepter in his hand—the glint lighting the room at random. Footsteps sounded down the hall, and Felipe appeared in the doorway with the letter José had sent earlier.

He held up the piece of parchment. "Are you going to tell me what this is about?"

"In a few moments." He pointed the scepter at the neighboring chair by the fire. "Take a seat."

Felipe's brow rose. "You're acting quite mysterious. And what is that in your hand?"

José smiled. "Just take a seat."

Felipe sat in the chair, staring at José with curiosity. The sound of the clock that lay on the mantle filled the room. *Tick. Tick. Tick.* Felipe fidgeted in his chair, adjusting his lapels. "*Dios mio*, José. You make me feel as if I've done something wrong."

"Perhaps."

"Well, if I have—"

"Patience."

A few short moments later, Armando stormed down the hallway holding up the same parchment in his hand. "What is this about?" Armando paused, his eyes zeroing in on the object in José's hand. "And what is that shiny object you are twirling?"

"Can you go fetch your sister, please?"

"No, I cannot. You summoned me from my offices, further delaying my business. I'm doing my best to squeeze all of my dealings in before the wedding, and it's driving me to insanity."

"Poor baby," José chided.

"What. Is. This. About?"

"Go get her, Armando."

Armando huffed and walked down the hallway. Standing from his chair, Felipe made his way to the bar cart. "Something tells me I'm going to need a stiff drink for this."

Armando and Joséfa's voices carried down the hallway.

"Do you have any idea how much I have to get done before the wedding?"

"That is precisely what I said to your soon-to-be husband, but he's acting like an ass."

Joséfa rounded the corner with Armando on her heels, her face set with fury. "What is this all…". She gasped, stopping suddenly in the doorway—eyes wide.

Armando ran into her. "Joséfa, what the hell is wrong with you?" he scolded.

"*Dios mio*," she whispered.

José smirked, still twirling the scepter in his hands, staring intently at Joséfa. "My dear. You look like you've seen a ghost."

"Agreed," Armando said. "What is wrong with you?"

Joséfa pulled her palms up, cautioning. "Would you please stop twirling the scepter in your hand, *mi amor?*"

"Oh. This?" José threw it in the air catching it with his other hand. Joséfa shrieked.

"Keep your voice down," Armando hissed. "You'll wake up Isabella." He turned to José, who smirked at them both. "What is this scepter you have, José?"

José glared at Joséfa. "*Mi amor?* Care to tell them?"

"Hah! What would Joséfa know about it?" Felipe asked, his face lined in bemusement.

José held his gaze on her. "Joséfa?"

Her eyes lit up like the sun as she pointed at the object in his hand. "That is the Scepter of Dagobert. It was created for the French King Dagobert the First in the seventh century. More importantly, it was recently stolen from the Basilique royale de Saint-Denis. *Es muy, muy veijo.*"

"And *muy, muy* expensive, I'm sure!" Felipe exclaimed. "How did you come to find it?"

"He didn't find it," Armando seethed. "He stole it."

All eyes in the room were trained on José. He smiled deviously and shrugged. "Pirate."

"*Pero,* José," Felipe began, "you have to get that out of here. Do you know what would happen if you were caught with such a thing? It is one thing to collect such objects, but it's quite another to steal them. And after receiving a pardon. Are you mad? How can you bring this into your home? No. *Their* home," Felipe exclaimed, pointing at Armando, whose face had gone pale.

"Indeed," José agreed.

"You agree?"

"I do."

"So, then, why bring it into their home?"

José's gaze bore into Armando. "Because I suspect this is not the only object of its kind in this house, my dear friend Felipe."

Felipe laughed. "*O si*! Armando is hiding a trove of rare stolen objects somewhere in this house. As if he has been busy running an underground treasure-seeking business all this time."

"Not just Armando," José said, redirecting his attention to Joséfa, "but his sister as well."

"Oh, come off it! Armando, tell him he's lost his mind."

The sibling duo remained silent and still. Armando took the barest step forward. "José speaks the truth."

"You see? It's all in your he—" Felipe's head snapped to Armando, "wait…*que*?"

Armando puffed out his chest. "He speaks the truth."

Tears welled up in Joséfa's eyes. Her bottom lip began to quiver. José could barely stand to look at her.

"*Mierda*," Felipe whispered in astonishment. "Joséfa, you cannot possibly tell me you were involved with this as well?"

"Of course, she is," José interjected. "She has all the historical knowledge Armando could ever need to be successful—to make sure that he was selling to the highest bidder and for the right price. No one would ever suspect a woman of possessing the knowledge of such things. And he never wanted me involved with his business because he didn't want to risk an *actual* pirate being so close to his thieving operation. If you need further confirmation, Felipe, I believe you will find a holding space just behind the panel on the left-hand side of the fireplace. Just give it a slight push."

Felipe set his drink on the bar cart and rushed to the panel. He pushed it gently, and the wall opened, revealing a small, dark storage room. Felipe stepped inside. "*Ave Maria purisima!*"

"How did you find out?" Armando demanded.

"Funny you should ask," José said indifferently as he twirled the scepter.

"*Dios mio! Aye, Dios mio!*" Felipe exclaimed from the depths of the small storage room.

"You see, you're not quite as smooth as you think, Armando. You never had to watch your back in your life, never had to think on your toes. When forced into such a situation, people tend to look over their backs. *You* were not looking over your back with le Grand."

"Le Grand?!" Felipe shouted from the storage room. He poked his head out, a golden tiara affixed on his head. "Certainly, you don't mean *Pierre* le Grand?"

"Yes, Felipe. The very same one." He turned back to Armando. "Did you actually think that you wouldn't be found out?"

Armando glared at José, his face turning beet red. "I didn't know I was being followed."

"No one was following you. You stuck out like a gypsy at a débutante ball. It took nothing at all to determine who you really were. Did you think a hat would cover your identity? You're in the business of moving rare treasures between pirates and treasure collectors, and you show your face on the ship of one of the most notorious pirates to ever live, thinking you won't be discovered? You're lucky it was me who spotted you."

"My goodness. But there are all types of treasure in here." Felipe's voice echoed off the walls. He stuck his head out again. "Just how long have the two of you been doing this?"

Armando and Joséfa exchanged a look. "Since a year after you were taken," she confessed. "We initially began the venture as a tactic to find you. Other merchants in Sevilla advised us secretly. They also knew Captain Rodgers had no interest in bartering with the treasure hunters. He preferred to keep those treasures himself. He also preferred to steal those treasures for himself while ships were en route to a potential buyer or while the potential buyer was out at sea. It took us years to attract his attention, but you all finally saw our ship. And we were finally able to save you."

"Save me and benefit from me. How convenient." José rose. He placed the scepter on the chair and walked across the room to her. "Why keep it from me?"

"I wanted to tell you."

"But you didn't because...?"

She looked over at Armando, the guilt heavy in her gaze. Armando stood straighter, tilting his head up. "She didn't tell you because I told her not to."

José rubbed a hand over his face. "You know what? Do I even know either of you anymore?"

"I might be asking you the same question," Armando retorted.

José raised a brow. "Is that so?"

"Yes, the José I know would never have succumbed to the life of a pirate in the first place. The *Admiral* I knew would have fought to get to San Juan as soon as possible. He would have fought for Joséfa."

José swiftly closed the distance between them, throwing Armando against the wall with a thud. "Don't you dare speak of what you do not know. Do you have any idea how hard it was for me out at sea? Hmm? Do you know the lashings I took when I discovered Captain Rodgers' precious treasure? When I kept him from raping young women? Trying to make it through the long days and nights hoping, wishing to see your sister's face, knowing that she may not want me as I am? A damaged soul traveling the sea to be forever tainted by the experience of piracy. You have no idea what it is like to have your life stripped from you. None. So do me a favor and spare me the criticism. I grow tired of your arrogance." José released him, slowly stepping away while Armando breathed heavily.

"Felipe, I think I need some space. Let us find my *pirate* friends. I feel like they might be better company anyway."

Joséfa stepped forward. "But José. I—"

"Whatever you're about to say, Joséfa, I do not wish to hear it. Spare me, please. Because I truly do not even know who you are anymore."

The tears welled up in her eyes. "You know me best."

"Do I?" José shook his head. "Am I making a mistake in marrying you?"

Joséfa gasped as she stared at him silently.

"Come, Felipe." José reached up and removed the golden tiara from his head, tossing it toward Armando. "To go with your golden scepter."

CHAPTER 38

"We sail the seas that lap the shores,
loving all the women, both rich and poor
who give us plenty of cherished nights
to go with the gold and treasures alike!

Now drink, me mateys! The night is young!
There's plenty of rum for everyone!
When pirates are serving the ladies and gents
your night will feel heaven sent!"

CHINO AND JOHN BELLOWED THE SONG AT THE TOPS OF THEIR lungs, mugs raised in the air as Felipe attempted to sing the words. The tavern was lined from wall to wall with the crew of *La Floriblanca*. Heavy with the smell of cigars and sweat, the thick air surrounded the crowd. José's mood had turned since meeting up with his crew at *La Taverna*. He drank away his worries, and Rodrigo was happy to keep the drink coming.

José's vision began to blur as two Rodrigos sat by his side. He hoisted his arm around Rodrigo's shoulder. "Now, this is how to celebrate the night before my wedding!"

"*Si, mi amigo.* I fear you will not feel as well tomorrow morning, but for tonight, we celebrate."

José raised his mug. "To the pirates who became friends and the fiancés who betray their *novios*!"

Rodrigo chuckled, clanking his mug against José's. "As I always like to say, there's a story there. I wouldn't shut her out for too long."

José slammed his mug down on the table. "Well, she'll be shut out tonight because I plan to celebrate well into the evening."

"Gaspar! We have a bit of a surprise for you!" Chino said as he approached the dark corner of the bar with John and Felipe on his heels. They parted ways revealing a woman whose breasts spilled from the top of her ruby red gown, the rouge on her face glowed in contrast to her jet-black hair—her lips painted the color of sin. She sauntered to José, placing herself upon his lap. José's head tipped back as he tried to take her in.

"Well, this is unexpected," he said, closing one eye to steady the double vision.

"I understand this is your final night of freedom before you're tied down with your *mujer* for the rest of your days," she said, eyes hooded.

"That it is," he replied.

"Then, perhaps I can show you what you will be missing." The devilish woman placed small kisses on his neck, trailing up to his ear. The men around him began to whistle and taunt José from the depths of the Tavern. José shifted uncomfortably, the chills climbing down his neck and over his arms. He placed his hands on her shoulders, gently pushing her away. "As lovely and delicious as you are and as good as you smell and as mad as I am at my beloved, I have to respectfully decline."

"Oh, come off it!" John chastised.

"You'll regret this in the morning when you look down and have a ball and chain around your ankle," Chino chimed in.

Felipe stood back, observing the scene with a knowing grin, saying nothing.

"I would certainly regret it if I did something I could not take back," José replied.

The woman leaned in, gently kissing his lips. José allowed the small moment of impropriety. He was a bachelor for a short time, after all.

"*Buena suerte, Don Gaspar,*" she whispered against his lips. She rose from his lap, sauntering away to another dark corner of the room.

"Gentlemen, pay up!" Felipe said to Chino and John, who grumbled a slew of curse words before handing their coin to Felipe. After pocketing his winnings, he patted José on the shoulder. "You're always a sure bet to do the right thing."

"Not always since I could have fought my way off of Captain Rodgers' ship, according to Armando."

Felipe tsked. "Pay him no mind. The man thinks he's far more important than he is. If I had to guess, he's likely envious of you."

"Envious?" he stared at Felipe.

"Of course. He knows you are brilliant and will likely figure out a way to best him in the trade of treasure hunting, not to mention you are marrying his secret weapon. He doesn't like losing control, and now you're forcing him to conform. He hates that."

"I would have to agree," Rodrigo said. "You are far more of a threat to his newfound business if you were to enter in the same line. He has to know this."

"Be that as it may…Felipe, would you please stop moving around."

Felipe looked at him awkwardly. "I haven't moved an inch."

"*Si, si*. You are moving. Just stand still."

Felipe bellowed in laughter. "No, *mi amigo*. It is the drink that moves you, and I think you've had enough if you plan on actually marrying the *Señorita de Mayorga*."

José sighed, rubbing his temples. "Yes, I plan to marry her. That is if she'll still have me."

Rodrigo bellowed with laughter, causing José to wince slightly, his head beginning to pound. "A woman comes across the ocean to save you, and you wonder if she'll still have you? I believe it is a safe bet, Gaspar. And if one little argument has your relationship casting itself overboard, it wasn't meant to be."

José nodded and lost his balance off the chair, hitting the ground with a thud. "Who the hell moved my chair?!"

"I think it's time for you to take your leave." Felipe pulled him up, placing his left arm over his shoulder as Rodrigo moved to carry him from the other side.

"Come. We procured a room upstairs in the event he shock-ingly took the woman's offer," he told Felipe.

That was the last thing José heard before the world went dark.

A slight nudge against his ribs provoked him enough to open his eyes. He immediately wished he hadn't. The throbbing pain beat like a drum at his temples. His eyes watered with the onslaught of light invading his senses. Another throbbing pain blossomed from the back of his head with every attempt at movement. His mouth felt like a pound of sand had been shoved down his throat as he lay on the floor of an unfamiliar room. Dusty boots stood in his immediate view. He followed the boots all the way up to their owner, who stared at him with a scowl. "I suppose it is a blessing that you slept here alone, even if it is on the floor," Armando said, glancing disapprovingly at the surroundings.

José moved to sit up, laying his aching head against the bed and resting his forearms on his knees. Armando moved to the table by the hearth, pouring a generous glass of water from the porcelain pitcher. He walked over to José, handing him what he knew he needed. José gulped it down in mere seconds, pant-ing between gulps. After a few attempts, he finally caught his breath. "Why are you here, Armando?"

"I came to apologize."

"For which part?"

Armando's lips thinned. "You know me well enough that this isn't easy."

"Which is why I will savor every moment of it."

Armando sighed. "I apologize for not telling you sooner."

And if I hadn't discovered your secret, Joséfa's secret, would you have told me?"

The guilt lay heavy in his gaze. "I had debated a while whether to tell you or not."

"But why keep me from it? From helping you?"

Armando moved toward the dusty window overlooking the cobblestone streets below. The air coming in from the small crack danced with the lapels of his coat. "I wanted it for me. I wanted it *just* for me. It always seemed like we were pawns in someone else's game, whether that be my father's merchant business, a soldier for a crown that was not ours..." He glanced back at José. "A pirate in someone else's crew. I just wanted this thing for myself."

"And what about Joséfa? What did she do this for?"

"I'm afraid that is her story to tell, *hermano*. I can only speak for myself." José nodded in understanding. A conversation to be had with her later then. "In any case, I am here on her behalf. She wants to know if you will still marry her today."

A long moment of silence passed between them. "And do I know who it is that I am marrying?"

"She is as true a person today as she was when she was but a young girl and as she was when you departed Sevilla."

"A true person wouldn't have lied to the one they're about to marry."

Armando chuckled.

"Just what do you find so humorous?" José demanded.

"You have much to learn if you believe you or your wife will share every detail of your life, unspoken feeling, or hidden emotion. There are some things in your heart and your soul that you will protect from anyone, even the one you love dearly. Things that can only be shared with the friendship of self and God."

"Be that as it may, I should hope lies of the level of treasure bartering would be something we wouldn't keep from each other."

"Touché. That is something we should have been straightforward about. For that, I am sorry. For that, I can guarantee Joséfa is sorry. But I ask that you go to her. Marry her. Marry her because I know you cannot live without her—and because you both deserve to be happy."

José sighed. "Of course, I'll marry her, you overbearing *cuñado*."

Armando chuckled as he made his way to the door. "Be ready by the time the priest is scheduled to be at the church. Given your current state, it may take a while for you to get yourself together. You reek of rum and bad decisions."

"To my recollection and in my defense, I was nothing but a happy drunk." José's brows furrowed. "By the way, how did you know I was here?"

"Ah. That is a delightful story. Isabella was up early for her morning pony ride with our stable hand. While prepping her horse, he spotted a female foot poking out from one of the stables. He discovered a woman of the promiscuous sort tangled in Felipe's legs, her ruby red dress barely covering her assets. Thankfully, Isabella was too busy fussing over her pony and was unceremoniously escorted out of the stables. I was escorted there to find out why my stables were being used as a brothel. That is when Felipe told me where the delightful woman had come from and where you were."

"Oh, come on, Armando. Are you that high on your horse to claim you have never taken a woman of promiscuous means, in a stable nonetheless? I recall a flock of women at your disposal in school, and I'm not just speaking of the students."

Armando smirked devilishly. "A gentleman never tells." With that, he exited the room leaving behind a parched and hungover José.

CHAPTER 39

Yo, José Rafael Gaspar Sariego, te tomo a ti, Joséfa Anita de
Mayorga Diaz,
como mi esposa.
Prometo serte fiel en lo próspero y en lo adverso,
en la salud y en la enfermedad.
Amarte y respetarte todos los días de mi vida.

Yo, Joséfa Anita de Mayorga Diaz, te tomo a ti, José Rafael
Gaspar Sariego, como mi esposo.
Prometo serte fiel en lo próspero y en lo adverso,
en la salud y en la enfermedad.
Amarte y respetarte todos los días de mi vida.

Light wisps of smoke drifted around them as they swayed to the music. He barely acknowledged the people around him as he lovingly stared into the eyes of his beloved. All fights of lost treasure and betrayal slipped away. His wife. They were finally married. Her smile had not stopped all day and still carried late into the evening. Unlike José, who was stunned into silence the minute she strolled down the aisle in a crisp white gown that would make la Reyna jealous, Joséfa had commanded the day with her bright smile and happiness radiating from her soul. He nearly burst at the sight of all of it.

"What are you thinking, *Señora Gaspar?*"

"*Señora* Gaspar," she said, mulling the words over. "I love the sound of it."

José chuckled lightly. "Yes, as do I. But you didn't answer the question."

"I am less thinking and more feeling at the moment."

He leaned down and gently kissed her lips. "And what are you feeling?"

She looked at him contemplatively. "I feel as if I am in a dream. One that I have had over and over for so many years. I thought this would never happen. I had lost hope so many times that we would find you." She shook her head, the smile fading from her face. "I will never forget the pain I felt day after day when we couldn't locate you." A tear reflected the light of the nearby bonfire as it trailed down her cheek.

He brushed his thumb across her cheek, wiping away her tear. "*No llores*. Do not cry. I am here. I am never leaving you." He leaned down to kiss her, her lips moving softly against his, tasting the tang of the wine and promises of tomorrow. Suddenly, her hands gripped his hair with desperation. His hands traveled lower to the base of her spine, crushing her against him. She pulled away breathlessly, her eyes hooded.

"And what are you feeling now?" he asked, his barely-checked emotions on full display for her.

"I feel like we need to be alone," she said, the blush on her cheeks visible despite the shadows cast by the bonfire.

Glancing to the side, José found most of the party either departed or lounging sleepily in wicker chairs, the smell of cigars drifting through the air. Armando and Pierre le Grand sat side by side with glasses of amber resting in their hands. Le Grand's presence was a bit of a surprise but a strategic one nonetheless. Piratical politics stop for no wedding.

As if sensing his thoughts, Pierre turned to him, raising his glass. "Congratulations, *Don* Gaspar!"

"Pierre le Grand," he said, bowing to him. He took Joséfa's hand and walked closer to them. "It is a pleasure to finally meet your acquaintance. I must confess. I wasn't expecting you to be at my wedding."

Pierre smiled with laughter in his pale blue eyes; his cheeks ruddy with signs of too much drink and his ruffled dirty blond hair. "I hope you will forgive the intrusion, but I couldn't resist. When I heard that *Señorita de Mayorga* was finally wedding her beloved, I couldn't stop myself from crashing the wedding. I knew it would be the wedding of all weddings." He turned his attention to Joséfa, raising his glass to her. "Congratulations, Joséfa. You look absolutely radiant."

"*Merci, Capitaine*! It is very kind of you to keep my brother company. He won't know what to do with himself now that he can no longer spend all his time watching my every move."

"Or mine," José muttered.

Pierre laughed heartily while Armando murmured unintelligibly under his breath. "Well, I will be sure to keep him preoccupied. We recently came across a shipment of excellent whiskey. I have taken the liberty of having a barrel delivered here as penance for my intrusion."

Where Pierre obtained the whiskey was a mystery, but José wasn't about to ask.

"And we will not object to such a gift," Armando exclaimed.

Pierre leaned closer to José. "I also hope to gain an audience with you soon, Gaspar…in regards to matters dealing with the family business."

He arched an eyebrow. "Family business?"

"Ah," Armando interrupted. "All in due time, le Grand. Let the newlyweds be. We shall discuss business tomorrow."

"And who says we will be available tomorrow?" José said with a smirk. A blush crept up Joséfa's neck to her cheeks.

While Armando did not seem pleased with the comment, Pierre laughed. "Of course, of course. In due time."

It seems Pierre wasn't the only one feeling the effects of his whiskey. José could make out the sounds of Felipe singing a song with Rodrigo and the off-key tones of what was sure to be Chino.

The evening sky's quarter moon cast its light upon the field before the house, painting it with the darkest of blues and speckles of light. José's hand traveled down to Joséfa's arm, intertwining his fingers in hers. "I believe we can sneak away to the guest house now. I doubt we will be missed." He leaned down, placing a soft kiss against her plump lips. "Come."

The guest house appeared at the end of the pathway, which sat at the outskirts of the plantation—a modest one-story house painted white. A small front porch with two wicker rockers decorated the front of the home. A warm light seeped through the shuttered windows as José and Joséfa approached. Joséfa, who hadn't uttered a single word on their walk down, held José's hand. Her grip tightened with each step.

The porch steps creaked underneath their weight as they approached the front door, Joséfa's hand shaking slightly in his. José turned to her taking her face in his hands. "You know, for someone who was awfully confident just a couple of days ago, you seem to be a little nervous now."

"*Yo?*"

"Yes, you."

Her chest rose and sank in quick succession. "Why would I be nervous?"

He leaned down, his breath hot against her lips. "It is normal to feel what you're feeling, Joséfa." He kissed the corner of her mouth and cheek, trailing kisses down her delicate neck, her breath tickling his ear.

"Not all of us have your…experience, you know," she whispered.

José pulled back, his gaze intent. "I can guarantee you whatever I experience tonight will be the first time I experience anything like it, for I have never loved another or wanted another as much as I have loved and wanted you." He took her hand and turned the knob on the door. A spacious living area greeted them. Two wingback chairs sat in front of a hearth, the fire bathing the room in a calm orange light. On the left, a door to the only bedroom in the guest house lay open to a four-poster bed with sheets so white they were visible from where they stood in the entryway.

José wasted no time. He lifted Joséfa tight to his chest, carried her to the bedroom, and placed her on her feet next to the bed. Their eyes bore into each other with love so immense he was sure his heart would burst. This beautiful woman who traveled across a vast sea to rescue him was now his. His hand traveled down her neck, skimming her collarbone as he lost himself in her beautiful hazel eyes. He leaned down, bringing his lips to hers in a searing kiss. "I plan to take my time with you, *mi amor*," he murmured against her lips. "I plan to consume you, taste you, drink every inch of you in." Pulling back slightly, her eyes held such passion, her body shuddering against him as her breath crested across his lips. "I live to bring you to your pleasure."

José claimed her mouth once more before slowly turning her to face the bed. With gentle hands, he began to untie her dress which fell to the floor in a puddle of lace at her feet. Trailing his fingers up her arms, he thrilled at the sight of the goosebumps that rose in their wake. His fingers moved to her stays, untying them while anticipation grew within him. As he placed gentle kisses on her neck, Joséfa gasped softly. It made him ache to devour her.

With her stays removed and sitting in a heap with her dress, he turned her back to him and was rendered speechless. Her olive skin seemed to glow with the firelight from the living room just beyond the door, her breasts full and perfect, her dark pink nipples pebbled and begging for his touch. An exotic line traveled down between her breasts to her soft abdomen. The soft curls of her womanhood were perfectly sculpted with the exquisite curve of her hips and thighs, making him itch to drag his tongue across them.

Words of devotion sprang forth. "You are a goddess," he whispered. When he reached for her, she stopped his hand.

Joséfa's sultry smile lifted her lips as she reached up to unbutton his shirt, her eyes firmly on his as she moved down the row of buttons. José's breathing hitched as she parted his shirt, tracing her delicate hands down the length of his arms as his shirt fell to the floor. Her hands boldly skimmed up his chest. She closed her eyes and placed featherlight kisses there as if in silent prayer. Holding himself still, his eyes bore into her with insatiable surprise as she slowly moved around him, kissing every inch of his skin. He hardened with aching need as her nipples grazed his back.

When she stood in front of him again, she reached up, pulled the pins from her hair, and tossed them on the neighboring nightstand. Her hair cascaded down her back as she shook out its length, her eyes intent on José. He could wait no more. "Lay yourself on the bed, *mi vida*." She moved with sensual grace laying herself before him. Standing to the side of the bed, he took in the sight of her—the beauty of her curves with all of their dips and shadows. *Mine.*

He climbed next to her, leaving his unbuttoned pants in a heap on the floor. A ragged breath escaped his mouth as his lips crashed into hers passionately and unapologetically, taking in every bit of her essence. They kissed with the urgency of many years of longing, waiting for this moment.

His hands trailed down her neck, coming to a rest on her breast. He palmed it while gently taking the nipple in his fingers, teasing it—kneading it. José drank her in as she arched into him, her moan escaping and driving his need for her. Breaking from their kiss, he moved down her body taking her pert nipple, ready and waiting for him, into his mouth. Her hands twined through his hair, pulling him to her with equal need.

As he worshipped her breast with his tongue, his hand traveled down her body, reaching between her soft thighs. Joséfa parted for him, and he groaned. She was more than ready for him, driving him mad with desire—a fierce longing calling him to worship her there. His thumb came to a rest at the apex of her thighs, moving in determined circles on her sensitive bundle of nerves. Her body convulsed with each rotation, her eyes hooded with lust; pure ecstasy upon her face.

"Yes, *mi amor.* That's it," he whispered. José placed two fingers inside her wet heat and continued his ministrations until her hips met his thrusts. "Come for me, *mi vida.*" She jerked in his hand, her release coating his fingers as she called his name in the night.

José could wait no longer to be inside her. He moved in between her legs, coating his tip with her desire. Putting an arm on the side of her face, he gently brought his forehead to hers, her breathing erratic. "Are you ready?" Her hooded eyes remained on his as she nodded. "This may hurt a little." Again, she nodded. That was all he needed before he slowly pushed inside her. She gasped at the sudden invasion as he broke through. For a few moments, he caressed her hair, kissing her waiting lips as he slowly moved further in, letting her adjust to him. When his restraint began to buckle with the feeling of euphoria rising within him caused by her delicious warmth, she reached down, grabbed at his backside, pushing him down to her. He exhaled, a shudder of relief rolling through him as he began to move inside her. Their repetitions beat like a drum as their bodies became one—each precious, passionate moment savored. His release built with intense pleasure as she tightened around his hard length, causing him to lose all focus—this goddess before him possessed complete control of his body. Her name escaped José's lips as his release shuddered through his body, losing himself in the moment of pure ecstasy.

When he could hold himself up no more, he dropped to her side, pulling her into him—the soft scent of jasmine lingering on her skin from the long day. After what seemed like an eternity lying in each other's arms, he whispered in her ear, "You are everything to me—my beginning and my end. I will never be parted from you until God Himself comes down from the heavens to take me. I will forever protect you so we have many more nights like this."

Joséfa lifted her head from his chest and kissed his lips. "We will have many more days like this, *mi amor.* I am by your side always. *Te amo.*"

"As I love you."

CHAPTER 40

JOSÉ TRACED CIRCLES ON JOSÉFA'S LOWER BACK, SENDING SHIVERS through her body as she lay unmoving against his chest. She relished the sound of his beating heart thumping in a steady rhythm. Whatever she imagined of making love to him did not compare. She was now and would forever be engulfed in him, twined in his body and soul. José Gaspar was now even more of an obsession. She would never get enough of him. Her fingers slowly glided across the ridges and crevasses of his abdomen, repeating their journey to the other side of his stomach.

"*Que estas pensando?*" he asked.

She propped her chin on his chest, looking up at him. "That it was better than I ever could have imagined."

He brought his cupid-bow lips to hers, kissing her once, then twice. "And which part was that, wife?"

Wife. She would never tire of hearing it. "Making love to you. I never imagined it could feel so overwhelmingly intoxicating." A rush of heat spread to her cheeks. She averted her gaze.

José grabbed her chin, lifting her head toward him while smiling softly. "Then I hope to always exceed your expectations for the rest of my days." He again brought his sensual lips to hers, making her toes curl. Breaking the kiss and leaving her breathless, he leaned back on the pillow, placing an arm behind his head, taking in all of her features, rubbing his thumb across her cheek as if needing to burn it into his memory for future reference.

She sighed. "I wish we could stay like this forever."

"*Iguamente*. But then, who would your brother use to identify his precious treasure?" He lifted his brow.

Joséfa winced, knowing that the subject was bound to come up. She just wished it wasn't so soon after they had made love for the first time as husband and wife. "I owe you an apology. I know it was wrong of me to keep it from you, but…."

"I understand," he interrupted.

Her eyes widened. "You do?"

"Yes." José's other hand traveled up her spine to twine in her hair, twisting and twirling about. "You do not need to explain any further. When Armando came to me before the wedding, he explained enough. Competing with a brother's love and what he wants for his life is hard. I understand why you did it."

"I would have done the same for you."

"I know you would have. And you very well may need to soon." He smirked.

"This is about the Dead Bishop's treasure?"

José propped his head in his hand, laying on his side, his dark hair falling across his face. "How did you hear about that?"

She rested her head on the pillow. "A drunken Rodrigo may have slipped last night after the wedding."

"*Maldita sea*. Damn it."

"You mustn't take it out on him, my love."

"He shouldn't have told you that."

"Why? Because you weren't going to tell me?"

"No. Because I wanted to tell you myself." He reached up, cupping her cheek. "I have gravely underestimated you. Yes, you are everything intelligent and intriguing, and your beauty is the muse artists dream of having at their disposal. But I refuse to treat you like you do not get a say. Moving forward, I promise that you get a say." He snaked an arm around her waist, tugging her close to him. Her bare nipples grazed his chest, sending a wild, uncontrollable heat to her core. "My life will be forever complicated by the past few years of my life, but with you by my side, I feel like we can overcome it together no matter what life may throw my way. I've always only had me. Made decisions for me. Now it is us. It is making decisions for us and for our eventual family. Hopefully. Soon."

She smiled brightly then. The thought of a family. Their children. She never gave it breath or hope. Now it was a genuine possibility. "Children. I like the sound of that."

A knowing smile bloomed across his face. "Then perhaps we should keep going."

She chuckled as he buried his face in her neck, licking up to nibble her ear, causing her breath to catch. "You know what else Rodrigo told me?"

His lips traveled down toward her chest. "I do not wish to hear about Rodrigo in my marriage bed, *querida*."

"Well, it wasn't so much what he told me but more about what I overheard." She gasped as his tongue reached her breast, making lazy circles against her nipple. "Your friend Rodrigo is an excellent storyteller, especially when he's telling stories about his lovers and their long, intricate nights."

José laughed against her breast. "I can only imagine what you must have overheard. Very well, then." He resumed his assault on her nipple, causing her to arch into him. "Let's hear it."

She twined her hands in his hair, pulling him back to meet her gaze. "Perhaps it's better if I just show you." Her hands slowly moved down his chest over the ridges of his stomach. José took in a sharp breath. Her fingers then traveled up his arms, circling his back, making their way slowly down the angles of his shoulder blades. She licked her lips and kissed his warm skin. He sighed, surrendering to her movements as her fingers worked their way back to his chest, leaving little raised bumps in their wake. Her heart hammered against her chest. Resting her hands on his waist, she pushed him flat against the bed. His gaze was full of lust and promise, making the heat between her legs near unbearable.

He grinned slightly. "I love the way you look at me. You have the most amazing hazel eyes—a sea of green and brown." He reached up, pulling her fallen hair behind her ear. "They have a tinge of blue when the sunlight hits them." She leaned into his hand but refused to be distracted by her mission.

She gathered her courage pulling the quilt down to the foot of the bed, revealing his manhood standing erect with need. Her featherlight touch traveled down the side of his hip where his hands lay. She wanted nothing more than to touch his hard length, but she resisted. Grabbing his hands, she moved them up her body. José gently kneaded her breasts in his hands, devouring her with his eyes. "My God," he whispered. "They are heavenly. Full. Soft. I will never tire of these."

She pulled herself from him. "Not now, my love. I am continuing my recreation of Rodrigo's story."

"It is an excellent tale so far."

She lightly laughed as she left a trail of kisses down his chest to his abdomen, licking just above his manhood. "This is the part of the story," she said in between swirling her tongue around the tip of him, pulling up only to continue, "I found to be fascinating." He gasped as she licked slowly up and down his length. He thrust up with need reaching into her hair and caressing her head as she took him in her mouth and began moving in a tantalizing rhythm. She wondered if she was bringing pleasure to her husband correctly. A moan escaped his mouth, and she worried no more as he began to thrust in her mouth with abandon until she pulled away from him. He let out an agonizing groan.

"You cannot finish yet. I'm afraid that is not how the story goes." The bed sank as she moved up his body, straddling him, desperate to take him into her.

Before lowering herself to him, he reached out and stilled her hips. "No."

"No?"

"No. You may be retelling the story, but no story is worth retelling if my wife is without her pleasure first."

The corner of her mouth lifted. José pushed her off him laying her flat against the bed, tracing his lips down to her nipple, circling and sucking, sending her body flinching with each rotation. He departed his task and traveled further down until his mouth was at the apex of her thighs.

"What are you—" but she couldn't finish her sentence. His tongue slid out from those cupid-bow lips and licked up her center until it reached her tiny bud. He paid no mind to her uncontrolled panting, her hands gripping the sheets as he continued to lick in circles filling her body with sensations she never knew existed. In a fit of ecstasy, she moaned—working her hands through his long, thick hair. When she thought she could take no more, two of his fingers thrust inside her. His tongue simultaneously picked up its pace, not letting up until she began to shudder, her hips rubbing against his face out of their own volition. He pulled his fingers from her body and knelt proudly between her legs, his erection glistening at the tip. She lost her breath at the sight of him, his wondrous body, his gorgeous eyes boring into her. At that moment, he became more animal than man. He reached down, stroking himself as his eyes raked over her body.

With courage she couldn't believe she possessed, she grabbed him by the waist, throwing him to the side. Moving to straddle him, she inhaled and exhaled in long steady breaths. His eyes were full of wonder and lust. "Now, it is my turn to bring you to your pleasure." She grasped him, sliding him inside her warmth.

José threw his head back in rapture as she lowed herself to him, his fingers digging into her hips. "*Dios*! You are so tight. You feel too good." She tipped her head back and began moving in the most natural ways. As if her body knew how to bring her husband to his pleasure, her thighs clasped his hips as she rolled to a beat drumming between their bodies that only they could hear. José's body met her every movement. He reached for her throbbing bud at her core, circling it feverishly and sending her over the edge as she tightened around him— shaking as the last of her strength left her body.

Suddenly and without warning, he flipped her on her back, gripping her thighs tightly. He pumped into her over and over until he careened over the edge to his own blissful end, tilting his head back in a loss of control.

Some moments later, after their breathing slowed and their minds slowly came to, he pulled back, looking at her, the sweat glistening from his brow—a smile breaking out on his glorious face. "Remind me to thank Rodrigo for providing you with such an inspiring story."

She laughed heartily and with such joy. José captured her lips as they continued to create stories of their own long into the early morning light.

Chapter 41

José and Joséfa strolled up to the main house in the late afternoon, two days after the wedding. They had spent the previous day with their limbs tangled, lounging in bed in blissful laziness and worshiping each other long into the night, breaking only to eat. José shifted slightly just thinking of it, the intensity coursing through his memory. A smile lifted his lips, thinking of the many days ahead of them just like those.

When they entered the house, they found Armando, Lorena, and Felipe in the sitting room. Rodrigo stood by the window overlooking the grounds. Their attention snapped to them as they entered the room.

"Have you all finally come up for air?" Felipe teased.

A beautiful blush crept up on Joséfa's neck. It made José ache to take her again. Lorena swatted Felipe's arm as he bellowed with laughter. José guided Joséfa to a chair next to Lorena and stood beside her, the rest of the group waiting for the inevitable conversation. José breathed in deeply. "Where would you all like to start?"

"Where ever you feel is best. I'd like to hear how my sister will play into all of this," Armando remarked.

José rested a hand on Joséfa's shoulder. "My *wife* will be making her own decisions on just how involved or not she would like to be. It is up to her discretion." He winked at her, causing a shy smile to appear. "The way I figure it, with Lieutenant Kearny watching my every move, there will be little we can do to broker deals with treasure collectors. I highly doubt I can move an inch without him noticing. He truly has it in for me."

"You mean he has it in for your wife," Rodrigo remarked.

"Hmph. Yes, that much is clear. It's as if he lies in wait to swoop in and take her from me."

"Silly man," Joséfa said, shaking her head. "His efforts would be better spent elsewhere."

"Perhaps it is best for you to have a conversation with him?" Lorena suggested.

"Over my dead body," José bit out.

"I think that's the point," Armando murmured.

José scowled at his brother-in-law. "I don't want Joséfa anywhere near the man."

"Lorena may have a point," Joséfa said. "Perhaps it is best that I speak with him. And don't give me that look, my love. You cannot claim that you would like me to make my own decisions and then turn around a minute later and do the opposite."

José crossed his arms over his chest but remained silent, only nodding his acceptance. "And then after we speak to him? What's the plan then?"

"Dead Bishop's treasure," Rodrigo said, a gleam in his eye.

"By the look on your face, there's no contesting you're a pirate, Rodrigo," Felipe remarked.

Rodrigo smiled slyly. "Just the prospect of attaining this treasure is an adventure. Just think. No one has seen it since…."

"1357," Joséfa said in bewilderment. "But where in the world has it been all this time, and why has it reappeared suddenly?"

"That's an easy one, *Señora Gaspar*. Captain Rodgers is no longer with us, and I assume the vultures are descending on his treasure haven as we speak. We will need to move quickly if we are to have a chance of finding it."

"You think he had it this whole time?" José asked.

"Oh, I know he had it. *Where* was the bigger question."

"And you know where?" Armando asked.

"When you are with a captain as sly as Captain Rodgers, you learn to study his movements during his downtime. The most important movements were *after* a raid. He was very secretive about where he went when he had to lay low. It just so happens that one day he left his map open. I found it curious that he pinned Bermuda. I have a feeling the treasure is there, among other items he may have wanted to keep hidden. We need to know where it is located and who is guarding it. There were more than just a few Rodgers loyalists, to be sure."

"Filthy pirates," Armando seethed. His eyes snapped up to Rodrigo. "Not you. You're not filthy."

Rodrigo cocked a brow. "Uh, thank you?"

"So, who's going after the treasure then?" Armando asked.

"Me, of course." Rodrigo looked over at José. "And you?"

The moment had come, and José still didn't know how to answer. On the one hand, he had his wife and his future. He had enough wealth on his island to sustain his entire lifetime and then some. He glanced at Joséfa, who held her breath, her eyes boring into him. He knew instantly. "I'm afraid I cannot go with you."

"You're sure?" Rodrigo asked with some surprise.

"Yes, I am positive. It's not the right time for another adventure, not with the Lieutenant hot on my heels. Things need to settle." He turned his attention to Joséfa. "And I would very much like to take my wife back to our home and have her appraise what we already have." *And to make love to her senselessly 'til she bares my child.* The thought filled him with warmth. "I'm sure our holdings may interest Mr. Janssen."

"I'm sure he would be *highly* interested. And with Joséfa's appraisal of the items, he'll be even more inclined to bid. He trusts her implicitly," Armando said, a look of pride crossing his features.

"And it appears I will be heading back to Sevilla with Armando and Lorena now that the dust has settled a bit. The ladies of Sevilla are likely missing me," Felipe sighed.

"Who? Your *Mamá* and your *Tía*?" José teased.

"Hah! Well, perhaps them too. My time here has been wonderful, but I am eager to get home."

José realized that these might be the last moments with his best friend, who was more of a brother to him. It saddened him.

"Unfortunately, we will not be traveling back to Sevilla just yet," Armando declared as he reached over and grabbed Lorena's hand, who smiled warmly at him. "We will need to wait for the arrival of our child."

Joséfa gasped. "You're pregnant?" Lorena nodded with tears in her eyes. The room erupted in congratulations. Joséfa leaped for Lorena, encasing her in a tight embrace. Felipe and José patted Armando on the back while Rodrigo poured drinks in celebration. "This calls for a toast!" he exclaimed. "To new beginnings!"

"To new beginnings!" everyone repeated.

Armando smiled widely from ear to ear. "I will speak with Mr. Janssen. Perhaps he would be willing to take you all to the island."

"And the crew and I can take *La Floriblanca* to Bermuda to track down the Dead Bishop's treasure. We'll return when we have it." Rodrigo threw back the rest of his whiskey, placing the empty glass on the bar cart. "I'll need to get back to town to let everyone know the plan and make preparations. If you all would like, I can drop correspondence to Mr. Janssen."

"And Lieutenant Kearny, if you wouldn't mind, Rodrigo. I want to meet him by the docks before we depart," Joséfa said.

"You're sure?" José asked her warily.

She took a deep breath nodding her head. "I'll have you all there with me, just in case. He won't do anything untoward."

"I did teach her how and where to punch a male long before we set sail, Gaspar," Armando assured him. "He couldn't do anything to her even if he tried."

"Lieutenant Kearny is a gentleman. I doubt very highly he would try anything."

"Hhmp. Until he does," José said, absentmindedly grazing his thumb over his bottom lip in thought. "No, I don't think he will either. The prospect of taking you from me one day when he sends me to the bottom of the ocean is too enticing."

Joséfa gasped. "Do not say such things, *mi amor.*"

José smiled gently. "No worries, *mi querida.* He will never be able to get to me." José pondered just how true those words were. It seemed Kearny was determined to have his wife. But at what cost?

Chapter 42

José's vessel, only to be met by an angry lieutenant and all of his men. Quickening steps sounded behind her. She glanced over her shoulder, finding Armando and Felipe hot on their heels, scowls on their faces when they saw Lieutenant Kearny at the bottom of the ramp leading up to *La Floriblanca.*

"Well, let's pray this goes as planned," she murmured.

José gripped her tighter to him, her arm wrapped in his as they walked up to the Lieutenant. Joséfa anticipated his adventurous life bringing some level of excitement. She hadn't expected that it would be as they set sail for his home on a hidden island. *Their* home.

She prepared to greet the guest she invited, but José beat her to it.

"Lieutenant Kearny," José said, bowing slightly at the waist. "Come to wish the newlyweds off?"

He ignored José, turning his attention to Joséfa. "I see you chose to ignore my advice."

"Lawrence," she greeted him. "Thank you for coming on such short notice." She pulled her arm from José's tight grip and stepped toward Kearny, motioning toward a part of the dock that was less occupied. "Might I have a word?"

Lawrence's brow shot up. He briefly glanced at José with a sniveling smile. "But of course."

José's eyes were ice cold as he stared him down. Joséfa squeezed his arm. "It'll be all right," she whispered. She walked forward, taking the awaiting arm of Lieutenant Kearny. She could still feel José's eyes on her back.

"I admit I was surprised to receive your message."

She smiled in what she hoped would be an authentically charming way. "I apologize for getting off the wrong foot, Lieutenant."

"Please, milady. Call me Lawrence."

Joséfa twitched a little at his insistence for such an informality but continued. "Lawrence. I understand your line of work and why it is important. I do not look kindly upon thieves either."

His brows furrowed. "So why on Earth did you marry one?"

She tried dearly not to bite back. *Hold your tongue. Hold your tongue.* Joséfa exhaled slowly. "I married the man I love." She stepped closer to him, looking right into his eyes. He fidgeted slightly with her closeness. Joséfa took a minor delight in that. "I have to insist that you cease your pursuit of him."

"Milady, you do realize he is not the man that you left? The man you rescued is a very different man. He is no longer an Admiral, pardon or not. He cannot offer you a life of worth. He is a changed man."

"Not to me, he isn't. Please. I beg you. Leave us be. Let us live our lives in peace. We are eager to move on from all of this."

He sighed, reaching up to brush a finger across her cheek. She remained stock still despite the urge to move away from his touch. "I can take you away from all of this. I could have the marriage annulled, stating it was pressure from a pirate. I will take good care of you. Give you everything a woman such as yourself deserves. Make you happy."

She shook her head. "You assume that I am not happy."

"How can you be? Look at all the trouble you're going through for him," he protested, nodding in José's direction. She prayed he wouldn't approach them.

"I go through the trouble because I love him. Dearly. And I pray you find the same thing with someone who cares just as much about you one day."

Kearny's face grew red. "The same thing? I didn't know thieving, murdering, whoring, female pirates were a *thing*," he bellowed, causing a few people to turn their attention to them.

Joséfa flinched at his vulgarity and the tone in which he delivered it. A series of footsteps sounded behind her, both Lieutenant Kearny's entourage and her own approaching on swift feet. José placed a hand on her lower back, fuming.

Lieutenant Kearny straightened. "Mr. & Mrs. Gaspar. I'm afraid I am here under orders." He glanced at Joséfa. "Although it is always a pleasure to speak with you. Be sure to consider my offer."

José started forward, but she grabbed him, stopping his progression. "What orders?"

A menacing smirk grew on his face. "I am here to take José Gaspar into custody by order of our Commander in Chief."

"I'm afraid you will not be able to do that, Lieutenant, seeing as how he has been pardoned," Armando called from behind with Felipe firmly at his side. "You seem to have forgotten what soil you are on."

Kearny's lips thinned out. "This does not concern you, Spaniard. Don't you both have some stolen treasure to barter on behalf of your precious treasure hunters?"

"Oh, how original," Felipe remarked with a roll of his eyes. "I will have you know that our business on these waters is honorable. We can have some of our wine exports sent to you before your departure. That way, you know what real wine tastes like." Felipe paused, tapping his chin. "But perhaps you cannot handle such expensive delicacies."

"You think I was born yesterday," Kearny bit out.

"Debatable," Armando murmured.

"I have my eye on this entire group, and one of these days, I will come for you all as well. In the meantime, I am here to take José Gaspar in for his crimes."

"And what crimes would those be?" José asked.

"The crime of killing, thieving," he glanced at Joséfa, "and stealing the maidenhood of a high-born woman."

"How *dare* you," Joséfa hissed.

"Calm down, *mi amor*," he said, patting her hand and looking lovingly at her with all the calm in the world. "If this was anything legitimate, I'm certain the good Lieutenant would have *some* type of paperwork, seeing as how he is here on behalf of," José quirked a brow and faced Kearny, "the Commander in Chief? Seems a bit high ranking for a *thief* like me."

"So, you admit it?"

José leaned in menacingly. "I admit nothing. Where are your papers?"

Lieutenant Kearny shifted from foot to foot, his face reddening with each ticking second. "I have no papers. I need no papers. You, sir, are a criminal."

"I am no such thing, for I have been pardoned."

"Doesn't mean you have changed your stripes, Gaspar."

"My stripes are just fine."

"The hell they are."

"That is enough!" Armando sliced through the tension between the two men pulling them apart before violence ensued. "Lieutenant Kearny, if you do not have any paperwork demanding his arrest, then I will have to ask you to leave them be."

"I do not need paperwork. He is wanted across half the globe."

"I'm afraid that is null, seeing as how the king pardoned him, and you have no power here. It is best that you be on your way."

Kearny stood glaring at José for a few moments before moving his attention to Joséfa. "One day, you will regret ever having married this man. Perhaps it will be the day justice prevails and he meets his end. When that day comes, you will always find a welcome with a man who would appreciate you."

Joséfa lifted her chin, having reached her limit with his advances. "What an incredibly romantic declaration. Quite useless but romantic nonetheless. Perhaps your efforts would be better used toward an *unmarried* woman, Lieutenant, for this one is gladly taken in every way that could possibly count."

Huffing his disapproval, Kearny bumped José's shoulder as he stormed off down the docks, his men following close behind him. The group breathed a collective sigh of relief as he moved further away.

José looked down at Joséfa questioningly. "What is it about you?"

"I'm afraid I don't understand either. It's not as if I have spent any time with the man. I suppose he has been busy creating a narrative about me in his head."

"I don't quite get it either," Armando chimed in. "I mean, she's no Helen of Troy."

Joséfa swatted her brother's arm. "Oh, hush. That wasn't very nice."

"He's right, though," José interjected. "You are no Helen of Troy."

Her mouth dropped in shock. "That's just—"

"Helen of Troy could not compare to your beauty," he said, leaning down to kiss her. She lost herself in his kiss, which José had never dared to do in public before.

"That's quite enough, you two," Armando huffed. "The honeymoon is over."

José pulled back slightly. "Who said it ever ended?" He brought his lips to hers again.

"Thank God I am on a different ship," Felipe exclaimed as he walked down the dock.

PART IV

The
Crossroads
&
Karma Driven
Illusions

CHAPTER 43

MR. JANSSEN BREATHED IN THE WARM, SALTY SEA AIR, A SMILE unlike any other upon his face as they stood on the shore. "Aaaahh! There's nothing quite like the open sea to reinvigorate the soul."

"I don't know that the open sea reinvigorates the soul as much as it reinvigorates the contents of my stomach," said Joséfa, looking a bit peaky as she carefully put one foot in front of the other.

The warm, powder-fine sand sank between José's toes as they made their way up the beach. The sun's afternoon rays bit into his skin, warming him with every step. The palm trees in the distance looked the same as he had left them. A few fishermen stood in the shallow waters in the distance down the shore, additional occupants to the island a new occurrence upon his return. José rubbed circles on Joséfa's back as he pondered who they might be. "I'm sure you'll start feeling better soon, *mi querida.*" The days at sea were long and challenging, with Joséfa not taking to the Caribbean waters quite the way she had taken to the Atlantic. Her demeanor was a little worse for wear. It relieved him that she would finally have a place to lie down that didn't make her seasick. They walked toward the pathway just through the trees, hands interlaced.

A curvy woman with a long dark skirt and a white tunic made her way down the pathway from the houses deep on the island, smiling brightly. José smiled in return when the woman's dark brown skin and hair bundled on top of her head came into view. She began jogging toward him, laughing.

"Gaspar! *Finalment regresaste.*"

José let go of Joséfa's hand, wrapping his arms around her in a deep embrace. "*Señora Perez*, it is so good to see you."

She pulled back, looking him over with motherly care, her brow furrowing. "We will need to make sure to fatten you up. You are looking too skinny."

José laughed joyously. "You always say that."

"Because I speak the truth." She glanced to his side, smiling, when she noticed Joséfa standing there—her face a display of pure curiosity.

José reached for Joséfa's hand, looking at her with a sense of pride growing in his chest. "*Señora Perez.* I would like you to meet Joséfa Mayorga Gaspar, my wife." Joséfa blushed deeply. He would never grow tired of seeing it.

Señora Perez's mouth dropped open, her gaze darting between José and Joséfa. She thrust her hands toward the heavens and then clapped like a child. "*Ave Maria purisima!* You are married. Thank the good Lord." She reached for Joséfa, kissed each cheek, and hugged her tightly.

Joséfa giggled with the onslaught. "It is a pleasure to meet you, *Señora Perez.*"

"Please. Call me Elena." Just as she had with José, she appraised Joséfa. "You are looking a little pale, *mija.* I take it the trip was difficult?"

Joséfa's shoulders sagged. "Very."

Elena nodded in understanding, gently squeezing Joséfa's hand in her own. "Very well. Let's get you some tea to settle your stomach and something warm to eat."

"Elena," José interrupted, motioning behind him. "This is Mr. Janssen. He is responsible for helping us arrive here."

Mr. Janssen bowed to Elena. "*Mucho gusto, Señora Perez.*"

She bowed to Mr. Janssen. "*Encantado de conocerte.*" Elena glanced behind Mr. Janssen. "*Y Rodrigo?*"

José fixed his gentle gaze upon her in understanding. "Rodrigo is with *La Floriblanca*. I'm afraid he will be gone a little longer."

Elena nodded, looking slightly disappointed but then quickly redeemed herself. "I take it we will be hosting quite a few of your men?" She beamed at Mr. Janssen. "How many rooms should I prepare?"

"I'm sure the crew would be happy to stay on the ship."

Elena *tsked*. "Nonsense, it is my honor to take care of you and your men. They are all welcome here. There is plenty of room. Plenty of food. They will stay in the cottages built for the crews."

"Cottages for the crews?" José asked curiously.

Elena gave him a mischievous smile. She quickly glanced at Mr. Janssen, unsure how much to reveal but proceeding when José gave her an encouraging nod. "I made the coin you provided us stretch quite a bit. You said to keep things going while you all were gone. And I also made sure to vet every living, breathing being that came through trying to settle on Gasparilla Island. Rest assured. Everyone who is living here is contributing and is sworn to secrecy. I made sure of it."

José was taken aback. "Did you say Gasparilla Island?"

"*Sí.* That is what I have named it. It is in your honor," Elena beamed. "It is better than *Rodrigorilla*. That would be a mouthful, and Rodrigo would not want it."

José laughed heartily. "Fair enough. It seems like you have the whole island in order." José grinned. "Why does this not surprise me?"

Elena smiled with pride. She motioned for the group to follow. "Come. I will show you the new grounds, settle you all in, and get you that tea I promised. And tonight, we will feast in honor of your nuptials."

"Sounds delightful! I do love a good celebration. And I have just the drink to make it memorable." Mr. Janssen beamed. "My men and I will be right behind you all. We need to fetch our goods from the ship," Mr. Janssen said as he returned to his crew. José nodded, threading his hand in Joséfa's as they made their way up the path. His heart suddenly kicked in his chest as he realized this would be the first time she would lay eyes on the world he had built. He kept sneaking glances at her as they ventured through the trail, the palms occasionally blocking them like a curtain covering a new world in wait.

She looked at him then. "What is it?"

He smiled. "I only dared to dream of you on this island. I never thought you would make it here."

She gave him a knowing smile in return, squeezing his hand. The last of the palms cleared, and José gasped. It appeared Elena was far busier than he could have ever anticipated. A row of small, well-built cottages greeted them. José counted fourteen of them built in a circle around a roaring fire. Chickens were scattered around the area. A pathway led to even grander houses that lay beyond the trees—the homes of Rodrigo, Chino, and John Gómez just beyond. José imagined more were added. "Elena, how on Earth did you do all of this?"

Elena radiated with pride. "Well, I will not lie to you and say it was easy work. It took many trips to Spanishtown Creek just around the way. I procured the men and supplies we needed to build such a town. With the war turmoil, they were more than happy to settle here away from all the racket."

"And you went on your own?"

Elena's brow rose. "Yes, on my own with some of the crew you left behind, of course.

"But the crew I left behind was injured or too old to take to the waters."

"Yes?"

"You could have been robbed!"

"*Sí?*"

"Or beaten!"

"Possibly."

From the corner of his eyes, José saw Joséfa hide her laughter behind her hand. "You could have been killed!"

"Oh, *si*?" She leaned a little closer to José. "I would have loved to see them try to take me down." She turned toward the cottages. José shook his head in disbelief. Elena provided them with a quick tour of the small cottages and the new grounds. A small river ran toward the back, where several women were washing clothing.

Joséfa's face carried nothing but wonder and astonishment. "This is amazing."

He chuckled. "Indeed, it is."

She glanced around. "Is our home near?"

José relished in the "our" portion of her question, loving how it sounded. He opened his mouth to answer when Mr. Janssen made it through the clearing behind them.

"*Señora* Gaspar. My men have the trunk you requested from the ship. Where would you like them to take it?"

Joséfa looked at José in question. "I'll lead the way," he answered.

On the opposite side of the campfire, away from the other path that led to the larger houses on the other side of the island, was a pathway leading to José's home. It took them a good few minutes to walk down the path, with Mr. Janssen's crew pausing every few steps and catching their breath, laboring with the weight of the trunk. José gave it a quizzical look. "Whatever did you bring?"

"It is a wedding present."

"A wedding present?" He leaned down, placing a gentle kiss on her lips. "I do not need such presents. You are enough."

She smiled warmly. "You will like this one. I promise."

With a few more paces, they reached a clearing, and Joséfa gasped. "*Dios mio.*"

José's nerves racked his body. "Do you like it?"

"Oh, it is wonderful, José. I had not expected it."

José guided her up the steps to the front door opening it and ushering her inside. The smell of dust and warmth enveloped them. The light of the fading day cast its light on the living area through the glass doors toward the back of the home.

"This is quite lovely!" Mr. Janssen called from behind them. "Shall we leave the trunk in the vestibule, Mrs. Gaspar?"

"Yes, please. Thank you so much for bringing it all this way."

Mr. Janssen bowed. "It was my pleasure. I look forward to spending time with you all at the celebration." He glanced back at his men in the entryway. "I'm sure my men are eager to return to the cottages and get some rest before they begin. I will leave the newlyweds be."

"Thank you, Mr. Janssen," said José.

"Not a worry. I look forward to talking about all things treasure with you later. Enjoy." With that, he turned around and left them in blessed silence.

Joséfa slowly walked around the room, taking in all the details. Her fingers touched the little trinkets on display on wooden shelving decorating the main wall of the sitting room. "He's right, you know," she said while observing.

He placed his hands in his pockets, slowly strolling her way. "Right about what?"

"The house truly is lovely."

José smiled. "I hoped you would like it. After all, I did build it with you in mind."

Her gaze met his. "That pleases me."

"I'm glad to hear that it does." He moved behind her, wrapping his arms gently around her waist. "Somehow, I knew you would explore the moment you entered the room. It's why I have these items on display. Each one of these items tells a story. I hoped you would take each of them in. My smart, incredible woman who always seems to know more than anyone about history."

She turned in his arms. "You flatter me."

"I speak the truth." His thumb traveled over the contours of her prominent cheekbone. "You are amazing, *mi vida*. I am so honored to have you here with me." He traced small circles on her cheek. "You must be tired. Do you want to rest for a while?"

She sighed. "I do. But there is something I wanted to give you first." She went toward the trunk Mr. Janssen's men had left at the front of the room and turned to him shyly. "Will you open this? I have been desperate for you to open it…well…for a while now. I figured this would be the perfect wedding gift."

Curiously, José moved to the trunk glancing at Joséfa for permission. When she nodded, he bent down, opened the latch, and gasped—tears suddenly blurring his vision. Inside the trunk lay row after row of books, his father's books from the library in his home in Sevilla. "I never thought I would see these again." Joséfa crouched down beside him rubbing slow circles across his back. He grabbed one of the books dusting off the spine and smiled.

"This one was his favorite."

"I made sure to take the trunk with me everywhere I traveled. You once told me that you can learn a lot about a person by the books they read."

José wiped his eyes with the back of his free hand. "It is true. It's as if a part of their soul is embedded within the book's pages. If they do not keep a book, they mustn't have cared enough to keep it. Literature calls to the soul. It can be the simplest line, but something calls us to it. I used to find solace in combing through these books multiple times, thinking, 'What lesson is my father trying to teach me?' and then rereading it to ensure I interpreted his message."

"Like trying to hear his voice through the pages?" she asked.

"Precisely." He moved his hand across the other books, reading the titles as he went. "It's as if those who love us are leaving behind pieces of them. These authors spoke to him, moved him, and made him laugh. Perhaps they helped him escape the world around him, if only for a few hours." He looked at Joséfa, his heart bursting. He reached up, placing a stray hair behind her ear. "Thank you. Thank you so much. You have no idea how much this means to me."

She leaned into his palm closing her eyes. "It was a lucky guess."

He chuckled, kissing her once before lifting her to her feet.

"Come. Let us rest for a bit." He took her hand, leading her to a staircase tucked in a hallway to the left, and ascended the stairs. Three doors decorated the hallway. José moved to the door directly in front of them, opening it to reveal a brightly lit room with the last of the sun's rays pouring in. The featherlight white drapes danced in the wind of the open windows. Elena, sneaky as she is, must have found someone to tidy up and open the space. The room was immaculately clean. The four-poster bed lay to the right, large and inviting—sheets clean and crisp. José guided Joséfa to the bed. He freed her tunic from her skirt, pulling the hem over her head. Her eyelids dropped, her eyes hooded. José kissed her softly. "Don't get any ideas, wife. You need to get your rest." He helped her remove her shoes and skirts, leaving her in her stays as he pulled back the sheets for her.

José made his way to the other side of the bed, placing his father's book on the neighboring nightstand. Propping a pillow against the headboard, he rested his shoeless feet on the bed and began to read as Joséfa's light snores reached his ears. He chuckled lightly. *I knew she would be asleep within minutes.* As she slept, he passed the time looking for hidden treasures within the pages of his father's favorite book.

Chapter 44

The bedroom was bathed in a warm light emanating from the right side of the bed, coupled with the moonlight streaming in from the window. Joséfa's gaze traveled to the source of the light finding José leafing through the pages of one of his father's books. He wore a fresh tunic and pants—his long, dark hair tied back off his neck. "Did you not rest?" she asked, voice raspy in waking.

José startled momentarily, relaxing when his eyes met hers. "I couldn't sleep, so I decided to pass the time reading." He brushed escaped hairs out of her eyes.

"And did you learn anything?"

"Oh yes."

Joséfa propped her head up on her hand. "Well?"

"Well, my father was nothing but intuitive if what I'm reading is correct. He left the lightest of marks on one of the lines on a page." He flipped back a few pages and began reading, *"Tyranny is not a matter of minor theft and violence, but of wholesale plunder, sacred and profane, private or public. If you are caught committing such crimes in detail, you are punished and disgraced; sacrilege, kidnapping, burglary, fraud, theft are the names we give to such petty forms of wrongdoing. But when a man succeeds in robbing the whole body of citizens and reducing them to slavery, they forget these ugly names and call him happy and fortunate, as do all others who hear of his unmitigated wrongdoing.*" José closed the book, shaking it slightly in the air. "Plato…"

"*Republic,*" she supplied. "Yes, I remember reading it a few years back."

"I would be lying if I said a chill didn't crawl down my spine reading it." He sighed. "I do not know if it excuses my wrong-doings or points out that those in power are just as guilty of committing the same crimes as those without it."

"Smart man, your father."

"*Si.* I miss him very much."

Joséfa reached out, squeezing his hand gently. The sound of distant laughter traveled through the open window. Joséfa bolted upright. "Oh, dear. Have we missed the celebration?"

He rubbed her arms. "*No te precupes.* Do not worry yourself, *mi amor.* While you were sleeping, Mr. Janssen's men dropped off more of your trunks. Elena took the liberty of placing some of your items in the washroom just down the hall, along with some heated water and soap for bathing. There's no rush. Afterall, the festivities are for us. We can afford to be casually late."

Joséfa leaped from the bed. "I will be quick about it." She entered the washroom down the hall after trying a few doors. A charming room greeted her, her clothes laid out with everything she might need to clean herself. After taking a few moments to indulge in washing the grime off her body, she dressed and made her way down the stairs. José sat on an armchair reading another one of his father's books. Joséfa couldn't help but smile. "Are you ready, my love?"

He looked up from his book, carefully taking in her dress. "You look beautiful," Placing the book on the neighboring table, he rose and enveloped her in a warm embrace. "I will never tire of holding you."

"And I will never tire of having you in my arms," she sighed, "but we need to make it to the festivities before the sun rises."

José pulled back, giving Joséfa his arm. "Shall we?"

The moonlight lit the trail, guiding them to the center of their wayward village. A lively group of sailors, fishermen and women greeted them—one of which was Elena rotating the pig roasting in the fire. Off to the side, a woman surrounded by laughing men handed out ale with a smile on her face seeming happy to make their fill. Mr. Janssen sat on a stump, bobbing his head back and forth to the rhythm of the fiddler who played by the firelight. A man drummed away beside him, matching the fiddler beat for beat. Everyone seemed happy—dancing and clapping away.

Elena looked up from her tasks. "Gaspar!"

Everyone noticed them at the head of the trail that led to their house. A collective cheer rose from the festive little group, and they were suddenly steered toward the fire to two tree stumps that sat side by side. Ale was placed in each of their hands. Elena appeared before them, cupping her hands on either side of their cheeks. "You all will want for nothing this evening. If you need anything, you just say the word."

José began laughing. "This is too much, Elena."

"Bah! This is what I live for. You wouldn't rob a woman of what pleases her, would you?" she smiled.

José's eyes gleamed. "I wouldn't dare."

"Then leave me to it." With that, she turned on a heel and walked away, dancing as she went.

Everyone sang, danced, and laughed. The ale began to course through Joséfa's veins—her body seemingly lighter and carefree. She danced with the other women by the fire, the music infecting her with a freedom she had never felt before. She closed her eyes, tilting them up to the sky, and when she opened them, she found her husband staring at her—his piercing gaze taking in every tantalizing movement of her body. She sauntered over to him and sat firmly on his lap without a concern for propriety. "Do you like what you see, my love?"

"Mmmm. Very much." He reached up, brushing her hair back from her face. "I've never seen you so carefree."

Joséfa froze. "Is it too much?"

José shook his head. "No, no. Never. I mean that as a compliment. I wish to see more of this side of you."

She tilted her head back to the moon. "It is as if I'm coming alive for the first time." She glanced around then, taking in all the people. Some of the women sat on the laps of gentlemen as she did with José. Other men played cards on tree stumps serving as tables and chairs around the grounds. Elena sat next to Mr. Janssen, laughing as he told her a tale with vibrant enthusiasm—her laughter making Joséfa smile.

"Tell me what you are thinking," José inquired.

José's thumb traveled back and forth over her upper arms, sending shivers down her body. "I think I may find myself happier here than in all my days in Sevilla."

José seemed taken aback by her declaration. "Truly?"

"Yes." Joséfa gestured around them. "Can you imagine anything like this happening at one of our balls or galas we used to attend?" She scoffed. "I certainly cannot."

He chuckled. "No, neither can I."

"Look how joyous these men and women are," she continued, the ale seeming to encourage thoughts to flow from her mouth. "When we were growing up, it seemed like most of the adults in the room were busy trying to posture themselves for some monetary or political gain, never truly revealing themselves to anyone—not even their own families. Does it make you wonder if we even knew them at all?" She looked down, finding José's eyes on her, stunned.

"I never thought I would hear you say such things, but it pleases me that you are so open-minded." José pointed to a woman just across the way, with bright red hair that flicked with deeper hues in the firelight, pale skin, and a bright smile as she admired the fiddler playing just a few feet away. "That there is Esmeralda. On one of our voyages, we discovered that her husband was hitting her violently night after night. He wasn't taking care of her, so she turned to prostitution to keep

food on the table. Sometimes, her bruises were still visible. But still, she worked."

Joséfa's snapped her eyes to him.

"No, not me. Rodrigo," he answered, sensing her question. Her shoulders slumped slightly. "But I digress. We decided to help her escape, having found her bloody and near death one evening. We took her on *La Diosa Ardiente* in the middle of the day when her husband was away doing Lord knows what and helped her escape here." José nodded in front of him. "See the other women on this island? They all have a similar story. Not all of them were prostitutes. Some are just poor, trying to survive. Widows. Friends who became lovers."

She glanced at him again. "Yours?"

He shook his head. "No. I will not lie. There were many times when I was tempted." He dipped his head shyly. "I am a man after all, and being away from you, knowing that you would have been my wife already, I would have taken you as mine, killed me inside." He looked up at her. "But I held on to faith, hoping I would see you again." His thumb traced her lower lip. "It was your face, only your face, I thought of when I brought myself to pleasure."

Joséfa felt heat rise between her legs. She looked away. "I wouldn't have blamed you if you did. It wasn't like I didn't know you had lovers in Sevilla."

"Look at me." She did—his eyes fierce. "When you said yes to being my wife at *El Palacio* all those years ago, I knew there would never be another for me." They sat there for a long moment. He sighed. "Did you?"

"Did I what?"

"Did you…well. Given that I did take your maidenhead, I know I am your first lover," he said thoughtfully, "but did you entertain taking on another man as your husband?"

Joséfa laughed heartily. "Have you met my brother?"

José's lips thinned into a grim line. "Good point."

"He even tried to have me marry Felipe."

José's eyes widened. "That bastard."

"I said no, of course."

"And you said no to every other man who also courted you?"

She reached up, placing an unruly strand of hair behind his ear. "When I said yes to being your wife at *El Palacio* all those years ago, I knew there would never be another for me."

He kissed her fiercely, making the heat rise in other parts of her body. He pulled back, placing his forehead against hers. "Come, wife. I think it's time we made our way home."

"But everyone is still celebrating."

"And they will continue to celebrate long into the night. I want our own celebration. Just you and me." He stood up, pulling her to her feet and taking her hand in his. They walked into the darkness down the trail to their home, leaving the rest of the island to their festivities.

CHAPTER 45

JOSÉFA AND JOSÉ WATCHED MR. JANSSEN'S SHIP FADE INTO THE horizon—the sea breeze, tinged with salt and the smell of fish, carried heavily on the winds as Joséfa leaned back in José's arms, wound tightly around her. "I would say he enjoyed his time here."

"To be sure. He certainly looked more relaxed here than I have ever seen him. He is a good man," José mused. "I feel terrible about how I treated him when I met him at the ball."

Joséfa leaned further into José's chest, sighing. "I am sure he has forgiven you. He doesn't seem to hold a grudge about it."

"Lucky for me. I'm sure the fact that I have many items he may be interested in has something to do with it.

Joséfa laughed, her fingers tracing idle circles on José's arm. "Yes, perhaps you are right. I'm sure Mr. Janssen will not be gone for long. He seemed very interested in the items you mentioned to him. I'm sure he would be keen to procure them."

"Yes, he did have a gleam in his eye when I showed him some of my treasure. Of course, I didn't show him *everything*."

She turned around in his arms, looking up at him. "You speak a lot about these treasures. I'm dying to know what they are."

He leaned down, kissing the tip of her nose. "I will show you everything in due time. Besides, I guarantee you know more about its history than I do." He moved his hands down her arms, twining his fingers in hers. "But right now, I want to sit and admire the sunset with you." José pulled her down to the blanket on the sand, a knapsack of items Elena was kind enough to pack for them sitting on top. Despite all the time they spent together in *Puerto Rico* and their journey across the sea together, they barely spoke of the difficult time apart. Joséfa was bound and determined to discover more, whether the stories of this time were good…or bad.

She made herself comfortable between José's legs as they gazed out at sea, José placing his hands in the sand behind them to prop them up. "You rarely talk about the time with Captain Rodgers." She felt José stiffen behind her.

"There isn't much to talk about. It isn't something I wish to relive."

"Fair enough. What about the time without Captain Rodgers? You mentioned a period when you and your crew needed to disappear."

"Actually, we came here. That is how this whole island started."

"But you didn't stay here the whole time?"

"No, we didn't." José paused for a moment. "Captain Rodgers was a deeply disturbed individual. Most of this you knew already, but I wasn't going to place my life in his hands if I could help it. So, Rodrigo and some of his crew's most trustworthy members decided to take matters into our own hands with the money we had acquired. We bought a ship."

Joséfa turned to face him. "You bought a ship." She looked around the shore. "But where ever is it?"

José laughed. "We do not keep it here. First, we didn't want to risk exposing our new venture to Captain Rodgers and some of his more loyal companions, and second, we didn't want to bring too much attention to Gasparilla Island. This was our sanctuary, after all. We keep the ship in the neighboring Spanishtown Creek. That is also where we go for goods and such. I will take you there soon. Beautiful town, Spanishtown Creek.

It has one of the most breathtaking bays. The waters are rougher than the Guadalquivir, but it reminds me of being on the water in Sevilla nonetheless."

She sighed. "Do you miss home?"

He kissed the top of her head. "Wherever you are is home to me."

A smile broke across her face. "What about the people, the food?"

"Sshhh. Let's not mention the food, or I might reconsider my feelings on the matter."

Joséfa giggled. "Very well then. Going back to your ship. What is the name of it?"

"*La Diosa Ardiente*."

"Ah, yes. I remember you mentioning it the other evening. It is quite a name."

"I hope it is. I named it after you."

"After me?" she asked incredulously.

José laughed as he held her a little tighter. "It is perfectly fitting. You are, after all, my Fiery Goddess. I've never encountered a woman quite like you before. Strong, independent, fiery. It's the perfect name for a ship."

"Good heavens. Please tell me that I'm not depicted half-naked on the bow of your ship.

"My mother told me never to lie."

Joséfa buried her face in her hands. "Oh, dear."

"Relax, my love. I only tease. We bought the ship from a merchant, woman on the bow be damned. We were pressed for time and needed to take the seas if we wanted our plan to work."

"Your plan? You mean robbing ships?"

"That is the life of a pirate, my dear."

Joséfa nodded. "Did you hurt anyone, José?"

He sighed heavily. "I will not lie to you and tell you that I never killed anyone to pursue the treasure we wanted. But I will tell you that I tried my best to injure and not kill. And I never ever threatened any women or children on board. That was Captain Rodgers' style, and I left it to him to hold that reputation.

"By the time we had our third raid, rumors circulated about the *El Pirata de la Misericordia*. I tried to exercise mercy as often as possible to live up to that name. A few men here and there refused to stand down. I made their deaths as quick as possible."

Joséfa didn't know what to make of it. She understood he had to do what he did to survive. He had no knowledge of the pardon or that they were searching for him. "Did you ever doubt we would come for you?"

"I knew you would never stop trying, but the years passed. I did give up hope. It was another reason I had to secure this life as a pirate and make the most of it.

"And what kind of items did you procure?" she asked. "They couldn't all be a treasure."

"Some were a treasure. Those were the ships we knew Captain Rodgers had his eyes on. We wanted to make sure to get to those before he did. But the other ships were merchant ships, much like your brother's, carrying goods across the seas." He breathed deeply and moved his hand up and down her arm. "Is this hard to hear? Do you think any less of me?"

"It bothers me, but I understand why you had to do it." She wrung her hands together. "It would bother me more if you continued to do it."

"You know, eventually, I will go out again."

"To what end, José? You know Lieutenant Kearny is out there right now, lying in wait for you. Why give him a reason?"

"We will handle Kearny."

Joséfa exhaled slowly. "Perhaps we should move on to other topics."

José leaned down, bringing his mouth to her ear. 'What other topics would you like to explore?" He took her earlobe between his teeth, biting down gently and licking it afterward for good measure.

She slapped him on the thigh. "Not that kind of exploration, Captain Gaspar."

He tightened his hold around her. "Perhaps I should take you inside and show you my secret room."

"Secret room?"

"Yes, the one with all the treasure I spoke to you about. You did want to see it, didn't you?"

Joséfa turned to face him, wide-eyed. "I'm surprised that wasn't the first thing you showed me."

"Oh, I had other priorities to show you first," he said, bringing his lips to hers. She relished the moment, a tingly sensation traveling to her core. His hand traveled up her thighs, the tips of his fingers tracing small circles across her flesh, her face flushing. "Perhaps I can remind you of those priorities." His fingers traced their way across her wet heat, evidence of her need for him. The tips of his fingers traced circles on her sensitive nub. She arched in his hold, her lips finding his.

"José," she breathed. "Someone will see us."

He continued his mission, causing her breath to catch, her release building. "This is *my* world," he whispered against her lips. "Let them watch my Queen unravel for her King."

She could hardly think. She buried her face in his neck as his fingers worked faster, her moans vibrating against his skin. She could feel the length of him on her thigh. Joséfa went over the edge, her hips pumping against his hand, his mouth coming to hers—her mouth catching his groan. "You are so beautiful," he whispered. "I will never get enough of you. Ever."

Joséfa could say nothing as she lay in his arms, coming back into her body. After a few quiet moments, José caressing her with a reverence heavy in his eyes, he stood, bringing her to her feet. Her legs wobbled as they regained their strength. "Come. Let me show you our treasure."

Joséfa packed their items in a daze and followed him up the path to their home. José's actions had made her mind dizzy, leaving words left unsaid. She would never get enough of him either, but if he continued down the path of piracy, she feared these moments would be few.

CHAPTER 46

José took the items from her hands as they entered their home and placed them on the sofa in their sitting room. He guided her toward the long hallway just off the stairs to the upper rooms. The dim light from the sconces set periodically on the walls cast their shadows upon the panels as they proceeded to a bookcase lined with books and trinkets sitting at the end of the hall. José grabbed a lamp on one of the shelves and lit it. He glanced behind her, his eyes scanning. Casting his glance down at her, his face grew serious. "What I'm about to show you, no one save Rodrigo and myself has laid eyes upon. You must never tell anyone about this room. That is for your safety and the safety of everyone here. Swear it to me."

She nodded vigorously. "I swear it."

He turned back to the bookshelf, focusing on the corner of the middle shelf. With great force, he pulled on something not visible to Joséfa's eye, and the bookshelf suddenly creaked open like a door. José held the lamp before them as they entered the darkness beyond. He ushered her in front of him, reaching for the bookshelf again and closing it. José made his way around the room as if he knew it by heart, lighting lamps as he went. As the light began pouring into the room, her astonishment grew— her mouth falling open and her breathing nearly coming to a stop. Before her stood a narrow space that ran the length of the house. In the back corner, gold coins, cups, gems, and other items of worth beyond her wildest comprehension lay in a pile several feet long and as high as her waist. Her gaze drifted to the right side of the room, which held shelf after shelf of golden crucifixes, cups, small ornate boxes lavishly decorated, tiaras—all manors of treasure. She could only imagine their worth.

Her eyes moved to the center of the room, where a long wooden table lay with various maps scattered on its surface. She walked toward them, moving her hands upon one to flatten it out. Various markings decorated the map in specific spots all over the area that surrounded their island. The detail upon it was breathtaking.

Joséfa hardly acknowledged José until he wrapped a hand around her waist from behind. "Say something," he whispered, his breath hitting her ear.

She huffed incredulously. "I can barely breathe, let alone speak." She turned to face him. "You've been busy."

He smiled, reaching to move his thumb over her cheek. "You could say that."

Something just behind José in the shape of a book wrapped in parchment caught her eye. Curious, she moved around José and reached for the object. Turning it in her hand, she found a single letter 'D' marked upon it. She turned it around a few times but found nothing else save the light roping crisscrossed upon it. She glanced at José, seeing him with arms crossed at his chest, a smirk on his face. She returned to staring at the 'D' when it dawned on her. She gasped, turning wide eyes to José. "There's only one missing treasure with this exact type of description." She pointed the 'D.' "Tell me this is what I think it is?"

He leaned in. "It's not what you think it is," he teased.

"José, people have been looking for this all over. However, did you come by it?"

José held his arms up and slowly whirled around. "Notice anything different about this room?"

She took in her surroundings again and noticed what she hadn't when entering, likely due to the enormous pile of distractions. The wood in the room was far older than the rest of the house. The panels behind the shelving were worn, the floorboards cracked in various places, and a thin layer of dirt scattered among the aging grains of wood. A window sat among the shelving, encased by a wooden wall just beyond it. "You built the house around the missing cabin of Amaro Pargo."

José nodded with a smile on his face. "I knew you would figure it out."

Her eyes moved to the other corner of the room, finding a chest with a carved pattern—*the* chest with the carved pattern. She held the book to her chest and moved toward it. Bending down, she traced the patterns with the tips of her fingers, the dust coming away with them as she trailed along. "It is as he had described in his will," she said in astonishment.

She heard José's footsteps slowly make their way across the room; the crunch of the sand and dirt sounded from beneath his feet. "Open it," he commanded.

Joséfa did as he asked, opening the chest without delay, the smell of dust and time hitting her nostrils with a flourish. José bent down with the lamp to help her see what lay inside. She placed a hand on her mouth to keep from gasping, her eyes unblinking. Silver, stones, diamonds, pearls, and some of the most beautiful gold jewelry she had ever seen lay before her, winking in the lamplight as if greeting her hello. "I cannot believe my eyes."

José's hand rubbed gentle circles on her back. "Believe it, my love. When I told you I had items I wanted to identify, this is what I meant. And this is just part of it. Everything in this room goes beyond the missing treasure chest of Amaro Pargo. There are items here no one has been able to find because…well…I found it before they could."

Joséfa's face suddenly felt cold. "I think I'm going to faint."

José quickly placed the lantern on the floor, grabbed Joséfa under the arms, and hoisted her up, cradling her to his chest. He walked her over to the table and gently sat her on it. He held her face in his hands, looking lovingly into her eyes. "Breathe, darling. Just breathe."

She nodded, closing her eyes, inhaling, exhaling—the drumming of her heartbeat decreasing with every breath.

"There you are. Just breathe." His hands moved over her hair, repeating their journey in soothing strokes.

When her nerves were finally calmed to the point of talking, she demanded. "Explain. I need to know how this happened."

José backed away and began pacing, his hands together behind his back. She gripped the edge of the table for support. "Pargo's will described a cabin. Most would assume this to be a cabin used for hunting or something similar. His family, treasure hunters, and half of *España* looked for his home, his hidden cave. As you very well know, none of them were ever able to find the chest. But it dawned on me that the man spent considerable time as a privateer in these waters obtaining silver and gold for the king of Spain. Why wouldn't the cabin be here? It would make sense. If I had a vast treasure of this size, I highly doubt I would bring it where it might be seized. Pargo was rumored to be an intelligent man. He, too, would have been very wary of bringing all of his fortunes with him.

"That thought was heavy on my mind when Rodrigo and I began looking for an island to hide our own treasures. As luck would have it, we discovered a cabin hidden here. When we entered, we found it decorated with little means for multiple people. A rug worn and dusted with time sat just under that table you are sitting on. It was a very nice rug which we found a little odd for such a small cabin in the woods. Call it intuition, but to this day, I'm still not sure what compelled me. I decided to lift the rug. Under it was a small door with a latch. When I lifted it, I was greeted with the chest. I still had no idea whose it was until I unwrapped the bindings of the parchment-wrapped book and read it with my own eyes." He chuckled. "I was just as astonished as you were."

"Rodrigo insisted that I build my house around the cabin and keep it hidden. He had no interest in guarding such a treasure and had his own to tend to anyway. He truly is the best first mate a captain could ask for. Any other man would have slit my throat on the spot. It is why I trust him implicitly and why I promised always to protect him and his kin. We decided to create that future here on this island so that all of our descendants can live and prosper."

José moved toward her, standing just beyond her knees. "We made a vow never to reveal the source of our vast income. We couldn't sell all the items for fear that someone would discover that we had found the lost treasure. We found someone trustworthy who we pay handsomely to melt some of the more recognizable items. Most of the other items we plan to sell to the highest bidder. And that's where you come in."

She shook her head, laughing. "You are mad if you think I can sell a single piece of the Amaro Pargo chest without being discovered.

"*Mi amor*, some of those items will have to be broken down."

"You cannot possibly!"

"We have to. For me to back away from the life I was thrust into and to provide for our family, we have to."

"But those are priceless treasures, José."

He cupped her face in his hands. "No. Those are just objects. *You* are priceless. Our future children are priceless. Our life together is priceless. Do not confuse the two."

Resigned, she tilted her head into his palm. "Perhaps Mr. Janssen is an option."

He smiled brightly. "Mr. Janssen is just one of many, my love. I have no doubt you will know what to sell and to whom at the appropriate time. You have my complete faith."

She placed her hand over his. "Very well."

"Yes?"

"Yes. Under one condition." The smile on José's face fell. "I want you to promise me that there will be an end to your piracy."

His hands dropped to the table on either side of her thighs. He looked pensively down at his boots. "I cannot promise I will stop tomorrow." He looked up at her then, determination in his gaze. "When I exit, I will do it on my terms and in a way I know will protect us. You must trust me on this."

Joséfa knew there was no further arguing on the matter by the way his brows furrowed, by the set in his shoulders. "I trust you. And I trust you will know what to do." She leaned forward, placing her lips upon his, sealing her vow. They proceeded to further their creed by making love on the long wooden table, maps be damned.

CHAPTER 47

SEVERAL MONTHS LATER...

JOSÉFA BECAME ACCUSTOMED TO HER LIFE ON THEIR LITTLE IS-
land. The constant chores—crops that needed tending, animals
that needed feeding, rooms that required a woman's touch in
their home—became oddly therapeutic to her. Even as she
gathered vegetables with Elena in the garden meant for their entire little village, she embraced the slight pain in her lower back
with a smile as she soaked up the rays of the afternoon sun. The
meals they ate provided so much more meaning and satisfaction
when prepared by her hand for her beloved.

In addition to the caretaking she had grown so fond of, she
spent endless hours notating all of José's wealth, developing a
strategy for how they may secure their future. She remained in
awe of the priceless items and the privilege of having them at
her disposal.

She was jolted from her reverie by the shouts of one of the
fishermen coming up the path. "*La Floriblanca* is back!"

Elena and Joséfa exchanged a glance, immediately setting
their baskets on the ground and making for the shore. It was no
surprise when they found José already there, observing his old
ship with a frown, his arms crossed at his chest.

"What is it?"

"I don't like the look of the ship. Something is wrong."

Joséfa placed a hand on her brow to block out the sun. Sure enough, there were deep, black areas riddled on the side of the ship. "What do you believe happened?"

"It could be any number of things, but my instincts tell me they were met with resistance, either while retrieving Captain Rodgers' items or on their return trip." He sighed. "Perhaps both."

Joséfa glanced at him then. She didn't like the worry that covered his face. She reached out, rubbing circles on his back. "Let us pray that no one was hurt."

"Or killed," he supplied.

There was nothing to do but wait for the arrival of the crew of *La Floriblanca*. A few hours later, a very solemn Rodrigo met them on the beach before the pathway to the village, Elena by his side, grasping his hand with a look of intense worry. He stared down at the ground, unable to meet José's eyes. He cleared his throat. "We…we lost Chino."

José's entire body froze. "How did this happen?"

Rodrigo shook his head. "It is a rather long story met with even more of a story after his death when your Lieutenant Kearny chased us down."

José stepped forward, placing his hand on Rodrigo's shoulder. "This is not your fault."

"He was my responsibility."

"Of course. No one would question that, but Chino knew the risks of this life, and you know that as well. Make no mistake, he wanted to go, and he went out doing what he did best."

"It should have been me."

Elena squeezed Rodrigo's hand. "Forgive me for being selfish, but I'm glad you are here and alive. That is also a gift." She reached up to wipe under his eye.

Joséfa's heart broke as she came face to face with the risky aspects of the pirate life. It all sounded romantic—the notion of the open seas, swords, stealing a priceless treasure. The reality of it stared her in the face, the grief heavy on Rodrigo's shoulders. It was almost too painful to witness.

"Come, my friend," José instructed. "Let us go to the house, we can get you something strong to drink, and you can tell me all about your travels."

The little group made their way up the path, some of the crew already getting settled in their quarters, some making plans to travel to Spanishtown Creek. Despite the blaring sun baking them from above, a gray cloud had descended on the crew. Everyone worked in complete silence, with not an ounce of laughter to be had.

"I will make my way to our home and get a nice bath put together for you, *si*?" Elena suggested.

Rodrigo reluctantly smiled. He leaned in, bringing his lips to hers. "*Si*, that would be nice. Once I have informed Gaspar of everything, I will be home."

Elena nodded as the rest of them headed toward their home. When they entered, José and Rodrigo settled in the sitting room; a light breeze traveled in from the open doors facing the ocean, the drapes dancing with the wind. Joséfa poured each of them a glass of whiskey and sat on the neighboring sofa.

Rodrigo inhaled deeply. "Chino was killed on the island while retrieving the treasure from Captain Rodgers' hide-out." He shook his head. "We were so close, Gaspar. So very close. We had everything in hand on our ship. Chino noticed someone had dropped one of the items and returned to retrieve it. That's when they emerged like spirits in the night, hidden in the bushes on the trail leading to the ship. They ran him through with a sword. Straight through his torso. I can still see his silhouette, half of the sword on one side of his being and the handle on the other. I don't think I'll ever get the image out of my head." He paused to take a deep gulp of his whiskey. "You would think that I wouldn't be as affected as I am with the many years at sea, the dozens of raids."

"Chino was a good man. And a damn good pirate," José said. "But you mustn't bear the burden of his death, *mi amigo*. He wouldn't have wanted that."

Rodrigo huffed. "My first solo trip. What a captain I turned out to be. I couldn't even protect my crew."

"Stop this. Stop this now. You are a fierce sailor. I am proud to have you by my side. This is the risk we take. This isn't a game. We all know that our lives are at stake. I will not permit you to take this all on yourself."

Rodrigo stared blankly at the floor and then exhaled deeply. "You are right. I do not believe he would want me moping about, either. He would probably give me a talking to of his own. The bastard."

José chuckled. "That he was. And tonight, we will hold a celebration in his honor. That's what he would have wanted." He glanced at Joséfa. "*Mi amor*, you wouldn't mind speaking with Elena to make preparations?"

"I would be glad to," she said, smiling warmly at Rodrigo. "But I think Elena is waiting for her dearest to make his way to their home. Make sure to have Elena come by the house whenever you all are…eh…finished resting." Joséfa could feel her face grow hot.

Rodrigo smiled knowingly. "I would be glad to, milady."

Chapter 48

As with most of the festivities in their little village, everyone attended and drank to Chino's memory. There were tearful tellings of adventures on the waters and some not-so-suitable, very risqué stories about Chino's extracurricular activities in the bedroom that were described in great detail. He couldn't help but notice John saunter off afterward with a woman or two, perhaps to recreate their story. José believed it would certainly take his mind off of Chino's death for a bit. Pleasure tended to do that.

He glanced around, frowning when he didn't see Rodrigo.

"He's down by the beach," Elena said, appearing at his side as if an apparition.

"I assume he's still having a hard time?"

Elena sighed. "Yes, it appears that not even I can distract him."

José rose from his tree stump by the fire. "I'll go find him." He smiled down at her. "Thank you, Elena."

She smiled sadly. "It is of no consequence. You know I love the man."

"He is lucky to have you. I'll send him up after I speak with him."

With that, José set off toward the beach in search of Rodrigo. He found him sitting in the sand, arms resting on bent knees, and took a seat beside him. They didn't speak for a while, choosing to sit in companionable silence. José admired the open ocean before them, noticing how the moonlight rippled across the water. The sounds of the waves reaching the shore were a welcome and soothing rhythm that calmed his nerves. He thought that was likely why Rodrigo came here, and he said as much.

"I needed to be away for a bit and clear my head," said Rodrigo.

"You are not still blaming yourself, are you?"

"It will be some time before I can fully come to terms, but our talk helped."

"Good."

After a few more moments, it was José who broke the silence. "This has also shaken me—so much so that I am contemplating my future."

Rodrigo tore his gaze from the ocean and looked at José with interest. "Oh?"

"Joséfa would have me quit the piracy if she had it her way."

"Ah. So, we're back to that, are we?"

"So it seems. But I would be lying to you if I said some part of me doesn't want the same thing, especially after Chino."

"You have lost men before, Gaspar."

"I know. This one is a little different, is all." He dug his toes deeper into the sand, sifting the grains between them. "And let's be honest, I'm not getting any younger."

Rodrigo laughed. "I can empathize with that sentiment." He inhaled deeply, his face deep in thought. "Perhaps it is time for me to get out as well."

José's eyes went wide. "*En serio?*"

"Very. I have the love of a good woman—a much younger woman at that. How I ever got so lucky, I will never know. But she will have aspirations of her own; children. I plan to make her my wife."

José felt immense joy for his friend, to have found love a second time after losing his first wife so tragically. He patted Rodrigo on the back. "That's wonderful, Rodrigo. Elena will make a wonderful mother and wife. Of that, I am sure. If she can spring a village up on an island all on her own, I daresay she could conquer the world."

Rodrigo chuckled. "Yes, that is precisely why I want to marry her. She is quite the gem. And to accept me with all of my faults—"

"We all have our faults."

"Yes, but mine are very deep. She knows all of it, and she has chosen to love me."

José sighed. "Well, perhaps we should convince a priest to live on the island."

"To live among the whores and thieves? You are out of your mind. No, no. I will take Elena to Spanishtown Creek and wed her there."

"Joséfa and I will go with you to bear witness."

"Thank you, friend." Rodrigo beamed. "I am fortunate to have met you in that dingy cell in Sevilla. My life would have turned out much differently if not." He turned his gaze to the ocean. "And now we must devise a different sort of plan."

"A plan?"

"Of course. To get out of piracy. Or did you think we could just walk away?"

José moved his hand over his chin pensively. "I hadn't really thought that far ahead, I suppose. But you are right. We will need to devise a solid strategy."

Rodrigo's lips grew into a mischievous grin. "I think I know just the plan, but I'm almost certain your Joséfa will not like it."

José's brows furrowed. "And why is that?"

"Because we will need to take on one more ship. One more raid. But I think it will work."

José listened intently as Rodrigo told him his strategy for exiting the pirate life, his nerves building in equal parts awe and excitement. "It's brilliant."

"Thank you, *mi amigo*. I've been thinking about it for some time.

"And you are sure about this ship setting sail in these waters?"

"I am positive. It is why I have been thinking endlessly about this. I have a very reliable informant of sorts who has given me great detail about the ship. This is a very rare opportunity. Very rare. Everything must go according to plan."

José nodded. "Then we go after the ship.

"This will no doubt pave the way for your beloved to barter what we have stored to the highest bidder."

"She will be ruthless in that conquest."

Rodrigo rose from the ground, holding a hand, pulling José to stand. "Come. Let us head back. I'm sure Elena will worry that I am sulking."

"She is worried you are sulking," he said, brushing the sand from his trousers. "But better to have her worry than not care at all."

"True."

They made their way up the beach, discussing their plan at length. A tiny spark of concern budded within José at having to explain this to his beloved.

"*Estas loco?*"

José had suspicions regarding Joséfa's reaction, and she had just confirmed them. Joséfa paced the length of the sitting room. He sat in his favorite armchair, casually sipping his rum, the liquor coursing through his body and calming his nerves. "It is a brilliant plan, *mi amor.*"

"It is a mad plan."

"It is that."

She threw her arms in the air. "You could be killed," she exclaimed. "You will be lucky if you leave with all of your limbs intact."

"Lower your voice, or everyone on the island is bound to hear you."

"Let them hear! *Dios mio.* This is madness. This is absolute madness."

José took another long gulp from his tumbler. "It will work."

"And what if it doesn't? There are a million things that can go wrong."

On her nearly hundredth lap, he reached out to grab her hand and pulled her down on his lap. Her lips began to tremble, her hazel eyes gleaming with unshed tears. "What happens if I lose you?"

He gently tangled her long deep brown hair between his fingers. "This will ensure that you do not lose me. This ensures that we have a future together, undisturbed."

"I can't lose you." The tears trailed down her cheek.

He reached up to brush them away. "You will not lose me. I expected your anger at the risk but not your tears. Surely you can see the logic behind the plan?"

She leaned into his palm placing her hand on the back of his and closing her eyes. "It isn't that I do not understand. It's a good plan."

"Then what is it, *mi vida*?"

She sighed as she took his hand from her cheek and moved it to her abdomen, opening her eyes to stare at him intently.

José froze, his grip on his tumbler in the other hand tightened. "Truly?"

She nodded, more tears escaping.

He dropped the tumbler with a loud clang on the side table and cupped her face. He smiled broadly. "I'm going to be a Papa!" He kissed her passionately and peppered kisses along her cheeks and neck before pulling back to look at her. Her smile was there. Barely. "Please," he pleaded, "please be as happy as I am right now, Joséfa. Please do not ruin this moment with worry. I cannot bear it."

She leaned down to kiss him, her tears coating his face. "I am beyond happy. Please do not mistake my worry for disappointment." She brushed back a hair behind his ear. "I am thrilled I will be a mother, but I want our child to have a father."

"And he will!"

Joséfa's brow quirked. "It could be a she."

"No, it is a he. I can feel it in my bones." He embraced her tightly, excitement traveling through every limb of his body. "But I will love him *or* her. I do not care. I promise to love our child endlessly. I'm going to be a Papa!"

She giggled into the crook of his neck. "Yes, you will be a great father." He drew gentle circles on her back as she relaxed further into his embrace. After a few moments, she whispered, "Just come back to me."

José closed his eyes, soaking up the warmth of her body against his, and made a promise he didn't know he could keep. "I will."

CHAPTER 49

The air, thick with the smell of the sea, made its way down to José's lungs. It was equivalent to breathing in water. Sweat beads welled on his arms, his sleeves rolled up to his elbows, and his jacket rested over his shoulder. "What a dreadfully hot day to be dressed like this."

"Well, I did tell you neither Elena nor I cared what I was wearing when we got married, but you insisted," he said as he fanned himself with a piece of parchment he obtained in the market where they currently stood waiting for their informant. Rodrigo pulled at the collar of his shirt, grimacing.

"I couldn't have my first mate getting married in something smelling of sweat and fish."

Rodrigo looked at him aghast. "I'll have you know that is the smell of hard work…and thievery."

"No one is contesting that." José gazed down the walkway riddled with various vendors selling their goods. He could see Elena and Joséfa observing several fabrics on display in a stall further down the way. She positively glowed, and his chest felt as if it would explode. He couldn't wait to see the swell of her soft stomach. Or the swell of her much larger breasts as he bit down on those pert nipples. He reached down to adjust himself.

"What did you say he looked like again?" he asked Rodrigo, distracting himself.

"He's a very lanky gentleman. He could benefit from a few good meals. A full head of bright red hair."

"And how do you know we can trust him?"

Rodrigo bit his lower lip. "Because he owes me for saving his backside."

José eyed him speculatively. "There's a story there."

"Indeed. I helped him and his lover escape."

"Escape what?"

"Being discovered." Rodrigo leaned toward José, amusement in his eyes. "You see, his lover is a sailor on the very ship we plan to raid. So, if you follow, our information comes from his bedmate."

The realization of his words suddenly dawned on José. "Oh…oh! Very well then."

A few moments later, the lanky man in question strode up to Rodrigo, grinning when his eyes moved over Rodrigo's attire. "Lopez. What on Earth are you wearing?"

Rodrigo rolled his eyes. "I feel like a court jester."

The man laughed enthusiastically. "You could certainly pass as one." His gaze moved to José, his mouth parting. "Holy God. Are you—"

"José, this is Jonathan MacNeal. Jonathan, this is—"

"Oh, I know who this is!" Jonathan beamed as he shook José's hand vigorously. "It is an honor to meet you, Gaspar. You are legendary." He leaned in, lowering his voice a few octaves. "Is it true that you singlehandedly killed an entire crew with one hand behind your back?"

"An entire crew? I wouldn't say—"

Jonathan held his hands up. "Say no more. I can see in your eyes that it's true. What about the triple virgins in Cartegena?"

"Triple virgins? Where in the world are you getting your tales?"

Jonathan blushed. "So, not true then. Good to know."

"Eh, Jonathan?" Rodrigo interrupted. "I'm afraid we are pressed for time with my getting married today."

"Oh, right! Your letter did say you were getting married. Congratulations, of course. William has recently announced that his wife is expecting. He asked that I send his regards and deemed that the information he gave me was still accurate. The ship is due to set sail in a fortnight," his face dropped into a frown. "Much to my dismay. I always dread when he is gone. No one there to keep me company at night."

"Yes, I empathize. That must be a challenge. However, wonderful news on the sailing, his marriage, and his child. Please be sure to send my congratulations to him."

"I most certainly will. He is due home in the course of a few hours. I will be glad to tell him. His wife is starting to show, and she is beautiful beyond words. We're all delighted."

José clamped down the questions sitting on the tip of his tongue while he observed the exchange with wry amusement. He plastered on a smile when Jonathan turned his attention to him.

"It was an absolute honor to have met you, Mr. Gaspar. Legend."

"Er…um…thank you," José replied uncomfortably. "And thank you for the information on the ship's departure. It is most helpful."

Jonathan bowed to both of them and turned to make his way through the crowded market.

"I don't even know what to make of that conversation. William… he's…"

"The sailor in question."

"Interesting." José shook his head. "Goodness. If only I could get the story down on paper, it would make for a most excellent book. It would sell faster than all the treasure we have on hand combined."

Rodrigo laughed. "That it would. Now, let us find our women. It's time for me to marry my bride, so I can get out of this ridiculous costume."

CHAPTER 50

THE COOL BREEZE CRAWLED THROUGH THE BEDROOM THROUGH the open window providing a welcome sense of relief. Their touch stuck with every graze as they slowly explored each other, the air so thick it could be sliced with a knife. Joséfa could do nothing more but thank God for the sun's departure as the light began to dim. Despite the lovely exchange of vows between Elena and Rodrigo, it had been a long, sweltering day of travel to and from Spanishtown Creek. Her heart was full for her friend and overjoyed that Rodrigo could find some joy, something to make him smile beyond the grief he felt for losing Chino.

She lay in bed with her beloved, wearing nothing at all— her initial shyness having subsided after the months they had shared in their marriage bed. They lay facing each other as José drew lines down her abdomen, the swell so incredibly slight. She was in a state of constant excitement and happiness, which she could not put into words. Yet, it was overshadowed by the looming prospect of possibly losing her husband. It had taken so long to find each other again, and even though it had been some time since their reunion, the days, weeks, and years with him would never be enough. She may lose him after all. That thought always made her stomach drop, and she tried to divert her attention away from it, but the plan was constant darkness surrounding her thoughts. She reached up, running a hand down the stubble on his chin that slowly grew. Despite her initial protestations, she was beginning to like it. Perhaps she would encourage him to grow it if he returned to her.

José turned his head, kissing her palm. "Tell me what you are thinking, *esposa*."

She moved her hand, gently dragging her fingertips across his brow and resuming their journey down his face. "It is strange to be so happy and yet to feel such dread at the same time, knowing that at this time tomorrow, I may never feel this way again."

His hand made its way up her arm, leaving chills in its wake. "I know it is pointless to tell you not to worry. You are far too intelligent for false promises, even though I will make them anyway." His hand cupped her face, the intensity growing in his gaze. "I will come back to you. I will fight at every turn and come back to you. And if I cannot come back to you in body, I will be here in spirit with all the power I possess in my soul, for my soul knows yours. They are one and the same."

Joséfa didn't want to waste these last moments arguing. She didn't want to shed any more tears or give in to the terror she often felt at the prospect of losing him. Instead, she would make sure that if these were her last moments with him, she would memorize them. She would take in every beautiful feature of his face—the straight line of his nose, the prominent lines of his chin and cheekbones, his deep brown eyes, and the way they seem to devour her even now.

Her hand slowly made its way over his olive skin, the tips of her fingers gliding over his neck and meeting with the firm muscles of his chest. José breathed in sharply, his eyes becoming more hooded with every passing second. With her eyes locked on his, she boldly moved her hand over the deep ridges of his abdomen to the delicious ridge leading like a beacon to his manhood. She wound her hand around him, his low groan making her slick with need between her thighs.

Like a serpent attacking its prey, he crashed his lips upon hers, his tongue twisting in a dance with hers in desperation she had never felt from him before. It consumed her, aching for him painfully. Her thirst for him was equivalent to going days without a single drop of water; he was the oasis she found waiting for her.

Her hand moved rapidly up and down his hard length, his breathing growing heavier. His heated gaze bore into her soul. She felt an immense power filling this strong, beautiful man with pleasure. His eyes closed as he tilted his head back. "Joséfa," he whispered reverently.

Suddenly, he grabbed her hand and moved atop her, placing her hand above her head and reaching for her other arm to do the same. "No," he breathed against her lips. He moved down her neck, his tongue and lips making their pilgrimage down her body to the center of her chest. A moan escaped her mouth as he took her nipple, circling it with the teasing tip of his tongue before sucking it greedily.

He drove her to insanity, alternating his attention between her breasts as the aching need grew. "José, I need you," she panted.

He kissed and licked his way down her abdomen, placing a loving kiss on the space where their child grew. "Tell me what you need, and it is yours." His eyes were filled with intense desire. "Tell me."

She couldn't bring herself to say it. Instead, she pushed on his shoulders, guiding him to the apex of her thighs. His light laughter vibrated against her thigh. "My sweet Joséfa. Cannot bring yourself to say what you want?" he teased.

She dragged her hand through his hair, the power she felt when unraveling him coming forth again. *"Besame."*

José smiled up at her as his tongue greedily parted her folds. She closed her eyes, her back arching involuntarily as a string of words in two languages left her lips. Her breathing became erratic, the air entering her lungs seeming too much and not enough.

José pulled back slightly. "Mmmm, so wet for me. I love the way your body responds, my sweet Joséfa."

She whimpered, prompting José to continue devouring her with his tongue as it traced circles over her sensitive bud. Her hips pumped against his face out of their own volition—her need building like water pushing against a dam until, finally, she succumbed to her pleasure. His hands spread across her hips and pinned her tightly to the bed as she came undone, the sensation overriding all of her inhibitions, her satisfaction expressed upon the screams coming from her lips.

Satisfied that she was thoroughly undone, his manhood proudly erect and waiting, José knelt between her open thighs, Joséfa breathing and wanton with anticipation. She watched him as he took each of her legs, slowly gliding his hands from her thighs to her ankles as he placed them on his shoulders. He lined himself up with her and thrust into her, moving his hips with abandon, hitting her in every sensitive spot inside. His hands dug into her hips, and he wildly continued to pound. His hips slapping the back of her thighs echoed against every corner of the room. José Gaspar was a man possessed by desire. She could not control the moans that left her lips. She did not want to. As her pleasure began to build again, she was consumed by him; he devoured her. They were one at this moment in an inexplicable way.

When Joséfa felt herself coming undone and squeezing around him, José threw his head back, calling her name as if in prayer, a hint of despair carried upon it. He gently placed her legs on the bed and collapsed by her side, panting wildly. Wrapping his muscular arms around her waist, he pulled her into him, his lips slowly pressing and sucking—their breathing returned to a steady calm. His eyes searched hers. "Was it too much?" he whispered.

She shook her head. "It will never be enough."

His fingers combed through her hair, setting it back behind her shoulder. "I love you, *mi vida*. I will always love you, whether I am here on this Earth or in heaven watching over you, over you *and* our child. All you have to do is close your eyes and feel me. I will be there. That I can promise you."

Her vision blurred as tears trailed across her face and down onto the pillow. "I love you, too," she lightly croaked. The sobs came then, wracking her body, for she no longer had the strength to hold them back.

He kissed up her tears and thoroughly kissed her again, taking in all her agony and pain. He held her tightly to his chest, rocking her gently. After a while, the sobs ceased as she fell asleep against him, possibly for the last time.

CHAPTER 51

THE SCORCHING RAYS BEAMED DOWN ON THE DECK WHERE Lawrence and his men waited—the waves lapping against the ship, sending them swaying from side to side. His blue coat rested upon his shoulders, causing rivers of sweat to soak through his garments with the onslaught of the humid tropical heat. He would stay in these clothes, sitting in this position for eternity if it meant achieving his goal. The loathing for his nemesis provided ample motivation. Today would be the day he takes down José Gaspar. He felt it in his bones.

He glanced over his shoulder, the half-moon shape of the bay surrounding them in the distance. They were far out enough to be seen but not rescued—just as Lawrence had planned. A few fishing vessels were scattered about. Fishermen wouldn't be an issue, but they would be perfect witnesses. He wanted everyone to know who was responsible for taking the most famous pirate to prowl these waters. Everyone would know Lieutenant Kearny brought him to his knees with his sword, for he was just as good a swordsman as Gaspar.

How a man like Gaspar could ever get by with such luck, how he had survived this long, was beyond Lawrence's comprehension. *Filthy Spaniard.* His hideout was somewhere around here. He would find it eventually. The protection of the people of Spanishtown Creek would only go so far. No level of torture was too high to obtain its whereabouts.

An image of the lovely Joséfa flashed in his mind, and his face grew hot with anger. How could a beautiful, intelligent woman such as Joséfa de Mayorga ever deign to marry such a thief? She was too good for him. He knew even Gaspar would agree—not that he would admit to having anything in common with the bastard. He thought pensively about the pain he was about to put her through. *She will move on from him…eventually.* He would give her plenty of time to grieve, and when enough time had come to pass, he would go to her. She would be his.

"Lieutenant, his ship has turned course and is approaching as planned." His second-in-command grinned evilly as he handed him his spyglass. "I am positive our disguise is working." Pleased with this report, he looked through the spyglass finding *La Floriblanca* in the distance. His adrenaline began to spike when he noticed the red flag, a skull and bones upon it, being hoisted into the air. This was all the confirmation he needed.

His crew busied themselves, their simple sailors' clothing cloaking the devils within, patiently waiting to take down the opposition; such a highly skilled crew in the art of combat. He could not be prouder of them. "Gentlemen, make busy and prepare the ship," he called from his position out of view, not wanting to risk being seen by the men on Gaspar's ship. "And do not give us away in the process. May God look favorably on your souls today." He noticed a few of them looking apprehensive; others moved about with the confidence of their stature. *As all his men should.* He didn't understand why any of them would worry. Gaspar's crew was used to a quick surrender from merchant vessels, the cowards always succumbing without a fight or foolishly fighting without an ounce of skill in weaponry. Not a single member of the USS Enterprise, currently disguised as a merchant ship, lacked in these skills. Gaspar and his men would find out soon enough.

As predictable as a fish to bait, *La Floriblanca* lined itself up with the USS Enterprise sending the first wave of cannon fire blasting through the ship's hold, their men scurrying on the deck like hundreds of dirty rats scouring for their feed. There was no feed on this ship, just certain death. He motioned to his men, who proudly raised the American flag, the merchant vessel cover blown wide open.

When his men began to fight back against the onslaught of Gaspar's imbeciles, Lawrence will admit—he didn't expect the type of skill he was met with, for he was never before granted the privilege of fighting them hand to hand. They were good—as good as any of the men he trained. He observed a few of his men drop to the deck with a thud, blood pouring from the various wounds as their opponent's sword drove through their bodies, the lights instantly leaving their eyes. Death had come to claim them, and a growing sense of unease grew in the pit of his stomach. Lawrence's eyes searched the frantic mess, attempting to find his target.

"The man you seek is right here, Lieutenant," a voice called behind him. He turned, finding Gaspar with a cocky grin on his face. "You mean to trick me?"

Lawrence withdrew his sword in a flourish, slowly making his way to the bow of the ship where Gaspar stood. Assessing. Calculating. He cocked his head. "It worked, did it not?"

Gaspar's smile grew before his sword lunged for Lawrence, but Lawrence was prepared, blocking him instantly. He had prepared for this moment for a long time, practicing endlessly until his limbs nearly fell off his body in pain. Countless hours he had spent with his men, envisioning Gaspar across from him. Even now, as they swirled and grunted their assault in a vicious tangle of swords—a few nicks gained and lost here and there—he replayed these scenarios in his head for inspiration. Him battling Gaspar this very same way when he discovered his secret haven, Joséfa looking on in terror later to be comforted by him when he drove his sword across Gaspar's neck. He was so close he could taste the victory. The energy drove his arm, meeting Gaspar's blow after blow after blow. The dance went on forever. He refused to let his body succumb.

"Retreat! Retreat!" he heard one of Gaspar's men call from behind him. He dared not take his eyes off Gaspar and continued his attack, retreat be damned. To Lawrence's shock, Gaspar ran to the ship's edge, yelling, "Rodrigo!" as he leaped off the side. A rope was thrown from *La Floriblanca* to him. Gaspar grabbed it in midair, slamming into the side of the neighboring ship, and was quickly pulled to the deck.

Lawrence saw nothing but red. He slammed his sword repeatedly into the railing, chipping away at the wood. Mad with the prospect of being so close to ending Gaspar once and for all, he regained his composure.

"Fire every last cannon on this ship! I want every last cannonball used! I want *La Floriblanca* at the bottom of the bay! Fire the cannons!" he bellowed. The remaining men moved quickly to follow his orders. He was becoming unhinged and couldn't care less. He would have his mark.

Within minutes, *La Floriblanca* became riddled with multiple holes, each bringing him such blissful contentment. They were so close to Gaspar's crew that he could practically taste their panic.

He watched as the men began to flee the sinking ship. Gaspar approached the railing staring straight at Lawrence. It was with no uncertain satisfaction that Lawrence saw the defeat in his eyes. The pirate knew he had been bested. "Surrender yourself, Gaspar, and I will grant you and your men the benefit of a quick execution!"

Suddenly, Gaspar stomped his way to the bow of the ship, bending down. Lawrence's eyes widened when Gaspar rose and began wrapping the anchor chain around his waist, glaring at him all the while his way. He jumped on top of the railing, struggling to stand with the weight, but keeping his gaze on Lawrence. "José Gaspar dies at his own hand! Not his enemy's!" He leaped over the bow of the ship. Lawrence gaped in horror as Gaspar's body hit the water, disappearing forever into the depths of the bay.

CHAPTER 52

GASPARILLA ISLAND, FLORIDA
1816

IVÁN GASPAR SAT MOTIONLESS IN HIS CHAIR, THE SILENCE IN THE sitting room deafening as José concluded his tale. "I quickly realized it would be either Kearny or me. He would not let me live in peace, and he would always try to find me, to find our family. When your mother told me she was pregnant with you, I was confident we had to follow through with *Tío* Rodrigo's plan to either take him down or disappear.

"As you know, your *Tío* Rodrigo is very resourceful. We obtained knowledge of a plan to lure us into a trap."

"The USS Enterprise disguised as a merchant ship," Iván provided.

"Correct. And because we knew of Kearny's plan, we devised a plan of our own to take over the ship before their ploy could be revealed." José paused, reluctant to reveal the next part to his son, who admired him. "To guarantee our freedom, it meant killing everyone on board."

Iván's eyes went wide. "All the men on board? Even the ones who asked for mercy?"

"All of them. Trust me when I tell you, they would have had no issue killing us all. They almost did." He paused again, the worry thick in his eyes as they pleaded for understanding. Joséfa reached across the space between them and squeezed José's hand, her gentle smile comforting him.

Iván took a few moments but then nodded. "Continue."

José sighed in relief. "Despite the efforts of my men, many of whom died trying, they were able to hoist their flag, thus shedding their cover. With a growing sense of dread, I knew it was up to our backup plan, which was shaky. I honestly didn't know if we would be successful, but for your sake and your mother's sake, I had to try. And I would die doing so if need be.

"Lieutenant Kearny was too busy seething at the thought of having lost the opportunity to kill me that he didn't notice how loosely the chain around my waist was. Anger can easily blind a man, and I was betting on his rage to overlook the small details.

"When I jumped over the side of the sinking ship, I sent up a silent prayer not only for me but for my men on board *La Floriblanca*. They knew the backup plan was in effect and were prepared to die for the opportunity to be rid of the pirate hunter. They gladly accepted the risks despite my asking several times, the efforts of which ended when some threatened me with a knife to the throat if I didn't take them at their word. I understood then just how much they wanted this, too.

"With the anchor chain having ample slack, I could maneuver out before it pulled taught. I knew I had precious minutes to swim underwater as far away from the ships as I could toward the bay of Spanishtown Creek. Having gone as far as I could, I reached into my pocket, pulling out a stalk of wild bamboo. It's native to this area and damned useful for breathing underwater. I was sure to supply our crew with the largest I could find."

Iván glanced at the wild bamboo prominently displayed in a vase in the corner hutch. "Huh."

José hid a smile behind his tumbler, taking another sip before continuing. "I was relying on the Lieutenant's disdain for the lower class, the hard-working fishermen of Spanishtown Creek who were out in the bay all day fishing to make a living and feed their families. He knew many of them were loyal to me. Swimming underwater took a toll on my body. I didn't know if I would survive it. Some of my crew were not as fortunate.

"When I finally made it to one of the fishing boats, I kept my head low to the water, bobbing as I hid from the view of the USS Enterprise until it left the bay heading for a town where their loyalties ensured my captured men would be hanged. They did not trust the people of Spanishtown Creek not to interfere on behalf of my crew, which they surely would have." José placed his empty tumbler on the side table. "Their deaths weigh heavily on my soul. Each day I continue to live is a privilege they did not receive." He sighed heavily. "By the grace of God and a well-built boat, *Tío* Rodrigo and some of the crew escaped *La Floriblanca* before it sank. I waited for them in hiding until they rescued me and brought me here to live out my days in hiding.

"And now you know everything. I pray you do not judge me for the life I was thrown into, my son. Everything I did, all the killing and thieving, I did for our family. I took many lives in that final battle. I would gladly do it again. Regardless of that, I ask for your forgiveness."

Iván's mouth lay open as he gaped at his father. He rose from the sofa and closed the distance to stand before José, placing his hand on his shoulder. "Papa, if it is my forgiveness you seek, know that you assuredly have it. You never have to ask for it. You have been a wonderful father and husband. It only pains me that the rest of the world will never know just how wonderful you truly are. But I am grateful for the lengths you went to in order to protect us. I can only imagine the burden you feel. My only hope is that I can be half the man you are one day."

He rose and embraced his son, Joséfa's sniffles sounding behind them. All his worry was for nothing, and although he still had many years before he revealed his tale to his daughter, he would savor the relief of knowing that his son's forgiveness was his.

José never cared whether the tongues of wicked men tainted his reputation. He thought this to himself much later in the evening as he and Joséfa sat on the beaches of Gasparilla Island, gazing up at the stars in the sky.

"I told you you shouldn't worry."

He admired her beautiful silhouette, the one he could paint from memory if he had any talent. "You are right as always."

"Hmph. Now you say this."

He chuckled. "When have I ever contested this?"

"There are not enough hours in the night."

They both laughed as he moved to sit behind her, pulling her between his legs until her back lay against his chest. "I can never thank you enough for this incredible life," he whispered.

"You never need to thank me, *mi amor*. I love you endlessly. I would do it all over again just for the chance of being with you, even if you died that day."

He clasped her chin, turning her head up to him. "And I love you endlessly as well."

José Gaspar made love to his wife on the beaches of his little haven, the stars bearing witness to their love. He remained grateful for every night he was awarded the honor of being by her side.

Chapter 53

Casa de Gaspar,
Summer 1836

While José couldn't come out of seclusion for the remainder of his days, José Gaspar gained a small sense of satisfaction from the tales about the battle in Spanishtown Bay. His son and daughter, grown with their own families, would tell these tales to them, his grandchildren not knowing that José Gaspar was the *Abuelo* they loved so much. The joy these tales brought him was immeasurable, and he would die happily knowing his legend was one of heroism for their small town, making sure to share the riches he obtained so the town could thrive.

"*Tío* José, do you want me to tell the others to leave?" his oldest nephew, Pedro de Mayorga, asked—the concern on his face evident. "You do not look so well." He placed a hand on his hip, looking so much like his father; may God rest his soul. It wouldn't be long before he was reunited with his overbearing brother-in-law and his lovely sister-in-law, Lorena. They raised their children on their quiet rancho in San Juan, with Alejandra returning to Sevilla when she was old enough to travel on her own, curious about her own family and life in *España*. Pedro remained behind running his father's business when it became too much for him. He was certain Armando would stubbornly outlive him. How wrong José was. He had survived them all.

It had been decades since he had seen his dear friend, Felipe, having met with him in Havana some decades ago when his health barely permitted. He learned of his best friend's passing from his daughter when he received a letter informing him of his tragic death. It pained him to know Felipe fell from a horse, having been likely too old to be on one in the first place. They said it was quick. José hoped it was.

While he understood Rodrigo's need for adventure, he couldn't understand his desire to come out of seclusion at such a late age. Elena had pleaded with him to stay on the island, but he was wooed by the life Captain Jean Lafitte offered in New Orleans and the surrounding seas. While he met his end at the tip of a sword, José felt he died on his own terms—at sea, with the freedom he sought his entire life instead of in a bed dying of old age as José was now—a prisoner in his own body.

His youngest granddaughter, Ana Luísa, now five, sat perched on his bed, her pleading eyes begging him not to let his nephew throw her out of the room. It had been an effort to tell his tales again to the little one, but he cherished these moments with each of his kin.

"It is fine, Pedro," he said, his throat sore and dry. "Let her stay with me a while, and I will send her to bed."

Pedro's lips thinned as he reluctantly nodded. "If you need anything, *Tío*, we will be just beyond this door. Just send her along to get us."

José rolled his eyes and shooed him along, Pedro scurrying out the door moments later.

"*Abuelo*? Did you really do all those things they say?" Ana Luísa asked him. She had been sitting at his bedside for hours; the other grandchildren had left to go to bed or to Spanishtown Creek with Alejandra some time ago.

It took a great effort to smile at her through the pain, his whole body from his head to his toes aching with age. It had been weeks since he left his bed, moving only to bathe or relieve himself with the aid of his children or grandchildren—

something his pride still had difficulty grappling with. "And what if I told you that I did?" he asked, his voice raspy.

Ana's eyes went wide. "I would say that is fearsome!"

José chuckled lightly, a cough leaving his lungs, jolting his body slightly up from the bed. The tiny face with eyes and hair, like his beloved Joséfa, looked upon him with concern. "Are you going to leave us now as *Abuela* did?"

His withering heart ached with the absence of his Joséfa, having been without her for just short of two years. José reached out and grabbed her little hand and squeezed it gently. "I cannot stay here forever, *mi niña*, but I promise you this. I will always be with you and all your brothers, sisters, and cousins. I will watch over all of you. I may visit you from time to time. You may catch my ghost following you around. Do not be afraid. It is just me or your *Abuela* looking over you. And we will watch over your children and your children's children until the end of time. I promise to look after all our kin. Tell them that."

Ana Luísa exhaled and then nodded. "That makes me feel much better." She reached to cup his cheek. "Sleep now, *Abuelo*. Tell *Abuela* we miss her and love her."

José patted her hand, the tears welling up in his eyes. "I will, *cariña*. I love you so much. I love all of you so very much." Ana Luísa gave him the greatest of hugs. As she headed for the door, she turned and smiled at him sadly as if knowing it would be the last time before softly closing the door behind her.

How did I ever get so lucky? This was his final thought as he lay in his room, comforted that his family was thriving and always would be. As he closed his eyes and took his final breath, his sweet Joséfa greeted him on the other side with a smile on her face.

EPILOGUE

TAMPA, FLORIDA
(FORMALLY KNOWN AS SPANISHTOWN CREEK)
PRESENT DAY

THE FAINT SOUNDS OF MUSIC DRIFTED THROUGH THE NEIGHBOR-hood on Bayshore Boulevard. Her heels clicked against the pavement as the parade beads clanked together on her chest. Each step brought an acute awareness of how long she'd been on her feet. The entire Gasparilla festival weighed heavy on her bones. The walking, the standing, the drinking. It all took its toll. She longed to sink into a lovely, comfy couch and hoped there'd be one at the end of this long evening walk.

The festival to honor the legend of José Gaspar, the infamous pirate who died in the bay, became a tradition. More than half of the city's occupants showed up for the event, and given the sharp, foul stench that rose from the ground, immediately causing her stomach to turn, they failed to find a restroom. Rows of cars lined the side streets; some parked for a twenty-dollar fee on lush St. Augustine grass in the yards closest to the parade route.

"Are we almost there?" Adelina asked, breathing heavily— the shooting pain driving into her feet like nails with every step.

The corner of James' mouth rose into a grin. "Yes, princess. Just a few more blocks."

She had suspected he withheld the time it would take to reach the after-party by foot. Adelina would never have agreed to walk had she known it would be *this* far out. *Just a few houses away from yours, my ass.*

Her body began to tense with each additional block she counted. The mist from the bay crawled across the quiet street, whirling in a dance with the wind. The faint outline of a man, almost an apparition, came into view. She stopped. The hairs on her arms stood tall. Her heart nearly jumped out of her body.

James walked back from ahead, putting his arm gently around her waist. His brows furrowed. "Do you need me to carry you?"

She couldn't move but not because of her throbbing feet. He stood just a few feet away. The man's deep, dark brown eyes full of awe pierced hers and dug into the depths of her soul.

"Do you see him?" she whispered. His long, brown hair reaching just past his shoulders. She gave him a once-over, taking in the rugged pants with rips and tatters lined with water stains that had long since dried. It wasn't unusual to see people dressed as pirates or débutantes for the Gasparilla parade. But this man's clothes looked from a different century altogether. No pirate costume could resemble this type of likeness. She met his eyes again, and a shiver ran down her spine.

James glanced at the mist swirling just above the sidewalk ahead of them. "See who?" He shook his head. "*Maaaaaybe* you've had too much to drink. Those last two shots we had? Brutal. Totally understandable if you're feeling it. No judgment. Everyone knows what a lightweight you can be sometimes."

Adelina rolled her eyes. "No, James," she hissed. "Look, just ahead of us." Adelina blinked a few times to be sure, but the man stood before her, becoming more apparent by the minute. Ignoring the pain emanating from her feet, she went in pursuit of the man.

"Uh…sweetie? Let's go now," James called after her. "It's late, and we've been drinking since the parade began. You're seeing things that aren't there and freaking me out. I know it's your favorite show, but this isn't an episode of Ghost Hunters."

Ignoring James, she continued down the walkway. With each step she took, a smile grew more expansive on the mysterious man's face. He stood a few feet from her now. A growing sense of familiarity consumed her. She feared one word would destroy the moment, but she had to know.

"Do I know you?" she asked. The man didn't answer. He gazed lovingly at her—almost in a fatherly kinship. As she approached him, he disappeared, fading into the mist as eerily as he materialized. Adelina looked at James standing twenty yards behind her and a space in front of her where the man had stood moments ago. *Maybe I did have too much to drink.*

Her eyes narrowed as something shifted in the shadows just ahead. The mysterious man emerged further down the walkway. She grabbed the bottom of her ball gown and quickened her pace, afraid he would disappear again. The man began to flee. The calm bay breeze blew her hair around her face.

"Adelina! Are you crazy?"

She dashed down the walkway, the pain in her feet almost non-existent now in her quest to catch up with the man. Just as he reached the retaining wall that hugged the bay, he glanced at her, smiling. He stared at the water as she approached him and leaped gracefully into the bay. A scream stuck in her throat. Adelina gulped the sea breeze, willing it to reach her lungs as she froze, staring at the water. Before she could even begin to understand what she was seeing, he was gone. She huffed, the set of her shoulders slumping in defeat.

"No one will ever get close enough, my dear," a voice called from behind.

Adelina gasped as she pivoted to see a man sitting on a bench, one arm stretched casually over the back. His peppered hair peeked slightly from under his fedora—the street light casting shadows on his face. He smiled at her tenderly. "I can see why he got so close to you, Joséfa." He studied her, taking in every curve of her face and her eyes.

"It's Adelina, sir," she replied in confusion.

"No, to *him,* you're Joséfa." He gazed at her intensely. "You have a piece of her soul and an undeniable likeness. You are his kin—a descendant of theirs. That is why he came to you."

"That's why *who* came to me?"

His gentle smile returned. "Despite the evening's celebration in honor of his legend, no one can confirm if he ever lived. Rumors constantly swirl through this town regarding his periodical appearances. Some believe he's real. Some do not. But *I* do. My family passed down his final words from generation to generation. His promise to watch over all his kin for eternity." The hairs on her neck rose. "And I, too, have seen him. His ghost still haunts the streets and beaches of Tampa Bay, his soul living beyond his ultimate demise."

Adelina's eyes went wide and her heartbeat quickened. She turned and searched for him again, finding nothing but the water lapping gently against the retaining wall.

"Gaspar," she breathed into the night.

THE END

Author's Note

The actual story of José Gaspar has been circulating through the area of Tampa Bay since the early 1900s. I became fascinated with the tale when attending college in the area. When I researched its origins, I found it interesting that José Gaspar's journey across the Atlantic mirrored my family's.

I became inspired and wanted to create my own Gaspar story. Other versions of José Gaspar were wrought with toxic masculinity and womanizing. I decided to right that wrong. After all, getting behind a character you don't particularly like isn't easy. Am I right?

If you loved the tale as much as I did, I highly encourage you to research the legend of José Gaspar through the Boca Grade Historical Society's website.

Scan QR Code to find out more about Jose Gaspar and John Gomez on the Boca Grande Historical Society's website:

And if you haven't found out already, Tampa's Gasparilla Parade & Pirate Fest is an annual event you don't want to miss. The event has been ongoing since 1904.

Scan QR Code for info about Tampa's signature event:

Thank You for Reading!

The Legend of Gasparilla has been a project that has taken years to develop. I truly hope you enjoyed reading it as much as I enjoyed writing it. I humbly ask that you leave a review!

Want more from the Gasparilla world? Sign up for my newsletter and received an exclusive never released *Farewell to Felipe* scene.

Scan QR Code to sign up and receive your bonus scene:

Acknowledgements

It's funny. I've dreamed of writing my Acknowledgements for as long as I can remember. There are so many people I have to thank that it's impossible to know where to start. The best place is with my wonderful, supportive husband, Brian. Thank you for being patient with me. I know it's not easy trying to juggle my creative consciousness sometimes, but you're doing a fantastic job. I love you. Keep that shit up, hunny!

To Brittany Cordero and Megan Todaro, we did it! Thank you for all the endless encouragement, cheerleading, crying, and emotional support you both have provided over the last few years. Words cannot express how much gratitude and love I hold in my heart for both of you. All the plotting, editing, reworking, and brainstorming took up so much of your time, yet you all still never stopped supporting me. This book is for you through and through.

To everyone in my Women, Wine, & Books Club, I heart you all so much for all of your support. Cheers!

To my beta readers, Ana, Josie, and Dimitra, thank you so much for your feedback. It was invaluable.

To Kathleen Foxx, you are an angel sent from above. Thank you for editing my debut novel and for your guidance. I learned so much from you and am grateful to have your stamp on this project.

I wouldn't be writing this at all if it weren't for the people who brought me into the world and helped raise me. To Mom & Mike and Dad & Hilda, thank you for being incredibly supportive no matter which crazy idea I had growing up. I hope that I've made you all proud.

To my sister, Annette, whose spiritual guidance has been priceless. I couldn't have completed this book or gone through this process without your "snap out of it" encouragement.

To Nikki Lynn, my sister from another mister who happens to be my brother from another mother, thank you....for, like, everything. I could write another book about how much you have helped me. Perhaps I shall! And, of course, to Ronnie, Sonia, Billy, and the rest of the Torres Fernandez family, I love all of you and thank you for being by my side.

To any other writer who is reading this right now and is considering writing that book. Do it. Everyone's writing journey is different, and there's not one right way to do it. Just get out there and make life happen. We'll all be behind you.

S. T. FERNANDEZ, also known as Stephanie, is originally from Orlando, Florida, and was born to two parents from *La Isla del Encanto*, Puerto Rico. She now resides in the beautiful small beach town of Ventura, California, with her husband and their two wiener puppies.

Stephanie is an avid reader of all levels of spicy, steamy romance—mostly in fantasy, historical, or paranormal genres. Just as much as she enjoys disappearing into a good book, creating a story that readers can disappear into brings her immense joy.

She is currently working on her second book in the fantasy romance genre, full of wonderfully diverse characters and themes. S.T. Fernandez's fantasy romance intertwines Puerto Rico's Taino indigenous culture's beautiful themes and language into a fantasy world. She is thrilled and excited to present it to readers when completed.

www.stfernandez.com

Instagram: @stfernandezwrites | TikTok: @stfernandezwrites
Twitter: @stfernandez | S.T. Fernandez Official Facebook
Group: Scan QR Code:

www.ingramcontent.com/pod-product-compliance
Lightning Source LLC
Chambersburg PA
CBHW020333010826
48970CB00010B/316